HE'S BACK...

The woman spun. Seeing Laila, she raised her gun.

"Marius sends his regards," she sneered at Laila.

Laila froze as the words sank in. The way her heart pounded it felt as though it was trying to beat its way through her ribcage. Marius had sent them. He was toying with her just as he had back in his arena.

The Fae raised her gun and fired repeatedly.

Laila's shield flickered and died. She'd expended too much energy fighting the Sorcerers, and her stamina was failing. Pain surged through her torso and left arm as the woman continued to shoot.

BOOKS BY
KATHRYN BLANCHE

Laila of Midgard series

Caught by Demons
Summoned by Demons
Infiltrated by Demons
Hunted by Demons

Hunted by the Holidays
(A Laila of Midgard Novelette)

SUMMONED BY DEMONS

LAILA OF MIDGARD
❖ BOOK 2 ❖

KATHRYN BLANCHE

First published in the United States of America in December 2018 by Kathryn Blanche
Library of Congress Control Number:
ISBN: 978-1-7326651-3-2 (Paperback)

Also available:
ISBN: 978-1-7326651-4-9 (Hardcover Edition)
ISBN: 978-1-7326651-5-6 (Electronic Edition)

Editing by The Crimson Quill
Cover Art by: Damonza.com

Printed and bound in the United States of America
First printing December 2018

Distributed by Ingram
www.ingramcontent.com

Printed by Lightning Source

Visit www.kathrynblanche.com

For a list of trigger warnings please visit: www.kathrynblanche.com

DEDICATION

Zachary Elliott
Whose lively spirit and beaming smile will
never be forgotten.

SUMMONED BY DEMONS

CHAPTER 1

Laila sprinted down the abandoned street, the cries for help growing louder. She squinted, straining her eyes against the oppressive dark of the Old City at night. The buildings loomed over her, their broken windows and boarded-up doors showing no signs of life.

She remembered the last time she'd followed cries for help in the Old City. Rather than finding a distraught woman, she'd found a Ghost that tried to kill both her and her partner, Darien.

Up ahead the sounds of a struggle echoed from a side street. Laila slowed as she reached the corner and cautiously peered around. There was a man trying to drag a woman into a running car. The woman wore a short dress that was torn in places, and a pair of stilettos that hindered her ability to flee. Her dark blond hair flowed wildly behind her as she whipped her head back to look at the man.

He grabbed her arm and threw her down on the asphalt.

"Get in the car!" he shouted, pulling a gun out of its holster and aiming it at the woman.

Laila stepped out from her hiding spot and readied a spell.

"Drop your weapon," she demanded, approaching the man, "and put your hands where I can see them."

"Who the hell are you?" he glowered, turning.

Laila twitched her fingers as she cast her first spell, which pulled the gun out of his hands. It skidded as it landed on the asphalt twenty feet away.

The man stared, mouth gaping, at his now empty hand that had held the gun. He quickly recovered and charged. She cast her second spell that hardened the air around him, trapping him in place. Laila could tell he was starting to panic as she took a step closer, her eyes narrowing.

"I'm going to release you, and I want you to get in your car and leave. Otherwise you'll find out what else I can do. Got it?"

His eyes were wide with fear. She released him, preparing another spell just in case, but he obeyed, scrambling to get in his car. The tires screeched as he drove off, and Laila noticed an unusual image that had been spray-painted on the bumper of the car, a three-faced skull.

She turned to the woman.

"Are you all right?" Laila asked, offering the woman a hand. She nodded.

"What happened? And why were you out here at night?"

"I-I live around the corner." The woman straightened her dress and brushed the hair out of her eyes. "I was on my way home from work when he pulled up next to me. He recognized me from the bar I work at, and I think he followed me. It's not the first time that's happened."

"Okay," Laila, frowned, "Why don't I walk you home?"

"Seriously, I'm fine." She turned as she, waved Laila off.

Laila raised an eyebrow. "A man just tried to kidnap you!"

She shrugged indifferently. "It happens. Well, out here any-way. I could've gotten away myself."

"Okay," said Laila skeptically, glancing around for any sign of the kidnapper. "Do yourself a favor and move back to the west side."

"Ha," she scoffed, "like it's that easy."

Before Laila could say another word, there was a shimmer of magic around the woman as she transformed into a hawk. It screeched at her before taking off and flying away down the dark street.

Laila shook her head. She hadn't seen that coming. Hawk Shifters were a type of Were, or a person with the ability to change into the form of an animal. But they were considerably more rare than other types of Weres in Midgard. In any case, though, she was grateful she'd been nearby to help the woman. She took one more glance in the direction the car had left before jogging back the way she came.

She hadn't told the others that she was stepping away. There hadn't been time. It was as if some instinct urged her to follow the cries for help. Now that the excitement had passed, Laila realized how rash her actions had been. What if something happened while she was away?

In her mind she could see Colin's look of disapproval. How was she supposed to explain that she'd abandoned her post because of some weird feeling she'd had? Laila was glad she'd been able to help, but now she cringed as she thought about the consequences.

Then again, the entire team was there for the drug bust. It was absurd, really. There was no reason they needed so many people onboard for this assignment; it was just a waste of their time. She'd been stuck in that dusty old apartment all day surveilling the alley. But when she'd heard the woman's cries for help, she couldn't just stand by and do nothing. She'd slip back into her post before anyone was the wiser. Besides, if the woman had been abducted, Laila would've been involved in the investigation eventually; it was her duty to protect the people of the city, both human and Supernatural.

❖

Ali shivered and shoved her hands deeper into the pockets of her worn black hoodie. Fall was on its way to Los Angeles, and while the days were still sweltering, the nights were beginning to cool down.

Checking the time on her phone, Ali noticed with irritation that the man she was waiting for was running very late. It was never a good idea to linger on the streets of the Old City, the mostly abandoned eastern sections of Los Angeles. There was not enough funding to send police officers out to patrol these sections on a regular basis, and as a result, illegal activity increased exponentially.

So long as the west side was not affected, a blind eye was turned on the Old City. The majority of humans and Supernaturals steered clear of it. The buildings weren't up to code, and that combined with the crime rate was enough to discourage most sensible people from occupying the Old City. Those who did choose to inhabit the Old City did so at their own risk. It would probably be cleaned up eventually, but for now criminal activity was rampant, from whorehouses and illegal arms dealers to black market dealers with designer drugs from the other worlds.

But that was exactly why Ali was there, except that her dealer was already more than fifteen minutes late. She fidgeted with the phone in her pocket. She considered calling the deal off. There would be others, and she was beginning to suspect that something wasn't right. Then again, if she left, she'd loose her opportunity.

Footsteps approached the opening to the alleyway. As they grew closer, Ali stepped out of the darkest shadows where she waited, watching the alley to make sure the drug dealer was alone. The last thing she wanted was a scene.

"Relax." The man smirked as he sensed her unease. "I had some business to take care of."

He was small for a human and stank of cigarettes, among other things. It took some effort on Ali's part to keep from wrinkling her nose.

"I was starting to think you wouldn't show," she murmured, the faintest of smiles playing on her lips.

The human looked her up and down, and she let him. Even with her drugged-out appearance she knew she was irresistible. As one of the Fae, she could use her magic to manipulate her appearance and even influence the thoughts of others. It was the biggest advantage she had over humans and Supernaturals alike, and she wasn't shy about using it. Ali could see him lower his guard ever so slightly.

"You have it?" she asked, pulling his attention back to the job at hand.

"Of course." He held up a small bottle of red shimmery liquid. Pixie blood, or pix as it was called on the streets. Pix is a highly potent and super-addictive magical drug. When consumed, pix could make an LSD trip look mild. A small quantity could get a Troll high for hours and quickly kill a human.

Ali reached for the bottle, but he snatched it back.

"Not until you make the payment." He grinned lazily.

Laila climbed through a lower window of a dilapidated building. She had a spell wrapped around her to help camouflage her in the dark. She'd be practically invisible, but still she glanced around to be sure she hadn't been followed. The last thing she needed was to blow their cover and piss off Colin even more.

Through the earpiece she wore, Laila could already hear that the exchange was in progress. Hopefully, no one noticed she was missing.

She climbed the steps silently, returning to the window where she'd been posted. She watched the exchange as Ali spoke with the drug dealer.

They had set the trap hours ago, waiting for this dealer to show. One of Ali's contacts had been sure this guy was being supplied by Demons, and while dealing was a serious offense, more importantly they were hoping to get some information on the Demons.

Demons are not a race, as the humans used to believe. They are a political group that rose to power in Muspelheim, the Realm of the Damned and the inter-dimensional prison commonly known as Hell. The term Demon could be applied to any person of any race or species who allied themselves with the group. Those who had actually been damned were known as Greater Demons, while supporters who had never been to Muspelheim, were classified as Lesser Demons. The Demons sought not only to escape, but to take revenge on those who had imprisoned them.

Five years ago, the Demons had attempted to take over Midgard, or Earth as it is known by its inhabitants. They almost succeeded, too, but the other realms intervened, saving the humans, from what is now referred to as The Event.

This aid broke an ancient contract that isolated Earth from the other worlds. With the contract broken, Earth was now open for travel between the worlds. No longer was it forbidden for humans to know of magic and the existence of Supernaturals. For the first time in thousands of years, it was possible for Supernatural Persons, or SNPs as Laila's team called them, to openly interact with humans. But with this interaction came new conflicts, and specialized law enforcement officers became mandatory to handle these situations. This was the beginning of the Inter-Realm Security Agency.

The Inter-Realm Security Agency, or IRSA, was a new program created by the U.S. government after the apocalypse to help combat any Supernatural or otherworldly threats in order to keep the peace on Earth. A few months earlier, Laila had relocated to Los Angeles after completing her training with IRSA. Since she joined the team in Los Angeles, she helped to dismantle a major operation organized by the Demons by going under cover as one of their victims. Unfortunately, most of the

Demons involved were still at large.

Laila watched as her fellow agent and roommate, Alastrina Fiachra, turned up her Fae glamour to hot and steamy. The Fae were masters of magic relating to illusion, emotion, and desire. Humans were particularly susceptible, and this one was putty in her hands. It was actually embarrassing to watch.

"You seem like an intelligent, resourceful guy," the Fae said, biting her lip. "I don't suppose you could help a girl out?"

"With what?" The man spoke in a daze. He was totally unprepared for Ali's charm. Laila felt a little bad just watching him, but she couldn't look away. She had to stay alert for any sign of danger.

It occurred to Laila that Ali could have a career as an actress if she ever got tired of working for IRSA. She smiled and shook her head as she pictured Ali strutting around a film set and ordering people around. The director wouldn't stand a chance against her powers of persuasion.

Ali continued. "I'm looking for a man named Marius..." she trailed off.

A goofy smile spread across his face. "I don't know who you're talkin' about, but if he left you, then the guy's an idiot." He was so drunk off Fae magic that he slurred his words.

Laila frowned. She doubted the guy had anything to do with the Demons. She didn't sense even the slightest trace of Demonic energy on him. Yet another dead end.

Disappointed, she watched as Ali finished the deal. The man's face morphed from giddy to horrified as Ali placed the man under arrest. But he recovered from his shock quickly, freed himself from Ali's grip, and bolted down the alley in Laila's direction.

Laila swiftly swung her legs over the windowsill and dropped to the ground two floors below, as gracefully as a cat, to block his path. The drop would've broken her legs if she'd been human, but Laila was an Elf, and her bones were naturally much stronger. Physically, she could run circles around any human athlete, which came in handy in her field.

She was nearly knocked off balance when someone shoved past her to tackle the drug dealer to the ground. It was her supervisor, Colin.

Ali wandered over, giving Laila a knowing look as she dropped her glamour. Laila gritted her teeth.

"Did you get him?" a male voice asked through her earpiece.

"Yeah. Go ahead and bring the car over, Darien." Laila watched Colin cuff the drug dealer.

It had been two months since Laila had freed herself from Marius, a Greater Demon who had somehow managed to escape from Hell. It was supposedly impossible to escape from Hell, but Marius had managed it. He was the one who'd organized the illegal fight ring that Laila uncovered. At the time she'd been forced into the fights as one of their gladiators. She escaped before they discovered she worked for IRSA and returned with backup to take down the operation, but Marius got away, and they had yet to pick up his trail.

Laila sighed. They didn't even know if he was in the area. For all they knew he could be in another state, or even another country. But if he was here, they would find him, because she would not stop until he was back in Hell where he belonged.

The agency had requested documents from the Fae city of Tír na nÓg, where Marius had been sentenced. They discovered that he was previously found guilty of Necromancy, magic that raised the dead. It was strictly forbidden in all the worlds and was also the kind of magic that had nearly destroyed life on Earth during The Event. Which was all the more reason to ensure he was back in Hell as soon as possible.

A black SUV pulled into the alley, and Darien stepped out from the driver's side. The fourth and final member of their team, Darien Pavoni, was most definitely dead. He had been since 1724, when he was turned. As with all Vampires, he had blood-red eyes and unnaturally pale skin that contrasted shockingly with his black spiky hair. Not one for a professional appearance, Darien preferred a wardrobe consisting mainly of distressed denim and leather. He looked more like he belonged in a band than in IRSA.

He sauntered over to the women. His characteristic cocky grin morphed into a smirk as he watched their supervisor read the drug dealer his rights.

"Didn't he just insist on coming as backup?" the Vampire mused.

Laila raised an eyebrow, and Darien laughed. He was ever the smart-ass.

"I'm just saying." He spread his hands in surrender.

Ali rolled her eyes. "Let's just load this guy up and get out of here. I don't know about you two, but I'm not interested in hanging around the Old City any longer than we need to."

Laila opened the door as Colin walked the drug dealer over. He situated the human in the back and shut the door before turning back to Laila, scowling.

"What the hell did you think you were doing abandoning your post?" roared Colin.

Of course, thought Laila as she realized he'd probably heard her leave. Colin was a Werewolf after all, and had excellent hearing.

"Saving someone," she replied, refusing to back down.

"You could've blown our cover!"

"But I didn't," she pointed out, "and I helped a Were in need. Besides, you had everything under control." She gave him a smile that didn't quite reach her eyes.

Colin snorted as he brushed dust off his clothes. "Someone on this team has to."

Laila clenched her jaw, just as Ali stepped in to change the subject.

"I don't think you'll get anything more out of him." Ali nodded towards the drug dealer. "It didn't seem like he knew anything, and all he had was this."

Ali showed them the red vial of Pixie blood.

"We'll see," Colin said. "I've got a good feeling about this one."

Laila twisted the vial in Ali's hand to reveal an image, a skull with three faces. It was the same image she'd just seen on the vehicle of the would-be kidnaper. Laila's frown deepened.

"What's this?" Laila asked the others, indicating the image. "I've seen it before."

Colin shrugged. "Probably just the dealer's stamp. And we'll be continuing this conversation later, in my office."

He hopped into the driver's seat of the SUV while Darien joined him in the passenger's seat. Laila rolled open the garage door of the building next to them, exposing another vehicle that appeared worn and desperately in need of a new paint job.

"We'll see you tomorrow," Ali called after them. "I'm beat, and it looks like you two have things under control."

Colin gave her a short nod before driving off, leaving the two women in the alley.

With a shake of her head, Laila walked around to the driver's door of the car. She clicked a button on the key fob and the air around the car blurred and shimmered as the vehicle's camouflage disengaged, and it changed to its normal appearance, a shiny new luxury car.

Laila smiled despite herself. It was a clever little enchantment that a Witch friend of hers had whipped up. It certainly deterred burglars and could help her to blend in. She had just bought the car a couple of weeks ago and was relieved that she no longer had to rely on the others for transportation. Up until that point, she had been stuck carpooling with whoever was available.

They slid into their seats, and Laila pulled smoothly out of the garage.

"What happened?" asked Ali as she pulled off her worn coat. "Where did you go?"

"I heard shouting down the street and found a male human trying to abduct a female Were. I scared him off, and the woman just went on her way." Laila shook her head.

The people of the Old City were something else. They rolled with the punches, and avoided law enforcement. They preferred to deal with whatever problems they faced in their own ways.

"Huh." Ali shoved the coat into the back seat.

"It gets stranger," continued Laila, pulling onto the main road, "The woman was a Hawk Shifter."

"Really? I've never met one before. But anyway, Colin seemed pissed."

Laila groaned.

"I'm sure he'll get over it, though," added Ali optimistically. "It was ridiculous to bring the entire team out here for this."

Laila turned down the street, weaving through the debris that littered the road.

"I'm not sure which is worse," Ali added, searching the glove box for a mint. "Colin feeling sorry for himself, or this." She waved her hand indicating the alley behind them.

"Well, at least he is more motivated this way. But seriously, what's with his attitude? These petty comments just don't seem like Colin."

Up until about a week or two ago, Colin had spent most of his time sulking in his office. Laila understood that he had been upset about losing Marius's trail. She knew better than anyone what the Greater Demon was capable of, but it irked her to watch him dwell on it and mope in his office instead of actually doing something.

She'd tried talking to him and had encouraged him to get out and do something social. It sounded as if she'd finally convinced him because he had left the office early, mentioning something about plans. Then, out of nowhere, he was suddenly intense and ready to go catch a Demon. The shift was sudden and refreshing at first, but now it was starting to grate on all of their nerves, and when Laila tried talking to him he kept brushing her off.

"He needs to get over the fact that you're a better fighter than he is." Ali popped a sugary mint into her mouth. "Think about it, he's a Werewolf. They are all about hierarchy and pack status. Normally he's the alpha, but then you come into the picture, and not only are you able to solve a case he's been stuck on for months, but he also put you into danger because of his stupidity."

"And?" Laila asked, wanting to hear the rest of Ali's theory.

Ali rolled her eyes. "Clearly he's trying to reestablish his dominance amongst us by taking point on *all* of the investigations. He's trying to prove that he is still capable of being alpha and leading the team."

"But we already know he can!" Laila shook her head, frustrated. "He founded this team."

"But he's got to prove it to himself."

Laila thought back to the night she had been kidnapped by the Demons. Colin had been there with her. Both of them had been jumped, but Colin had been left behind. The Demons had claimed he was not as valuable a fighter as Laila was.

Perhaps Ali was right, but it should have been a blessing that *he* had not been locked up in a cage like an animal. *He* hadn't had to fight and kill for his survival. But apparently Colin did not see it that way.

Laila was torn. Deep inside she could see his potential, and from what the others told her, he'd been a great leader. But since her arrival, he'd made one bad decision after another. Despite any poor decisions, though, he was still their leader and deserved their respect.

Laila could feel a headache coming on. She stretched her neck as she waited at a stoplight. At least they had made it out of the Old City.

Before The Event nearly wiped out human civilization, a number of cities existed on the eastern side of the 405 freeway, including Hollywood and the affluent city of Beverly Hills. Now it all lay in ruins and was simply named the Old City. In fact, most of the Los Angeles area was abandoned. Only the west side north of the airport had been rebuilt for habitation.

During The Event, most of humankind had been wiped out by a horrific plague of Zombies raised by Demon Necromancers. These Zombies were virtually unstoppable killing machines. The only way that they could be destroyed was to end the Necromancer's spell that was raising them. This was one of the reasons that Necromancy was on the list of offenses that could land a person in Hell. It was far too dangerous, not to mention disrespectful to the dead.

Prior to The Event, Midgard had been isolated and completely unaware of the other worlds that existed in dimensions alongside their own. However, when the kingdoms of the other worlds discovered that Necromancers were behind the attack, they knew they couldn't stand by as the Demon Necromancers laid waste to Midgard.

Laila had only been working in Los Angeles for a few months, but already she had seen her fair share of action, including the incident in which the Greater Demon Marius had kidnapped her. Working for IRSA hadn't been her first choice of careers, but she found it fulfilling in a way. She was of more use here than back home in the Elven city-state of Ingegard, and she liked knowing that she was making a difference.

Finally, she pulled into Ali's garage. The sign painted above it read Fredrico's Automotive Repairs. The building had once housed an automotive repair shop, as well as legal offices on the second and third floor. Ali had bought and renovated the building, but never painted over the old sign, since she found it charming and nostalgic.

Wearily they entered the kitchen.

CHAPTER 2

Ali fished around in the refrigerator for food while Laila searched the cabinets. They were pretty empty, though, with only cereal and junk food remaining.

"Frozen pizza?" asked Ali as she sifted through the freezer.

"Sure."

Between the two of them they could stumble through a pasta recipe without burning down the kitchen, but when they were busy chasing Supernatural criminals all over the city, culinary proficiency ended up low on the priority list.

As Ali preheated the oven, her sister Erin joined them in the kitchen. She wore a pair of black yoga pants and an old band t-shirt.

"How did it go?" she asked, scooting onto one of the stools at the island.

Ali sighed. "We didn't learn anything useful."

"That's not entirely true," pointed out Laila. "What about that insignia? The one on the vial?"

Ali rolled her eyes. "Okay, so we found a picture of a weird-looking skull, but that's about it." She folded up the empty pizza boxes and shoved them into the recycle bin.

"And I saved a Hawk Shifter," added Laila.

"Okay, okay," muttered Ali, "so, it wasn't a total waste of an evening, but we should be out there saving people and tracking down Demons. I don't know what Colin hopes to accomplish with little drug busts like this."

Erin shrugged. She appeared to be in her pre-teen years by human standards, but looks were deceiving when it came to Supernaturals, who often lived much longer lives than humans. Laila looked to be in her mid-twenties, but was in fact 83, and quite young in the eyes of most Elves. Erin was only a few decades younger but, for mysterious reasons, had stopped aging. The inability to reach physical maturity was only one of several issues Erin was facing.

As a Dragon, Erin should be able to shift from human form to her true Dragon form. She should also have the ability to use magic. However, all of these abilities seemed to be just as stunted as her growth.

Ali had determined that it had something to do with the fact that Erin was raised in a Fae family and had no contact with other Dragons and their methods of training their young. It wasn't for lack of trying, but the Dragons were closed off. Especially when it came to the subject of raising their young. Laila had even asked her mother, an Elven diplomat, to aid in their search for answers. She had supposedly connected with a relative of sorts, who was supposed to contact Ali, but so far there had been no word.

"Come on!" Ali said to the oven, staring at the appliance's display as the temperature slowly rose. "Do you think I could just stick the pizzas in now?"

"Yeah, if you want to burn them." Erin slid off her stool and searched the freezer.

Ali ignored her little sister and impatiently stuck the pizzas in anyway. Erin rolled her bright green eyes and shook her head. Her short black hair swayed with the movement. Like Laila,

Erin had short hair, but while Laila's was a neat and profession-al-looking shoulder-length bob, Erin's was choppy and messy. Erin's hairstyle had been a personal style choice, unlike Laila's, which had been the result of a fight gone wrong. In a life-or-death moment, Laila had been forced to chop off her hair or be cut down by a Werecat. She lamented the loss of her long auburn hair, but slowly it was growing out again.

Erin helped herself to a generous portion of ice cream while Ali frowned at her.

"Well, *that's* a healthy dinner."

Erin stuck her tongue out and retreated to her stool. "It's dessert. Don't expect me to wait around until three o'clock in the morning to eat with you two."

Laila's focus drifted away from their conversation as she re-ceived a new alert on her phone. She groaned.

As a recent update to their database system, all field agents now received alerts when they were assigned to a new case. Laila was pretty sure that the true intent behind the new system was to control her life. She was bone-weary and had struggled to get a good night's sleep lately. The constant ping of new cases popping up during the night wasn't exactly helping either. The ever-pres-ent stack of cases was beginning to take its toll. She didn't mind the work, and at least it kept her mind off her own troubles. But lately she was beginning to feel the effects of too much work and too little sleep.

Laila suddenly realized the other two were looking at her.

"Um, sorry. Did you say something?" Laila glanced from one sister to the other.

Ali chuckled. "I was just wondering if you wanted to go out this weekend. We've been so busy lately. I feel like we haven't done anything fun in ages."

"Oh, right."

Laila hadn't even thought that far. She was tempted to lay on a couch and binge watch movies all weekend, or go into hi-bernation, although she should probably find time to cram in a little extra work. But she was reminded of Colin's obsession with work and was suddenly put off.

"Sure." Laila set her phone face down on the counter so she wouldn't have to look at the new alert. "Did you have something in mind?"

"Not yet, but I'll plan something. I—"

"Ali! Seriously!?!" Erin pointed to the oven.

"Ah! Crap!" Ali snatched up a pair of oven mitts and pulled out a pair of slightly burnt pizzas from the oven.

Erin was doubled over, laughing so hard that she almost fell off her stool. Laila laughed until she cried and wiped the tears from her eyes. She tried to find some self-control, but it was late, and restraint was in short supply.

"You guys!" Ali groaned, staring at the slightly blackened pies.

Not willing to wait another thirty minutes, the two of them scarfed down their extra-crispy pizzas in a matter of minutes. With her appetite satisfied, Laila climbed the stairs to her room.

Laila stayed in one of the guest rooms on the second floor. The room was a decent size and even had a walk-in closet, but Laila's favorite part was the attached bathroom. It had beautiful mosaics of sea creatures, which reminded her of home, back in the Elven city-state of Ingegard. That was one thing she missed about Alfheim—the art. Human art just couldn't compare, and Laila was convinced it had something to do with a lack of magic in Midgard.

After she'd returned to Los Angeles, she and Ali had had a long talk about housing. Ali had finally convinced Laila to stay, and they came to an agreement about rent. Laila was relieved that she didn't have to find a new place to live, and she honestly enjoyed living with the sisters. It made life in the city far less lonely.

Turning the faucet in the shower to hot, she discarded her filthy clothes into a hamper and stepped into the shower, relishing the warmth of the water. As she stood there washing the grime away, she thanked the Gods that her life in the city had finally reached some level of normalcy.

Thirty-three-year-old Alice Lawrence parked along the curb of her worn little house which she shared with her ten-year-old son. It had been a long day of work at the grocery store, and she was ready to go home and go to sleep.

She unlocked the front door, expecting the sounds of her son's video games to greet her. Instead, there was nothing but silence.

"Aaron?" She peered into the living room. His backpack rested by the sofa, but her son wasn't sitting in front of the television as he usually was.

Maybe he'd actually listened to her and gone to bed on time? She checked his bedroom, but it was empty, and the bed was still made. She continued to the kitchen, switching on lights as she went.

Her stomach dropped, and she stared in horror.

Furniture was broken, and objects were strewn about. There had been a fight.

Alice's hands shook as she dialed 9-1-1, her eyes never leaving the bloodstained corner of the counter.

CHAPTER 3

Laila circled the Vampire, watching for his next attack. Although Elves were fast, Vampires were faster. She needed any information his body would give her in that instant before he attacked.

As she expected, there was a slight shift of his weight before he lunged. He intended to grab her, but she stepped out of the way and aimed a cut at his ribs with the dagger she held. He dodged at the last moment and was already circling her by the time she had reset her position.

In a flash, he grabbed the front of her shirt and swept her feet out from under her. She fell to the ground, the impact jarring, but she had expected it and was able to reduce the shock.

As his fangs lowered closer to her neck, she shifted the balance of the Vampire above her. Using her body weight, she threw him to the side and rolled on top of him. Instantly she had a dagger pointed at his heart.

Darien gave her one of his signature smart-assed smirks from his position below her.

"Getting a little sloppy?" he asked with a sneer. "I almost got you that time."

"'Almost' being the keyword." Laila winked, and patted his cheek.

The last couple of weeks Laila and Darien had begun sparring together to help keep in fighting form. There was a small gym in the IRSA building, which they utilized. Since their sessions had started, Laila had quickly discovered the advantages and disadvantages to having an undead sparring partner. With the Vampire's ability to heal within seconds, Laila quickly learned there was little use in pulling her blows. And even though Laila could use her magic to heal her bumps and bruises, it was taxing, and it gave her all the more incentive to avoid getting hit.

"I, um, hope I'm not interrupting." A man watched with amusement from the doorway.

Laila glanced up, recognized the man, and smiled. "Torsten!"

She helped Darien up before embracing the Dwarf who had wandered into the gym.

He was short, only about waist height compared to her. His work clothes were plain and covered in metal shavings, and his long curly hair was pulled back out of his face in a ponytail. Torsten, like Laila, had been imprisoned by Marius. Although he had managed to avoid entering the fight ring, Torsten had been held captive for much longer than she had, serving as a weapons smith.

"How does the new job suit you?" she asked.

His expression was uneasy. "That's what I wanted to speak to you about..."

After his rescue, Colin had arranged for a position to be created in IRSA for Torsten. He had hoped that someone with a better understanding of Supernaturals and otherworldly weapons would be able to help develop new means to safely apprehend larger, more dangerous beings. This was important, especially for those without magic, and his inventions were receiving a lot of praise from the higher-ups in Washington, D.C.

The Dwarf glanced between Laila and Darien before continuing.

"I may have a lot of experience in creating weapons, especially ones that target certain tougher kinds of Supernaturals. The trouble is that my skill can only go so far. If I had a Witch helping me, I could make a lot more progress with these inventions."

"Have you spoken to Colin about this?" she asked, folding her arms.

"Not yet." Torsten sighed. "I thought I would run it by you first to see if it would be asking too much."

"I don't think it would be an issue," Darien chimed in as he retuned their equipment to its proper place. "Your department is one of the areas that IRSA is struggling with the most. I just don't know who we could bring in for that sort of thing that IRSA hasn't already considered."

"I might." Laila wiped the sweat from her eyes on a towel. "I could find out if they'd be interested once you get the go-ahead from Colin."

"Thank you." The relief was apparent in his expression. He wandered off in search of Colin while Laila turned her attention back to Darien.

"Did you manage to get any information out of that drug dealer we picked up last night?"

He shook his head. "Not a thing. Not even a rumor of Demonic activity."

"That's what I was afraid of." Laila sank onto a bench. It looked like they were back to square one.

Darien joined her on the bench.

"How about that logo?" she asked, hopefully.

"What logo?"

"That skull with the three faces," She tried to jog his memory. "It was stamped on the vial of pix."

"Right," he said slowly. "No, I haven't gotten around to that yet. Maybe I'll send a picture to the support staff and have them research it."

Laila nodded. She wondered if she should inform him that the same logo was on the attempted kidnapper's car from the night before, but Darien spoke again, interrupting her train of thought.

"I've been contacting my informants to see if they've heard anything about Demonic activity. It troubles me that they've been so quiet. I've got this feeling that dark times are coming." He shook his head.

"Is that a Vampire thing?" Laila asked lightheartedly.

"Kind of." He frowned as he packed up his gear.

Laila had rarely seen him so serious. Whatever was going on, it seemed to bother the Vampire deeply. She hoped for all their sakes that Darien was wrong.

Laila's phone chimed, and she checked the screen. With the upgrade to the new notification system, assignments were color-coded based on their level of importance and urgency. This notification was orange, which meant the assignment was fairly high-priority.

"Duty calls." Laila stood and grabbed her gym bag.

Five minutes later they had changed into their street clothes and were climbing into Darien's SUV. Darien pulled up the address on the GPS and pulled out of the parking garage.

"So, what do we have?" he asked, turning onto the street.

Laila flipped through the transcription of the call to the dispatcher. "Looks like a ritual of some sort. An SNP reported it. He heard strange noises from an abandoned storefront on the border of Culver City and checked it out. The man, a Vampire, said that he saw someone tied up and smelled blood, but it looked like there was magic involved. He's waiting in a parked car down the street from the warehouse and he's on the phone with dispatch."

She selected an auto-reply to dispatch, informing them that they were on their way. The dispatcher would be able to trace her phone and update the witness on their location.

They pulled down the street and spotted a person waiting by a car. He waved them over. As they drew closer, she could see the characteristic red eyes that marked him as a Vampire.

Laila rolled down the passenger window.

"Did you report a strange incident in the area?" she asked.

"Yeah, in there," he said as he pointed to a building across the street. "They're still inside."

"Okay, stay back here in your car. We're going to check it out now, but we have a few questions for you, so please stick around."

He nodded.

Darien parked the car and they cautiously crossed the street. Both of them wore their bulletproof vests, but Laila readied a shield spell, just in case.

As the two of them crept closer to the building, they could hear the low buzz of voices and the shuffling of footsteps. They reached the door, and Laila peered through a crack into the building. People shuffled back and forth frantically as Laila searched for the cause. Perhaps a spell gone wrong.

"Everyone out!" shouted a voice, whose owner was hidden from sight. "Take him with you!"

"Shit!" she hissed to Darien. "They're making a run for it."

Darien kicked the door in, startling those within.

"On the ground! Hands where I can see them!" he roared, bursting through the doors.

Chaos erupted. Men fled in every direction. A few of them drew guns from concealed holsters and fired at them. Laila threw her shield up, scrambling to think of a spell that could contain the men, but nothing would work, there were just too many of them to be contained by a single spell.

Someone flung a metal object at them. It bounced off her shield and rolled on the floor. It was a canister of some kind.

"Tear gas!" shouted Darien, shoving Laila out the door. She conjured a second barrier of air around them to keep the gas out, but the distraction had been enough, the room was empty, and the screech of tires signaled that they were getting away. By the time Laila and Darien could make it to the SUV, they'd be long gone.

"Great," she muttered.

"I'll be back."

In an instant Darien was gone, probably running at superhuman speeds to get a description of the vehicles, or to check around the back.

Laila reentered the building, examining the room. The gas was already starting to dissipate, but she kept her shield up. There was a circle of chalk on the floor with runes drawn around it. She had no idea what language it was, but maybe Torsten could help them identify it. There was fresh blood on the ground as well, but no sign of the individual it came from.

She reached out to feel the energy of the space but recoiled with a hiss. The magical energy of the room was tainted. There was a sick feeling in the air of corrupt magic.

There was something else, another source of magical perversion in the room. The energy signature was unmistakable to Laila. There had been a Demon present in the room.

CHAPTER 4

There was no mistaking it. She'd know that energy anywhere. Faint traces of it had even clung to her after she'd been abducted by Demons. It wasn't particularly strong, so they would be looking for a Lesser Demon.

Greater Demons who managed to escape from Hell had the energy signature of Muspelheim forever burned into their skin, which was really the only sure way to identify a Demon, since any creature could technically be one. Lesser Demons would not necessarily have a Demonic energy signature, but many of them had residual bits of Demonic energy clinging to them from being in close proximity to a Greater Demon. Laila could identify this energy signature, but only if she was searching for it amongst the network of magic in the area.

They'd finally found a Demon, but now there was no telling where they had fled to. Laila took a deep breath to calm her nerves.

"They're gone," grumbled a voice behind her.

Laila jumped and spun around, a spell at the ready, but it

was just Darien.

"Whoa, easy there." He held his hands up in surrender.

"There was a Demon here," she explained shakily.

"What?" he said incredulously.

She nodded.

"Did you see them?" he asked as he turned to look at the pool of blood.

"No, there was too much going on. I only just picked up on the energy signature."

Something wet dripped on her shoulder.

"What the—?" she started.

She glanced up and saw more liquid seeping through the decaying boards of the floor above them. Someone was moving up there.

The stink of gasoline hit her nose.

"Get out!" she screamed, shoving Darien towards the door.

He took off running so fast that he was little more than a blur in front of her, surging through the doorway and across the street beyond.

Somewhere above she heard flames roar to life as the gasoline ignited. Laila threw up a shield around her to protect herself from the flames as the fire quickly spread. She had almost made it to the door when an explosion tore through the building. Her shield took the brunt of it, but the force of the blast thrust her forward, sprawling on the street.

Laila lay there for a moment, dazed. Her shield was gone, obliterated by the explosion, and the flames were licking dangerously close to her clothing. She groaned.

"Get up!" barked Darien from across the street. He stood by, unable to venture closer to the fire.

Laila shook herself out of her stupor and picked herself up off the ground, scrambling away from the flames.

When she'd made it across the street to where Darien stood, she turned and watched the building as the fire consumed it.

"Gods!" breathed Laila, her heart sinking.

She pulled out the phone and called 9-1-1, requesting fire trucks at the scene.

"No, no, NO!" she cried as the evidence burned before her eyes.

She started to prepare a spell to put out the fire, but Darien grabbed her from behind and jerked her around, breaking her concentration.

"Stop it!" he said. "It's too big. Let the firefighters deal with it."

He released her, and she staggered back as she watched the building burn.

The fire crews eventually arrived to extinguish the flames. There was nothing more they could do.

At least they had a witness. They questioned the Vampire there on the street, but he hadn't seen much. His vague descriptions were nowhere near enough for a sketch artist to work with. They thanked him for his cooperation, and Darien passed him one of his cards in case he remembered something later. Then they sent him on his way.

Laila sat on the curb, staring at the unfortunately small list of notes she'd taken while they questioned the witness.

"Come on, let's get out of here." Darien squeezed her shoulder. "The others will want to know what happened."

Back at the IRSA headquarters in Los Angeles, Laila and Darien stepped out of the elevator and onto the third floor of the building where their offices were located.

"Meeting!" called Darien as they walked down the hall and into the conference room on the right. "Ali, Colin, we need to talk."

There was a shuffling of footsteps down the hall. Colin and Ali entered the room but paused in the doorway.

"Rough night?" Colin arched an eyebrow, wrinkling his nose at the smell of smoke.

"You could say that." Laila took a seat in one of the chairs, not caring if the ash on her clothes rubbed off on the upholstery.

The others found their seats, and Laila glanced at Darien, waiting for him to begin. When he didn't respond, she took a deep breath.

"We were out on a call on the border of Culver City. It was something to do with a strange ritual of some sort, but the participants scattered when we showed up. After they'd gone—well, most of them—I realized that there were energy signatures from a Lesser Demon."

"Didn't you follow them?" demanded Colin.

"Yes," explained Darien, "but they were too fast. They escaped in the direction of the Old City before we could stop them."

"Well, most of them did," said Laila. "One of them dumped a canister of gasoline and set the building on fire with us inside. Firefighters are there now, and the police are on their way to keep people out. We'll have to see how much evidence remains in the morning, when the fire is put out."

Colin stood up and massaged his forehead with his fingers.

"So, let me get this straight," said Colin through gritted teeth. "Not only did you let the Demons escape, but you also allowed them to destroy the evidence?"

He slammed his chair into the table.

"What the hell am I paying you for!?!" he growled.

"Seriously?" Ali, raised her eyebrows in shock. "They could've died, and all you care about is the Gods-damned evidence?"

Colin ignored her and stormed out of the room.

"What the hell was that?" muttered Darien. "He's getting to be a real ass, you know." He shook his head in disgust.

Laila and Ali exchanged concerned glances. Something was definitely going on with Colin, but Laila wasn't in the mood to face him right now. They had bigger problems at the moment.

The next day was Saturday, but there was far too much work

for Laila to enjoy the day off. She woke up early and helped the investigative team as well as a team of firefighters who combed through the remains of the building. All that remained were blackened boards and debris in a heaping pile. They had to proceed with caution as smoldering coals were possibly hidden amid the rubble.

They searched for any surviving evidence as well as the cause of the fire. Most of the evidence had been destroyed, though, and the fire had even cleansed the area of the Demonic energy. The firefighters did discover the remnants of a crude bomb that someone had left on the second floor. That explained the explosion that occurred shortly after the fire started. Other than that, there was little revealed by the initial search.

By the time the afternoon rolled around, the head of the investigative team pulled her aside.

"Look," she said to Laila, "we've got this under control. I'll let you know what we find, but this is your day off. Get out of here and decompress."

Laila nodded and wiped the sweat from her face with the back of her hand. Realizing she was covered in soot from head to toe, she cast a spell that flicked most of the ash off her.

She returned to her car and considered her options. There was so much to do, but the investigator was right—she needed a break. She started the engine and headed towards the beach.

CHAPTER 5

After circling the neighborhood three times, Laila finally found a place to park. She walked down the sidewalk and to the beach. The late summer heat was nearly intolerable, but the off-shore breeze brought her some relief. Even so, Laila was sweating by the time she walked through the door to Lyn's Charms and Remedies, the oceanfront shop her friend owned.

Upon first glance, the shop appeared messy, filled with little bits of junk. But to the eye familiar with magic, each knick-knack filling the crowded shelves was a powerful tool. Lyn had told her that she had enchanted many of the objects herself, while some she had bought from other Witches. Once created, the objects could be used in complex spells without draining the spell-caster. Laila had experienced a bad reaction to magic exhaustion and had ended up in the hospital for several days, so she understood the value of these enchantments.

Lyn looked up from the book she was reading behind the counter.

"Hey! It's been a while!"

The Witch looked at Laila's work clothes that were singed

and blackened in places.

"Whoa, what happened?" Lyn examined her filthy clothes. "Why don't you come up to my apartment? I can make us some tea."

"Sure." Laila wandered over to the counter, glancing at the book Lyn was reading. It was old and in poor condition. Lyn had it propped up on foam blocks to keep the spine from cracking. The language was unfamiliar, but Laila assumed it was about magic.

"Oh," said Lyn, following her gaze. "That's just something a friend lent me. I'm looking for something specific, but the book is so dull, it's hard to read."

She stepped around the counter, locked the front door, and flipped the "open" sign to "closed."

Lyn waved Laila through the beaded curtain at the back of the shop. It led to a small hallway lined with books and other odds and ends. At the back was a staircase to the second floor.

Lyn showed her into a small living area and kitchenette. The furnishings were modest, but the view was breathtaking. A large window ran along the entire wall overlooking the beach.

"Wow," Laila marveled at the view. "This is amazing."

"This is why I could never move away from the ocean." Lyn smiled dreamily at the expanse of ocean stretching as far as the eye could see. "What kind of tea would you like?"

"Chamomile, if you have it."

"I definitely do." Lyn opened a cupboard and pull out two mugs. "Find a seat anywhere. Don't worry about your clothes. I've got a spell that will take care of it."

While Lyn rummaged through her cupboards looking for the tea, Laila searched for an available seat. Like the shop, every surface of Lyn's apartment was taken up with magical objects, books, and a variety of magical tools. Laila moved a stack of books to the floor and sat on the plump sofa.

"How have you been?" Lyn called over her shoulder. "I feel like it's been ages since I last saw you."

"I'm feeling much better now. I was probably still recovering from my magic exhaustion last time we met."

"That's right!" She put the kettle on the stove and joined Laila. "So, did you ever find the guy responsible?"

Laila shook her head. "Unfortunately, no. But we're still looking."

"I'm sorry." Lyn frowned. Laila just shrugged.

"Any luck with the research?" she asked the Witch.

"Yeah, I've been meaning to call you about that."

After Laila and the team took down the illegal Demon-run fight ring, she had discovered a letter mentioning an object called a Charon's Obol. She'd looked into it herself, but didn't find much, so about a month ago, she'd asked Lyn for help.

The Witch folded her arms and leaned against the counter.

"Honestly, I didn't find much more than you did. A Charon's Obol is an offering for the Ferryman who guards the river Styx. It allows the souls of the dead to cross over to the afterlife."

"Okay," said Laila, "and what would a Greater Demon want with one?"

"That's what stumped me too, until the other day. Why would a living person want to willingly cross into the realm of the dead? I mean, there are other ways to cross over that are much simpler. Then I came across this text talking about the history of Muspelheim, and how the Gods sealed it off from the rest of the worlds. The problem is that they needed a way for the souls of the dead to be released, and so there is still an open connection from Muspelheim to Styx."

"So, you think they are trying to escape that way?" asked Laila, surprised.

The kettle whistled, and Lyn got up, nodding.

"The problem is that the Ferryman is not easy to bribe. It would take more than an ordinary Charon's Obol to convince him to take them back to the world of the living. They would have to prove that their soul traveled to the land of the dead by mistake."

"That's why they need one that is blessed by Hades," mused Laila.

"Exactly!" exclaimed Lyn. "It's essentially a pardon for a prematurely dead soul. I believe those are extremely rare."

This was a lot to take in. They'd found at least one way that the Demons were possibly escaping. More questions echoed through her mind. Lyn brought over a tray laden with mugs of steaming tea and a plate of cookies and placed it on the coffee table.

"I've got another problem now," added Laila, shifting in her seat.

"What's that?" asked the Witch, biting into a cookie.

"What do you know about rituals?" she asked, unsure how much she should say about an ongoing investigation.

"That's a pretty broad question," pointed out Lyn. "There are so many different rituals, with so many purposes. You've got to be more specific."

"I encountered one that involved blood," said Laila, thinking back to the blood pooled on the floor of the building.

"That's dark magic," Lyn frowned. "The practice of blood sacrifice is connected to black magic and generally frowned upon. In many cases it's even taboo. Especially if the blood comes from a non-consenting victim."

Laila picked up her tea, staring at the flecks of leaves swirling in the water.

"The one I saw last night sounds like that, but the scene was destroyed before evidence could be collected. I don't know what they were doing, but at least one of them was a…criminal. A Lesser Demon."

"Well, shit," Lyn muttered. "Um, I do have some books that talk about blood sacrifice, but most of them are very old, and I can't read many of the languages they're in either. They're just too old."

"You know," began Laila, "my roommate Erin studies languages. She's been pretty bored lately and would probably give you a hand."

"Really?" Lyn asked over her shoulder. "What languages?"

"I'm not sure. I'll text her and see."

While Laila sent the message to Erin, Lyn searched through bookshelves and stacks around the room. Laila's phone chimed with a new message that contained a list of languages. Laila passed the phone to Lyn.

"Oh, wow." The Witch glanced at the list. "Do you think you could take a couple of books with you?"

"Sure, especially if it helps us figure out what these Demons are up to." They needed all the help they could get.

Lyn passed her a stack of dusty books, which she placed on the sofa beside her.

Laila glanced out the window at the setting sun. The clouds were colored in a blend of pink, orange, and purple and were reflected in the surface of the ocean.

"Speaking of work," Laila added, "I'm looking for a Witch to help develop new technology for the agency. Would you be interested?"

Lyn wrinkled her nose.

"Not really." Lyn took a sip of her tea. "I like my current setup. I might know someone who would, though—"

She got up and rummaged through a drawer in a desk. Lyn returned with a business card, which she passed to Laila.

"You could try this guy. His name's Donald. I met him at the local Witch gatherings. He's usually trying to promote the combination of technology and magic, but he's a little odd in my opinion."

"Thanks." Laila pocketed the card. "I'll see if I can arrange a meeting with him."

Laila's phone chimed again. This time the text was from Ali. *Where ARE you? Don't forget we're going out!*

"Oh no!" groaned Laila, grabbing her things.

"What is it?" asked Lyn.

"I'm sorry, I've got to go, I completely forgot I promised to go somewhere with Ali tonight. How much do I owe you for the research?"

Lyn shook her head and smiled. "We can discuss that later. Go on, and watch out for the traffic."

Laila grabbed the stack of books, and Lyn showed her back downstairs to the shop.

The traffic was heavy, but Laila didn't have far to drive. Fifteen minutes later she walked through the garage door with the stack of books for Erin.

"There you are!" huffed Ali, waiting in the kitchen.

She already had her hair and makeup done for the evening.

Laila carefully set the stack of books on the counter, while Ali eyed the thick tomes.

"A bit of light reading?" the Fae asked as she made a face.

"They're for Erin. Lyn needs some help with the translations."

"Oh, good. She's been bored out of her mind lately and playing way too many video games." Ali shook her head. "Hey Erin!"

Erin entered the kitchen, and her eyes lit up.

"Whoa!" Erin opened the first book and skimmed the page. "Do you know how old these are?"

Ali shrugged.

"Ancient," she said with a reverent expression. "They are literally ancient. They're probably worth a fortune."

"Do you think you can look for anything having to do with rituals involving blood or sacrifice?" asked Laila.

"That's pretty gnarly. Sure, but it'll cost you," Erin flashed her a wicked grin.

"Erin!" Ali frowned disapprovingly.

"How much?" asked Laila, feeling suspicious.

"You do my chores for two weeks."

"Deal."

Laila offered her hand solemnly, and Erin shook it. The Dragon picked up the books with a hasty 'Thanks' before retreating to her bedroom.

"Hey! Be careful with those!" Ali yelled after her.

"I will," called the Dragon over her shoulder.

Ali rolled her eyes. "You really shouldn't give in to her like that."

Laila laughed. "Well, it's the least I can do if she's helping. Plus, it'll give her something to do."

"Well, we definitely won't be sitting at home reading dusty old books tonight. By the way, you are not going to wear another boring tank top out. I bought you something new for tonight to help spice up your wardrobe a little. Consider it a gift." Ali winked.

With her curiosity piqued, Laila climbed the stairs and checked her room.

"What in Thor's name…" she trailed off in shock as she examined the clothing on the bed.

Sitting on her bed was a steampunk, over-bust corset. It was mostly made of sturdy black canvas with brown leather accents. There was a jacket that went with it. Ali had also picked out a black pair of skinny jeans and brown knee-high boots to go with it.

With the corset in hand, Laila marched back down the hall.

"What in Thor's name is this!?!" she shouted from the balcony while waving the garment in the air.

"It's a corset," said Ali with a smug grin.

"What's it doing in *my* room?"

"Oh, relax! Trust me, you'll look great. Just put it on. Please?" Ali gave her a look with big puppy-dog eyes.

Laila rolled her eyes and was about to turn back down the hall when she stopped.

"What kind of club did you say we're going to?" she shouted down the stairs.

"A Vampire club," Ali yelled back.

"Great," Laila muttered.

CHAPTER 6

"Wow!" Laila stopped in her tracks. They were still a block away from the club, but they had already found the line. It consisted of a blend of SNPs, punked-out teens, sorority girls, and Vampire wannabes, complete with fake fangs and all.

"Are you sure about this?" Laila asked under her breath.

"Oh, come on. It'll be fun!" But Ali's wavering smile betrayed her waning confidence. They had been to a variety of Supernatural as well as human-owned clubs, but this was their first Vampire club.

They took their place in the line and waited, taking in the people around them. As per usual, they got a number of second glances, but these were of curiosity and fascination rather than the regular looks of disdain. Supernaturals may be common, but there were many humans who retained a strong mistrust of outsiders.

Laila watched the bouncers. They seemed to be turning away most of the humans. She pointed this out to Ali.

When they reached the front of the line, though, the bouncer had no issue with letting them through. Laila suspected that

Ali might have used magic to influence them. Then again, Ali was gorgeous and dressed to kill in a little black dress that clung to her curves.

Whenever they went out, the men flocked in hordes to Ali. Laila knew she paled in comparison, but she was completely fine with that. She preferred to avoid that kind of attention.

Ali, on the other hand, had no shortage of lovers, and kept several of them on speed dial. But then again, Ali was not the kind to become emotionally involved in her relationships.

Passing through thick velvet curtains, they stepped into the bar. It was elegant and dark, the colors ranging from blood-red and silver to black. The furnishings and decor were Victorian in style, but with a Gothic twist. It was exactly what Laila thought of when she heard "Vampire club."

They waded their way through the crowd. Unlike the line outside, the patrons within were mostly Vampires. The rest of the crowd was human, and attractive.

Laila had no problem with Vampires. After all, Darien was her partner. But the sheer number of them in the vicinity left her uneasy. She glanced at Ali, who seemed unaffected.

They stepped up to the bar and ordered a couple of drinks. For once, Laila wished that human alcohol had more of an effect on her.

"I wonder how large this place is." Ali indicated an archway in the back of the room.

"Pretty big," the bartender chimed in, passing them their drinks. "There's a dance floor through there, and a second one below. There are also guestrooms for hire in the event some of our patrons need lodgings close to sun-up."

From the vibe she was getting, Laila suspected that the rooms were likely used for other purposes as well. She paid for their drinks, and the bartender left to help another customer.

"So, what do you think?" Laila gestured to the room.

"I think I want to find that dance floor." Ali, eyed the men in the crowd hungrily.

"Are you sure you're Fae and not a Succubus?" Laila joked, referring to a type of SNP that fed off sexual energy.

"My great-grandmother was a Succubus," said Ali thoughtfully.

"Wait, really?" asked Laila, stunned.

Ali didn't respond. She just sipped her drink nonchalantly and headed towards the dance floor.

"Ali!" called Laila, rushing after her, "you're joking, right?"

She couldn't tell if Ali was messing with her or not.

"You can't just drop a comment like that and walk away!" howled Laila incredulously.

Ali laughed and headed for the archway in the back of the room. It led to a short hallway lined with antique sconces. As they approached the curtains at the other end, they could hear the steady thrum of music.

Equally as large as the front room, the dance floor was surrounded by archways branching off. The lights were low back there, but Laila could make out seating areas.

The center of the cavernous room was a standard dance floor with pulsing lights and writhing bodies. Once again, the vast majority of the people surrounding them were Vampires.

Ali and Laila stood in a small alcove by the door, watching and listening to the music while they enjoyed their drinks before diving straight into the crowd. The Fae was in her element, dancing and swaying with the music. Laila didn't find it nearly as satisfying, but she knew Ali enjoyed the company.

Ali subtly nodded towards a Vampire who could have easily passed for an underwear model. "That guy over there keeps looking at you. He is definitely interested!"

"What?" Laila took a step back.

"You should totally go talk to him!" She had an excited gleam in her eye that made Laila wary.

"Oh no. No, no, no. We are *not* going there tonight."

"Come on, Laila, it's been months. It's time to move on."

Laila shifted her weight, taking a sip of her drink to avoid answering.

The last man she had been remotely involved with had toyed with her feelings, then left without a word. She knew that it was illogical to feel as miffed as she was. After all, she and Jerrik were never officially together. But the Dark Elf's abrupt departure still stung.

A wicked grin spread across Ali's face, and before Laila could stop her, the Fae strode over to the sexy Vampire.

"Damn it, Ali!" Laila hissed, hurrying after her.

When she gracefully slipped into the group of dancing Vampires, they certainly didn't object. Not wanting to get separated this early in the night, Laila reluctantly joined her.

The music was loud and conversation was practically impossible, saving Laila from having to make small talk with the gorgeous Vampire who was now beside her. Without looking at him, she could feel his gaze boring into her, a little too intensely.

She noted that he was not the only one. In fact, there were several Vampires who were looking at both her and Ali with interest. It wasn't long before Laila grew uncomfortable and left with the excuse of buying another drink.

As inconspicuously as she could, she slipped out of the crowd and into the hallway. She paused for a moment to gather her nerves, leaning against the wall. It wasn't often she was spooked this badly. She often dealt with creepers when she was out, but this was something else entirely. Perhaps it was the feeling that the Vampires watched her like an appetizer?

The staccato clack of stilettos caught her attention. A female Vampire approached.

"You look a little tense," she pointed out. "Is everything all right?"

"I'm fine." Laila forced a grin and stood up straight.

"It's your smell."

"What?"

"Your smell is what draws our attention," she said, stepping closer. Laila could see her nostrils flare as she inhaled, smiling.

"Oh?" Laila took a hesitant step backwards.

"Like a fine, exotic wine," purred a voice behind her. Laila gasped and spun around finding herself face to face with the sexy Vampire from the dance floor.

"It's very alluring," added the woman with lust in her eyes.

In the moment Laila had turned to look at the woman, the man placed his hands on her arms from behind.

Ordinarily, Laila would have moved away. Instead, she found herself melting backwards into his lean, muscular body.

"You should join us tonight," he whispered, trailing his lips down her neck, lingering over her vein. Laila's pulse quickened, but this time it wasn't in fear.

"What are you?" Laila gasped. Never had she heard of Vampires with such ability to charm.

The woman caressed her cheek. "Come with us, and we'll show you what else we can do." Her voice held the promise of lusciously dark pleasures.

The male gently spun her. Using a finger, he slowly tilted her chin up, and leaned in for a kiss. It was divinely sensual, and she didn't want him to stop.

The buzzing of her phone brought her back to reality. She glanced at the screen and found a message from Erin reading:

Can't contact Ali. Please call ASAP. It's an emergency.

"I—I have to go," stuttered Laila, sliding from the Vampire's grasp.

The woman looked rather irritated. The man grabbed her hand, stopping her momentarily.

"If you change your mind," he said, brushing her hand with his lips, "you know where to find us."

Thor's hammer, thought Laila as her heart skipped a beat. She nodded before rushing off to find Ali, cheeks flushed. She found Ali back on the dance floor where she had left her.

Laila waved her over.

Ali grinned. "Did you and that guy just…"

"He blasted me with a seriously strong wave of Vampire

charm. I didn't even know they could do that!"

"What!?!" Ali's jaw dropped.

"Yeah, like on a scale of normal to Fae, this guy was off the chart." Laila still felt a little dazed.

"Are you okay?" Ali asked, suddenly concerned.

"Yeah, it felt good. Maybe a little too good." Laila shook her head, blushing. "I think he left a standing invitation."

Ali grinned and did a little victory dance while Laila worried how far that might have gone if her phone hadn't rung…

"Right," Laila said. "More importantly, I think something's up at home. Erin sent this." She showed Ali the message.

"Shit." Ali checked her phone. There was a long list of missed calls. "We better go. She doesn't call unless something is really wrong."

They hurried back out of the club and to Laila's car. Once inside and on the road, Ali called Erin and put the phone on speaker. It rang twice before Erin answered.

"It's about time!"

"What's going on?" Ali asked.

"There's some guy just standing at the door. I don't recognize him at all. I told him to leave, but he's still out there, snooping around the house."

Ali and Laila exchanged glances.

"We're on our way. Just don't let him in," Ali told her as Laila sped up.

"Ugh, yeah, because I was definitely about to invite some weirdo in for a cup of tea."

Laila could picture Erin rolling her eyes on the other end of the line.

"You know what I mean!" Ali snapped, exasperated.

"Whatever, just thought you should know." And with that, Erin hung up.

CHAPTER 7

Laila pulled up along the curb in front of their home to find a man sitting on the doorstep. She didn't recognize him at first glance, but she sensed a familiar energy. It was one of the perks of being an Elf and working with elemental magic. She could read the energy of others, and sometimes even determine what they were. Ali climbed out of the car before Laila could finish parking and stormed up to the man.

Laila sighed and followed her hot-headed roommate.

"If you're looking for an auto mechanic, this shop has been closed for years," Ali all but shouted, a warning tone in her voice. If there was one way to set off Ali's temper, it was to put her family or friends in danger.

"Ali—" Laila warned.

The man gave Ali an appraising and slightly annoyed look, but Ali continued.

"—so clearly you have no business here—"

"*Ali!*" Laila hissed. But the Fae ignored her to continue her rant.

The man stood. He was very tall, with an angular face and a

defined jawline. His nose was slightly crooked as if it had been broken before and his skin was tan from time spent in the sun. The shoulder-length brown hair rustled in the breeze, and even in the darkness, Laila could make out the piercing blue eyes that watched her roommate. Laila suspected he was muscular under his brown coat. But that's not what made Laila's stomach clench in dread, it was the fact that she knew he was a potentially dangerous male Dragon.

In his true Dragon form, it was entirely likely he could roast them for dinner without a second thought. For now, at least, he was in human form, but he was still no doubt a force to be reckoned with. All creatures from the other worlds knew better than to piss off a Dragon.

Laila silently prayed that her clearly insane friend would shut up before she became a silk-wrapped, flash-fried entrée.

The Dragon raised an eyebrow and waited for Ali to finish her lecture on loitering. When Ali paused for breath, he finally spoke.

"My name is Frej Ilmarinen. I'm here to train Erin."

"Oh." Realization dawned on Ali's face. She glanced from Laila back to Frej.

"Please excuse my roommate's confusion," Laila said with her best dignified smile, giving Ali time to compose herself. "You see, we were not expecting your arrival."

It had been weeks since Laila's mother, Ragna, an Elven politician with contacts in the Dragon Kingdom, had informed them that someone with ties to Erin's birth parents would be contacting them. They had expected some written form of contact. Instead, it appeared the Dragon wished to introduce himself in person.

"I am so sorry!" A mortified blush spread across Ali's cheeks. "Please come in!"

Ali ushered their guest into the house. Laila seized the opportunity to leave the awkward conversation and to park her car in the garage.

She took a moment to examine her appearance in her visor mirror. Once she was as presentable as she was going to get, Laila cautiously slid out of her car, eased open the garage door and slipped into the short hall leading to the kitchen. She silently edged into the room, pretending to make herself busy by searching for some snacks.

"Erin!" Ali called down the hall on the other side of the great room where she stood with their guest. "Come here, please, I want to introduce you to someone."

The Dragon waited as footsteps approached from down the hall. Erin poked her head around the corner.

"Erin," Ali began, "this is Frej Ilmarinen. He's here to help mentor you."

"If she can be trained, that is," Frej added, still frowning.

"What do you mean *if?*" Erin crossed her arms, giving him a look.

"You mean if, *sir*," the man interjected sternly. "If I'm going to take you on as my pupil, I ask that you show me due respect." His stance bespoke a military background.

Erin stared with her mouth gaping like a fish. Slowly, she recovered, giving the man a seething look. Frej ignored her and continued.

"Not all Dragons who reach your age without receiving any training can even access their powers. They simply remain blocked."

Laila watched as he continued. By Elven standards, Laila found his response to be honest, but curt. But the Fae, and those raised in Fae society, were a lot more sensitive as a whole. Laila bit her lip and exchanged glances with Ali, who was stunned.

"Who the hell do you think you are!?!" Erin's temper erupted. "You come in here, demanding I call you 'sir,' then you tell me that there could be something wrong with me? Ugh, newsflash! I didn't ask to get abandoned by your *stupid* society!!!"

The look of horror on Ali's face told Laila that this was not at all how she imagined this moment going.

"Let's get something straight." Frej's voice rumbled like thunder. Even from across the room, Laila could see how his sky-blue eyes shone. "I have better things to do with my time than to attempt to train some angsty and entitled child. So, if this is going to be a waste of my time…"

Erin made a rude gesture and headed down the hall. Ali seemed at a loss for words, and even Laila wished she could sink back into the cupboards.

The downside of living with two sisters was the family drama. Laila usually was good about staying well away from any arguments, but it was too late for her to sneak out of the room. Instead, she silently watched as her friend's hopes for opening up her sister's future unraveled.

"I'm so sorry!" Ali said, trying to calm the fuming male Dragon. "Erin has no idea what she is saying."

"I should've known—" He began heading towards the door, but Ali held up her hands.

"Please don't leave yet. It's my fault for not preparing her for this." Ali spoke with confidence, but Laila knew the Fae well enough to hear the desperation in her voice. She didn't use her Fae magic to charm him, which was wise. But it seemed her determination alone softened the Dragon's heart just enough that he stopped before the door.

"Hey!" Laila interjected, stepping forward. "Why don't you come get a drink with me? I'm sure you could use it after traveling through the inter-dimensional security checkpoints."

Drinking with a pissed-off Dragon was definitely not at the top of her list of things to do, but if it would buy Ali the time to talk some sense into her sister….

Frej looked her up and down thoughtfully for a moment. A flicker of amusement crossed his eyes as he took in Laila's corset. Laila stood her ground.

"Very well," he said flippantly. "I could use a drink."

Ali cast her a grateful glance as Laila grabbed her keys from the kitchen counter.

CHAPTER 8

Laila waited patiently while her companion looked over the drinks menu of the Irish pub. She already knew what she wanted anyway. She'd often stopped here after work with Ali. She placed an order for a basket of fries while Frej made up his mind.

Laila watched the Dragon. His clothes were definitely from Alfheim. He wore a knee-length greatcoat. The brown fabric seemed sturdy enough, but there was delicate gold embroidery along the cuffs and lapels. His boots were nicely polished as well, and there were no signs of wear on his pants or tunic. He carried himself like a soldier, but his clothes suggested he was well-off, or more so than the average soldier at least. His appearance attracted some odd glances from other customers, but the Dragon ignored them.

Other than Erin, Laila had spent very little time with Dragons. She knew that they held similar values as Elves and tended to put a lot of emphasis on order, education, and culture. But they were closed off and rarely welcomed outsiders. Her mother had mentioned that Dragons could be secretive about many aspects of their lives and cultures when it came to outsiders. They could take a human form or Dragon form, and they had some magical abilities. Beyond that, Laila knew them by their reputation to be easily angered, and that they were more likely to roast you now and ask questions later.

Frej glanced over at her.

"What do you get out of this, anyway?" he asked in the common tongue of the other worlds.

"Excuse me?" The question was so sudden it caught her by surprise.

"I mean, why are you helping Ali and Erin?" He folded the menu and placed it on the slightly sticky bar.

"They're my friends," she said, a little confused. "Of course I want to help them."

"Have you known them long?"

"I met them when I moved to Los Angeles about four months ago. Why?"

He chose his words carefully before he answered.

"It's an odd situation to be called upon to train a young Dragon like this. Until a couple of months ago, I wasn't even aware of Erin's existence."

Frej examined the condiments sitting in the basket in front of them.

"Aren't you a relation of Erin's?" Laila asked, watching, as he picked up a bottle of ketchup to read the label.

"No, not by blood. I was a friend of her father's." There was a pained tone to his voice. "He was a good man. I was away on business when her parents were killed. I knew they had an egg, but I assumed it had been destroyed."

Laila was tempted to ask more, but she didn't wish to pry. Luckily, a waitress arrived with her basket of fries. She munched on one while Frej eyed the basket with interest.

"Go ahead, help yourself." She gestured to the fries while she poured a healthy serving of ketchup into the basket.

"What are those?" he asked skeptically.

"French fries." By his expression, her explanation didn't help. "They're deep-fried potatoes. Just try one."

He cautiously ate one and shrugged with disinterest, but Laila noticed he quickly went back for another. Before she knew it, he was inhaling the basket.

"Is this your first time in Midgard?" Laila asked with amusement.

"No," he replied stiffly, "but my previous visit was very rushed, and there was no time for such meals."

The bartender took their drink orders, and Laila quickly added a couple of burgers to their order. It was already clear that the two of them would make fast work of that single basket of fries.

"So, what exactly *are* you doing here?" He glanced sideways at her. "You're a bit far from home, aren't you?"

Laila thought for a moment. How much was wise to tell him? She had no idea who this man was. Then again, if all went well, he would be spending a lot of time around the house. He probably had a right to know what she did for a living.

"I work for the Inter-Realm Security Agency. Ali and I are both agents who work here in the city with any Supernatural-related issues."

"I see." He gave her a more thorough examination. Laila couldn't help but shift under his gaze. She saw a small spark of amusement flicker across his face.

"So," he continued, "what exactly does that job entail?"

"Just that I help to keep the peace in situations that the human police may not be prepared to handle."

The bartender passed them their drinks, and she thanked him. Turning back to Frej, she noticed he was still watching her with that unreadable stare. It was so blank and reptilian, the way he observed her. Laila attempted to change the subject to something other than herself.

"So, this block that Erin has on her magic, is this normal for your kind?"

"Generally, no." Frej took a cautious sip of his beer. "It only happens amongst young Dragons who are not exposed to elemental magic. I suppose that Erin suffered this block because she was raised in a Fae household where the only magic she had exposure to was glamour and charm magic."

Laila frowned. "I've lived with them since I arrived, and in that time she would've been exposed to elemental magic." After all, Elves used elemental magic, meaning that each spell she cast was in some way connected to the elements. Those Elves who trained for years were able to branch out into other magic as well, but elemental magic was always the strongest.

"It could be that she's past the age where she should've had exposure." He shrugged as he ate the last fry in the basket.

"So, it really could be too late for her?" Fear blossomed in the pit of her stomach. If Erin could not be unblocked, so to speak, Erin would remain trapped perpetually as a child, with no connection to any of her inherited Dragon traits.

"Calm down, Elf." He gave her a wolfish grin. "I only said that to scare the girl and to see how serious she is about this training. There's no reason she can't break the block. It may take time, but she has to be determined. If she isn't willing to put in the work, then by all means her magic will be bound forever."

Before Laila could speak, their food arrived. Whatever retort Laila was about to say vanished as she watched Frej poke at his burger, searching for an appropriate method to eat it.

Pretending not to notice his dilemma, Laila silently picked up her veggie burger and took a bite. Frej quickly followed her lead, and within seconds half of his burger was gone.

"I haven't eaten since I left Alfheim," he said, sitting a little straighter and holding his chin up. He attempted to slowly consume the rest of his meal with dignity. Laila couldn't help but laugh.

"Were you at work when I arrived?" The Dragon eyed her rather revealing corset.

Laila nearly choked on her burger. "Oh no, definitely not.

We were out at a club."

"With Vampires?"

"How—?"

"I can smell them."

He waited for her to continue.

"Ali wanted to check out this new Vampire club. I discovered the hard way that Elf blood is, um, apparently a delicacy."

"Did they attack you?" Frej asked, suddenly concerned.

"No. I think they had other plans." Laila couldn't prevent the heat from creeping into her cheeks as she remembered her encounter in the hallway. "Besides, I've been training with a Vampire lately. If push came to shove, I could've stood my ground against the two of them."

"The *two* of them?" he asked with interest.

She searched for the words to form an appropriate explanation that would salvage her reputation, as a bemused smile spread across his face. Laila grinned at him sheepishly and shrugged.

Frej laughed, a sound that rumbled throughout the bar.

Laila noted that he was actually very good-looking, particularly when he smiled. His most striking feature was his azure eyes. Despite their intensity, she couldn't help but feel there was something pleasant about them, friendly even.

"You mentioned," she started, "that you didn't know Erin was alive until my mother contacted you. Ali told me that her parents had spent years trying to find any relative they could, so how is it possible that you never heard a thing?"

He paused as if considering how much to say.

"I'm often away working for the royal family." He stared across the bar as if looking for something in the distance. "It is possible that I didn't hear simply because I was away."

Laila was skeptical, but before she could voice her opinion, he faced her, serious.

"Believe me, though." The pain returned to his voice. "If I had known that Brandr's daughter was out there alive, nothing would have stopped me from finding her. The only reason it took me as long as it did to arrive here was that I was tied up and didn't receive the full message until a few days ago."

A commotion near the door pulled her attention away. She peered over the crowd to see two unruly men nearly at blows. Human conflicts were not her responsibility, but it felt wrong to stand by. She excused herself and squeezed through the gawking bystanders.

"I don't care what's going on," the bartender boomed, approaching the men, "I want both of you out of my pub!"

One of the men rounded on the bartender, swinging a wild right hook. It was poorly aimed, but the slow human bartender never saw it coming. She intercepted it, grabbing his wrist and twisting his arm behind him. The position wouldn't hurt him, but it wasn't particularly comfortable either.

"I suggest you listen to him," she said to the drunk. "If not, I've got friends with LAPD who would gladly escort you to a cell to sober up."

She let the man go, giving him a slight shove towards the door.

"Go home, Elf bitch!" the other man called. "Go back to your own world!"

The man spat at her feet, making a rude gesture. The other one stared at her, fear and hate written on his face. She stood her ground, though, and the two men took their cue to leave.

Of course, she sighed. The spitting. *What was it with humans and spitting?* she wondered, irritated. They always seemed to spit at you when you annoyed them. She couldn't even recall another type of creature that expressed rude displeasure with spitting. Not even Trolls.

Laila returned to her place at the bar, aware of the hushed conversation and glances directed her way. She finished the rest of her drink in one go, before speaking.

"It might be a good idea if we leave," Laila muttered, barely loudly enough for the Dragon to hear. It wouldn't be beyond the realm of possibility for one of those guys to return with friends, and she would really prefer to avoid that.

Frej shrugged but didn't protest. Laila handed the bartender some cash. It would more than cover their meal.

After making sure that no one was lurking in the parking lot, Laila climbed into her car, with Frej close behind her.

"I'm sorry." She sighed. "I should've let those men be."

"Do you get that treatment often?" He indicated the bar. "I mean, humans acting like that?"

"Often enough." She glanced at the Dragon seated in the passenger's seat.

"I'm sure you could find a more pleasant job back in Alfheim," he commented, "so why stay here when the humans treat you like this?"

"It's not all bad." She fidgeted with the keys on the key ring. "I've got a great team here, and Midgard really needs the help right now. I'm actually making a difference here."

She thought back to Marius, freely roaming somewhere in Midgard. She couldn't let Demons like him take control of this world.

"This probably sounds crazy," she continued, "but I feel like I'm supposed to be here."

Frej watched her, his expression unreadable.

"You're far more interesting than I gave you credit for," he admitted thoughtfully as Laila started the engine to head home.

"Why do you say that?" She watched him from the corner of her eye.

"Most Elves I've encountered wouldn't be bothered to live here in this world."

Laila laughed. She could tell he was watching her again with that same unreadable, expression. Laila waited for him to say something, but he seemed content to spend the remainder of the drive deep in thought.

Minutes later, they stepped into the great room to find Ali waiting for them.

Frej, appearing to be in a cheery mood, clapped Ali on the

shoulder.

"We'll start lessons in the morning," he announced with a grin.

"Oh! Great!" Ali said, surprised. "Please, I've got a guest room on the second floor. You are welcome to stay there."

She escorted the Dragon upstairs, leaving Laila standing in the kitchen. Laila took her time hanging up her keys and helping herself to a glass of water. Ali hurried back into the kitchen with a look of awe.

"How on earth did you do that?" she asked, laughing. "I thought he was leaving for sure!" Ali was practically jumping up and down with excitement.

"Honestly, I don't know." Laila had no clue why he had changed his mind, but she remembered their conversation about Erin's father, Brandr. Perhaps he had never intended to leave.

Laila climbed the stairs to her room. She was just heading down the hall when Frej stepped out of the guest room wearing nothing but a towel. Every muscle on the Dragon's toned chest and broad shoulders was defined in a way that made it difficult for Laila to keep her eyes from wandering.

"I—I'm glad you decided to stay." She hid her embarrassment and made sure to keep her attention on the Dragon's face.

"That's good to hear," he smiled before heading down the hall to the bathroom. Laila hurried to her own room, thanking the gods it was an ensuite.

CHAPTER 9

Laila woke once again from a night of restless sleep plagued by nightmares filled with Demons and small concrete cells. It was clear she was not going to get any more rest that night. Throwing off her tangled blankets and climbing out of bed, she opted to take a leisurely shower.

While she waited for the water to heat up, she pulled off her pajamas and examined her toned body. It was covered in a handful of bruises and scrapes from her training sessions with Darien. She sighed and called up her magic to heal herself.

If she twisted around, she could see four long scars that raked down her back. They were a reminder of a near-death encounter in the Demon-run fight ring.

Mysteriously, a Goddess had appeared to her. Laila had never learned the Goddess's identity, but she had healed her, leaving scars in a silvery bluish-white color. They reminded her of moonstones, like the moonstone in the pommel of the dagger she'd found when she returned to save the rest of the captives. Laila was not entirely sure how she had found it, but she had used it to rescue Torsten from the Demons.

She brushed her fingers over the curious scars once more before stepping into the shower.

Memories of the night before returned, reminding her that there was now a male Dragon living down the hall.

With a groan, Laila used a bit of magic to pull the excess water from her hair, drying it, and then pulled on a pair of jeans and a T-shirt from her closet.

After slapping on a bit of makeup, she headed downstairs. The other three were already there, sitting at the long dining table in the far corner of the great room with a variety of breakfast foods sitting before them.

"'Morning," Laila called to the others, pouring a steaming mug of coffee. She joined them at the table.

Ali and Frej greeted her, but Erin sat glowering at her plate while the local news played in the background. Laila had a feeling it was going to be a long day for all of them. Maybe she would head in to the office after all, if only to escape.

"Ugh!" Erin scowled at the television. "I don't understand why you are always watching the news. It's depressing!"

Ali shot her sister a look before returning her attention to the female news reporter on the television.

"—Anyone with information on the boy, named Aaron Lawrence, is asked to contact the authorities," said the reporter, before switching to a different topic.

"What was that about?" Laila asked, leaning against the counter.

"A human boy was kidnapped." Ali regarded the television grimly. "See, this is exactly why I want a new security system installed."

Erin gave Laila a desperate look. Laila shrugged. Ali tended to be over-protective of her sister at times. Laila tried to stay out of their family conversations, but she had to admit that a little extra security wouldn't hurt.

They ate in awkward silence until Laila couldn't handle it any longer.

"So, what's the plan for today?" Laila asked the others. Frej was the one who finally responded.

"I will begin Erin's education on Dragon culture and custom. Perhaps if we have time, I'll introduce her to some basic magic. But first things first. I need to determine what her element is. It shouldn't take long, but we'll need room to work."

Ali and Laila cleaned up the mess from breakfast while Erin and Frej cleared away more space in the living room, pushing the furniture aside.

Laila started towards the garage door, but Ali stopped her.

"Where do you think you're going?" Ali hissed at Laila. The Fae glanced over her shoulder at Frej and Erin.

"I—"

"There is a strange Dragon in our house, giving Erin her first-ever magic lesson. You can't leave me here alone with them!"

Laila shrugged. "You can come with me."

"Seriously!?!" Ali shook her head incredulously. "Please stay! If something goes wrong, I want to know there is someone I can trust to intervene and save my sister, and my house for that matter."

Laila watched the two Dragons preparing for their lesson.

"Fine," said the Elf, "but I'm going to get my laptop from the car. The investigative team should have uploaded photos from Friday's crime scene, and I want to see if the runes survived the fire."

Ali nodded and took a seat on the couch. Laila retrieved her laptop and set it up on the table in the corner of the kitchen where she could still observe, but from a distance.

"Now," began Frej, "unlike Elves who can use all elements, Dragons each have the ability to utilize one element. That element is not only the basis of their magic, but also their Dragon type."

The master and pupil sat on the floor across from each other. Frej continued.

"There are four Dragon types: fire, air, water, and earth.

These traits are inherited, but since your father's element was fire, and your mother's element was earth, we won't know for certain until we test your abilities."

Despite herself, Laila found she was more focused on the lesson than the screen in front of her. Then again, it wasn't often an outsider was able to observe anything to do with Dragons.

"What kind of Dragon are you?" Erin asked.

"Air."

"Can you still breathe fire?"

"No, only Fire Dragons have that ability."

Laila and Ali exchanged glances. At least now they knew he wouldn't huff, and puff, and burn their house down.

"Any more questions before we begin?" Frej asked.

Erin shook her head.

"Good." He pulled out a cloth sack that Laila had not noticed earlier. From it he produced a rock, a candle, a small glass bottle filled with water, and a feather. He passed the rock to Erin.

"I want you to hold it between your hands like this." He demonstrated. "Now, study the rock. Take in every detail of it so you can form a picture in your mind."

He watched quietly while Erin examined the rock before continuing.

"Close your eyes and form a picture of that rock in your mind. Recall everything about it—every detail is important, every bump, curve, and color that you saw.

"Now, as clearly as you picture that rock as it is, imagine it crumbles in your hands, reduced to a pile of sand."

They watched as Erin's brow creased in concentration. The minutes ticked by, but nothing happened. Frej offered suggestions, but still nothing happened.

"Next, we'll try fire." He struck a match, lit the candle, and placed it in front of her. "This time I want you to memorize every detail of the flame. Consider the way it moves, its color, what shape it takes, everything. Then I want you to close your eyes again, see the flame in your mind as it is, then picture it growing so it burns twice as high."

Erin tried, but nothing happened. Laila glanced over at Ali, whose frown was deepening. Ali's grip on her coffee mug was so tight that her knuckles were beginning to turn white.

"That's okay," Frej told them, digging around in his bag once more. "Just because her parents' elements were earth and fire doesn't necessarily mean that hers will be too. She could've inherited air or water abilities from an ancestor."

He repeated the process with the feather, trying to get Erin to move it with air, as well as to shape the water. Still there was no result.

Frej pushed Erin, working with each element over and over to no avail. Finally, after two hours, Erin had had enough.

"Stop!" she yelled. "This isn't working. Nothing is happening!"

"Losing your temper is not going to help you," Frej pointed out coolly.

Erin folded her arms and glared back at him.

"Fine. We'll come back to this later."

They moved on to history and culture, but this time Frej asked for a room with more privacy.

Ali shrugged and suggested they use the small office next to Erin's room.

Laila moved the furniture back into place. With the bulkier pieces, she used her magic to shift them. Ali returned just as she was moving the last sofa back into place.

"It looks so simple when you do it." Ali indicated the furniture.

"I've been using elemental magic for decades, though. Erin's just beginning."

"Do you think she'll get the hang of it?" she asked anxiously.

Laila nodded. "Of course she will! She just needs time," she added quietly. "I think this is new for both of them."

"What did he say last night when you were out?" Ali asked, leaning against the counter.

"Not much more than he told you." Laila glanced down the hall. "He mentioned that it would be possible to train Erin, but he wasn't exactly giving information away freely."

"Sounds like a typical Dragon." Ali shook her head.

"He did seem pretty interested in why *we* were here in Los Angeles, though." Laila thought back to their conversation.

"Do you think he's here to spy on us?" asked Ali suspiciously.

Laila considered the thought. It had occurred to her as well, but she was fairly certain that he wasn't working with the Demons. At least not directly. He could be reporting information back to the Dragons, but that wouldn't make much sense. After all, the Dragons had been among the first to extend their help to the humans during The Event. Why would they be interested in spying for information that they probably already had access to in other ways?

"I don't know," said Laila finally. "We should probably keep an eye on him and see how things progress. If it appears he's a threat, then we'll deal with him then. For now, we'll just have to watch what we say around him."

Ali nodded in agreement.

CHAPTER 10

"I heard you had a date with a Dragon Saturday night." Darien smirked as he and Laila circled each other in the gym.

Laila dodged as he cut at her diagonally. She narrowly avoided the cut to her stomach that followed.

"I never realized you were into those dangerous types." Darien gave her a wicked look.

Darien was an insufferable womanizer, although he was never anything less than professional when it came to his female colleagues. However, it was for that reason that she and Darien often worked as partners. Laila could help keep the Vampire on track, while having a partner who was unnaturally fast and strong. Plus, Darien knew far more about local human and Supernatural history than anyone else on the team.

Ignoring the bait, Laila feinted a cut to the left. As she had planned, the Vampire recognized her tactic. He moved to block her attack, but she feinted again and cut back to the left side. The shock on Darien's face was priceless as he stared at the training knife poking his ribs.

"And I never realized Vampires were so attracted to my

blood," she whispered. "Funny how those details are overlooked."

Darien frowned. "How did you–?"

"Ali and I went to a Vampire club Saturday night as well."

"And you didn't invite me!?!" Darien made a show of his offense.

"Well, I didn't think I would require backup to fend off a club full of hungry Vampires!"

He tried to cover it, but Laila could still see the laughter in his eyes. She scowled.

"Plus," Laila continued, "I didn't know you had magic."

"I don't," Darien replied, confused.

"Then how—"

"Sorry to interrupt." Torsten stuck his head into the gym doorway. "I just heard Colin was looking for you both."

Laila and Darien exchanged looks.

"He's in the conference room," Torsten continued.

Whatever he wanted was probably urgent if he was calling a meeting out of the blue. Darien and Laila grabbed their bags and were heading out when Laila paused.

"I almost forgot. I have a lead on someone to assist you. I gave the guy's contact information to Colin earlier."

"Thanks." Torsten smiled before heading back to his workshop.

Still in their sweaty workout clothes, Laila and Darien took their places in the conference room with Colin and Ali. The room was larger than her office and filled with a big table surrounded by chairs. A television-sized monitor allowed for videoconferences and presentations. Covering one wall were maps of Los Angeles and the surrounding areas. A tablet rested on the table with a file open.

Laila glanced at the first photo in the file and frowned.

"Isn't this the missing boy from the news?" she asked Ali, as she looked up.

Before Ali could answer, Colin took command of the room.

"It is. LAPD contacted me this morning regarding the case.

They seem to think there could be SNPs involved, and I'm inclined to agree. I wanted the three of you to take a look at the file and see if there is anything that stands out about the crime scene."

Darien scrolled through the photos, stopping at one. "Was all this blood from the boy?"

"We're not sure. LAPD took samples, but the test results haven't come back yet."

Laila examined a photo of the boy. Why would an SNP want to kidnap a human boy and possibly injure him in the process? There was nothing that stood out as particularly Supernatural about the crime scene. Laila mentioned this to the others.

Colin shrugged. "The doors were all locked, and there was no sign of forced entry."

"So?" asked Darien. "The kidnapper could've had a key."

Colin selected a photo. It appeared to have been taken by the back door and showed multiple sets of large footprints leading away from the house. Some of them appeared to be larger than the average male human's. It was possible they belonged to an SNP, but someone was grasping at straws.

"This is not substantial evidence to support an SNP connection," said Laila with a frown. "We don't have time to take this case."

Colin turned to her. "We've been asked by the LAPD to take a look at it, and considering all they do for us, I am willing to at least examine the crime scene. I am assigning all of us to this case. This isn't a problem for you, is it, Agent Eyvindr?"

He gave her a withering glare, daring her to challenge him. Where did this come from? She'd done nothing but put the safety of the team and the city first. In the last few months she'd shown nothing but dedication, but now this?

"No, sir," she replied with all the Elven poise she possessed, trying to keep the offense out of her voice. She sensed the others bristle beside her.

He returned his attention to the rest of the group. "We'll be leaving immediately to examine the scene and speak with the mother."

He glanced disapprovingly at Laila and Darien in their workout clothes.

"Once you change, that is," Colin added with disdain.

Laila and Darien hurried back down to the small locker room.

"Did you piss him off of something?" asked Darien when they were out of earshot.

Laila shook her head. "No, not unless he's still upset that I left my post during the drug bust."

"Meh, I doubt that'd be it." Darien paused as they reached the doors to the locker rooms. "I don't know, I've always thought he was a little high-strung, but this is something else."

He turned and entered the men's locker room as Laila stood there in the hallway for a moment. She wondered what could possibly be the cause of Colin's irritable moods, but came up blank. With a sigh, she entered the women's locker room to change.

When the team arrived at the house, they found the mother waiting for them outside by the front door.

"Alice Lawrence?" Colin asked as he walked up the pathway. The woman nodded

"My name is Colin Grayson. My colleagues and I are with the Inter-Realm Security Agency," explained Colin, stopping short of the door.

"Yes, I was told to expect you. Please come in." She unlocked the door and invited them inside.

As Laila passed the woman, she noticed that there were heavy bags under her red, swollen eyes. She seemed fragile, as if a breeze might knock her over.

"I've been staying with a friend," she explained as she

switched on the lights. "I don't feel comfortable staying here by myself at the moment."

Ali nodded and gently asked if she could answer a few questions from her and Colin. Meanwhile, Laila and Darien examined the crime scene.

Luckily, it had remained untouched since the LAPD's investigation. A cleaning crew had yet to arrive, so Laila and Darien went to work.

Aside from the blood splatters and signs of a struggle, the small, older kitchen was clean and well maintained. The refrigerator was covered in pictures of Alice Lawrence and her son, Aaron. Compared to many of the situations she had dealt with, this family seemed so ordinary, aside from the fact that the boy had gone missing in such a frightening way.

"Well, I can tell you that the majority of this blood isn't from the boy," Darien said to Laila as he examined a bloodied corner of the counter and took a whiff of it. He shook his head in disgust. "This is definitely from an SNP, and I'm tempted to say from Jotunheim by the smell."

"Well, I suppose that proves that SNPs were involved," Laila concluded, a little annoyed that Colin had been right.

Laila took a deep breath and exhaled, allowing her senses to open to the magic in the space. She searched for remnants of a spell or something to determine why the boy had been abducted.

She continued to search the space but found nothing aside from faint traces of magic around the door that would have been from a spell to unlock it. That was enough to prove that a Sorcerer had been present too. They took additional photos and notes, as well as blood samples.

Finally, they returned to the living room where the others were wrapping up.

"Thank you for your time, Ms. Lawrence," said Colin, shaking her hand. "We will do everything we can to help find your son."

"Thank you." She wiped the tears from her eyes.

Ali hugged the woman, and when she pulled away, Laila noticed that Alice Lawrence had calmed down a little. Laila suspected Ali had used a hint of magic.

They piled back into their black SUV, Colin grimacing and rubbing his eyes.

"Everything okay?" asked Darien.

"Yeah, just a headache." Colin pulled out a bottle of pills.

"Should I drive?" offered Darien, frowning.

Colin shook his head. "I'm fine."

He started the engine and pulled away from the curb.

"Well, you were right about this case." Darien sighed. "Some of the blood in there is Supernatural."

"We'll see what the lab comes back with and if we get a match with one of the registered SNPs on file." Colin slowed to turn a corner. "The mother doesn't appear to have connections with any SNPs though. The father died during The Event, so at this point, I can't see a motive."

A thought occurred to Laila that chilled her to the bone.

"What if the purpose of this kidnapping was to pit humans against SNPs?"

Realization dawned on the rest of the team.

Ali shivered. "It could destroy what relationship humans and Supernaturals have."

"We need to keep this quiet," said Laila. "At least until we find the ones responsible. The media would blow this way out of proportion."

The others mumbled in agreement.

"We'll keep these suspicions to ourselves until we know more about what happened here." Colin glanced at the others.

Ali sighed. "This isn't much to go off of."

CHAPTER 11

Just as the team pulled into the garage, both Laila's and Darien's phones chimed. Laila opened the notification from the support staff.

"We've got to go," she said to Darien. "Someone's reported another ritual. This one's in the Old City."

They climbed out of the SUV along with Ali and Colin. But rather than heading towards the elevator, Laila saw Colin get into his personal vehicle.

"Everything okay?" she asked suspiciously. It was too early for him to be heading home.

"Just a meeting," he added hastily as he checked himself in the visor mirror.

"Do you have a second to talk?" Laila asked.

"Don't you have somewhere to be?" He shot back.

"Come on Colin!" hissed Laila her hand gripped he door, preventing him from shutting it. "What's gotten into you?"

"You're one to talk," said Colin pointedly, "You were the one that left your post in the middle of a drug bust. And now you're ignoring an urgent call. I suggest you get going."

Laila opened and closed her mouth before climbing into Darien's SUV. He was right, she needed to go, but it seemed strange to her that he was leaving so early in the evening.

"It's a date," explained Darien as they pulled out of the parking garage.

"What?" she spluttered.

"Yeah, I overheard Colin on the phone earlier."

"I didn't know he was dating," she said, genuinely surprised.

Laila didn't know how to feel about that. A month ago, she would have been happy to see him leave work early every now and then, and to see that he was moving on from the death of his late wife. But with his recent attitude, she felt more annoyed than happy for him.

"With all the cases we've had lately, how can he justify extra time off?" she asked bitterly.

"That's the thing," Darien brooded, "I've been watching him lately, and I don't think he has the same caseload as we do."

He pulled onto the 405 freeway going north. Luckily there was no traffic at this late hour.

"What do you mean?" pried Laila.

"I mean, he doesn't seem to have as many cases as we do. He hasn't stayed late in weeks, either."

"Maybe it has to do with the headaches?" Laila suggested. It seemed more reasonable for Colin to take off early because of a medical issue than a date.

"You noticed those, too?"

She nodded. Tonight wasn't the first time she'd seen him take those pills.

"But doesn't it concern you, given our work?" she asked.

Darien paused. "Honestly, I think it's just Colin being Colin. He should probably see someone about those headaches and make sure there isn't something health-related going on. I don't know what to do about attitude, but I'll admit it's getting to be an issue. If it was one or two outbursts then okay, whatever. But this?" He shook his head at a loss for words.

Darien exited the freeway and entered the dark streets of the Old City. This location was only a little deeper into the Old City, but far more abandoned. It was surprising that the ritual had even been reported, especially since the people of the Old City were less than fond of the authorities.

"This is it." Laila pointed towards a building up ahead. It was a hotel of some sort, and the front doors had been kicked in. They strapped on their bulletproof vests and got out of the car, shutting the doors as quietly as they possibly could, not wanting to give themselves away if there was anyone still in the building. Laila prepared a shield spell as they approached.

Darien glanced cautiously around the corner, then waved her forward. They entered the dark and silent hotel lobby.

"I smell blood," said Darien. "Lots of it."

Laila conjured a glowing ball of light. In the middle of the lobby was another large chalk circle that looked identical to the one at the previous ritual site. At the center was a body lying in a pool of coagulating blood.

Darien took a step closer, but Laila grabbed his shoulder.

"Hold on," she cautioned. "There could be an active spell around there. Give me a minute."

Darien turned his attention to watch the lobby around them as Laila fell into a trance. Reaching out with her magic, she searched for spells or magical creatures. Around the chalk circle floated bits of a spell that had already been completed. It had been an intense spell, whatever it was, but by now it was completely harmless. The faintest traces of Demonic energy lingered in the air.

"Okay." She pulled out her phone to request an investigative team to join them.

Darien approached the body, giving it a quick examination.

"He's a young male in his teens," said Darien. "Looks human, but the smell's a little off. If I had to guess, I'd say he was a reptile Shifter. His throat was slit."

"Looks like whoever did this is gone," Laila glanced around

the deserted room.

"Yeah, looks like he's been dead for about twenty-four hours."

She walked around the circle and snapped photos with her phone to document the crime scene, just in case someone decided to blow up this scene as well.

A faint sound behind her made her freeze. The noise was like someone sliding a heavy box across the floor. Jamming her phone back into her pocket, she searched the darkness behind her. The sliding noise continued, then abruptly stopped.

"What was that?" asked Darien, looking up from the corpse. "I—"

"Watch out!" he shouted looking into the gloom where Laila's light couldn't quite reach.

There was a flash of movement. Laila dove to the side as a massive scaly head lunged at her. It recoiled and lunged again. Jumping at the last second, Laila ran a couple of steps across its scaly back before landing nimbly on the floor behind it.

"Where did *that* come from?" Darien stared in horror at the giant snake.

"Maybe they brought it for that ritual," suggested Laila, regrouping as the snake-like creature swiveled its head to look at her. "I think it's a Lindworm."

Lindworms were similar to giant snakes with two stubby legs and stunted wings. They lived in the mountains of Svartalfheim. She'd never seen one in person before, but there weren't that many species of giant snake-like creatures in the worlds.

This one was large enough to swallow her. It was nearly three feet in diameter, and there was no telling how long it was, since the coils vanished into the darkness.

It struck again as Laila sprinted towards the far side of the room, giving her enough time to draw her gun. Ducking behind a pillar, she took aim and fired at its head.

The Lindworm hissed and flinched, but the scales on its body were like armor, and the bullets barely dented them. It lashed out, striking at the pillar with its tail. There was a loud boom, and Laila scrambled to find cover as she was showered with bits of plaster.

"Why is it only attacking you?" asked Darien, throwing debris at the Lindworm and trying to get its attention. It hissed at him before returning its attention to Laila.

"You're dead!" replied Laila. "Why would it want to eat something that's already dead?"

"Good point!" said Darien thoughtfully.

She lost track of the Vampire as she ducked to avoid the next attack from the Lindworm.

"Catch!" he shouted from her left, tossing her a long, thin object. It was a sword. Darien must have retrieved it from the car.

"Thanks."

Darien unholstered his gun. He fired at the underbelly, and this time the snake reacted. The skin underneath was softer.

The Lindworm recoiled and retreated. When Darien stopped to switch magazines, Laila advanced and attacked. She sliced the creature along the underbelly. The cut was deep, but the blade was no match for the thick layers of muscle and tissue. The Lindworm struck at her again, but she sidestepped, cutting as she went. She sliced across the creature's face and over one of its eyes.

The Lindworm unleashed a high-pitched, ear-shattering screech. It coiled around itself, causing its tail to lash around, knocking over piles of dusty furniture and cracking the tile floor. Laila dove out of the way behind a large stone planter to avoid being crushed.

They needed something larger to stop the Lindworm than a sword and bullets. Laila searched the room and found a large, broken piece of steel from a table leg. She sprinted towards the snake but caught its attention in the process. The Lindworm attacked, and she had to dive down and slide across the tile to avoid it. But when it rose to strike again, Laila saw her chance.

She used her magic to hurl the steel stake through the underside of the snake. It struck just below the skull and embedded itself deep within the Lindworm. It hissed and thrashed, spraying dark blood all over Laila before it collapsed in a pile in front of her.

Lovely, she thought, as the blood dripped down her clothes.

There were footsteps by the door, and Laila looked to find the investigative team entering the lobby. They paused, looking from Laila to the Lindworm and back again.

"And this is why we're not first responders." The man from the investigative team eyed Laila, covered in Lindworm blood.

Laila didn't bother to pick up her car from the office. Instead, she had Darien drop her off at the house.

"Here." He tossed the bloodstained towel she'd been sitting on at her. "Wash it, burn it, I don't care what you do, just get rid of it! That blood *reeks!*"

Laila hadn't really noticed. Then again, Darien's nose had a different sensitivity to blood. She wadded up the towel and shoved it under her arm.

"See you tomorrow," she said, shutting the door.

She entered through the garage. One glance at the empty parking spaces told Laila that Ali was still at work. In the laundry room, she was about to strip down out of her blood-splattered clothes when a noise in the kitchen reminded her that Frej was home, too. Instead, she just removed her boots. They were covered in blood as well, so she set them in the sink to wash later.

"What happened!?!" asked Frej, horrified, as she entered the kitchen. "Are you hurt?"

Laila shook her head. "I'm fine. It's from a Lindworm."

"I see." Frej, still looked confused.

"I'm going to go…" She gestured towards the stairs.

"Oh, right."

Laila climbed the stairs to her room. In the bathroom, she

stripped off the bloody clothes and shoved them into a plastic bag. She took a long shower, scrubbing twice to make sure that no Lindworm blood remained.

As she shut off the water and dried herself, she thought back to the crime scene. There had been no body at the first crime scene, probably because they'd interrupted the ritual before they'd killed the victim, although there had been some blood at the scene. It was possible they had taken the body to dispose of elsewhere. She had a feeling that the ritual had something to do with the Lindworm's appearance, but why a Lindworm? And how did they manage to transport it?

A knock on her bedroom door caught her attention.

"Just a minute!" she called, pulling on a silk robe hanging on a peg in her closet.

She opened the door to find Frej.

"Oh, so sorry," he stammered, looking away. "I just came to tell you that I made dinner."

"Oh, um, okay, thanks, I'll be down in a minute." She started to shut the door.

"Wait." He stopped her. "I just wanted to say that I'm sorry for how I behaved that first night. I was irritable and rude."

"Thank you," she said, keeping her expression neutral. "But the ones you should be apologizing to are Erin and Ali."

"Yes, which I did this morning. However, I thought it was also prudent to let you know how sorry I am."

He paused as if he was going to say more, but decided against it, excusing himself as he gave her a slight bow.

Laila shut the door and stood there for a moment. She was not accustomed to people bowing to her. At least he seemed polite. Unlike with the Vampires the other night whose presence left her hair standing on end, she did not feel entirely uncomfortable around him. Still, she knew better than to trust him so soon.

CHAPTER 12

Laila awoke with a start. Her heart was pounding, and she was covered in a cold sweat. Recognizing her room, she sighed with relief. There were no concrete walls or steel bars.

Rolling over, she glanced at her phone and groaned. It was seven a.m., meaning she had only been asleep for a few hours. There was also a list of new messages from work. She scanned through them. Three were new cases she needed to look at, and one was a notification from the investigative team, to inform her that the photos from last night's crime scene had been uploaded into the database.

Hoping for a distraction, she flipped through the photos. Most of them documented things she and Darien had already noticed, but one picture caught her eye. It had been taken off to the side of the circle by a bench. Lying on the floor under the bench was a small plastic bag with drugs inside. On the bag was a black image of a three-faced skull. The same image they had found on the vial of pix last week.

Looking more closely at the image, Laila noticed that there was no dust covering the bag. It had only recently been placed there. Perhaps it had fallen out of someone's pocket during the ritual?

Whatever the case, this symbol was turning up far too frequently. Someone in the investigative team was already assigned to research it, but perhaps it was time for Laila to look into it herself.

She rolled over and stared at the ceiling. Laila knew that she couldn't go back to sleep. She would only be plagued with more nightmares anyway. So instead she got up and headed down to the kitchen.

She made as little noise as possible, knowing that her housemates would not be up for hours. The fact that Laila and Ali mostly worked nights meant that their sleep schedules were all a little off.

Pouring water into the kettle, she placed it on the stove and switched on the burner. Then she picked through their box of tea, trying to decide what kind she felt like drinking. She found a blend with chamomile and dropped the teabag into her mug. Hopefully the tea would help relax her and she could go back to sleep.

She stood there, watching the flame of the burner as it heated the kettle.

"You're up early."

Laila spun around suddenly to find Frej leaning against the kitchen island behind her.

"Sorry," he said hastily, "I didn't mean to startle you."

"You're up awfully early too," she pointed out, yawning.

"I'm always up early. It's a habit." He stepped around the island to examine her more closely. "Is everything okay?"

Laila shrugged off the comment. "I just had trouble sleeping, that's all."

She turned away from him to remove the kettle from the stove. Silently, she added water to her mug, but she could still feel him watching her.

"It's more than that. I can hear you talking in your sleep at night. You are haunted by something, or someone, in your past."

He paused for a moment as he waited for an explanation, but Laila ignored him and continued to stare at her tea.

He seemed to take a hint and didn't pressure her further. Instead he offered her companionable silence. Laila actually found his presence soothing. It was better than standing there alone.

After a time, Laila took a deep breath and replied, "About three months ago, I was abducted by Demons in a stakeout gone wrong." She lifted her head to face him. "While I was imprisoned, they forced me to fight the other prisoners for their amusement. Some of them I hurt pretty badly."

Frej's brow furrowed as his concern deepened. She continued.

"I was able to escape. I had to kill a couple of the Demons in the process. I returned and freed the other prisoners, but the man behind the operation got away."

Frej said nothing, but the worry in his eyes was too much for Laila. The pity there made her uncomfortable. She turned away, cradling her mug in her hands.

"I don't know why I told you that," she added, frowning. "It's nothing for you to worry about."

"Did you speak to anyone about this?"

She hesitated. "No. I don't like talking about it."

"You should," he replied seriously.

Laila chanced a quizzical glance at the Dragon.

"I know what it's like to have a job that puts you directly in the line of fire, and I know that it's important for you to talk to someone who can help you through this. It's not healthy, even though you think you can manage."

She considered his words for a moment.

"It doesn't make you weak to talk about this," he added, "but it'll help you to work through this trauma."

Laila nodded. Colin had tried to get her to see a therapist after her abduction. She had refused, thinking it would dredge up more of the horrifying memories. But the memories and the flashbacks came no matter what she did. Perhaps speaking with someone was a good idea.

They stood there in silence once more as Laila drank her tea. By the time she was done, she felt considerably better.

As she placed her empty mug in the sink, she remembered with embarrassment that all she was wearing was a pair of thin cotton and lace pajamas. Not that Frej was any closer to being fully dressed than she was. All he wore was a pair of long pants. His disheveled hair just brushed his bare shoulders. His body rippled with muscle, and a warm, musky scent clung to him.

The Dragon grinned, noticing her gaze. Laila could feel her cheeks flush with embarrassment.

"I should try to get some sleep," she said, trying to act natural. "After all, I'll probably have a long night tonight."

He nodded in agreement.

Laila beat a hasty retreat to the second floor, noticing that the Dragon watched her the whole way.

Later that day, Laila stood in the kitchen with Ali watching as Erin attempted once more to discover her element. Erin had spent days attempting to access her magic, with no progress.

"I think she's stopped trying," Ali whispered to Laila. "She has that look on her face. The one she gets when she's shutting down."

Laila watched as Erin scowled at the candle in front of her.

"You need to search deeper within yourself," Frej instructed her, barely covering his exasperation.

"I am! There's nothing there!"

"You need to concentrate," insisted Frej.

"Maybe you're just a crappy teacher!" Erin snapped at him.

"Erin!" Ali glared at her sister. "Apologize!"

"Sorry," she grumbled.

Laila could feel the tension growing in the room. They'd all been irritable lately. But if Erin couldn't get through this first obstacle, she would never be able to begin her training.

"May I?" Laila asked, joining the Dragons where they sat on the floor. Frej nodded, and so she continued.

"Erin, perhaps you need to look at this differently. It's not a matter of forcing something out of you. Think of it as expanding and connecting to the magic around you. Here—"

She motioned for Erin to join hands with her.

"Now I want you to close your eyes and focus on your breathing, like we do when we practice yoga."

Laila counted their breathing until Erin was at a slow, relaxed pace. With both of them keeping their eyes closed, she continued.

"Now, as you exhale, I want you to imagine that you are expanding yourself outward, into the space. Imagine you are reaching way outside of yourself and feeling everything around you. Feel all the furniture, the floors, the walls, everything.

"As you reach out, you might start to notice the magic. I sense it as tiny strands connecting everything around us. It's delicate here, as if the slightest breeze could disrupt it, but it's still here nonetheless."

"I can feel it!" Erin said with excitement. "It's like a spider web."

"Exactly!" Laila grinned and opened her eyes. "This is the network of magic. When you want an element to obey, you work through these strands. It's like you're a puppeteer."

"Okay, then." Erin picked up the rock. "How do I make this crumble?"

"Reach out and grasp the strings—"

"With my hands?"

"With your mind. But if it helps, you can use your hands too, for now. Grasp the strings surrounding it and pull them apart."

"I—I can't," Erin frowned. "They keep slipping away."

"Try the candle instead," she suggested, passing the candle

to Erin. "This time, try grasping that string at the top of the flame, then pull."

Erin reached out and pulled the invisible strand with her fingers. Ali gasped as the flame grew.

"You did it!" Laila beamed.

"I did it?" Erin opened her eyes and saw the tall flame before it shrank back to a normal size. "Ha! I did it! I actually did it!"

She hopped up and ran to Ali, who gave her a big hug.

"I knew you could." Ali grinned.

As Erin chattered excitedly with her sister, Laila and Frej stood.

"Thank you," he said softly. "I never even thought of explaining it like that."

"It was nothing," she insisted, but inside she felt rather smug, considering the humility written on the Dragon's face.

Yet as quickly as the expression came, it vanished, replaced by his usual unsettling, stare.

"I think this is cause for celebration!" Ali beamed at her sister. "I know we haven't done anything with just the two of us in ages. Why don't we plan something fun this weekend?"

Laila headed towards her bedroom to get ready for work, but by the time she'd reached the second floor, Frej had caught up to her.

"Laila," he said, "thank you. I've never had to train someone before. I think I have just as much to learn about teaching, as Erin does about magic."

"I've known Erin a little longer, that's all."

He opened his mouth as if he was going to add something but thought better of it. Instead, he returned downstairs.

Laila suppressed a grin. There was something endearing about the way Frej seemed so awkward at times.

Her phone chimed, and Laila glanced at the screen. It was another case assignment.

CHAPTER 13

As the car skidded around the corner, Laila took hold of whatever she could to stabilize herself. The siren blared as Darien maneuvered his way through the late evening traffic.

She'd been finishing a report back at headquarters when she received the call. Since Colin and Ali were wrapped up with another missing persons case, Laila and Darien were left to deal with the other issues that came up. So, she and Darien were sent out, rushing to a minimart where an ongoing conflict with an SNP was occurring.

LAPD was already on site, but they had called IRSA after realizing some of the individuals involved were SNPs. They were handling the situation as best they could while Darien and Laila were on their way, but she had been informed that hostages were involved.

Darien slammed on the brakes as an oblivious driver failed to pull over. Thank the Gods Laila was wearing her seatbelt, otherwise she would've gone sailing through the windshield.

"Move!" he hissed, not that the driver could hear him. Finally, the car pulled over, and they hurried on their way.

They pulled into a parking lot where police officers were surrounding a building. Through the window, Laila could see two armed individuals with a couple of hostages held at gunpoint.

Laila and Darien jumped out of the SUV and headed over to the commanding officer.

"Have they made any demands?" she asked.

"No, they haven't said anything, other than to stay back. We were waiting until you arrived."

"Thank you." She glanced at Darien. "If I can get closer, I could immobilize them."

"You make it sound simple," he chuckled darkly.

"Let's hope it is. Cover me."

Slowly, she crept closer. One of the two was actually a woman, a Fae. The second was a burly male and appeared to be human, but appearances could be deceiving. Both were dressed like they belonged in some sort of biker gang. They were also armed with automatic weapons. Standing in front of them were the three human hostages. Between the hostages and the walls of the minimart, there was no way the police could get a clear shot.

The female biker noticed Laila's approach.

"Stop there, or we blow their brains out!"

"Easy, now." Laila held her hands up showing she was unarmed. "I just want to talk."

She reached out with her magic to freeze the air around them. To her horror, she realized that nothing was happening. There was a shield around them.

The bikers laughed.

The male was some kind of Sorcerer.

"Why are you doing this?" she asked, trying to buy some time while she thought of another plan.

"We're done talking," the woman snapped, glancing at her cell phone. "This is what happens next. We're going to get in our car, and you are going to let us. We'll give you two hostages, but the third comes with us to ensure no one follows."

Laila gritted her teeth. With the shield around them, bullets would be useless. Reluctantly, she nodded and retreated back towards Darien and the others.

"They've got one hell of a magical shield around them. Until he drops it, we won't have a chance at taking them out, and they know it," she informed the others.

"So now what?" an officer asked.

"We let them go and hope we can track them. If they don't know we're after them, we can find out where they're going and separate them from any remaining hostages. If the shield comes down, then we take any opening we have."

The officer nodded and relayed the news to the others.

Laila watched closely as the biker pair and their hostages emerged. Slowly, they made their way to a beat-up truck. They shoved two of the hostages out of the way, who ran towards the line of police.

As they approached, Laila reached out again with her magic to check their shield, when she noticed the remaining hostage, the one they were dragging towards the truck, was masked in a glamour.

"Wait a minute. That hostage is a plant!" she yelled.

The officers fired at the truck, but the shield widened to cover it. The woman fired at the officers, and they ducked behind their vehicles for cover.

"Shit!" Darien swore as the truck sped off.

CHAPTER 14

Darien and Laila leapt back into their SUV and sped after the bikers. Three LAPD squad cars pulled out closely behind.

"This doesn't make sense!" Darien yelled over the screech of the siren. "Why would they go through all that trouble to presumably rob a minimart? They should have been long gone by the time we got here, especially with a Sorcerer on hand. Were they waiting for us to show up?"

"I don't know, but let's just focus on not crashing for now!" Laila gasped, as Darien swerved around another car, nearly heading into oncoming traffic.

"Relax, my reflexes are a lot better than these humans'."

Laila ignored the comment and got on a radio with the LAPD.

"It looks like the perpetrators are headed towards the Old City. Can we set up a barricade ahead of them?"

"We're already ahead of you," came the crackling reply. The officer gave her the location while they followed the SNPs, who were headed directly into the trap.

They drove down a long street lined by buildings, with no alleyways or side streets. Up ahead police cars created a barricade with flashing blue and red lights. The truck in front of them drove over a spike strip, shredding its tires. The truck skidded to a halt.

Right behind them followed Darien and Laila, stopping just before the spike strip. The agents dove for cover under the dash as a round of bullets thundered into the car.

"So much for them surrendering," Laila muttered, glancing at Darien.

Laila summoned her shield and cautiously sat up. The three perps were running for the cover of an old warehouse.

"Let's go!" she shouted, leaping out of the car.

Covered by her shield, Laila and Darien hurried towards the building. A dozen police officers followed.

"Surround the building!" she ordered the officers. "But do not enter!"

The officers rushed to cover the building, while she and Darien entered cautiously into the foreboding gloom.

Darien paused, checking the air for the scent of the perpetrators' blood.

"That way," he mouthed silently. They headed down a hallway and into a massive storage room.

The room was filled with dusty old boxes piled high on towering shelves. There were several aisles and plenty of space to hide.

"They've split up," Darien whispered. He motioned for Laila to search one aisle while he took another.

She conjured a light above and maintained the shield surrounding her. She prepared a third spell, this time offensive, a blast of wind strong enough to knock a Troll off its feet.

Searching between the boxes, she started down the aisle. Her ears searched for the slightest sound, as dust drifted in motes around her. She had to stifle the urge to cough.

Halfway down the aisle a rustling sound from behind made

her turn. A spear of ice shattered on her shield. She attacked with a blast of air, but the Sorcerer deflected it.

Another attack came from the opposite side. Laila groaned, realizing the plant was also a Sorcerer.

With a steady stream of attacks from both sides, Laila poured more energy into strengthening her shield. Taking on one Sorcerer was hard enough, but two?

Laila sent a blast of fire at the biker guy, followed by an ice dagger to the leg. He blocked the fireball but missed the knife. He dropped to the ground, howling in pain.

Laila turned to the second man. She threw another handful of ice daggers she had conjured. He threw up a shield. However, like most Sorcerers, he didn't expect an attack from below.

Reaching into the concrete with her magic, Laila opened a crack big enough to trap his foot. It was taxing but broke his concentration long enough for Laila to magically immobilize him. She approached and cuffed him, in case she lost her hold on him magically.

There was a click and a spin. The biker took aim and fired with his machine gun. Laila braced herself as the bullets ricocheted off her shield. He moved closer and closer while Laila struggled to keep her shield up. She retreated to the end of the aisle, ducking behind an old forklift.

"Darien!" she yelled. "Where the hell are you!?!"

A noise to her right drew her attention. The Fae biker chick stood twenty yards away. Laila could sense the charm magic as she laid another heavy dose on Darien. He was standing just beside her and was like putty in her hands.

"Snap out of it, you idiot!" Laila snarled, but the Fae just laughed.

"Come along," she called to Darien, who followed the Fae like a lovesick puppy. Laila started to follow after her, but another barrage of bullets sent her ducking back behind a crate.

Holding out her hand, Laila shot a crackling bolt of lightning at the Sorcerer. It struck him with a bang.

Not waiting to see if the man was dead, Laila rushed after the Fae, determined to save her partner.

She followed them down a hallway.

"Freeze where you are!" Laila shouted.

The woman spun. Seeing Laila, she raised her gun.

"Marius sends his regards," she sneered at Laila.

Laila froze as the words sank in. The way her heart pounded it felt as though it was trying to beat its way through her ribcage. Marius had sent them. He was toying with her just as he had back in his arena.

The Fae raised her gun and fired repeatedly.

Laila's shield flickered and died. She'd expended too much energy fighting the Sorcerers, and her stamina was failing. Pain surged through her torso and left arm as the woman continued to shoot.

Darien snapped out of the trance as Laila fell to the ground. He grabbed the Fae by the neck and slammed her into the wall. The gun flew out of her hands, and she was nearly knocked unconscious.

Laila watched as the Fae pulled a knife from her boot.

"No!" Laila screamed. With some of her precious remaining energy, she stopped the Fae's hand, only a hair's breadth away from Darien's chest.

The Vampire roughly knocked the knife out of her hand, spun her around, and cuffed her.

It was then that the police made their entrance. Darien passed the Fae off to a female officer to keep an eye on her.

"Be careful," he warned. "She'll try to charm you."

Laila cautiously stood as Darien rushed over to her.

"How badly are you hurt?"

"The vest stopped the bullets aimed at my chest, but not the one in my arm." She pressed her hand over the wound, trying to stop the bleeding.

As the scent of her blood hit Darien, his expression changed, and he clenched his teeth.

"Can you heal that?" he asked. He seemed to be fighting his bloodlust. Laila had never seen him react this way. Then again, this was the first significant wound she'd received while working with him.

She shook her head, taking a step back to give them some space.

"I—I can't, I used too much magic back there." She glanced down and to her horror, saw that she was quickly losing blood. She leaned against the wall, sagging to the ground.

"If Vampires have healing powers," she added as the room started spinning around her, "now's the time to use them."

"Not unless you wish to join the undead." He retreated further down the hall.

"No offense, but I'll pass."

The female officer passed the Fae woman back to Darien and whipped out a handkerchief, tying it tightly over Laila's wound.

"Don't just stand there!" the officer yelled at him. "Go get help!"

Darien nodded, dragging the Fae around the corner.

"And for Thor's sake, keep an eye on her!" Laila warned him. She rolled her eyes at the female officer. "Men!"

There was commotion down the hall, and Darien swore.

"What's going on?" Laila asked through clenched teeth.

The paramedics arrived, rushing to stanch the flow of blood.

"I need help!" Darien shouted. "I've got a suspect down!"

What was happening? Laila wondered as another pair of paramedics rushed past her with a gurney.

The paramedic currently helping her led her away to an ambulance. As she was being loaded in, she saw the female perpetrator strapped to the gurney and covered in blood.

"What happened?" Laila shouted frantically. "Darien!"

"Miss, you're losing a lot of blood," said the paramedic. "We need to go."

"But my partner!"

The paramedic shut the doors of the ambulance, and the rig

drove off.

She tried to explain to him that really, she needed to eat, and then she could heal herself so she could get back to work. Laila needed to find out what happened with the Fae woman. She was Laila's only link to Marius. She couldn't lose this lead; not now.

The paramedic gave Laila a skeptical look but found her a protein bar. She wolfed it down, but the food wasn't enough to help the magic exhaustion, and soon the ambulance pulled into the loading bay of a hospital.

Unfortunately, it was a human hospital and not the one by her office. The staff cleaned and dressed her wound while Laila explained again that she just needed to eat in order to replenish the energy she had lost.

To make matters worse, Darien wasn't answering his phone. She left a series of text messages and voicemails asking him to call her back.

Eventually, Ali showed up to take her home. A nurse walked Laila out to the car, even though Laila insisted she was fine.

Once they were on their way, Laila turned to Ali.

"Did you bring it?"

Ali held up a paper bag with a grin.

Laila opened it, and the scent of Mexican food wafted through the car.

"You are the best friend ever!" Laila, bit into a burrito.

"It sounds like you had one hell of a night." Ali pulled another burrito out of the bag. "Darien called and filled me in."

"That was a pretty close call." Laila shivered. "It's a good thing I had a bulletproof vest on, otherwise that might have been the end of me. I've been trying to get a hold of him. Did he see what happened with the perps?"

"Darien said that both of the men were dead. One was accidentally shot by the other, and the last was electrocuted or something."

"Shit, I should have backed off with that lightning bolt. I didn't mean for that to happen." Laila shook her head.

"He would've killed you," Ali reminded her firmly.

"What about the woman?"

"She had another knife on her that was concealed. The crazy woman managed to slit her own throat before Darien realized it, and she died on the way to the hospital."

Laila set down her burrito and rubbed her palms against her eyes, wincing as she moved her injured arm. Just because the Sorcerers had been trying to kill her didn't mean he had deserved to die.

"She mentioned Marius," explained Laila as she turned to Ali. "He's here. He must be in the city, and he knows who I am."

"Easy," said Ali, "we don't know that's the case. Maybe someone caught on to the fact that we've been searching for somebody named Marius?"

"I don't know," sighed Laila. It seemed like too much of a coincidence.

Ali changed the subject. "Where was Darien when you were getting lead pumped into you?"

Laila finished her burrito and tossed the empty wrapper back into the bag. "Busy getting his ass charmed by the Fae."

"He what?" Ali snorted.

"Oh, yeah! She really had him. If I hadn't had to go save lover boy's butt, I wouldn't have this." She gestured to the bandage on her arm.

"Sexy ladies always have been his weakness."

Laila laughed. After all, what was there left to do at this point? She and Darien had made it out alive, and once she recovered from the magic exhaustion, Laila would be able to heal herself. But then again, Marius was still out there, and they had once again lost their only lead.

"Wait," Laila said as they turned a corner. "This is the way home. Aren't we going back to the office?"

"Yeah, like I'm taking you back to the office all beat up." Ali rolled her eyes. "I'm dropping you off, then I'll head back in and help Darien. You're going to need some rest if you expect to heal yourself by the morning."

Laila sighed. Ali was right. Food alone was not enough. She would need plenty of sleep.

"You were shot!?!" Erin's jaw dropped.

"I'll be fine. Seriously, I don't get why everyone is making such a big deal." Laila chucked the bottle of pain pills the human doctor had given her into the garbage can and rummaged through a cabinet of Alfheim medications.

Ali turned to Frej and Erin. "Could you two keep an eye on her? I'm going back to the office, and I don't want Laila following."

"Of course," Frej said solemnly.

"I told you, I'm—" Laila began, but the world started spinning and she had to hold onto the counter to stay upright.

"And *that's* what I'm talking about," Ali grumbled as she and Frej both surged towards the injured Elf.

"I've got her." Frej wrapped an arm around Laila to steady her. Ali sighed and left through the garage door.

Reluctantly, Laila allowed Frej to guide her up the stairs and to her room. She noticed he had some flour smudged on his green tunic from whatever he and Erin had been cooking.

"Does this sort of thing happen a lot in your line of work here?" he asked as they reached her door.

Laila shrugged. "Not really. This is the first time this has happened to me."

"Will you be okay from here?" He gestured towards the door. Laila nodded and bid him goodnight before stepping into her room.

Beyond the point of ordinary exhaustion, Laila pulled off her work clothes and chucked them into the laundry hamper. She paused to examine the nasty purple bruises spreading across her chest where her vest had stopped the bullets. Then there was the bandage on her arm that covered the stiches she'd received. Laila was tempted to heal herself a little, just enough to help her sleep, but knew it was a terrible idea. She'd already overexerted herself today, and if she used too much magic before she had time to properly rest from the magic exhaustion, she risked landing in another magical coma. The human doctors had seen to the worst of her injuries, so even though they were still painful, they could wait.

Instead, she crawled into bed and drifted off into a deep sleep.

CHAPTER 15

The magic exhaustion hit her harder than she had expected. She was unable to summon the energy to heal herself in one go, instead she had to wait and do it in phases. She'd healed her arm enough to use it and drive to work. Thus, the next afternoon Laila found herself stuck in the office sorting through files.

There was a new file: the autopsy report on the perpetrators from the minimart robbery. She still didn't understand what they hoped to gain from the robbery, and as far as she'd found, all they'd taken was a few hundred dollars in cash and a pack of cigarettes. It just wasn't logical, unless it wasn't about the robbery. What if the robbery was the bait set by Marius to get her attention, and lure her into a trap where the Sorcerers could take her out? If so, they'd nearly succeeded.

Opening the file, she skimmed through the notes and photographs for anything useful. The first one was unenlightening, but the second caught her attention. On the back of the Sorcerer's right shoulder there was a tattoo of a three-headed skull.

Laila opened another window on her computer and compared the photo of the drugs found at the ritual crime scene to the man's tattoo. The skull images were identical.

She stood up and looked out the window of her office. It was only early afternoon, and the sun blazed down on Los Angeles. She looked off into the direction of the Old City.

What was this symbol, and why was it at so many crime scenes lately?

Her laptop chimed, and she glanced at two more notifications. The first was about the lab results from the blood samples taken from the kidnaping crime scene. The sample wasn't a match for anyone in IRSA's database, but it was confirmed that the blood came from some sort of SNP from Jotunheim.

There'd also been an update to the file on the ritual victim she and Darien had found. Laila opened it, but it was only an amendment to his address. It looked like he'd been living in a building in the Old City, just a few blocks from where he'd been killed.

"Hey," said Ali from the doorway, frowning. "I thought you were supposed to be resting."

"This is resting." Laila waved at her laptop. "I'm staying in the office instead of going out."

Ali shook her head. "Sometimes I think you're more stubborn than my sister. Driven, that's for sure, but as stubborn as a Fire Salamander in winter."

Laila chuckled. "Ha, those were the days, back when our biggest event of the week was rounding up Fire Salamanders."

"Yeah, Darien's got another missing person case. He was abducted in much the same manner."

"Human?" asked Laila.

"Vampire. He lived in the Old City."

Laila glanced at her computer screen, and a thought occurred to her.

"They still haven't found that missing boy, right?" she asked.

"No, unfortunately."

Laila returned to her desk and pulled up the file on the missing boy. The date he went missing was the same day as the first ritual. She flipped the laptop around and slid it towards Ali.

Laila took a deep breath. "I think you should search the dumpsters near the area where the first ritual occurred. The one where the building burned down."

Realization dawned on Ali's face as she made the connection. "You think he was involved?"

"There wasn't as much blood at that scene, and a body was never found."

It was still grasping at straws, but the house was only a few blocks from the ritual site.

"Okay." Ali stood up and headed for the door. "I'm going to bring Colin up to speed. He can shift into his wolf form and help search for a body."

"I'll come too," said Laila, getting up.

"By the Morrigan, I swear I'm gonna tie you to that chair." Ali planted her fists on her hips. "I have another assignment for you. You're going to go home now, and since I know you won't take the time to rest, you can drive Frej to pick up some supplies from Lyn's."

Laila's jaw dropped.

"Don't argue with me, either. I'll deal with Colin."

"So, this is what it's like to be Erin," wondered Laila out loud.

"Ha!" Ali grinned. "You should be thanking me. I wish someone would give me an excuse to go home early."

Laila rolled her eyes. "Well, I don't recommend getting shot."

"I'll try to avoid it. Now go on, get out of here. I told Frej ten minutes ago that you were on your way."

"Wait a minute." Laila turned on the Fae. "You did what? You planned to send me with him."

"I have no idea what you're talking about." Ali couldn't quite hide her grin.

"You're a crappy liar. You know that, right?"

"It's a good thing I don't play poker, then." Ali winked. "He is totally into you, by the way."

"You're joking, right?" Laila rolled her eyes.

"Oh, believe me," said Ali smugly, "I can tell. Don't you see the way he acts when you're in the room? Plus, he doesn't seem like the kind of guy who runs away unexpectedly."

Laila raised an eyebrow.

"See?" Ali continued slyly. "He's already *way* better than the last one."

Laila rolled her eyes. "He's a Dragon! In his other form, I probably look like an appetizer, for Thor's sake!"

"Oh, I bet he finds you tasty!"

"Ali!"

A sound in the hall caught Ali's attention.

"What the—" Ali started, glancing over her shoulder.

Laila joined her in the doorway. There was a man at the far end of the hall searching through Ali's office. Laila reached out towards him with her magic, but he was unfamiliar.

Human, Laila mouthed to Ali.

Stop it! Ali mouthed back. She knew Laila was using her magic.

There were a number of humans who worked in the building, both on the investigative team and as support staff. Laila knew them all by face, if not by name, and this man was not one of them.

Soundlessly Laila and Ali crept down the hall, pausing outside Ali's office.

"Stop right there," Ali said, blocking the doorway. Behind her, Laila prepared a spell in the event the human turned violent.

The man stared at Ali in shock. He was probably in his late twenties and scrawny. His short brown hair was a mess, and his clothes were slightly wrinkled.

He swallowed hard, looking as if he was going to speak.

"I—I," he began, but the words appeared to be stuck in his mouth. Instead he blushed and looked away from Ali.

"You better have a good explanation for this." Ali gestured

to the office. "Who are you, and what are you doing in here?"

Torsten rounded the corner.

"What's going on?" He cautiously approached Laila.

"Looks like we've got an intruder." She gestured into Ali's office.

Torsten glanced into the room and swore in Dwarvish.

"Donald!" he thundered. "What are you doing in here?"

"I—I got lost," he stuttered, avoiding Ali's gaze.

Torsten shook his head and sighed. "Ladies, this is Donald. He's my new assistant."

"Ah." Realization dawned on Laila. "You must be the Witch that Lyn mentioned."

He muttered something Laila couldn't catch.

"What was that?" she asked.

"Um, I prefer Tech Wiz."

"Sure…" She glanced at Torsten, who rolled his eyes.

"I don't care what you call yourself," the Dwarf huffed, "but I've got a stack of cuffs that need enchanting."

The human nodded and awkwardly slipped around Ali. He added a hasty apology before rushing after Torsten.

"Well," Ali said, stunned, "that was weird."

Laila snorted. "He was terrified of you!"

"Did I miss something?" Colin asked, rounding the corner.

"Ali nearly made that poor man pee his pants," Laila snickered.

Colin cleared his throat. "Enough screwing around. We've got enough work here. We don't need added distractions."

"Speaking of which, we should go," said Ali to Colin. "Laila and I think the missing persons cases and the rituals are linked. I want to go search for a body while it's still light out."

Laila waited until they left before heading down to the garage as well. She also grabbed her laptop on the way out to finish her work later.

CHAPTER 16

"So, what are you looking for?" Laila asked Frej while pulling out of the driveway. As promised, Laila was helping Frej with his shopping.

He read aloud from a list. Some of the items were mundane, like canvas and wood. They could find those at a hardware store. Other items were more obscure and otherworldly, such as a collection of Alfheim herbs.

"What is all of this for, anyway?" She glanced at the list, and the variety of unusual herbs.

"I figure I should take precautions since Erin's a Fire Dragon. The herbs are for a fireproofing we make back home."

"I don't know about the herbs," Laila admitted, "but we should stop by my friend's shop. She'll have some charms that might work. Otherwise we can find fireproofing sprays at the hardware store."

She pulled down the street and towards the beach. Frej folded the list and returned it to the coat he wore. Laila noticed it was different from the greatcoat he had on the night he arrived. It was dark blue with a wide embroidered collar and cuffs that were lighter shades of blue and white. It might be the peak of men's fashion back home, but it definitely stood out in Los Angeles. Then again Frej didn't seem like the kind of guy who cared about fitting in with the Los Angeles crowd.

As Laila circled through the streets, she regretted arriving so close to sunset. Apparently, the rest of the city had thought to go to the beach as well. The streets were crowded, and Laila had to park several blocks away.

"Sorry," she explained. "It looks like we are going to have to walk from here."

"You say that like it's a bad thing," he replied cheerfully.

He opened his door and was hit with a wave of ninety-degree-plus heat.

"Oh," he said.

"Welcome to L.A.!" Laila chuckled. She locked the car and engaged its camouflage to blend in with the other beat-up cars nearby. Frej raised an eyebrow but followed her without comment.

"How's Erin doing?" she asked.

"In areas of history and culture, she excels. She's very smart."

He paused, curiously watching a group of humans pass them on their way to the beach.

"What about the magic?" Laila hoped things were going better now that Erin had managed to find her element.

Frej sighed. "That area is still difficult for her. I don't think it's for lack of trying, but I think she will struggle with it for some time."

"She only just discovered how to access her magic the other day," Laila pointed out.

"Even so, her control over it is much weaker than usual for most Dragons. I just hope that improves with time."

He wrinkled his nose as a man walked past him smoking a cigarette. He shook his head.

"How are you?" He indicated her shoulder.

"Partially healed, but the magic exhaustion makes it difficult. It was a pretty close call."

"I'm starting to think you go looking for trouble." He gave her a small smile.

"I don't have to. Trouble seems to find me these days." She sighed. "Some days I think I'm in need of a vacation."

They rounded a corner, and suddenly the beach was in sight. Laila glanced sideways at Frej, observing his reaction.

"Wow," he said, shaking his head. "That's amazing."

Laila nodded in agreement. It was hard to not be amazed by the crashing waves and the endless expanse of ocean. Naturally there were oceans back in Alfheim, but they seemed tame by comparison. Perhaps it was due to all the magic there. But on Earth the oceans raged with a wild energy. It was beautiful to watch.

Of course, this particular stretch of beach was overcrowded with human beachgoers. Laila and Frej had to slip through the crowd in order to make it to Lyn's shop. Even inside, the shop was crowded with curious folk.

Lyn was busy explaining the difference between two potions when they arrived, so the two of them waited patiently.

"What is all this?" Frej motioned to the shelves.

"Enchanted artifacts." She pointed to the runes etched into an old-fashioned fountain pen in front of them. "Lyn's a Witch. She enchants them with spells."

Lyn finished helping the line of customers at the register before joining Laila.

"You didn't tell me you were seeing anyone," she whispered excitedly to Laila.

"Lyn," she said loudly, "this is Frej. He's Erin's tutor. He has a list of herbs he is looking for to help fireproof their practice space."

Lyn shot her a quizzical look.

"We discovered yesterday that Erin's a Fire Dragon." He passed her the list. "I just wanted to take some precautions for when she practices."

Lyn scanned through the list before passing it back to the Dragon.

"None of these look familiar to me, but I've got some fire-proofing spells and potions that might work instead."

She gathered a collection of items from around the shop and set them on the counter. One by one she explained each object and its use. After a debate on whether it would be more beneficial to use a spell or a potion, Frej decided on a potion that could be sprayed around the practice space.

"I've got more in the back room somewhere. Laila, do you think you could give me a hand?"

She followed the Witch through the beaded curtain. Lyn pulled her towards the back, out of earshot from Frej.

"Spill it. I want all the details. What's up with you and hunky Dragon boy out there?"

Laila rolled her eyes. "There is nothing going on between the two of us."

Laila picked up a smooth glass sphere from a dusty cushion to examine it more closely.

"Sure there isn't. You're just hanging out on a beach with six and a half feet of gorgeous male Dragon."

"Yeah, I guess so. I haven't really paid attention to his appearance." The glass ball changed color in her hand from clear to black. "Why does this change color like that?"

"It's a truth crystal," the Witch giggled. "Which means you most certainly *have* taken notice of him."

Laila blushed and quickly returned the truth crystal to its cushion while Lyn selected a large bottle from a crate.

"Here we have it!" Lyn and Laila emerged from the beaded curtain.

"Great. How much do I owe you?" He pulled out a pouch of coins.

"Um, I usually only take U.S. Dollars, but how about a trade? The potion for two of your scales?"

Frej considered it for a moment before reaching in his pocket and removing two blue scales that were flat and as big around as Laila's fist.

"You just carry those around?" Laila asked incredulously.

He shrugged. "It's not the first time I've traded with scales."

Lyn stared at them in awe before wrapping them in a piece of cloth and stowing them behind the counter.

"Here you go." She handed him the bottle, looking very pleased. Laila wondered what she would do with the scales.

They were heading out the door when Lyn asked, "By the way, Laila, did Erin find anything in those books yet?"

"What books?" asked Frej.

"Ancient books on magic," explained Laila. "Lyn asked for her help with the translations—"

Laila's phone rang. She glanced at the number but didn't recognize it. She frowned but answered the call.

"Hello?"

"Laila, it's Orin. I've got a problem."

"What is it? What's wrong?"

"Someone broke into the club," the Fae said darkly. "I think you'd better see this for yourself."

CHAPTER 17

Laila rushed as fast as she dared through traffic towards Orin's club. Since she wasn't driving an official IRSA vehicle, she didn't have lights or a siren. That meant she was stuck fighting the traffic like everyone else.

"Who is this person?" Frej asked, cutting through Laila's irritation with the driver in front of her.

"Oh, Orin? He owns a club that Ali and I go to."

She glanced over her shoulder before changing lanes to pass the painfully slow man in front of her.

"He also helps us out occasionally," she added. "He's in with the elite Supernatural crowd in Los Angeles. He has a lot of useful contacts."

"I see."

She pulled into the parking lot behind the club. Frej followed her as she walked through a side door that was unlocked.

"Orin?" she called into a hallway.

Orin stepped into the hallway. His brow was furrowed, showing his concern, something unusual for the Fae. Ordinarily he was cool as a cucumber.

Noticing Laila, his expression changed immediately to delight.

"Laila!" He accepted her hand. "Thank you for coming."

Rather than shaking her hand, he planted a delicate kiss on it. Orin was ever the flirt.

"I hear there is some sort of emergency?" Frej asked, stepping in. He stood with his arms crossed and didn't bother with introductions.

The Fae dropped Laila's hand, raising his eyebrows. But he kept whatever comment he had to himself.

"See for yourself." Orin led them into the main bar area.

Bottles of liquor that were ordinarily neatly arranged on shelves had been smashed on the floor behind the bar, but that wasn't where the damage ended. Someone had taken a hammer to the dance floor, slashed leather seats, and had even broken the lighting equipment. Spray-painted onto the dance floor was a message:

You haven't seen anything yet. Leave while you still can...

"Thor's hammer!" Laila gasped. She pulled out her phone and began taking photos. Even Frej was stunned silent.

"What happened?" she asked tentatively.

"When I closed up last night, I engaged all of my usual security features so that if something like this were to happen, the security company would be alerted and the police called. But when I came in, the alarm was disabled."

He sighed and sank onto a ruined sofa before adding, "I called you as soon as I saw this."

Laila nodded.

"Any idea how they managed to get around your security system?" Laila asked, taking notes on her phone.

"Nothing seems to be physically damaged, if that's what you mean."

"Did your cameras catch anything?"

"Not much. They spray-painted them all. I can show you what they did catch."

He led them to his office, which appeared to be untouched.

"How did they miss the office?" Laila wondered out loud.

"I paid a Witch to charm the door. Intruders will overlook it, even if they know it exists."

That sounded like a pretty handy spell, but it was a small blessing when she considered the damage the rest of the club had sustained. Luckily, his insurance would cover it, but the club would be closed for weeks.

Orin pulled up the footage from the break-in on a large computer monitor. Laila watched as the front door opened and dark figures rushed into the building. They scattered, rushing to cover the cameras. They were all dressed in black and wore masks to conceal their features. Laila played back the recordings several times, noticing something off about the action. She paused the video.

"Look here." Laila pointed to the screen. "During the initial rush, you can't see that spot where your alarm panel is located. It's obscured by all the bodies. There is just enough time that someone who knew the code could disable it.

"Also, the intruders knew exactly where every camera is located before they entered the building. They didn't spend much time searching for them."

"You mean these could be my employees?" Orin looked at Laila in shock.

"Perhaps. Or maybe they were able to get information out of your employees. How many of them know the security codes?"

"Three of my bartenders have them." He frowned.

"I want you to call them and see if you can get them down here right away."

"You might not have to," Frej said from the doorway. "Someone just walked in. He's in bad shape."

Orin and Laila rushed back into the bar, carefully avoiding the pile of glasses and booze.

"John!" Orin hurried to find the man a seat.

He had been beaten pretty badly. Laila called for an ambulance. She also asked for the police.

"John," Orin repeated. "What happened?"

The man winced as he felt the bruising on his face.

"Last night I was heading to my car when some guys attacked me. They dragged me down the alley behind that old café and started beating me. They wanted the security code for the alarm."

He glanced at Orin. "I'm so sorry. I gave it to them. I thought they were going to beat me to death. I just woke up behind a trash can. I'm so sorry, man."

"That's okay," Orin said. "We're getting you help."

"Is there anything you can remember about the men who attacked you?" Laila asked.

"Um, they were human, I think. One of them had this funky tattoo on his wrist. I could see it between his shirt and his glove when he grabbed me. It looked like a skull, but with three faces."

Laila frowned and pulled out her phone, flipping through the photos.

"Did it look like this?" she asked, showing him the picture of the three-faced skull from the bag of drugs the investigators had found the other day.

"Yeah, that's it."

"Did they say anything? Any names?"

The man shook his head. "That's all I remember."

"Thank you," she added as the ambulance arrived.

"What's going on here?" Two LAPD officers entered the building. They stared at the damage.

"I'm Special Agent Eyvindr. I believe we've met?" She vaguely recognized the men. She showed them her badge, and they nodded.

She continued, "There was a break-in last night. It sounds like humans were involved."

She explained to the officers what she had discovered so far.

When she mentioned the wrist tattoo and showed them a picture of the image, the older officer stopped her.

"Hold on, I know that one. It's from a gang called Di Inferi. I think they disbanded during The Event. The department should have files on the known members, though."

"Clearly, they haven't disbanded," said Laila, frowning. "Their drugs have been showing up all over the city, and they were involved in that minimart robbery last night."

The officers exchanged shocked looks.

She repeated her explanation when a human detective arrived. Thankfully, the detective took charge of containing the scene. He assured Laila that he would report their findings to IRSA.

She wandered over to Orin and Frej who stood examining the message on the dance floor.

"Why would someone do this?" Frej crouched down by the message.

"This is the most popular Supernatural club in town," Orin pointed out as he poured himself a drink from one of the few unbroken bottles of liquor. "If they wanted to send a message to the community, this is a pretty good way to do it."

Laila shuddered. This was all she needed. Another human-Supernatural conflict.

"Shall we go?" she asked Frej. "The humans have this under control for now."

"Thank you." Orin embraced Laila.

"Of course," she said with a sad smile. "I'll let you know if I find anything."

CHAPTER 18

"There." Frej started a timer. "The others should be back by the time it's done."

He'd insisted on cooking dinner while Laila sat at the kitchen table researching the Di Inferi gang. She wasn't having much luck, though. Most of the information was pre-Event. Still, at least she now knew what the symbol stood for. Erin was home as well, supposedly reading through the books from Lyn, but Laila could hear faint sounds of a video game echoing down the hall.

She shut the laptop and gently felt her arm. Reaching out with her magic, she began the process of healing the wound once more.

Frej loaded the last of the dishes into the dishwasher and shut the door. There was silence for a moment as he stood there watching her.

Laila stretched her arm and moved it around. The stiffness and residual bruising were gone. Her shoulder was more or less back to normal, but she felt a wave of fatigue. The magic exhaustion still hung over her.

"Laila," said Frej seriously, "I've got something I wanted to ask you—"

At that moment, Ali entered from the garage.

"Wow," Ali commented. "That smells amazing!"

"Apparently, Frej can cook." Laila waved at the oven cheerfully.

"Really?" Ali walked around the kitchen island to peer into the oven. "Well, you can cook as much as you like!"

Laila and Frej finished setting the table while Ali chased Erin out of her room to get cleaned up for dinner. When the timer went off, Frej pulled the dish out of the oven and set it on the table. The others gathered around and dug in.

"Gods, this is good!" Erin exclaimed through a mouthful of lasagna. "We are never buying that frozen stuff again!"

"This is very good," Laila admitted.

Frej grinned and sat a little straighter.

"I actually wanted to ask the three of you something." He paused, watching the three women. "I have to go back to Alfheim for a few days later this week. There is a ball for the king's one hundred and fiftieth birthday, and I am required to make an appearance."

"Well, aren't you fancy!" Erin giggled.

"I was actually hoping that Laila would come with me."

Laila nearly choked on her lasagna.

"Now, that sounds like fun!" Ali said excitedly. "Of course you should go, Laila!"

"I—I really can't. There is so much work to do at the office. Marius—"

"Don't be ridiculous." Ali rolled her eyes. "The rest of us can cover for you. After all, how often do you have a chance to go to a ball?"

Frej watched Laila patiently, waiting for her response. This seemed far too personal for Laila. It probably wasn't appropriate at all considering he was Erin's teacher.

Ali nudged her under the table, reminding Laila that she was supposed to say something.

"I'll have to speak to Colin about it first."

Frej nodded and returned to eating his dinner, satisfied.

When they had eaten as much as they possibly could, Ali shooed Frej out of the kitchen before he could offer to help with the cleanup. He left with Erin to continue a lesson they had started earlier. Ali tried the same with Laila, but she insisted on staying.

"Any luck with the search?" asked Laila.

Ali shook her head. "We didn't cover much ground today. Colin said he had a meeting or something, so we had to end early. We'll keep searching tomorrow."

"Sure it was a meeting," added Laila wryly. "Colin's probably off on another date."

"What?" asked Ali as she nearly dropped the dish she was scrubbing.

"According to Darien, that's why he's been leaving early lately."

Ali unleashed a string of profanity in the tongue of the Fae.

"I swear," continued Ali, "I'm going to report him."

"I'm sure there's a good reason—" started Laila.

"Oh, come on now! Don't defend him!" Ali glared at her. "He's been treating you the worst of all of us lately. You're not a soldier, you don't need to follow him blindly."

Laila was at a loss for words.

"Look," Ali sighed, "I just don't like watching you put up with this. I know it affects you too, and it's okay to say it. You're allowed to admit our boss is an ass."

Laila knew she was right. But there was still a part of her, the part that believed in the good in people, that felt that there was something more to Colin's story, something they didn't know. It was growing more difficult for her to ignore his comments though, so she'd been avoiding him around the office. She could try to speak with him again, but she didn't imagine that going too well.

Changing the subject, Laila informed Ali of her visit to

Orin's club, and the damage. Ali listened in shock. By the time Laila had finished, Ali had sat back down at the table.

"I need to write up my report still," Laila explained. "But the LAPD should get back to us with any new developments."

"Gods, I should give Orin a call."

"I think he'd appreciate that."

Laila retrieved a bottle of Fae liquor from a cupboard as well as two shot glasses. She poured Ali a shot, sliding it across the table before pouring a shot of her own. It was from their small stash of Alfheim beverages. They didn't normally drink like this, but it had been a long week.

"This is why I can't leave the city," Laila explained before downing her shot.

Ali stared at the liquor before her, then knocked it back as well.

"Don't be ridiculous," she said. "I was totally serious when I told you to go earlier. This might have been one hell of a week, but the work can wait. At least for now. Plus, we are going to need all the allies we can get if this comes to a fight with the Demons."

Ali had a point. This ball could be a valuable opportunity to strengthen their ties with the other world communities.

"I suppose you're right." Laila poured them another round. "I'm sure it'll be an interesting experience too."

"Going to a ball with a handsome Dragon escort…some women have all the luck!" said Ali dreamily.

"Luck?" Laila scoffed, "I took half a clip of bullets the other day. I wouldn't call myself lucky."

"But you're alive!" added Ali cheerfully.

Laila chuckled and shook her head.

Ali lifted her glass. "To unexpected opportunities and to the friends who help us through them."

CHAPTER 19

The next day Laila was once again stuck in her office, filling out her report on the vandalized club and searching through the information the LAPD had sent her way.

The electronic files from the LAPD on the Di Inferi gang were also mostly pre-Event, but there were a few reports that were more recent. Included in the files were photographs from the gang whose sign matched the tattoo on one of the perpetrators' wrists. She searched through the photographs, not expecting to recognize anything, when one picture caught her eye. It was more recent that the others, dated only a couple weeks ago. It was from a traffic camera that caught a gang member as he ran a red light. She didn't recognize either of the men in the vehicle, but she printed the picture and pinned it to a bulletin board.

She left her office and headed towards Colin's. He needed to know about the connections, and she had to speak to him about time off. Not that she was looking forward to doing the latter of the two. She knew he'd disapprove.

"Hey." She stood in the doorway of his office. "Do you have a minute?"

He nodded, and she took a seat.

"Do you remember this symbol?" She showed him a picture of the Di Inferi gang's sign. "It's turned up at multiple crime scenes lately."

"Okay," he said.

"It's from a gang known as Di Inferi. I think they're the ones behind the robbery at the minimart and the break-in at Club La Fae."

"And how did you make this connection?" asked Colin, rubbing his temples.

"Tattoos of the symbol were found on men at both locations."

Colin pulled out the bottle of pills and took one. "Did you figure out why they would target those locations?"

"I think the minimart was a distraction to keep as many people occupied as possible and to send a message from Marius. I think it was a bonus that it gave SNPs negative media attention—"

"What does Darien think of all this?" Colin frowned at her.

"I haven't told him yet," admitted Laila. She was about to add more, but Colin cut her off.

"Look, you're drawing connections where there are none. Maybe that tattoo is popular right now. You think you see Demons everywhere. You're just being paranoid."

Laila stared at him in shock.

"Now, wait for Darien to get to the office. He knows this city better than you do. I'm sure he'll agree with me."

"Excuse me?" snapped Laila, furious.

"Clearly your lack of experience is clouding your judgement." He opened a bottle of pills again and swallowed two more.

Laila was .05 seconds from blowing a gasket then and there, in her supervisor's office. How dare he belittle her like that! Just because she didn't have the definite proof yet didn't mean she wasn't onto something. Not to mention that she'd been in training to observe threats back in Alfheim since Colin was a child.

Ali was right—she didn't need to follow Colin blindly. Why should she just stand here and let him walk all over her?

But then a thought occurred to her. Laila needed his approval to take time off work if she was going to travel back to Alfheim with Frej. Perhaps she could manipulate Colin and convince him to give her the time off?

"You know what, Colin," she said, doing her best to look distraught, "I think you're right, I'm feeling a bit paranoid, and this injury didn't help."

She made a show of wincing as she moved her arm. It was completely healed, but Colin didn't need to know that.

"I think I need a few days to return to Alfheim and clear my head. Maybe I'll even talk to some healers there."

"Sure." He returned his attention to his computer. "You're of little use to us until that shoulder is healed anyway. You should be more careful out there next time."

Laila nodded innocently. "Thank you, Colin, this means a lot. I'll be back no later than Sunday."

"Sure." His attention was already back on whatever he was reading on his computer screen.

Well, that was easier than expected. She was still livid, but more than ever she was determined to prove this connection.

Darien arrived a half-hour later, and Laila motioned for him to come into her office. She shut the door quietly and turned to the Vampire.

"I've got to tell you something," she explained.

Quickly, she explained her discovery about the Di Inferi tattoos, the link between the minimart robbery and the club, and how she believed the Demons were involved. She also pointed out the drugs found at the ritual scene as well as the attempted kidnapping.

"This seems like more than a coincidence," said Darien, taking a seat, "but why this secrecy?"

He jerked his thumb at the closed door.

"Colin thinks I'm losing my mind, and I'm done with his bullshit."

Darien gave her a bemused smile. "I don't know where this Laila came from, but I like her."

Laila rolled her eyes. "Look, I think they're working for Demons."

"Go on," Darien urged.

"I've looked into this gang. They've got a history of small drug deals and the occasional battery charge, but nothing like these recent crimes."

She picked up her laptop from the desk with the Di Inferi file open and passed it to Darien. While he scanned through it, she continued.

"Now suddenly they've got SNPs involved and are committing very public crimes that are increasing the tension between humans and SNPs. This is a completely different direction. It only makes sense that there's a new chain of command, and I think there are Demons at the top of it."

Darien thought for a moment. "I don't think that's crazy, and I've been thinking for a while that the Demons were probably involved with a local gang, or gangs for that matter. But we need more proof to connect them to the ritual scenes where you actually detected a Demon."

"What about the woman from the minimart shootout? She mentioned Marius."

"Sure, but we need something more concrete, and we can't get a confession out of her now. If we can prove this connection, that's enough for an arrest warrant for anyone involved in the gang."

"Well, we know that the gang was involved in at least two crimes so far," pointed out Laila. "Why don't we speak to LAPD and see if we can track down some of the other members involved with the break-in?"

From there they could try to find a link to the rituals.

"Okay," said Darien, "I'll make some phone calls and see if I can arrange something. Maybe you can meet with them tomorrow during the day."

Laila shook her head. "I'm going to be out of town for a few days."

She explained how the sudden trip to Alfheim had come up, and the conversation with Colin about the time off.

"So, Colin doesn't know about the ball?" asked Darien slyly.

"No, and let's keep it that way. I feel like I'm in enough trouble with him for now."

Dairen said nothing, just nodded with approval.

"I'm really sorry to leave you with this," Laila frowned.

Darien shrugged. "Don't worry about it, and don't worry about Colin either. I'm going to try to convince him to see a doctor about those headaches. I think it's also time he and I had a talk. It bothers me that he's been so obnoxious lately."

"Maybe you'll have better luck than I've had," Laila shook her head. "Okay then, looks like I'm going to go home to pack."

"So, is this thing like a date?" asked Darien smugly.

"No!" she snapped, glaring at the Vampire.

He rose from his seat.

"Okay then," he said, winking. "Have fun with your 'not date.'"

CHAPTER 20

Laila pulled her duffel bag out from under her bed while Erin chattered away about the day's lessons. Ali and Colin were out of the office by the time she finished speaking with Darien, so Laila headed home alone to pack.

Finding Erin looking dejected that Ali was going to be home late, Laila invited her to help pick out a dress for the ball while she asked Erin about her lessons. The young Dragon sat cross-legged on the bed as she explained her frustration over a list of spells Frej had given her to practice, and how many historical events she had to memorize from Dragon history.

"I don't suppose Frej's mentioned anything about what you wear to a ball in those lessons?" Laila dug through a rack of dresses in her closet.

"Nope, he hasn't said a word about fashion."

"Any suggestions?" Laila asked.

Erin slid off the bed to look in Laila's closet. "I think you should take that long black dress you have."

"That's what I was thinking." Laila removed the dress from the rack and held it up. She looked in the mirror while Erin leaned against the doorframe of the closet and sighed.

"Do you think I'll get to go to the Dragon Kingdom next time?" Erin stared forlornly into the mirror.

"Of course!" Laila set the dress down on her bed. "It's the kingdom of your kin. He probably just wants to give you more time to prepare."

"I don't know…" Erin picked at her nails. "It's probably better if I never go. I can't even figure out a basic spell."

The sorrow and embarrassment in Erin's eyes were heartbreaking. Laila knew that she was struggling with her studies, but in this moment Laila could see all of her insecurities bubbling to the surface.

She sat on the bed and patted the spot next to her, motioning for Erin to sit.

"You're worried about your lessons."

Erin paused for a moment still leaning against the doorframe. She nodded, avoiding eye contact.

"Do you want to talk about it?"

Erin hesitated before joining Laila on the bed. "Normally I'm a fast learner. That's how I know so many languages. And when it comes to these lessons, I can study the history of my kind, I can learn about theory, but when it comes to actually using magic, I just feel like an idiot! I try, but it doesn't work."

"It's a lot of new information, that's all. Remember, you can't force magic. You have to coax it to work. You just have to trust yourself. You can do it. I know you can, and Frej does too."

"It's really hard." Tears welled in Erin's eyes.

"Yes, it is. But it would be boring if it was easy."

"I don't think magic could be boring ever. Well, except when Frej's teaching it."

Laila laughed, and she noticed a faint smile creeping to the corner of Erin's mouth.

"Just you watch," Laila said, nudging Erin in the ribs. "I'm going to make a complete fool of myself at this party. I'm probably going to trip over my dress on the steps."

Erin snorted. "I'm pretty sure Elves can't trip. It's like in your DNA to be graceful."

"We'll see. Court life is pretty treacherous. My mother attempted to get me into etiquette courses, but I kept sneaking off to the training grounds instead. At least in a fight you *know* who's trying to attack you."

"Swords are cooler anyway," Erin pointed out. "I'd rather have a sword than a frilly dress. I want to start martial arts lessons soon, so I can be a badass like you someday." The Dragon flopped back on the bed, staring at the ceiling.

"Speaking of swords…" Laila walked over to a dresser where a dagger rested. It was beautiful and looked more ornamental than anything. The hilt was made of intricately twisted pieces of metal that encased a blue moonstone pommel. More than decoration, the blade was honed to a lethally sharp edge, but never once had she needed to clean or sharpen it.

She had discovered it when she raided the Demon's illegal fight ring. She wasn't entirely sure how she had found it. In fact, it felt more like *it* had found *her*. All she knew was that it was there in her hand when she needed it.

After the incident, she had given Torsten the blade for inspection. She had never seen anything quite like it, and the language carved into the blade was unfamiliar to her. Torsten was able to determine that the metal was incredibly rare, and only found in a remote region. As to who could have crafted the blade, he had no idea. He fitted it with a simple but elegant black leather sheath, but she hadn't worn it since.

In the moment, she felt drawn to it. She moved to touch it but snatched her hand back quickly.

Were her eyes playing tricks on her, or did the moonstone glow when she touched it?

Cautiously, she picked up the dagger, but nothing happened.

"I wouldn't take that if I were you." Erin watched her as she held the dagger. "From what Frej's told me, Dragons are kind of funny about foreigners walking around armed in Schonengard.

They seem rather protective of the capital city."

Laila shrugged and wrapped the dagger, sheath and all, in a scarf before adding it to her bag.

"It's just in case. Besides, it's decorative, and I don't own much jewelry."

"Whatever, I'm just saying…"

Laila changed the subject.

"Have you made any progress with those books Lyn sent over?"

"Nothing about blood sacrifice rituals." Erin made a face. "They've got a lot of different spells and things, and they are actually pretty interesting, but so far nothing about portals either. I've still got two more that I haven't even looked at, though. I'll try to read them while you're gone."

"See, now that's what I don't get." Laila strode over to her closet returning with a small box of jewelry. "You've learned how many languages…?"

"Seven."

"But you get frustrated with magic."

Erin shrugged. "I don't know, languages are easy because they have patterns. You learn the patterns and you can apply them to similar languages."

It was normal for the children in Alfheim to learn three or four languages. But then again, their lifespans were much longer than humans, which left more time to learn languages. Seven languages were still a lot, though, especially considering Erin had learned three or four of them while living here the past few years.

"Magic has patterns, too. You just have to work with it more."

Erin nodded, but seemed lost in thought.

Laila always found Erin unusual in a way. Sometimes she acted like the child she appeared to be on the outside. Other times Laila caught glimpses of the woman trapped inside. It was not the first time that she wondered how different Erin would be if she had been raised by her own kind.

"All packed?" Ali asked sleepily over her cup of coffee.

"Yep." Laila hefted her small duffel bag onto a chair.

She noticed that Frej didn't have a bag, only his usual coat. But then again, they were headed back to his house. Laila supposed that he had no real reason to take anything with him.

Ali finished her coffee and set the mug in the dishwasher. She attempted to stifle a yawn, but Laila caught it.

"Are you sure you're up to driving us to the airport? We could call a taxi."

"You're worrying again," Ali pointed out. "I told you, Darien and I have things under control. Colin will hardly even notice you're gone."

Laila sighed.

Ali gave her a pointed look before turning to Frej. "It's your job to remind her of that."

Frej chuckled. "You say that as if I have a shred of control over what Laila does."

"Are we going or not?" Laila called over her shoulder, heading to the car.

Thirty minutes later Laila stood on the curb of the inter-realm terminal of the Los Angeles International Airport, watching as Ali's car disappeared into the distance.

She and Frej entered the sliding doors to the building and were blasted with a cool, air-conditioned breeze.

The inter-realm terminal was similar to the ordinary flight terminals. It was filled with small shops, fast food eateries, and cafés to occupy travelers while they waited for their departure times. But rather than airline check-in counters, there were designated portal check-ins.

This particular location only had access to three of the worlds: Alfheim, Svartalfheim, and Jotunheim. Naturally there were no portals to Muspelheim, the Realm of the Damned. It was also rare to find portals to the Realm of the Gods, or to Vanaheim, the Realm of the Ancient Ones.

The portal here would take them to Ingegard, the city-state of the Elves. From there they would have to take a second portal to Schonengard, the capital of the Dragon Kingdom.

As usual, the check-in lines were long. There was also the security checkpoint, where the inter-realm customs and immigration screenings were performed. Despite the crowds, they made good time. They had a bit of time before their departure, so they found two available chairs to occupy while they waited.

Laila noted that Frej had been unusually quiet throughout their check-in process. As they sat there observing the other travelers and waiting for their names to be called, Laila realized he was watching her.

"Something's making you tense," he stated.

"Um, I guess," Laila managed, surprised by his sudden declaration.

"Are you nervous?"

"It's just…." She paused, biting her lip. "This will be my first time returning to Alfheim since I left."

It had been a rather scandalous event for her family. They still struggled to accept her decision.

"I know it sounds ridiculous," she continued. "But I guess I'm worried that if I return to Alfheim, I won't come back to Midgard."

The Dragon watched her thoughtfully.

"I don't think it's ridiculous," he said finally. "It was a life-altering decision to come here to Midgard. It would be so easy to return home, back to the way things used to be. Yet in your heart, you know your duty is elsewhere."

"Yes, exactly! How did you—"

"I've spent decades in a constant state of travel. Sometimes I wish I could settle down, but every time I get comfortable, I'm called away. If I'm completely honest, though, I'd have to say I enjoy this lifestyle. I always wonder what would happen if I were to return to Schonengard for good."

Laila nodded. It was the most he had mentioned to her of his personal life. There was a longing in his voice. Sure, she had her own struggles adjusting to human society. But then again, she had Ali and her other teammates and friends. Who did Frej have?

"Frej Ilmarinen and Laila Eyvindr," called a female voice over the intercom.

"Here we go," Laila muttered, grabbing her bag.

They walked up to the final checkpoint with their inter-realm I.D. cards. The woman waved them through the doorway into a large chamber.

Armed guards watched from their positions along the side-walls. There was a bulletproof glass window above them from which additional border patrol guards watched the far wall, where the portal stood.

The portal was large enough to drive a semi-truck through and appeared to be made of rippling, rainbow-colored liquid. Upon closer inspection, one would see that it was in fact made entirely of magical strands that linked the worlds together.

Laila and Frej stood before the portal, bathed in its light.

"Shall we?" Frej asked.

Laila nodded, took a deep breath, and stepped into the portal.

CHAPTER 21

The magic brushed against her like a veil of feathers as she stepped through the portal. She resisted the urge to scratch her nose and pushed her way through the strands until she was standing in the space between the worlds.

The room they left in Los Angeles was connected to the other world by a bridge of tightly woven magic, strong enough to walk across. The rippling rainbow of colors that created the bridge was the only light in the space between the worlds. It was a dark abyss, and if anyone fell from the bridge, they would keep falling for eternity. Here, time meant nothing. The only thing physical and tangible was the magic connecting the worlds.

Portal travel was always disorienting for Laila. It made her nervous, and it was difficult to breathe. She and Frej quickly made their way over the long bridge. When they reached the veil on the other side, the magic caressed them, almost willing them to stay.

Laila gasped as she stepped through the magic and back into Alfheim. Beside her emerged Frej, mirroring her look of relief.

"Welcome!" An Elven man stepped forward in official-looking clothes. "You've arrived in Ingegard. If you would allow me to check your travel documents…"

They handed over I.D. cards and the Elf examined them closely.

"Welcome back." He passed the cards back to them. "Will you be staying in Ingegard, or continuing on to another destination?"

"To Schonengard," Frej said, returning his card to an inside pocket of his coat.

"This way, please."

The Elf led them through a series of corridors until they reached an arching chamber lined with portals to the various capital cities in Alfheim.

He led them across the room and indicated a portal.

"Here you are. You may enter whenever you are ready."

"Thank you." Laila gave him a polite smile and adjusted the strap of her bag before following Frej into the portal.

Unlike the inter-realm portals, the local portals were filled with dazzling light, especially in Alfheim where the magic saturated everything. It was like walking into a kaleidoscope. The bridges were also shorter and narrower. Rather than falling endlessly through space if you stepped off the bridge, the local portals would dump you in a random location between the two portal entrances. It was still hazardous, though, since people had been known to get trapped in walls or appear deep underground.

This time when they emerged, four guards approached them. Laila glanced sideways at Frej, who stepped forward to meet them.

"Sir Ilmarinen!" called one of the guards when he recognized Frej. He and the others saluted the Dragon, who returned the gesture.

"Can I call you a carriage?" another asked quickly.

"That would be great," Frej said, shaking his hand.

Laila arched an eyebrow at Frej. *Sir?* She mouthed at him stunned. He shrugged. Laila watched as he strode away with the guards and wondered how many other secrets he was keeping. Titles were one thing, but she truly knew very little about the man she was traveling with.

They followed the detail of guards through a tunnel leading to the city. The building that housed the portals was built along the wall that surrounded the city, just to the side of the city's gate. The two of them climbed into a carriage provided for them by the guards, and Frej gave them one last nod before the carriage pulled away along the main road.

"I didn't realize you were a knight." Laila looked across at him with interest. He nodded and stared out the window. Clearly whatever was laying in the gutter was more interesting than his past.

"Why didn't you tell me?" she asked, unsatisfied with his response.

"Because it doesn't matter, it's just a title." He waved dismissively as if they were talking about something as insignificant as the cobblestones the carriage was rumbling over.

Laila stared at him, but clearly he was done discussing the topic. She resisted the urge to sigh as she looked out the window at the passing city.

They were leaving the wall and slowly making their way toward the heart of the city. The buildings were mostly made of the same worn, yellow stone bricks that paved the streets. Schonengard had an ancient and archaic feeling to it, but there was also something that reminded her of the old villages of Europe she'd seen in pictures and movies. As they moved further from the gate, there was a shift in appearance as the buildings' inhabitants decorated the fronts of the buildings with small, potted gardens, or painted designs around the doorways and windows.

Not only did the architecture remind her of Midgard, but so did the people. After all, the Dragons had a human form and a beast form, just as the Shifters in Midgard. She wondered about the history of the Dragons, and if their ancestors could've possibly come from Earth.

Like the Shifters in Los Angeles, all the Dragons she saw were in their human form. The sidewalks were too narrow for them to navigate in their scaled forms, although she imagined that they could squeeze through the streets. Laila also noted that the buildings were only built to accommodate Dragons in human form. Yet high above she could make out large, winged creatures, soaring on updrafts, they were Dragons in their true forms.

The further they rode, the nicer the buildings became. Many of them had decorative metal fences with small, manicured gardens. Others were painted and had elegant plaster details. Some were even large enough to have their own courtyard; it was into one of these that the carriage turned.

"Here we are." Frej hopped down and offered Laila his hand. She took it and climbed out of the carriage.

The courtyard was relatively plain compared to some of the others. There were rows of well-maintained roses along the perimeter and the cobblestones beneath the carriage had been laid in elegant twisting patterns. Aside from that, there was little in the way of ornamentation. It was simple but maintained, and not as flashy as some of the other buildings.

Frej paid the driver and waved him off while an elderly man approached from the house.

"Welcome home, sir!" He paused, noticing Laila.

"Alfred!" Frej embraced the man. "This is a friend of mine, Laila Eyvindr. Laila, this is my butler, Alfred."

"Nice to meet you." She extended her hand. The butler ignored the gesture.

"Welcome. I'll take your bag, if you please."

A little awkwardly, Laila handed it over to him, before the butler bowed and ushered them inside.

The furnishings inside the building were antique but well cared for. There were a variety of old statues, paintings, and tapestries as well, from ages past. Laila had the impression that Frej had inherited the house and its contents. He didn't strike her as the kind of person who cared what his furniture looked like, so long as it was functional, and while the furniture was practical, it make the place seemed dark and cavernous rather than welcoming. She imagined he didn't have guests often, especially if he was traveling constantly. It was certainly a change from the warm, homey feeling of her home in Los Angeles though.

From the entryway, Laila could see a study to the left lined with bookshelves. To the right was a dining hall, large enough to seat twelve. In front of them was a set of double doors that were shut beside a long, curving staircase.

Frej paused by the study.

"Laila, I have some work to take care of. It shouldn't take long. Alfred will show you to your room so you can get settled in, and then we'll have lunch."

"Of course." Laila followed the butler who was already climbing the staircase.

When she reached the landing she paused by a large archway that led to a chamber. Inside were large sheets of metal that were polished and neatly arranged. It took her a moment to realize that it wasn't a sculpture, but a massive suit of armor for a Dragon in their scaled form. While the armor had been well maintained, she did notice a number of scratches and dents.

Up ahead Alfred coughed, pulling her attention away from the armor. He showed her to a room at the end of the hallway.

"This will be your room for the duration of your stay. Lunch will be in a little over an hour. I will call for you when it is ready."

"Thank—" she began, but he had already left, "—you."

She rolled her eyes and set her duffel bag on the edge of a large bed. The room was bright and open at least. There was a vanity, and a wardrobe, as well as a set of chairs and a small table by a hearth. A door led to a bathroom with a large, polished stone tub. Along one wall was a large tapestry. In it was woven the image of two Dragons spiraling through the clouds in a night sky.

After taking time to examine the room, Laila got to work

unpacking her bag. She was laying her clothes out on the bed when there was a knock on the door.

"Come in," Laila called, a part of her hoping it wasn't the stuffy butler.

In strode an older woman. Her curly, grey hair was attempting to escape its low bun. Her face was round and pleasant, and there was a youthful glimmer in her eyes. She wore a simple, blue, floor-length dress.

"Sorry to interrupt, my dear," she said cheerfully. "My name is Hanna. I'm the housekeeper."

She curtsied. Laila returned the gesture with a bow.

"It's nice to meet you, Hanna. I'm Laila."

"Here," she bustled over to the bed, "let me help you unpack these things."

"Oh no, it's fine—"

"Nonsense!" She waved Laila off, so Laila took a seat on the bed.

Laila's mind was swimming with questions, and Hanna seemed friendlier than the butler, so she chanced asking one of them.

"So far I've only heard people speaking in the common tongue here. I thought Dragons have their own language."

Hanna chuckled. "Oh, we do, but it fell out of fashion generations ago. Only scholars use it now."

She turned to Laila.

"Didn't Frej mention that to you?"

"Not exactly."

The older woman placed her fists on her hips and asked, "I suppose that's not the only thing he's neglected to tell you, now is it?"

Laila's reaction seemed to be enough of an answer.

"Oh, that boy!" She threw her hands in the air.

Laila would not consider Frej to be a boy in any way, but Laila had the impression that he would always be a boy in Hanna's mind.

"I tell you," Hanna continued, "these Dragon men are all completely ridiculous. Well now, don't be shy. Ask away!"

Laila grinned. Hanna might be old, but she was feisty.

"Is Frej a knight?"

Hanna beamed. "Yes, he is. He's a knight of the highest order. He was born into a noble family, but his parents died young. Frej became the head of the household when he was little more than a boy. The few relatives remaining were more interested in the family's money than supporting him, so Frej made the decision to handle the affairs on his own. There were a number of family friends that helped him though, not to mention my husband, Alfred, and I."

"I'm sure that was very difficult for him." Laila watched the woman as she hung one of her shirts.

Hanna nodded.

"Oh yes, and for a while he managed well enough. But he's got an adventurous streak in him. He joined the army and went off on all sorts of crazy missions, leaving Alfred to oversee the house. His birth may be noble, but he's earned his title all on his own."

Laila processed the information. Suddenly it made sense that he would go to another realm just to train Erin. It seemed he and Erin had far more in common than Frej was willing to admit.

"So, Alfred is your husband?" The idea seemed a little far-fetched. After all, Hanna was so pleasant, and Alfred… well, to be blunt, he seemed to have a stick up his ass.

"Oh, yes. We met here when I first moved into the household as Frej's nanny. There used to be more of us here, but since Frej is rarely home, Alfred and I are the only remaining staff."

"That seems like a big job to maintain the house."

"It's not that bad. And despite his quirks, Frej is a lovely man and he's like a son to me. I couldn't bear going anywhere else."

She held up Laila's black dress and made a face.

"Oh dear! Is this what you were planning to wear to the

ball?"

Laila nodded.

Hanna frowned at the garment, but carefully hung it up.

"Right," she said. "I've got to go check on the lunch. It will be ready in fifteen minutes. Afterwards, we'll talk more about that." She waved her hand at the dress before hurrying out of the room.

Laila didn't understand what was wrong with the dress. It seemed perfectly fine to her.

She finished unpacking her things before wandering downstairs in search of lunch. She had skipped breakfast and was starving. As she went, she examined the halls for anything that might reveal more about Frej. Close to the stairs, across the hall from the archway was a portrait of a man, woman, and little boy. The man bore a striking resemblance to Frej, although his eyes were grey. The little boy's eyes were bright blue, just as the woman seated behind him. She was beautiful, with fair skin, and pale-blond hair that cascaded around her shoulders in loose curls. There was something that seemed very fragile about her though. Laila wondered if Frej was the boy with the bright blue eyes. If so, that would mean that the other two were probably his parents.

After descending the staircase and rounding the corner into the dining room, she paused. There stood Frej, who appeared to be getting a lecture from Hanna. Frej was ordinarily self-assured and confident, but now he ducked his head like a guilty school-boy and took a tentative step back.

Realizing she had intruded, Laila silently edged out of the doorway. She had almost made it to safety when Hanna called.

"Laila! Don't think I can't see you. Come on in here before the soup gets cold."

"Sorry to intrude." Laila reentered the dining hall.

Hanna directed her to a chair. Frej gave her a sheepish look as she seated herself.

Once she was settled, Hanna brought her a steaming bowl

of soup. It was thick and filled with root vegetables. Laila resisted the urge to immediately shovel it into her mouth.

"Oh!" Hanna searched the table. "I forgot the rolls!"

She left for the kitchen, leaving Laila and Frej alone at the table.

"Um," started Laila, glancing at the bowl of soup in front of her, "do we eat?"

"Only if you wish to incur the wrath of my housekeeper." He gave her an amused look.

"Right…" Laila glanced over her shoulder before setting her spoon back down.

They sat there while the seconds ticked by on an old clock in the corner.

"Hanna tells me you require suitable clothing for the events this weekend."

Laila shook her head. "Oh, not really. I've brought a dress—"

"Nonsense!" Hanna returned from the kitchen with a basket of bread. "No offense, my dear, but that dress is far too plain and simple. You are going to a royal ball, and you need to dress like it!"

"I can take you," added Frej quickly, "to shop for gowns, that is."

Laila caught his nervous glance in Hanna's direction. She seemed pleased with the idea, though.

Tentatively, Laila agreed. She had not brought much gold with her, only what little was left from her travels to Midgard.

"Excellent!" Hanna clapped her hands together. "I'll have Alfred prepare the carriage while you eat."

CHAPTER 22

As the carriage rumbled its way through the city, Laila saw more pedestrians in human form walking to and from various buildings. She noticed that the clothing the Dragons wore was intricate, colorful, and made from the finest materials. The ladies wore dresses comprised of multiple layers of rich and colorful fabrics adorned with ornate embroidery. Their waists were synched tight with corsets and the skirts were so wide that they bushed the frames of the doors as they moved in and out of the shops. As artistic as the gowns were, they appeared far to gaudy for Laila's taste, not to mention absurdly impractical.

Amid the sea of fluffy, cake-like dresses the men were clad in a slightly less ostentatious manner. Like the women though, the Dragon men wore several layers of clothing topped with colorfully embroidered vests and coats. The day wasn't particularly cold though, and Laila wondered how they weren't sweating through their layers.

Laila glanced down at her knee-high black boots, t-shirt, and brown leather jacket. She suddenly felt as plain as a chicken in a sea of peacocks.

What in the worlds am I doing here? she thought. There were so many other women Frej could take to that ridiculous ball. Why would he choose her? It was not as if he had been terribly forthcoming with information. Why else would he have chosen Laila, if not to help her understand the culture? Was it for political reasons?

"In recent years fashion and designer clothing has become very popular," Frej explained, following Laila's gaze.

"I see." Laila stared at a group of ladies exiting a café with large, feathered hats.

"It's absurd, really," Frej continued. "They spend everything they can on their wardrobes, just to show that they can fit into the latest fashion craze. I'll never understand it. And every year there's a new company everyone wants clothing from."

The carriage pulled to the side of the street. They were at the entrance to a long, pedestrian-only street lined with expensive-looking shops. Like the clothing, the shops here were painted in vibrant colors. A variety of flowers grew from window boxes while vines creeped up walls. There were lanterns lining the street and the shops had elegant signs hanging above the doorways. The windows of the shops displayed everything from jewelry to clothing. There were also bakeries and restaurants of many varieties.

"There's a nice store up ahead. Many of the women shop there." Frej led the way down the street.

Laila followed, trying to ignore the disapproving looks from the Dragons they passed. It didn't escape her notice that she was the only woman wearing pants. They arrived at a storefront, and Frej held the door open for her.

"After you."

She stepped into the shop. It was larger than it appeared from the outside. Racks of gowns in every color lined the walls.

"Just a moment!" called a woman from behind the counter. "I'll be right with you."

The group of women the shopkeeper was helping glanced

over their shoulders at Frej before talking excitedly in hushed whispers. If Frej noticed, it did not show.

Laila crossed her arms, watching the women as they gathered their packages and left, casting skeptical and judgmental looks her way. Although she was slightly irritated, Laila kept her expression neutral.

The shopkeeper invited them in to sit on a couple of upholstered chairs. She was middle-aged and rail-thin. Her expression was severe and suggested that she took her job as a seamstress very seriously. While her dress was relatively plain compared to the gowns on display, it was elegant and suited her perfectly.

"Now tell me, what occasion are we preparing for today?"

"We will be attending the King's ball and other festivities this week," explained Frej. "Miss Eyvindr requires appropriate attire."

"I see." The woman eyed Laila's outfit and wrinkled her nose.

Laila crossed her arms. Her clothing wasn't that bad, at least it wasn't one of the lace-coated deathtraps that the other women wore. With dresses like that, she had no idea how Dragon women were supposed to run and defend themselves, or how they could even manage to pick up a dropped handkerchief for that matter.

"It's a little last-minute," the seamstress explained, "but I know we can find you something."

She clapped her hands, and two apprentices entered from the back room. The three of them got to work sorting through the racks of dresses. After some debate, they agreed on a stack of dresses, and then beckoned for Laila to follow them into a dressing room.

"Please remove your clothing," instructed the shopkeeper. "You can leave your things on that chair over there."

Laila did as she was instructed and was left standing before them in her underwear.

"I do love working with Elves," sighed the shopkeeper. "You have such graceful lines."

"Oh, um, thank you," Laila replied awkwardly.

The assistants nodded in agreement, then got to work, layering on the first gown. It was the color of autumn leaves, and quite beautiful. The embroidery was some of the finest Laila had ever seen. When the assistants finished adjusting the dress and stepped back, the shopkeeper frowned and shook her head.

"Oh, definitely not!"

Laila glanced in the mirror and was dumbfounded—the dress was beautiful! She had no idea what the shopkeeper was talking about.

Before Laila could object, the two assistants were stripping the dress off and replacing it with another.

The next one was a light steel blue. It had a lace pattern with the slightest hint of silver, and a sweetheart neckline. Intricately woven silverwork capped her shoulders instead of sleeves. Its skirt flared out with delicate feathers that rippled when she moved.

"Yes!" the shopkeeper cried, and pulled away the curtain.

Frej was sitting on a chair reading a book. He glanced up when the curtain opened, and nearly dropped his book.

"Wow, you, um…" he faltered.

Laila spun, allowing the skirt to flare out.

"Do you think it would work?" Laila asked, suddenly concerned.

Frej nodded and looked like he was about to say more when the shopkeeper ushered her back into the dressing room.

Hanging the dress on a separate hook, the shopkeeper and her assistants returned to their task.

They repeated the process over and over. By the time they had gone through the pile, the shopkeeper had found two gowns that she deemed appropriate as well as a midnight blue cloak made of thick velvet.

The assistants gathered up the cloak and the two gowns the seamstress had approved and carried them to the counter.

"These will suit you well enough for the other events," explained the seamstress when they joined Frej in the other room. "But they simply won't do for the ball."

Frej frowned. "Do you know somewhere else where we could look?"

The shopkeeper held up her hand. "If you trust me, I can make the most beautiful gown for your lady. It would be exquisite, and I would have it delivered to you the morning of the ball."

"Oh no," said Laila hastily, "I'm not... I mean... we're just friends."

The shop keeper gave her a skeptical look. Frej cleared his throat as he quickly turned away to examine a gown on a mannequin.

"Yes, something custom would be great!" he concluded.

Laila raised her eyebrows. That sounded way more expensive than she could afford.

The shopkeeper made some calculations on a sheet of paper while Laila reached for her purse.

"Your total will be one thousand and sixty-four crowns."

Laila caught herself on the counter. One thousand and sixty-four crowns? That was more money than she made in four months working with IRSA. She only had a couple hundred on her at the most.

Frej passed the shopkeeper a large coin purse.

"What are you doing!?!" hissed Laila.

"You didn't think I would actually make you pay for these, did you?" he asked, shocked.

Laila's jaw dropped.

Frej counted out the remaining change and accepted a box with the neatly folded dresses and cloak.

"Now don't forget," the shopkeeper added as they were leaving. "She needs accessories as well!"

The door clicked shut behind them.

"I really don't," Laila insisted. "I have jewelry and shoes back in my room. I really don't need anything else."

Frej gave her a questioning look.

"And I'm going to pay you back for those dresses, too!" she added, poking him in the chest.

Frej arched an eyebrow. "Are all Elves like this?"

"What?"

"So stubborn?"

"Excuse me?" Laila took a step towards him. "I am entirely capable of paying for my own clothes, thank you very much!"

Frej stared at her in shock.

Laila turned on her heel to put some space between her and the Dragon, when Frej's deep laugh stopped her.

Whirling around, she glared at him.

"I'm sorry!" he said, trying to compose himself. "It's not funny, really. I just didn't expect you to have that reaction when I bought these dresses."

Laila arched an eyebrow.

"You see," he explained, "I don't give women gifts often, but it's always been my impression that women, well, *like* these kinds of things."

He took a step forward, looking into her eyes before continuing.

"I didn't mean to offend you. Seriously. If I hadn't invited you to this event, you wouldn't need to buy anything. It's the least I can do."

His eyes mirrored the honesty of his words. Immediately Laila felt ridiculous for making such a big deal over the dresses.

"We have some time before dinner," pointed out Frej. "I'm going to hand this package off to my driver to take home. That way we can walk through the city. I'm sure the fresh air would do us both good."

As they wandered through the streets, Frej pointed out various restaurants or bakeries he was fond of. He told her of the time from his youth when he and a group of fellow boys had attempted to climb a statue in the middle of a square, before a grumpy old woman in a nearby house caught them.

The longer they walked and talked, the more Laila's tension eased.

"I'm sure you have many stories from your rebellious youth," Frej remarked as they rounded a corner onto a smaller street.

"Not really." She paused. "There was that time I disguised myself as a boy to escape from this awful dance teacher. One of the guards thought I was a message runner and immediately put me to work running messages all over the city. I was on my way to deliver a message in the palace when I ran into my father."

"Did he lecture you?"

"No." Laila laughed. "He gave me three more messages to deliver and reminded me that if I wasn't home in an hour, my mother would be suspicious."

"Well, that's not bad."

"No, but he knew that dance teacher was horrible. She was scary too." Laila shivered at the memory.

She glanced up. Far above the rooftops she saw a lone white Dragon gliding over them. The sunset painted its scales in brilliant shades of gold and pink.

"Why are all the Dragons in their human forms within the city?" asked Laila as she watched.

Frej paused. "I've never really thought about it. I suppose it's just easier to navigate the city in human form. It takes a lot less space to house one of us as a human too. I can't even imagine trying to crawl through my house in my other form. Usually I just shift in the courtyard if I intend to fly anywhere."

That made sense to Laila. It was probably a lot easier to build a house for a human that it would for a fully-grown Dragon in their true form.

"It's getting late." Frej glanced at the quickly fading sun. "Why don't we stop for dinner? There's a tavern just a block away. It's usually crowded, but the ale is worth it."

CHAPTER 23

The tavern was crowded and noisy. They squeezed their way in between tables until they found an unoccupied booth in the back. They seated themselves and waved over a waitress to order dinner and a couple of pints.

They settled in quietly as they waited for their food.

"I'm sorry." Laila glanced over at Frej.

He looked up in surprise. "For what?"

"For overreacting about the dresses."

Frej started to speak, but Laila stopped him.

"I know you had the best intentions. I'm just not good at this sort of thing."

"What do you mean?" Frej asked, frowning.

Laila bit her lip. "I mean this whole wearing dresses and attending balls and parties thing. I'm a warrior, not a socialite."

The waiter delivered their drinks. Laila accepted hers and immediately took a sip.

"There's nothing wrong with that," said Frej softly. "But some battles are fought with words."

"Which is what politicians are for," Laila pointed out.

"Sure, but many of the politicians here stay locked behind their thick stone walls." Frej smiled sadly. "They don't always understand how dire a situation is simply because they don't see it, or it doesn't affect them. They might've heard about Demons escaping Hell, but they don't understand the situation like you do. You've spent the past months dealing with this issue directly and you've seen what the Demons are capable of, but the people here haven't.

"You see, this is where my job comes in. I fly out across the country serving as the eyes and ears for the queen. I fight the battles and I see firsthand the consequences of political decisions, whether good or bad. It's my job to tell the court what needs to be changed for the good of our people. If I didn't, they'd sit in their fancy mansions having parties while the rest of the country struggled. This time I've brought you to help me explain that we need to prepare for the Demonic threat, before things escalate as they did during The Event."

"You may have that kind of power," said Laila, "but I don't. I'm no one. I'm just an ordinary Elf. No titles, no noble heritage, nothing. Why should they listen to me?"

"Has it ever occurred to you that this is exactly why your opinion *should* be heard?" He cocked his head and watched her reaction.

Laila sighed and took another sip of her ale. It was much stronger than anything she had had during the last year from Midgard. The flavor was bold and rich, but not overpowering. It had a sort of nutty taste that reminded her of autumn.

Frej sat there patiently, waiting for her to respond.

"Is that why you brought me here?" Laila asked finally. "To explain to a bunch of nobles what it's like in Midgard?"

"Not exactly," he admitted.

Laila waited for his explanation, but at that moment the waiter returned with steaming hot plates of food. They were piled high with roasted vegetables that were native to the area. Laila's contained only vegetables, but Frej's was also piled with meat. Elves were generally vegetarian. That's not to say that Laila never consumed meat, but the idea of raising animals for slaughter repulsed her.

A band set up in a corner of the room and started a merry tune. Laila and Frej listened as they ate their meal. The food and drink improved Laila's mood, and the music lifted her spirits.

"So, what will I be expected to do at these parties?" Laila asked Frej. She leaned back against the booth and crossed her arms.

"Well, the first night is just the welcome party. There's the usual talking, dancing, and refreshments.

"The second night is the actual ball. It's more formal. Usually there is a reception hall when you first arrive, and then a dinner. After the dinner comes more dancing and music. At some point the king will address those present. Then the last night is a farewell party."

"Couldn't they just condense this into one night? Is it really necessary to continue this for three days?"

Frej smiled at her. "Think of the first night as a rehearsal for the actual party. You get introduced to everyone, see how everything's going, and get prepared for the real event. The last day gives any traveling nobility a chance to recover from a long night of drinking before they have to travel."

Laila snorted. "If the drinks at the ball are as strong as this, then the next few nights could be more interesting than I expected." She waved her almost empty glass.

Frej laughed and rested his head against the wall behind him. Rarely was he so relaxed back in Los Angeles. It suited him. Laila noticed a softness in his features as his shoulders relaxed and his bright blue eyes shone.

She thought back to the night he arrived on Ali's doorstep. Never would she have thought that only a few weeks later she would be traveling to the Dragon Kingdom with him.

"What's so funny?" he asked curiously.

"What? Oh, nothing. I was just thinking."

"About what?"

"How much happier you are here."

Frej laughed. "Not really, I—"

A boisterous voice cut his explanation short.

"Frej?" the man bellowed. "Is that you?"

Frej's face lit up as he recognized the Dragon.

"Mavrik!" Frej slid out of the booth. "Gods! It's been years!"

The men embraced, clapping each other on the back.

"I take it you're back for the ball?" Mavrik asked with a big grin.

"Yes, just for the next few days."

"I don't mean to interrupt. I just can't believe you're actually here!"

Frej shook his head. "Where are my manners? Mavrik, this is Laila. Laila, this is one of my oldest friends, Lord Isaac Mavrik."

Lord Mavrik bowed deeply. He was even taller than Frej and had darker brown hair. While it was clear that Frej had spent many days in the sun, Lord Mavrik's complexion was fairer and his eyes a deep shade of ruddy brown. His presence was authoritative, but his smile was warm and playful.

When he took Laila's hand to kiss, Laila noticed his hands were rough with calluses. She could tell he trained with weapons often.

"You should join us." Laila waved at their booth with a smile.

He glanced at Frej, who nodded in agreement. Then he slid beside Laila on the bench.

"So, tell me, how does a gorgeous lady like you end up in a tavern with a rascal like him?" He jerked his thumb at Frej with a sly grin.

"Frej's been helping a friend of mine back in Los Angeles. That's how we know each other. As for why I'm here, you'd have to ask Frej."

"Los Angeles?" He turned to Frej. "What have you been doing in Midgard? I didn't think we were sending anyone over there anymore."

"This is a personal matter," explained Frej, glancing around. "Do you remember Brandr?"

The lord nodded grimly.

"He has a daughter."

"What!?! How come no one's heard of this?" he said incredulously.

"She was raised by the Fae couple who found her egg. No one ever came forward to help, so she has a pretty severe magical block."

The other Dragon gave a low whistle. "Wow, I wish I would have known. How did you find out?"

"I live with the girl and her adopted sister," Laila explained. "My mother has some connections in court here, and asked around."

Frej nodded. "I heard about this after my last mission and came to train the girl as soon as I heard."

Lord Mavrik sat back as he processed the information.

Laila had to give him credit. The Elven nobility she had encountered back in Ingegard were generally stuffy and egocentric. But Lord Mavrik was quite different, down-to-earth and genuinely concerned. Perhaps Dragons weren't as standoffish as she had thought.

"Enough about my troubles, though." Frej, finished off his drink. "How have you been? Have you set a date for your wedding yet?"

"No." He waved his hand dismissively. "My fiancée called it off. She decided she wasn't interested in an arranged marriage, and honestly, I don't blame her."

"But you've been betrothed since you were children!" Frej shook his head in disbelief.

Lord Mavrik shrugged. "To be honest, I'm relieved. Now I can search for a wife on my own terms."

"Every woman in the city will be vying for your hand!" Frej laughed.

"Exactly!" He grinned triumphantly and winked at Laila. "So, if you get sick of that old bore…"

"Drinks for my Lord's table, compliments of the owner," said the waiter, sliding three more pints onto the table with a bow. Lord Mavrik nodded to him and tipped him a silver coin.

Frej slid one of the drinks over to Laila.

She shook her head. "Oh no, I really shouldn't."

"You're on vacation," Frej pointed out.

Lord Mavrik chuckled. "A toast! To old friends and new!"

He and Frej raised their glasses, and Laila hesitantly followed suit.

"So how does an Elf end up in Los Angeles?" Lord Mavrik asked.

Laila explained how she had accepted a job with IRSA and had been transferred to the city. She also included a description of the city's condition and the struggles her team was facing. By the time she was finished, the Dragon's brow was creased in thought.

"I hadn't realized how chaotic things are over there." The lord exchanged a troubled glance with Frej, who nodded in agreement. "The other lords should be made aware of this, as well as the king and queen."

"Exactly my thinking," said Frej. "We helped the humans fight the Necromancers during The Event and it seemed like enough at the time. But with the possible threat of continued Demon involvement…. I think it's wise to consider an amendment to our alliance with the humans."

"Any conflict in Midgard could trickle over here," sighed the other Dragon.

"So far I haven't heard reports of Demon activity in the other states." Laila stared at her drink. "But Los Angeles is one of the largest and most powerful Human cities. It has access to a lot of resources, and powerful humans. That makes it a target."

A grim silence hovered over the group. They sat there listening to the band play, and eventually changed the subject to the upcoming festivities.

They sat there chatting until the band had finished their set, and their glasses were empty. By the time they paid, the group was in high spirits. Particularly Laila.

She knew it was the magic in the air. Magic was present in all of the worlds and connected everything. But in Alfheim, the magic was much stronger. It called to Laila and filled her with energy she lacked in Midgard.

She inhaled the cool night air as she and the two Dragons stepped into the night. It was late, and the streets were deserted. They wandered their way through the city towards Frej's home, laughing and joking as they went.

Suddenly she sensed someone behind them. She was about to turn when her body stopped, frozen to the spot.

"Look what we have here!" called a voice behind her. Laila's pulse raced as she realized they had walked right into a trap.

CHAPTER 24

Laila swore internally. She should have known better. She shouldn't have had that second drink. Now she, Frej, and Lord Mavrik were frozen, trapped in the air surrounding them.

There was the soft clack of footsteps, and a man appeared in her field of vision. He was tall and wiry. His hair was cropped short and his clothing was worn. When he grinned, Laila noticed a gold tooth. She could tell he was the one controlling the spell.

In addition to the man with the gold tooth, she could sense the presence of three others surrounding them.

The man surveyed her two companions.

"It looks like luck is on our side, boys," he called to his companions behind them. "Looks like we've caught ourselves a couple of nobles."

While he gloated, Laila concentrated on the spell holding her captive. It was the same spell she often used against the criminals she faced. Luckily, she also knew how to break it. She reached out with her mind until she found the strands of magic binding her in place and got to work unraveling the spell. It was similar in theory to untying a knot.

The robber gestured, and his buddies got to work stripping Frej and Lord Mavrik of their valuables.

"Thank you kindly, gentlemen." The words dripped like venom. "I assure you, all donations are much appreciated."

He turned his attention to Laila.

"You're a pretty little thing, aren't you?" He leaned in to smell her hair. "An Elf too. I do like Elves."

His breath stunk like a Troll's ass. If she hadn't been frozen in place, she would have gagged. He reached up and stroked her cheek as Laila unraveled the last strand of his spell.

She kneed him in the groin, the force of the blow jerking his head down. She met his face with an upper cut, followed by a right hook. He dropped like a rock.

His cronies stared in shock.

"Don't just stand there, you idiots!" he moaned, scrambling away. "Do something!"

Two of them rushed her. She spun out of the way, tripping one and knocking him into the other.

The third grabbed her from behind, choking her. She elbowed him in the stomach and the face before throwing him over her shoulder. His legs sailed through the air, and he landed on the leader, who was attempting to stand. They collided painfully with a grunt.

One of the first men had recovered and grabbed her from behind, pinning her arms to the side, as the other approached. She lashed out, kicking him in the stomach.

He doubled over with a groan. Her next kick was aimed at his face. She felt the heel of her boot connect with his chin. His eyes rolled back into his head, and he toppled backwards onto the cobblestones.

Before one of the other men could recover, she blasted fire at the feet of the man holding her. He yelped and shoved her painfully into the wall of a building. Her head hit the brick with a painful crack, and stars danced across her vision.

She shook her head, clearing it just in time to see the man attack her with a jagged knife.

Laila knocked his hand out of the way as he cut once, twice, and the third time she grabbed his wrist in both hands, bringing it down on her knee. It wasn't quite hard enough to break his wrist, but it did loosen his grip. Twisting the knife around, she stabbed him in the thigh. He screamed as he crumpled.

Taking a moment to recover, Laila conjured ice daggers and aimed them at her assailants.

"Return what you stole from my friends." The men stared at her blankly. "Now!"

They scrambled to empty their pockets onto the cobblestones.

"If I ever catch you again, I will hand you over to the authorities," she growled. "Consider yourself warned. Now leave."

Hastily, they retreated back the way they came. Laila waited to drop her ice daggers until they had vanished into the night. There was a gasp as the spell broke on Frej and Lord Mavrik.

The men stared at her as she passed them their belongings. After a minute, Lord Mavrik spoke.

"Thor's hammer, that was amazing!" He turned to Frej. "Did you know she could do that?"

Frej shook his head. "I knew you were good. But—"

"You just took down four fully grown male Dragons!" Lord Mavrik interjected.

Laila shrugged. "They weren't that good. Seriously."

"I'm not sure how to repay you," he said, still stunned.

"Don't worry about it." Laila waved him off. "We should get going though, just in case they return with their friends."

Lord Mavrik talked about the experience the rest of their way to Frej's house. When they arrived, Frej insisted Mavrik take a carriage the rest of his way home. The lord reluctantly accepted. Once they had seen him off, Hanna and Alfred fussed over the two of them.

Before Laila could protest, Hanna whisked her off to her

bedroom.

"Oh, you poor thing!" Hanna exclaimed as she inspected a bruise spreading on Laila's head and shoulder from the impact with the wall.

"It's fine, really," insisted Laila.

"You can't go to the ball looking like that! If you wait just a moment, I'll fix you right up."

Hanna hurried out of the room, mumbling about water.

Laila glanced in a mirror, examining the bruising and cuts for herself. She called up her magic, and within seconds the bruising was gone.

She sighed as the magic drained her. The magic exhaustion of a few days ago made the task more taxing than usual.

Momentarily, Hanna returned with a bowl of water. She took one glance at Laila, and chuckled.

"Of course! You're an Elf. Naturally you are good at healing."

After the housekeeper had determined that she was properly healed, Hanna got to work showing Laila where she had hung the gowns and cloak that Frej had purchased earlier that day.

"Thank goodness Frej had sent them home before that encounter with the bandits. I'd hate to think of the shape they'd be in after that."

Hanna hung them back up and added, "I noticed that you are still missing a ball gown."

Laila nodded. "The seamstress said she is making something special and will deliver it the morning of the ball."

"Oh, that will be lovely." Hanna nodded excitedly. "The seamstresses make such beautiful gowns here. They never disappoint!"

When Hanna left, Laila changed into a thin cotton t-shirt and pajama bottoms. Exhausted, she was about to crawl into bed when there was a knock on her door.

"Laila?" a voice called. "It's me, Frej."

Laila padded over to the door with bare feet. She opened it and found Frej standing alone in the hallway.

"I hope I didn't disturb you," he said, noticing her pajamas.

"Oh no, it's fine."

"I just wanted to thank you."

"It was nothing. Seriously."

"How is your head?" he asked, searching her face for signs of bruising.

"All healed." She tucked her hair behind her ear and away from her face. "See? Nothing to worry about."

Frej nodded.

Laila leaned against the doorframe. "I'm used to it, really. It's kind of an occupational hazard for me. At least this time I knew what I was up against. Sometimes I'm dealing with Supernaturals I've never even seen before."

"Well, at least there will be guards at the parties. You won't have to worry about safety there."

"Hopefully," Laila added with a smile.

They stood there silently for a moment.

"Well, have a good night then," said Frej abruptly. "Hanna will wake you in the morning. You'll want to sleep in. These parties tend to go late."

"Thanks, sleep well."

"You too." He gave her a slight incline of his head.

Laila shut the door and returned to her bed. As she lay there, her thoughts were plagued with worry for the day ahead. Would she make a fool of herself? Were the Dragons even open to hearing the struggles of Midgard, or would they scoff at Frej's decision to invite her? She didn't know how different the Dragon's customs were from that of the Elves or the humans, so what if she offended somebody? The thoughts continued to cycle through her mind, but eventually she drifted off to a fitful sleep.

CHAPTER 25

Ali drove the van down the street in the late evening sun. Colin, in his wolf-form, trotted back and forth down the various alleys searching for the scent of a decaying corpse.

They'd been at it for the better part of the day with no luck, so they'd expanded their search radius.

She was glad that Laila had decided to go to the Dragon Kingdom with Frej. Not only because Laila needed a break, but because Ali wanted to know as much as she could about the Dragon Kingdom, and if Ali couldn't go herself, there was no one she trusted more to give her honest opinion. Eventually Erin would leave to further her training there, and Ali knew it. The thought constantly loomed in the back of her mind like a dark cloud, but she trusted Laila to be frank in her assessment of the city and the people there.

She sighed. For years she had hoped for a way to connect Erin with the Dragons, but now that it was here, she worried that it would all happen too fast. Erin was all she had left, and she knew it would be difficult when the time came for Erin to leave.

Colin loped out of yet another alley and shook his head. Ali pulled the car forward as he proceeded down the road. Suddenly, the wolf stopped and sniffed the air. He took off down a side street, howling as he went. He'd found something.

Ali followed him and pulled the SUV over to the side of the road. She parked the car and pulled on a pair of gloves as she approached Colin, who was shifting back into his human form.

Even Ali could smell the rotting body.

"In here?" She pointed to the dumpster.

"Behind," he said, finishing the transformation.

She passed him a pair of gloves before searching the area behind the dumpster.

"Goddess," she whispered as she spotted the body.

It was small, most likely a child, and the flesh had been partially eaten away by rats and other creatures that lived on the street.

"These people are monsters." She pulled out her phone and sent a request for the investigative team.

"It's hard to say," said Colin from the other side of the dumpster, "but I think it's the boy."

It took almost forty minutes for the investigative team to arrive, during which time Ali and Colin took photos and entered notes into the database. The investigative team loaded up the body to transport it to the morgue.

"Do you think you could catch a ride with them to the office?" Colin asked her as he checked his phone. "I'm supposed to be somewhere."

"What? Another date?" Ali asked, annoyed.

"That's none of your business." He walked towards the SUV.

"Oh, really?" she said. "Because when you push your work on the rest of us to make more time for your love life, it sort of makes it my business."

Colin's face was turning red, and the investigative team was staring at them. Ali continued with a warning in her voice.

"I don't care about your love life. Go have fun. You deserve it." She stepped in close. "But don't you dare do it at our expense."

"Enough!" snapped Colin. "This is my break, and if you have an issue with the way I run my office, you can always transfer somewhere else. I do my duty to this position and to my job, and at least you won't find me sleeping with my informants."

That was a low blow. Ali was still struggling with the guilt of Carlos's murder. She'd never intended for him to become an informant, but over the years his information was just too valuable to pass up. It was because of that information that he'd been killed.

Colin turned and climbed into the vehicle.

"Just remember, you'd be better off with me as a friend than as an enemy," she snarled.

It was a threat, but if Colin heard it, he didn't react. He pulled away from the curb and back towards the west side.

Ali clenched and unclenched her fist. She took a deep breath, and pushed down the urge to hit something.

The supervisor of the investigative team stood beside Ali and watched as Colin's car disappeared around a corner. She was human, and Ali couldn't recall having a conversation with her that wasn't work related.

"What was that about?" The woman cast a concerned glance at Ali. "I've never seen him just leave like that."

"I don't know, but I swear I'm going to find out," said Ali venomously.

But it would have to wait. Right now there was a body of a little boy on its way to the morgue.

What kind of person would kill a child? Ali shook her head.

She just prayed to the Morrigan that she would have the strength to put up with Colin's bullshit until this case was dealt with.

CHAPTER 26

"Good morning!" called Hanna from the doorway. She strode over to the windows of the dark room with the familiarity of one who has spent years in the same house.

Laila flinched as she pulled back the curtains.

"Oh, how late is it?" Laila asked, trying to clear away the cobwebs of sleep.

"Close to noon, I'd imagine, but not to worry, dear, there is plenty of time to prepare for the evening."

Laila sat up and glanced out the window. Through the archway of the courtyard she saw there were people rushing back and forth on the street. Tunics and aprons in a variety of colors were embordered with household and royal crests, marking them as staff from the larger households as well as from the palace. Presumably they were preparing for the first night of the parties.

Laila threw back the covers and swung her legs over the side of the bed.

"I've brought breakfast for you, dear." Hanna wheeled a cart over to a chair by the fire.

"Thank you."

"Frej had a meeting in the city. It seemed silly to have you sit in that large dining room all by yourself. Here you are." She transferred a dish from the tray onto the table as Laila seated herself.

It was a simple porridge, but considering Laila's nerves over the evening ahead, a plain breakfast was probably the best idea. While she ate, Hanna disappeared into the bathroom. Laila could hear the sound of the tub filling.

It felt odd for her to be waited on. Her parents' house was fully staffed, but Laila was still accustomed to doing things herself. She had the feeling that it made Hanna happy to care for and fuss over someone when the house was empty so often.

After breakfast Laila took her time bathing. She lounged in the hot water with a hint of rose perfume. It relaxed her body and removed any stiffness from the previous day's encounter with the would-be robbers.

While she soaked, numerous scenarios played out in her mind, each one reminding her of how out of place she would feel that night. Why in the worlds had she agreed to this? At least no one there would know her. There would be no embarrassing stories dredged up from her youth, and no history to refer to. She would be just another young woman in the crowd.

The water began to cool, and Laila considered heating it up with a spell. But she knew that there would be much to do to prepare for the evening. Instead she thoroughly scrubbed herself and rinsed before climbing out of the tub.

Laila wrapped a towel around herself and looked into a full-length mirror. She may be tall and thin, but she was strong, much stronger than a human, although as with most Elves she was not visibly muscular. She'd been through worse situations than a ball, so why was she so anxious?

Hooking a damp lock of hair behind a pointed ear, Laila debated what she would do with her hair for the evening. After some consideration, she settled on drying it and decided to ask Hanna for help later.

Makeup, on the other hand, was something she could handle. Twenty minutes later, she was finished, and changed into a spare t-shirt and her jeans.

She headed down to the first floor to find something she could help with. Hanna was in the entrance hall discussing the carriage with her husband.

"Of course the carriage is suitable!" huffed Alfred, throwing his hands up in exasperation. "It's carried this household to and from events for decades."

"But that is exactly my point." Hanna crossed her arms and shook her head. "Perhaps we could rent a newer one?"

"Where are we supposed to find a carriage to rent on such short notice? Even if I can find one, do you know how expensive that is?" he said exasperated.

"What's wrong with the carriage?" Laila asked.

"Absolutely nothing!" Alfred retorted, glaring at Hanna.

"It's old and horribly out of fashion," sniffed Hanna.

Laila cocked her head to the side. "It looked fine to me."

"See!" Alfred nodded contently. "Even Miss Eyvindr agrees with me."

"Oh, all right," Hanna sighed. "We've spent long enough debating the issue anyway."

Alfred excused himself to check in with the stables, leaving the women in the entryway.

"Is there anything I can help with?" Laila asked.

"Oh no, everything is perfectly fine. The only thing you need to concern yourself with is getting ready for the party tonight."

"I still have hours. Surely there's something I can help with in the meantime."

Still, the housekeeper insisted there was nothing for her to worry about. Frej was still out attending to business, so Hanna helped Laila find a few tomes from Frej's study to read. Laila carried the stack up to her room and used the afternoon to read up on Dragon formalities and etiquette.

CHAPTER 27

Laila stared at her reflection in the mirror, speechless. She actually looked like a highborn lady. Hanna had pinned her hair up in an elegant fashion. She had also made some changes to Laila's makeup and helped her into one of the new gowns.

Laila had chosen to go with the first dress she found at the dressmaker's shop, the steel blue one with silver neckline and sleeves. It was graceful and beautiful, but it wasn't too delicate. She didn't feel like a silly girl who was off to a party, but instead like a woman who was ready to take on the cutthroat intrigue of court. She felt infinitely more confident.

"Come on now, don't dawdle. We don't want you to be late!" Hanna said, pinning the cloak around Laila's shoulders. She then ushered the Elf down to the entry hall.

Laila's heart skipped a beat when she saw Frej. His formal attire complemented hers surprisingly well. The grey coat had complicated black embroidery, and his boots were freshly polished. The tight pants didn't escape her notice either.

Frej stood by the door discussing something with Alfred. His back was mostly to her, and he didn't notice her approach until she was halfway across the hall.

"Shall we go?" asked Laila.

Frej spun around. "Oh, yes, we should be going."

They climbed into the carriage and started towards the castle.

Frej was distracted, even more than he usually was. He frowned, staring into space, lost in thought.

"Is everything okay?" she asked. To be honest, she was a little disappointed by his reaction. She didn't know what she had expected him to do, but he'd hardly glanced at her.

"Huh?" He turned his head. "Oh, sorry. I had a meeting with an old colleague of mine today. It seems that a lot has been happening in my frequent absences. The increasing crime rate in the city, for example."

Laila frowned. "Is this going to affect your work with Erin?"

"It shouldn't. At least not for now. There are plenty of people here who can deal with it. But it is something I should discuss with the queen later. I have a feeling she's not completely aware of this, and we've had difficulties in the past with certain groups of criminals in the city."

"Does this have to do with last night?"

He nodded. "I've never had an issue like that in Schonengard before. Maybe in some of the shadier areas near the gate, but not up here by the palace. I'm afraid the thieves are growing too bold."

They sat there quietly for a moment before Frej continued.

"I'm sorry. I don't want to sour the mood. We're going to a party after all." He changed the subject, telling Laila about the other people of interest she was likely to meet.

There was a long line of carriages leading up to the castle, so the journey was much slower than she expected. They waited but were making little progress.

"How much further is the palace?" Laila leaned out of the window, trying to assess if the carriage was moving anytime soon.

"Not far, maybe three city blocks."

"We could walk."

"Walk to the ball?" Frej snorted.

"Well, at least we wouldn't be crammed in the back of a carriage."

Frej chuckled but made no move to get out. Laila shrugged and continued to study the woodwork of the carriage. After another ten minutes without much progress, Laila opened the door and stepped out.

"Where are you going?" he asked.

"To the palace," she said simply as she smoothed the skirt of her dress. "unless you want to sit here all night. Besides, fresh air would be nice."

Frej shook his head, smiling as he followed suit, then offered his arm. She took it, and they made their way on foot past the line of carriages.

Laila noticed that more and more people were watching them the further they went. Some laughed, others scoffed, but she saw more than one man stare after them longingly, as if he couldn't stand to be trapped any longer in a carriage with his wife discussing curtains or some other trivial matter.

"Walking to a ball?" sniffed one woman from her carriage. "I've never seen anything so outrageous!"

The outer walls of the castle were massive, and if Laila remembered her history lessons correctly, they'd been built to keep out attacking Ice Giants from the desolate mountains to the north. There had been a war when she was a child where the Ice Giants had fought once more to expand their territory and claim the Dragons' kingdom as their own. There had been peace in the kingdom for many years now. Still, the fortifications were a reminder of troubling times.

The palace itself was an entirely different matter. It had been rebuilt after the war to welcome in a time of peace. The palace was something straight from a storybook, painted in shades of orange, pink and blue. Marble statues adorned the rooftops and flanked the marble steps to the palace doors. Stained glass windows glittered in a rainbow of colors from the light within. The guards who were dressed in their formal uniforms wore tunics of white with four Dragons in their scaled forms intertwined, representing the four elements of their powers. It was the royal crest of the Dragons.

Even the staff seemed rather surprised at their unorthodox arrival. They quickly recognized Frej, though, and immediately ushered them into the palace.

On the inside, the palace was even more opulent, with rich carpets and wallpaper. The floors were constructed of marble, and the ornaments adorning the ceilings were covered in gold leaf. Ornately carved wooden tables, antique chairs, and large portraits lined the walls of the entry hall. A set of massive marble steps led from the entry hall up to a second floor wide enough for twenty men to stand abreast.

There were maids and butlers waiting to take any coats and cloaks. Laila allowed a maid to take her cloak before continuing onward with the crowd.

They followed the other guests through the entry hall and up the staircase. On the landing was a massive set of double doors that led to a ballroom where everyone was gathering in a sea of vibrantly colored fabric. Laila's dress lacked the wide skirts that the majority of the women wore, something she was relieved about. She felt elegant without looking gaudy as many of the women in their poufy dresses and elaborate hair styles did.

Tension grew in her shoulders as she entered the cavernous room and took a deep breath. The people around her would be oblivious to her anxiety. After all, she was an Elf. She had been raised from the day she was born to keep her head high and her face masked, especially in a crowd of nobles.

She also reminded herself that this was not so different from working undercover.

A massive crystal chandelier hung from a ceiling that was painted like the sky during a brilliant sunset. The floor was made of polished marble inlayed with the royal seal in gold in the center of the room. There was a banquet table with refreshments along one wall which was draped in a gold table cloth that matched the drapes framing the long row of windows behind it. Against the opposite wall was an orchestra. Large vases decorated tables and lined the walls with floral arrangements of pale blue and yellow flowers. The far wall held a raised dais with two thrones above which hung a massive banner with the royal seal. Laila glanced around the crowd, but the king and queen had yet to arrive.

She cast a sideways glance at Frej who was looking around at the crowd, smiling and nodding at those he recognized. They made their way through the crowd, pausing as Frej exchanged pleasantries with the other guests, and to introduce Laila.

Most of the people there were Dragon nobility. There were a few other SNPs, mostly from other Alfheim nations, but thankfully no one she recognized.

The Dragons she met were all polite, but she had the distinct impression that she was being judged. Elves had a certain reputation amongst other Supernaturals. Stereotyping was a given, but Laila had yet to determine what exactly the Dragons' stereotype of the Elves was.

"Miss Eyvindr," called a voice behind her.

Laila turned to find Lord Mavrik, bowing deeply. Laila curtsied in reply.

"Lord Mavrik, it's good to see you again. I hope you had no further difficulties getting home last night," she said softly.

"No trouble at all. How are you feeling? I take it you are all healed?"

She nodded. "I couldn't show up here looking too battered and bruised. It attracts too much attention, and then I would spend the night explaining why I was fighting in the streets."

"I have the distinct impression you'd rather be out on the streets than in here."

"Is it really that obvious?" She glanced at him sharply.

He shrugged. "You're a warrior, like Frej, and he loathes these things."

"He does?"

Laila glanced at Frej, who was engaging an elderly couple in conversation. He wasn't relaxed, but neither did he seem as uncomfortable as she felt.

Lord Mavrik chuckled. "I've known him a long time. I practically had to drag him to formal events when we were younger. But since his employment with the queen, he's gotten used to them out of necessity."

Laila shook her head. "Are all of you so cryptic?"

Lord Mavrik stared at her blankly.

"I don't mean any disrespect," she continued, embarrassed. "But your kind in general seem to be very private individuals.

Not that it's a bad thing, but it's difficult to get information. Especially from Frej."

Lord Mavrik laughed. "I suppose you're right. We do like our secrets, although Frej is particularly…enigmatic. He's always been like that, but I suppose that all his confidential missions haven't helped him in that regard."

A pair of older men approached to greet Mavrik. After a brief conversation, the men moved on to another group.

"So Frej is employed specifically by the queen?" Laila cocked her head.

"Our queen has an extensive military background. The king has less experience with such matters, so naturally the queen oversees his army."

This was news to Laila. She supposed it made sense, and it certainly piqued her curiosity.

"I should have known you'd find us, Mavrik," Frej chuckled, joining them.

"Someone has to keep an eye on you." Mavrik winked. "Besides, you're here with the most beautiful woman in the room, whose debt I just so happen to be in."

"You're just happy to have been the damsel in distress for once." Frej winked.

"I make a very pretty damsel," the lord said thoughtfully.

"Yes, a pretty ugly one." Frej snickered.

Laila rolled her eyes.

Lord Mavrik glanced across the room. "Speaking of damsels in distress, Lady Irene looks horribly bored of listening to that old man drone on. I'll see you two later."

They watched the lord saunter across the ballroom.

"You do look lovely," Frej turned to her. "I'm sorry I didn't mention it before."

"It's okay."

"No, it's not." He caught her hand. "I've been distracted since we arrived. I'm very glad you agreed to come with me."

Meeting his gaze, Laila's stomach fluttered. But she remembered the last man to look at her like that had left without a word. Did she really want to go down that path again?

She felt the urge to say something, anything, but before she could, she saw a familiar face over Frej's shoulder.

"Shit," she swore, causing a Lady next to her to scowl at her. Laila murmured an apology to the woman and stepped to the side to conceal herself and hoped she would not be recognized.

"Is everything all right?" Frej asked, confused.

"Sort of, I—"

"Laila? Laila, is that you?" a woman's shrewd voice called.

Laila groaned inwardly. Outwardly, she plastered on a pleasant smile.

"Mother! I didn't know you would be here."

CHAPTER 28

Lady Ragna Eyvindr observed her daughter and crossed her arms. Ragna was elegance incarnate and had a voice as musical as a harp. She wore a black velvet dress with green and orange accents and an embroidered bodice. A late middle-aged Elf who had dedicated her life to politics, Ragna often rebuffed Laila for not following in her footsteps.

It had been almost a year since they had last seen each other. Laila had to resist the urge to run straight through a portal back to Midgard.

"Is Father here as well?" asked Laila hopefully.

Ragna shook her head. "I was chosen to come as the Elven representative, and he had other duties to see to. The question is, what are *you* doing here? Please tell me you've decided to end all of that Midgard nonsense."

"No," Laila said as politely as she could muster. "I'm here as a guest with a friend."

"I'm Sir Frej Ilmarinen," Frej introduced himself, stepping forward with a bow, "of Her Majesty's inner circle. I'm pleased to make your acquaintance."

"Ah yes, of course." Ragna curtsied in return. "I apologize for my daughter's unusual tendencies. She's always had a mind of her own."

"Yes, I find it to be one of her most flattering traits." Frej smiled at Laila. "If you'll excuse me, I'm going to find us some drinks."

Once he was out of earshot, Ragna spoke.

"A knight of the queen's inner circle is a high honor," she pointed out. "He's a good match, even if he isn't a lord. Matches outside of our kind are unusual, but not unheard of. This could work quite nicely."

"We are not courting!" Laila snapped sharply.

"Don't be ridiculous! He invited you to a major celebration where everyone of importance in the kingdom would see the two of you together. Of course he's courting you!"

Laila sighed. It was impossible to argue with her mother, and Laila knew it. Luckily, there were many people of importance that Ragna needed to speak with. She excused herself quickly with the promise that they would continue their conversation later. Laila silently hoped that they wouldn't.

She glanced around, looking for Frej. She spotted him halfway across the room when everyone fell silent.

"Ladies and lords," called a voice from the doorway. "Their Majesties King Ingemar Hildegard and Queen Regina Hildegard."

The crowd parted, leaving a pathway for the king and queen. The orchestra struck up a song, and the two proceeded to their thrones, their subjects bowing as they passed. They ascended the dais and turned, facing the crowd.

The queen held herself with a sureness that came from years of military training. Laila could see the scars from past injuries on what little skin was exposed by her sweeping scarlet gown. She was handsome, but more importantly she was strong.

Her gaze swept over the crowd, assessing and analyzing. Laila could see she was the sort of person who rarely relaxed and was always on guard.

On the other hand, the king was proud in that way most politicians are, hiding behind a mask of benevolence and confidence. Laila often had trouble reading politicians for that reason. They hide behind so many masks that their true intentions can rarely be discerned.

Observing his appearance, Laila found nothing of interest, save for a large diamond pendant surrounded by a golden Dragon on a heavy gold chain.

The room fell silent as the king spoke.

"Esteemed guests, it is our pleasure to have you here for these three days of celebration. I invite you to enjoy our excellent selection of food and wine, as well as the music that has been prepared for this evening. Thank you!" His manner was easy, and his smile was genuine, from the looks on the faces of the other guests, Laila could tell he was well liked.

The lords and ladies clapped, and the orchestra started up again.

"I see your mother has moved on." Frej appeared at her side.

"I had no clue she would be here," said Laila, mortified. Frej passed her a drink.

"I didn't realize you are from a noble family."

"I'm not. My mother's title is more or less ceremonial. It was given to her for her service to the crown. She owns no lands, and I don't stand to inherit her title."

"I see. She seemed very…" He paused, searching for a word. "Aloof?"

"You mean Elven?"

"Well, I—"

"Oh, believe me, I know." Laila glanced down at the drink in her hands, wondering if it was strong enough given the circumstances.

"Clearly you're different, though," Frej pointed out.

"What do you mean?"

"I've seen you at home with Ali and Erin. You are comfortable around them. You are open with them the same way they are with you."

Laila shrugged. "I suppose that's because I've been living on Earth, and with Fae roommates."

"In any case, it suits you." There was a gentleness in his eyes as he said it that warmed Laila's heart. She blushed.

"What in the worlds are you two doing?" Lord Mavrik asked cheerfully, appearing from amid the crowd. "The dancing has begun, and here you are standing around talking."

"Oh no, I don't dance." Laila watched the group of dancers skeptically. "Plus, I have a drink in my hand." She waved it for emphasis.

Frej and Mavrik exchanged glances. There was some silent agreement between the two of them. Lord Mavrik bowed.

"I'd be honored if you would join me for this dance."

"Oh no," Laila said, taking a step back. "I don't even know this dance."

"Lucky for you, I know *all* the fashionable dances." He gave her a disarming smile.

Laila gave Frej a desperate look.

Frej just grinned. "That sounds like an excellent idea! I'll hold this for you." He took her glass.

Laila reluctantly allowed the lord to guide her to the dance floor. They joined the others on the dance floor in a waltz. Lord Mavrik held her close as they spun around the dance floor.

"See?" he asked as they danced. "It's not so bad, is it?"

Laila didn't reply. She found the dance distracted her. It pulled her attention away from the room. Perhaps it was a good thing. It kept her focus off her mother and the other nobles. But at the same time, she preferred to know exactly what was going on around her.

"Why dance with me?" Laila asked. "There are so many other women here. Surely any one of them is a far better dancer than I am."

"But none of them are as lovely as you are. This also looks

good for both of us."

"How?" Laila didn't see how twirling around the room could possibly do her any good.

"It shows you off to the other nobles in the room. Since most of them haven't met you, they may feel more inclined to make an introduction and eventually an alliance.

"Conversely, the others see me interacting with a beautiful Elven diplomat and showing I've got strong political ties. It may help me to catch the eyes of a few bachelorettes in the room."

"Really?" Laila raised an eyebrow. "You're using me to make the other women jealous?"

"An excellent plan, isn't it?" He grinned.

Laila resisted the urge to stomp on his foot.

The Dragon spun Laila around before speaking.

"By the way, you seem even more tense now. Did something happen?"

"You could say that," Laila said bitterly. "My mother's here."

"And this is a bad thing?"

Before Laila could reply, the Dragon spun her away. Laila realized that the dancers had formed a circle and the women were weaving in and out of the men. She quickly joined in with the other women. Eventually she made it back to Lord Mavrik.

"Yes, it is. A bad thing, I mean." Laila shook her head. "She's under the impression that Frej's courting me."

"Are you so sure he isn't?"

Laila missed a step and stared at him, her mouth agape. Lord Mavrik laughed out loud.

"Frej may be bad at showing it, but I can tell he has an interest in you. You're also the first woman he's ever brought to any of these events."

Laila took in his observations. She was beginning to suspect as much back in Los Angeles. But since their arrival, Frej had made no effort to show his feelings.

While Laila was lost in her thoughts, the song ended. She didn't realize it until a man approached them.

"I hope you don't mind if I cut in?" the stranger asked. His coat and trousers were dark grey with silver embroidery. His hair was black as jet, and he was incredibly handsome.

The smile he gave Lord Mavrik was friendly, but Laila could feel Lord Mavrik stiffen as he gave Laila a wary look.

"Surely you don't intend to hold her captive the entire evening?" the man mused.

When he didn't move, Laila gently nudged Lord Mavrik in the ribs. She didn't want to make a scene. He hesitated before stepping away and cast Laila another concerned glance before heading in Frej's direction.

The stranger bowed, and Laila curtsied in return. Then the dance began.

Quickly she noticed that he was also a very good dancer. But as he led her through the steps, he guided her in a very different way. He felt demanding and dominating. She was growing more uncomfortable by the second.

"I haven't seen you here before, Miss…?"

"Eyvindr."

"Miss Eyvindr. I hadn't known there would be two Elven emissaries."

"I'm not here as a representative, sir. I am a guest of Sir Ilmarinen's."

"I see," said the man. Laila noticed a slight change, his steel grey eyes growing slightly colder. But as suddenly as the change came, it went.

Laila guarded herself, willing her expression to remain the perfect Elven mask of indifference. Whatever this man was up to, Laila didn't like it. She made a mental note to ask Frej and Lord Mavrik about him later.

"So, tell me, how do you like our city?" he asked.

"It is quite different from the other capitals in Alfheim, but every kingdom has its own preferred style."

"So, the city does not appeal to your tastes?"

"That is not what I said." Laila wished he would stop speaking.

"Oh, that's all right. Sir Ilmarinen is a well-meaning man, but I wouldn't expect him to know the proper places to show a fine woman such as yourself." He gave her a disarming smile.

"And you do?"

The man grinned and pressed against her. "I have connections to all the finest establishments. I could show you far more than Sir Ilmarinen knows exists."

"I am not here for sightseeing."

The song ended, but the Dragon held her to him a moment longer than necessary before releasing her.

"If you change your mind, I'll be here." He finished with a bow.

Laila curtsied and gave him a curt "thank you" in reply before stepping away from the dance floor.

She wove through the crowd, hoping the Dragon was not following her. She did not glance over her shoulder, worrying that it would draw the man's attention. Instead she kept her focus on Frej and Lord Mavrik, until she reached Frej's side.

"Who was that?" she asked the two men, who visibly relaxed at her return.

"Lord Viktor," Frej said with distaste. He passed Laila her drink, which she quickly downed and set the empty glass on a table.

"He comes from a very old and powerful line of Dragons," Lord Mavrik explained. "He seems to be involved with a lot of unsavory people lately. There's nothing anyone can prove, but…"

"The point is," continued Frej, "we know he's constantly plotting against the others, but we've never been able to prove it. He's a real snake."

"That was my impression." Laila shuddered inwardly. She was about to add more when Frej suddenly bowed to someone behind her. Laila spun, finding herself face to face with Queen Regina of the Dragons.

CHAPTER 29

Laila blinked at the monarch for a moment, then bowed instinctually. In her rush to adhere to protocol, she bowed as a soldier rather than as a lady.

She lifted her gaze to find a curious expression on the queen's face. After a moment, she turned to Frej.

"I'm glad you could join us. I trust your obligations in Midgard are keeping you busy?"

"Yes, my queen, the girl is progressing, but slowly."

The queen nodded. "That is to be expected. There is so much time to make up."

"If I may," began Frej, glancing at Laila, "I'd like to introduce Special Agent Laila Eyvindr of the Inter-Realm Security Agency. Both Laila and the girl's adoptive sister work for the organization."

The queen returned her gaze to Laila intently.

"It's a pleasure to make your acquaintance," the Queen of the Dragons said.

To Laila's surprise, she offered her hand. Laila took it, grasping it firmly.

"And an honor to make yours, Your Majesty," Laila replied.

"So tell me, Special Agent Eyvindr, how are things in Midgard? Do the humans continue to recover from The Event?"

Laila hesitated. "They do, but there is a lot of uncertainty. Tensions are rising between the human and Supernatural communities, and the recent conflict with the Demons is particularly troubling. Not to mention the fact that the Greater Demon involved is still at large."

"What?" The queen frowned, glancing at Frej. "Why haven't I heard of this Demonic activity?"

"I only just discovered this after I arrived," he explained. "I believe we've been staying out of human affairs for too long. I understand the reasoning behind the initial decision to remove our citizens from the earthly embassies better than anyone, but it's left us blind to these new developments. Based on my observations, it's time the Dragons offered their assistance in dealing with this threat."

The queen nodded pensively. "I'll think on this. The presence of Greater Demons in Midgard is certainly unsettling."

The queen headed back into the crowd to converse with the other guests.

"So, what do you think of my queen?" asked Frej as Laila watched the monarch go.

"She seems like an interesting woman." Of all the others present at the party, Queen Regina seemed to make Laila feel the most comfortable. Laila wondered about her past. Lord Mavrik had mentioned she had a military background.

"I believe you two would get along very well," mused Frej.

"Oh, they certainly would," added Lord Mavrik. "But that reminds me, I need to speak with some of the other lords. Please excuse me."

Lord Mavrik quickly vanished into the crowd, leaving Laila and Frej alone.

"Shall we?" He indicated the dance floor.

Laila was not particularly excited to get back on the dance

floor, especially after her encounter with Lord Viktor. But she knew it would be rude to refuse. After all, Frej was the one who invited her to the party.

She nodded and followed Frej, joining in with the next dance. To her surprise, Frej was a good dancer. He talked her through the dance as they went. By the time they were on their third dance, Laila was beginning to relax and even enjoy herself. She smiled and laughed as her worries melted away and she forgot about the surrounding nobles. All that existed in those moments were the two of them as they glided around the dancefloor.

His grip was firm, yet not demanding, as he led her through the dance. As his dazzling blue eyes met Laila's, her breath caught. She was entranced by their brilliant color and gentleness as they glanced down at her lips. Laila blushed, and tore her eyes away. Could it be that Frej was interested in courting her?

When the orchestra took a break, they wandered back over to the refreshment tables in search of drinks.

"We have a lovely Elven wine, if you would prefer." The servant held out the bottle so Laila could read the inscription.

Laila accepted his offer eagerly. She was very fond of Elven wine. It had been a long time since she had last had any, though. Unfortunately, it was not common in Midgard. Its alcohol content was much higher than in human wines, so imports were heavily controlled and stores rarely stocked it. Not to mention Elven wine was very expensive, and the cost of importing it would be higher than she was willing to pay in Los Angeles. She decided she would have to bring a couple of bottles home with her when she left Alfheim.

As the evening wore on, various lords, ladies, knights, and other notable people approached them. Many of them were curious, having never seen Laila before. Others were interested in Frej's assignments and voyages. Laila did notice that he avoided mentioning his reason for traveling to Los Angeles. She decided to ask him about that once they were alone.

The more she spoke with the other guests, the more Laila got the impression that Dragon women were not trained in combat as often as the women were in the other kingdoms. At first, she attributed the observation to the fact that there was little need for nobility to be trained for battle during times of peace. However, she also noticed that every guard she saw was male.

Laila yawned. Perhaps she was just tired. She reminded herself that it was not necessary to analyze every detail about the Dragons.

"Shall we go?" Frej asked, catching her yawn. "I think the party is winding down."

"Sure, if you are ready."

He nodded with a little too much vigor. He was clearly done chatting up nobles for the evening.

They slipped out of the ballroom and headed down the marble staircase. Frej called for the carriage as Laila asked for her cloak.

While they waited, another set of footsteps echoing off the marble caught their attention. It was Lord Viktor.

"Leaving so soon?" he asked, looking all too much like a wolf on the prowl. Or in this case, a Dragon.

"Perhaps, but I don't see how that's of any concern to you," Laila responded, careful to keep her expression neutral.

The Lord looked her up and down.

For all of Laila's training, men like Lord Viktor never ceased to make her feel uncomfortable. The kind of men who think you owe them your attention. The men who won't take no for an answer, and instead think you are joking because there is no way any woman would possibly say no to them.

"I had so looked forward to speaking with you, Sir Ilmarinen." The Lord approached, diverting his attention to Frej.

"I'm not sure what we could possibly have to discuss," said Frej mildly. He made some attempt to keep his composure, but Laila could sense his ire close to the surface. Lord Viktor could too.

The lord smiled. "Now what could I possibly have done to offend you? I haven't spoken to you all night."

"Frej, would you mind checking on the carriage?" Laila asked, looking for a way to remove Frej from the situation before it escalated.

Frej hesitated reluctantly before exiting the hall. Laila turned her attention back to Lord Viktor.

"I'm not sure what game you are playing here, but I would like it to stop."

"I have no idea what you are taking about." The Dragon stepped closer, too close for Laila's liking.

"Playing the fool doesn't suit you, Lord Viktor." Reluctantly Laila took a step back. She clenched her jaw as she felt her back press against the wall.

The Dragon grinned, giving her a predatory look. It was cold and lustful. The hair on Laila's neck stood up straight.

"I'm not sure what is so appealing about that knight." He reached up to touch her cheek. She smacked his hand away.

"You clearly have the wrong idea about me," she hissed. "I will bring harassment charges against you so fast, you—"

"On what grounds?" He smiled darkly. "I've done nothing."

Laila kept her expression neutral.

"No, I don't think I have the wrong idea," he sneered. "In fact, I know exactly who you are, Miss Eyvindr. I also know you walked away from a fight with four thieves, relatively unscathed."

"Then you know what I can do." A hint of a threat crept into her tone.

"Oh yes, and I can offer you so much more," the words rolled off his tongue like silk. "I can make your life very comfortable if you come work for me."

"Wow!" She laughed. "You really don't know the first thing about me, do you?"

She conjured a shield of air and shoved him an arm's length away from her before continuing.

"This conversation is over. I'm leaving."

"Think about my offer," he called as she pushed the door open.

Laila ignored him and stepped into the night.

Solemnly, Frej helped her into the carriage. She could tell he was waiting until they were out of the castle gates before speaking, but his concern was palpable.

"What happened? Are you okay?"

"He wants me to work for him. He knew about the attack last night. I think he's keeping tabs on us," Laila said grimly.

"That wouldn't surprise me," muttered Frej.

"Do you think he's connected to the Demons?" In Laila's opinion, he would fit right in.

Frej shook his head. "I don't think he'd be that dumb. He's nothing if not clever, which is why no one's ever connected him to a crime before."

Laila was beginning to understand Frej's frustration with the lord.

"Lord Viktor aside, did you enjoy the evening?" Frej asked.

"Yes, actually, I did." She was surprised.

"I'm glad." Frej smiled, and the warmth in his eyes made her breath catch.

The carriage came to a stop in front of Frej's home. They climbed out of the carriage and opened the door to find Hanna striding towards them.

"Welcome back!" she called cheerfully. "I see you both survived the first party."

Frej chuckled. "Yes, although Lord Viktor is up to his old games again."

"That scoundrel!"

Frej shrugged. "But there is nothing to do about it at the moment."

Hanna shook her head as she helped Laila out of her cloak.

"Well," she said, "I've just left tea for the both of you upstairs. I'm sure you are both ready to turn in. I'll just leave you be."

She started to leave, then paused.

"Oh, by the way, Laila, I've taken the liberty of cleaning a few of your things. They should be dry by morning, but I've left replacements for you in the meantime."

"Oh, um, thank you," Laila replied, slightly confused. After all, she had plenty of clothing to last her for the duration of her stay, but if Hanna was offering to do some laundry, who was Laila to refuse?

They bid Hanna goodnight as she retreated through a door and out of sight.

Frej walked Laila up the stairs and to her room. When he reached the door, he paused.

"Well, I'm glad you were able to enjoy yourself at the party tonight."

"Yes, it was very nice."

They stood there awkwardly for a moment.

"Well then," said Frej, "I should, uh, probably go."

"Right, yeah, it's kind of late," Laila added lamely with a half-smile.

"Okay, good night then."

"Good night." Laila shut the door, feeling much more ridiculous than she had two minutes ago.

She sighed and stood in front of the mirror. Reaching for the zipper on the back of the dress, she found nothing. She turned to examine the back of the dress in the mirror to find a series of complicated clasps.

"Crap."

CHAPTER 30

She twisted and turned, trying to unclasp the hooks that trapped her in the gown, but it was useless. She would need Hanna's help if she didn't want to damage the dress.

Opening the door to the hall, she hoped to find the housekeeper, but the hall was empty.

"Hanna? Are you there?" she called. Of course not, Hanna had mentioned she was going to bed.

"Is everything all right?" asked Frej, opening his door. He stood there wearing a pair of pants and a thin, loose tunic.

"Oh, um, yeah, I'm just having some trouble with the clasps." She pointed at the back of her dress. "Do you think you could...."

"Oh, right." He entered her room, pulling the door shut behind him. "Here, let me see."

She showed him the back of the dress, where the series of little clasps hooked together. His fingers brushed gently against her back and a warm feeling blossomed in her stomach.

She thought back to the way he held her as they danced, and how easily he had smiled. In those moments, nothing else had mattered. She had forgotten her anxieties, and her self-consciousness, and the threat of Demons. She had been so happy to just live in that moment…

Lord Mavrik said that Frej had never brought a date to a public function before. So why her?

"Why did you invite me here?" Laila asked suddenly.

Frej paused in his task.

"I thought you might find it interesting, and I wanted to bring someone who understands the situation in Midgard."

"Then why not invite Erin or Ali? Surely they would benefit from seeing the city more than I would."

When he didn't answer, Laila turned to face him. His bright blue eyes shone, framed by his wavy brown hair. He looked at her with an expression she couldn't read.

She took a step closer, and he didn't retreat.

"Why did you bring me here?" she asked again, quietly, needing to hear the answer from him.

"Because I wanted you to see my life in the way I was able to see yours in Los Angeles. I hoped that showing you all of this might help you to understand who I am."

He hesitated before continuing.

"I've known since the moment you asked me to go have a drink with you that you were no ordinary woman."

The tenderness in Frej's eyes made her heart skip a beat. She could not deny that she was attracted to him. Being so close to him was maddening, but she willed herself to be still.

"I can't stop thinking about you," Frej continued. "I know I am very bad at this, at showing you the way I feel, but I think you are an amazing woman. I invited you here to have a chance to get to know you better."

He took her hands in his. But as a man of honor, he made no other move to touch her. He searched her face, waiting for her reaction.

Laila felt torn. It was a relief to know for certain what Frej was thinking. But at the same time, she was still hesitant. What would he expect from her? Would he leave her on a whim as Jerrik had?

Laila could feel the tension growing between them. She desperately wanted to yield to it.

"Frej, you know my life is complicated. My life is constantly in danger. I'm not like the ladies here who sit around going to social events and drinking tea." She watched him closely.

"Of course, and I wouldn't want you to be anything but what you are."

"Even if I'm stubborn at times?" She arched an eyebrow.

"Yes," he laughed. "Even so."

That spark was back in his eyes, the way it always was when he smiled. It was completely disarming.

She reached up with one hand to brush his shoulder-length hair from his face. As her hand reached the back of his head, she guided his mouth down to hers.

The kiss was tentative and lingering. It was as gentle as the caress of a summer's breeze, but it ignited a fire in the pit of her stomach.

She pulled away and looked into the Dragon's eyes. In them she saw a lust that mirrored her own. The wild look in his azure eyes made Laila lose her breath. The floodgates had opened, and Laila experienced a tide of emotions and feelings she had tried to lock away.

Taking a step closer, she lifted her mouth for another kiss. This one was deeper, more explorative than the last. Each of them was searching, demanding more. Frej wrapped his arms around her, pulling her to him. She wanted the moment to never end, but finally they surfaced for air.

The fire within urged Laila on. She needed more.

She grasped his tunic and slowly pulled it over his head, exposing his tanned, muscular chest. As she reached out, he caught her hand and spun her around so her back was to him. Frej wrapped an arm around her waist, using the other hand to caress her neck. He leaned down to kiss the point where her neck and collarbone met. Laila gasped.

So painfully slowly, he unclasped the remaining hooks of her dress. When he had finally finished, Frej slid the sleeves off her shoulders, allowing the dress to pool around her ankles in a flutter of blue lace, leaving Laila to stand there in nothing but a pair of panties.

Frej paused a moment and traced a finger over one of the long, blue-white scars that ran over her back.

Laila stepped away from the dress and turned to face him. He watched her as he slowly untied the drawstring of his pants. They fell to the ground revealing that he was wearing no under-garments.

With her pulse racing, Laila stepped into his embrace. Her body pressed against his, and her need intensified. Frej brushed her lips with his own before lifting her with a guttural growl.

He carried her to the bed and gently laid her down. The panties were quickly discarded as Laila surrendered herself to him.

Sometime later, Frej and Laila lay resting on the bed. He traced his fingers over the scars on her back curiously.

"What are these from?"

"A Werecat tried to maul me during a fight," she mumbled. "A Goddess healed me afterwards and left me with those scars."

"A Goddess? Which one?"

Laila shook her head. "That's the funny thing. I can't re-member anything specific about her."

"Well, they're beautiful in any case. I've never seen anything like them."

Laila lifted her head from where it rested on Frej's chest. She excused herself to take care of personal needs.

As she finished washing up in the bathroom, she reached for the pajamas she'd left on a hook. Instead of cotton, her hand met smooth silk.

She conjured up a light, revealing a midnight blue nightgown.

Now she understood why Hanna had mentioned that she was doing laundry. Hanna was not the kind of woman to forget that Laila would need help getting out of her gown either. Clearly Hanna had her own method of playing matchmaker.

Laila smiled and pulled the nightgown over her head. It was rather short, the hem falling just below the curve of her bottom, and it was simple yet sexy.

She returned to the room. Frej turned his head and appeared ready to speak, but stopped short as he noticed the oh-so-short nightgown.

As she approached the bed, he was suddenly wide awake, and aroused. He pulled her on top of him.

"How are we ever going to sleep tonight?" Laila chuckled.

Frej inhaled deeply as he ran his hands down her sides and over her hips.

"We have all the time in the world," he said so deeply, it was almost a growl. "We don't have anywhere to be until tomorrow night."

He gave her a wolfish grin, as she leaned in for a kiss.

CHAPTER 31

"Darien, this is serious!" Ali, scowled at the Vampire who was laughing hysterically in the passenger's seat next to her.

"I'm sorry," he apologized, "but I can't believe you actually said that to him!"

After the argument with Colin the night before, Ali had asked Darien for his help with an assignment. Colin had been holed up in his office, and Ali didn't particularly feel like talking to him, let alone dragging him out to the Old City.

"Well, good for you," said Darien. "I'm glad you stood up to him. Laila has a tendency to just take his crap, or forgive him, or something."

"She's too hung up on hierarchy," Ali explained. "I think she's worried he'd fire her."

Laila had only been there a few months, whereas Ali had been there for a few years. She was less concerned about losing her job, and more concerned that Colin's distractions would interfere with the safety of the team if this got any worse.

"So where are we going?" asked Darien.

"One of my contacts found a body in the Old City. Normally they don't report them to me, but I asked them to notify me of any potential murder victims."

Behind them, two more vehicles for the investigative team followed. Ali turned down another street and found a man waiting at the curb. She pulled over and got out of the car.

The man didn't say anything as she got out of the van, he simply nodded. While the hoodie obscured his features, Ali knew it was her contact, J.D. He rarely showed his face, self-conscious about the scars that covered it. It was part of the reason he'd retreated to the Old City.

"Down there?" she asked, indicating the alley.

He nodded again.

She pulled out a flashlight and headed down the alley with Darien. Piles of trash and old cardboard boxes littered the place. There was a rolled-up tarp halfway down the alley, which Darien approached. With a gloved hand, he pulled away the corner of the tarp, revealing the body.

"He's been dead a while," said Darien, looking up at her.

Like the boy they'd found, this corpse had been picked at by scavengers. Ali waved the investigative team over.

She froze as a bloodcurdling scream echoed through the night, like the cry of a banshee.

"Morrigan," breathed Ali, "what was that?"

"Let's find out." Darien stood and removed his gloves.

They left the investigative team to collect the evidence and set out on foot in search of the source of the scream.

"I hear something down this way," said Darien, jogging up the street.

Ali knew he was slowing his pace for her sake, so she pushed herself a little harder and rounded the corner. From here, she could hear frantic cries.

"Somebody help me! Please!" a woman's voice sobbed.

Ali was left behind as Darien rushed to find the source of the voice. Seconds later she heard him.

"Over here," he called from a side street.

Ali sprinted towards his voice and found a woman hunched over a figure in the dark, sobbing.

"What is it?" asked Ali as she approached.

"My sister!" cried the woman. "Please help her!"

Ali took a step closer and realized the figure that the woman was hunched over must be her sister. Her dark blond hair and clothes were covered in fresh blood from her slit throat, and her eyes stared lifelessly at the sky.

"Please!" the woman begged.

Ali glanced at Darien, but he shook his head. There was nothing they could do.

"She's gone," whispered Ali, gently. "I'm so sorry."

The woman shook her head, holding her sister's body closer. Ali whispered a prayer to the Morrigan, to watch over the soul of the deceased.

"How did this happen?" she asked the woman gently.

The woman didn't respond.

"Please," urged Ali, "we work for the Inter-Realm Security Agency. We can't find who did this if we don't know what happened." She showed the woman her badge.

The woman held Ali's gaze for a moment, then finally she spoke.

"I was stopping by her house for a drink like I do some nights, but when I got there, I saw a white van drive off in a hurry. I got closer and realized the door had been kicked in and that she was gone.

"I shifted—I'm a Hawk Shifter—and tried to follow the van, but I wasn't fast enough. I lost them near this area, but I kept searching for hours until... until I..."

The woman broke down, overwhelmed with grief.

"This was where you found her?" asked Ali as she glanced around the alley.

The woman nodded and wiped her eyes with the back of her hand.

"Did you see the people who did this?" Ali looked over the

body for anything that might help to identify the killer.

"No, I just found her like this," the woman sobbed. "She told me someone was following her, but I didn't listen. I just thought she was being paranoid."

Ali helped the woman up and over to the curb while Darien called the investigative team and informed them of the second body. Wrapping her jacket around the woman's shoulders, Ali reached for her magic to help calm the woman. Her breathing slowed slightly.

Darien motioned for Ali to follow him back into the alley where he continued to examine the body.

"What do you think?" asked Darien. "Her throat was slit just like the victim I found at the ritual site, and I don't think it's a coincidence that she was found so close to another victim either."

Ali nodded. "We should take the body back and see what the medical examiner says."

She took a deep breath and glanced at the woman sitting at the curb.

"I want to ask her a few more questions, then we should take her home. I don't want her to try flying home like this."

"Didn't Laila mention a Hawk Shifter the other day?" asked Darien as he stopped what he was doing.

"You mean the night of the drug bust?" Ali glanced up.

Darien nodded.

"I think so." Ali, tried to recall the conversation as she removed her gloves. "Do you think it's related?"

"Maybe, but I guess we'll have to wait until she gets back to ask her about it."

Ali looked at the woman again. Hawk Shifters weren't common, it seemed like too much of a coincidence.

"I'll get the SUV," said Darien. "I need to lead the investigative team over here anyway."

In a blur he was gone, back the way they'd come.

Ali tried to get more details out of the woman, but she was

so distraught, she had a difficult time remembering much more. She hadn't encountered any Elves lately either. When they took her back to her house and called a friend to come stay with her, Ali left her card with the woman, asking her to call if she remembered anything else.

By the time they made it back to headquarters and Ali had finished her report, it was almost dawn. Wearily, she drove home and parked in the garage.

The house was silent as she entered. She dumped her purse on the counter then walked past the staircase and down the hall to Erin's room. She opened the door noiselessly and found her sister asleep in her bed. There was a stack of books on her bedside table, and a translation guide sat open on the bed next to Erin. Ali picked it up and set it on the stack before pulling the blanket up around Erin's shoulders.

She left the room and climbed the stairs to the third floor and entered her room. Ali walked past the bed and over to the far wall where a little shrine she'd made sat on a side table. The centerpiece was a crow carved out of onyx, and on either side of the figure sat portraits of her mother and father.

Lighting some candles, she closed her eyes and took a deep, ragged breath.

"By the Morrigan, I ask for the strength to protect my sister. I ask for guidance to find these murderers, and the power to bring them to justice before more lives are lost. I may not be your most devoted servant, but I'm doing my best to keep the people of Los Angeles safe."

A noise at the window caught her attention. It was a crow tapping on the window. The bird took flight into the darkness of the early morning. Perhaps the Goddess was listening after all.

CHAPTER 32

Laila awoke with a start, but relaxed when she found Frej curled around her. One arm was wrapped loosely around her waist, and his nose was nestled in her hair.

She smiled as she lay there, relishing the moment.

She'd had another nightmare, but this one was different from the usual ones. In the dream, she was back in Los Angeles, flying over the city. It was amazing at first, but when she looked down at the streets below, all she saw was death and destruction. It was so clear in her mind that it felt real, but she reminded herself that it was just a dream.

"Good morning," said Frej softly. He pulled her close and nuzzled her ear. Laila twisted, meeting his lips with a kiss.

"What time is it?" she asked groggily.

"Noon. Maybe later."

"We should probably get up." Laila slid out from under the blanket, but strong arms pulled her back.

"Why? There's no rush." He gently kissed her shoulder.

They were both startled by a knock on the door.

"Laila?" called Hanna through the door. "Are you up yet? I

brought you some breakfast."

"Right." Laila exchanged a frantic glance with Frej. "Ugh, just a minute, I—"

The door opened, and in came Hanna pushing a cart.

"Oh!" Hanna winked, as Laila and Frej clutched the bed sheets to themselves. "It's a good thing I brought breakfast for two, then!"

Laila stared, mouth agape, as she watched Hanna lay out their breakfast at the sitting area by the fireplace.

"By the way," Hanna said, "a messenger came with a letter for you, Frej. I've left it on your desk."

"Thank you, Hanna."

"Of course, dear. Now don't wait too long, or the food will get cold."

Hanna left the room and shut the door behind her.

"Well, then." Laila slid out of bed and examined their breakfast. It smelled delicious, and Laila hadn't had much to eat the night before.

"Is everyone in your kingdom as casual with these sorts of things?" Laila gestured to the bed.

"Not exactly. I suppose we are a little less subtle than Elves generally are, but Hanna's different." He retrieved his pants from the floor before joining her.

"How so?"

"We don't have a typical master-servant relationship. She's been like a mother to me since my parents died, and she has no children of her own. Like most mothers, she's been hoping that I'll settle down and…"

"Oh." Laila blushed.

"I don't mean… Well, we…" He sighed. "It's too early to discuss these things."

"Yes." Laila stared mortified at her plate. It was not that she was against the idea of marriage, but at this point in her life, she was nowhere near considering *that*.

Frej wiped his face with his hand.

"So, what's for breakfast?"

Laila walked into the courtyard in high spirits and a clear mind. Frej had business to take care of that afternoon, so Laila had gone for a walk through the vibrant city.

She returned to find an unfamiliar carriage waiting in the courtyard. Assuming it was someone meeting with Frej, Laila attempted to quietly slip through the door. It clicked softly as she shut it, and when she turned around she found herself face to face with Alfred.

"There you are!" he exclaimed with a disapproving frown. "The seamstress has just arrived. Hanna took her to your quarters."

"Oh, shoot!" Laila had completely forgotten, and by Alfred's expression, he could tell. "Thank you!"

She rushed up the stairs and found four women waiting for her—Hanna, the seamstress, and the two assistants.

"I'm so sorry to keep you waiting," said Laila as she entered the room.

"That's all right," replied the seamstress. "We weren't waiting long. We've brought the dress early so that there is time to make any necessary alterations if need be."

The seamstress rose and indicated the gown lying on the bed. It was nothing short of beautiful. It was cream-colored and dissolved to a dusty gold at the base. The cut of the dress was simple, floor-length, and form-fitting with a swooping neckline. Upon closer inspection, Laila saw that the entire dress was embroidered with an intricate pattern with the finest silver thread Laila had ever seen.

With the help of Hanna and the two assistants, Laila tried on the dress. The seamstress frowned and gave her assistants instructions on where to pin. Before Laila could even sneak a peek in the mirror, the seamstress ordered her assistants to remove it.

The two girls then got to work altering the dress.

The seamstress turned to Laila.

"Tell me, what were you planning to do with your hair and makeup?"

"Oh, I don't know. I hadn't really thought about it."

The seamstress frowned. "Well then, if I may, I would like to assist you."

Laila glanced at Hanna in surprise. The housekeeper nodded encouragingly.

"Thank you, that would be great." Laila returned her attention to the seamstress, wondering what that would entail.

"I'll fetch everyone some tea," called Hanna as she left the seamstress and her assistants to their tasks.

The seamstress sat Laila on a chair and called for one of her assistants to join her. The two women curled and painted and brushed for the better part of an hour. Hanna periodically stopped in to admire their work before leaving them again.

When they had finally finished, Laila asked if she could see herself. She was curious to see how the two women had transformed her.

"Not yet," said the seamstress with a smile. "Not until we are completely finished."

In the meantime, the other assistant had completed the alterations to the gown. The assistants carefully slid the garment over her head, paying special attention not to mess up her hair or makeup. They stepped back, allowing the seamstress to make the final adjustments.

"Might I see your jewelry?" she asked Laila, as she critically examined the work of her assistants.

Laila went to the wardrobe and brought out the small box of jewelry she owned. The seamstress sorted through it with a frown.

"Hmm. This was not quite what I was thinking. Luckily, I've brought a few things with me. They are pieces on loan from a jeweler I know, and so long as they are returned in the same condition, there will be no charge."

She opened a chest that was sitting by the door and pulled out a wooden box. Inside was a delicate silver necklace that twisted and curled like a vine. Small diamond leaves studded the necklace, and there was a pair of matching earrings.

"Oh, those are lovely!" exclaimed Hanna.

"Yes, they are." The seamstress examined them fondly.

From the chest, the seamstress also produced a pair of shoes that fit Laila perfectly.

"There is one more element left," explained the seamstress. She opened a bag, producing a coil of silver wire. "You see, I'm an Earth Dragon, with a particular talent for working with metal. That is why I like to include silver and gold in my dresses. This is a little trick I learned from my jeweler friend."

Laila felt a shift in the magic floating through the room. Slowly, the silver wire rose like the head of a snake. It reached towards Laila, coiling around her chest. It twisted and turned with a life of its own. By the time the seamstress was done, the wire had formed a curling bodice that complemented the jewelry. It was thin and subtle, but beautiful.

"Now you may look in the mirror," the seamstress declared, beaming.

Laila stepped into the bathroom to look in the full-length mirror. She stared at her reflection, speechless.

For all the time spent, Laila's makeup was relatively natural-looking, with slight hints of silver and gold. Her auburn hair hung loosely in curls that fell just above her shoulders. Every movement she made caused a shimmer of light to be reflected off the silver, like moonbeams. She practically glowed.

"You look wonderful, dear!" said Hanna next to her, clapping her hands. "Oh, I wish I could see their faces when you enter that ballroom."

Hanna sighed.

Laila returned to the bedchamber where the seamstress and her assistants waited with their things.

"So?" asked the seamstress. "What do you think?"

"It's amazing, all of it. But why are you going through all of this trouble?"

The seamstress laughed. "I've heard that there are designers in Midgard that dress up celebrities for formal events. I hope to begin that trend here in my own kingdom. So, if anyone asks you who you are wearing, please give them my name: Alke."

"I'll make sure I do." Laila grinned.

Hanna showed the women downstairs and to their carriage, leaving Laila in her room. A thought occurred to her, and she followed Hanna into the hall.

"Is there a scrying glass?" she asked the housekeeper.

"Oh, sure," she called over her shoulder. "It's in the study, dear!"

Sure enough, she found one resting on the desk of the study. She picked it up and focused on Ali, then reached out to the magic of the mirror. She blinked and found herself looking into the living room back in Los Angeles.

"Hey!" said Ali in the mirror. "How are things?"

"I'm all ready for the ball!" Laila, stepped back a few feet so Ali could get a better look at her dress.

"Oh my gosh!" squealed Ali, "You look amazing! Erin, get over here!"

The two sisters gushed over the dress and bombarded her with questions about the Dragons. Laila answered as many as she could, but it was getting late, and they would be leaving soon.

"I've got to go," explained Laila, glancing at the carriage pulling into the courtyard, "but how's the investigation going?"

Ali sobered. "More bodies and few answers, but don't worry about it. Darien and I have got it handled for now. I'll fill you in when you're back."

"Okay," said Laila reluctantly.

"Seriously, Laila, just enjoy yourself, and I expect you'll give me all the details when you get home." Ali winked.

"Fine," Laila laughed, "stay safe and I'll see you soon."

She ended the spell and replaced the mirror where she had found it before rushing back to her room to grab her cloak.

As she opened the wardrobe, a pale blue glow caught her eye: the moonstone in the hilt of her dagger. A peculiar humming filled the room, and Laila was suddenly filled with the urge to have the dagger with her.

Laila snatched her hand back. She knew of enchanted weapons, but the dagger had never had that effect on her before. It was like a premonition. Something in the back of her mind urged her to bring the dagger, that it was necessary.

She backed away, pacing back and forth. Generally speaking, she didn't get premonitions like this, but she had been warned from an early age to trust them.

Eventually she gave in, strapping the dagger to her thigh with the sheath Torsten had made for her. Her skirt was just full enough to hide the blade.

Immediately, Laila felt relieved. She shook her head, feeling slightly ridiculous.

She found Hanna waiting anxiously for her in the entryway.

"I've just sent Alfred to check on Frej. They should be coming any moment."

As she spoke, Frej and Alfred appeared at the top of the staircase. Frej's pants and shirt were cream colored. Over that he wore a large cravat of gold lace and a dark blue greatcoat with a pattern embroidered in gold thread. His brown boots were polished, and his shoulder-length hair had been pulled back into a low ponytail. He held himself with grace and dignity. When Frej spotted her, he paused a moment. When he continued, he couldn't take his eyes off her.

"I believe that I'll be arriving with the most beautiful woman at the ball." He bowed. "Are you ready?"

"Yes," said Laila, blushing as she looked up at him, "we should probably go now."

As Laila settled herself in the carriage, careful not to damage the dress, she caught Hanna giving her husband a joyous look. Alfred didn't exactly reciprocate, but Laila swore there was a twinkle in his eyes.

❖ 195 ❖

CHAPTER 33

Laila and Frej stepped through the grand entrance of the palace and climbed the stairs to the ballroom. Laila noticed that people watched them as they passed. On the streets, crowds of people from the city had come to watch the carriages arrive. But here, even the nobles stared at her.

Looking around at the beautiful gowns that the other women wore, Laila noticed that the others looked like they had been crammed into fluffy layers of silk and satin. They had tightly cinched corsets that left their bosoms popping out, and wide, sweeping skirts that were so large they took up the space of three people. Their hair was done up in complicated braids and buns, and their makeup was painted on thickly. Even some of the men wore makeup.

By comparison, Laila's appearance was much simpler, and more natural. But Laila felt much more comfortable than the others appeared. There was no way she wanted to be crammed into one of those contraptions.

In her opinion, Laila felt that her dress represented Elven fashion beautifully. Elegant, but not at all gaudy.

They reached the ballroom to find the king and queen seated on the dais watching the early arrivals venture out to the dance floor.

Laila approached the monarchs with Frej, bowing deeply.

"I see you've returned from your personal duties in Los Angeles," observed the king.

"Only for the festivities, Your Majesty."

"And who is this lovely Elf you've brought along?"

"This is Special Agent Eyvindr," Queen Regina informed him.

"Any relation to Lady Eyvindr?"

"She is my mother, Your Majesty," Laila provided.

"Miss Eyvindr works for the American government," added the queen. "She's a special agent with the Inter-Realm Security Agency."

"I see." The king glanced between Laila and his wife. "I suppose you've been keeping Sir Ilmarinen in line over there. Good for you."

After speaking with the king and queen, they joined a crowd forming to watch the dancers.

A familiar figure wove through the crowd towards them. It was Lord Mavrik, dressed in crimson with gold embroidery and accents. He bowed and winked his way through the party guests.

He paused when he reached Laila.

"My dear, you could rival a Goddess with your beauty!" He took her hand and kissed it.

"Don't say that too loud," she warned. "I don't want to anger any of them."

"Well, you're certainly the envy of the ladies here tonight. They can't decide whether they are jealous of your looks, or jealous that you are here with Frej, or both."

Laila cast a questioning glance at Frej. He ignored her, but Mavrik caught it.

"So, you didn't know you were invited to the ball by the court's most eligible bachelor?" he asked with a crooked smile.

"Oh, really?" Laila teased noticing a blush creep up on Frej's cheeks.

"Oh, yes," continued the lord. "Every mother has been trying to set him up with their daughters, and every eligible lady was batting her eyelashes at him."

"They only like my title, and my proximity to the queen," Frej muttered.

"Don't forget your looks!" Mavrik winked.

Frej's expression was a mixture of discomfort and exasperation. Laila couldn't help but giggle.

"Well, I also think the women are quite jealous of your bold fashion statement." Frej, indicated the dress.

She laughed. "Well, I suppose it will make the seamstress happy, but I really don't like that kind of attention."

"I heard you two had a run-in with Lord Viktor last night in the entry hall." The lord's expression darkened. "What was that about?"

Frej's jaw clenched. "He's been expressing his interest in Laila."

"There's something off about him," Laila added with distaste.

"I have a feeling that he won't give up that easily though." Frej scowled. "He had that look. The chase is on for him."

"Then we'll be ready," said Lord Mavrik confidently.

While Frej and Lord Mavrik disappeared in search of refreshments, Laila watched as people greeted the king. Among them was Ragna Eyvindr. Laila winced as her mother spotted her, but she willed herself to stand her ground. After all, there was nowhere to run.

"Gods above!" her mother exclaimed. "You look beautiful! I always knew there was an elegant woman hiding somewhere inside you."

Laila bit her tongue to stop her sharp retort. Her mother continued.

"I spoke to your father this morning and he sends his regards. He would have found a way to come if he'd known you would be here. Your absence has been very difficult for him, you know."

Laila looked away, feeling guilty. She'd always been closer to her father than to her mother. After all, they had more in common. Laila regretted not taking more time to call him. Even so, she didn't regret her decision. Los Angeles was where she was needed.

"Did you enjoy yourself last night?" asked Laila, changing the subject.

"Yes, I suppose so, although I did notice you left rather early."

"Well, I'm not exactly used to these kinds of events."

Ragna frowned and stared over her daughter's shoulder.

"Laila, you seem to have caught Lord Viktor's attention. No, don't look at him," her mother said as Laila started to move her head. "Don't encourage him."

"It's probably too late for that," mumbled Laila. "He made me thoroughly aware of his presence yesterday. How do you know him?"

"His reputation is known to many of the kingdoms. He—" Ragna stopped short and pursed her lips. "He's coming this way."

"Crap." Laila shut her eyes as if it would make all of this court nonsense go away. She opened them to her mother's disapproving glare. Clearly, swearing was not on the list of acceptable behaviors at balls.

"Lord Viktor." Ragna gave him a tight-lipped smile and a short bow. "How are you enjoying the party?"

"It's a fascinating event." He stared directly at Laila.

"I believe you've met my daughter?"

"Your…?" He looked from Laila to Ragna. "Of course, I see the resemblance."

He returned his attention to Laila.

"Would you care for a dance?" The way he asked was polite, but the look in his eyes was dark. He offered his arm.

"I'd rather not."

Ragna grew still as Lord Viktor's eyes flashed with annoyance.

"Perhaps later then?" he added stiffly.

Laila smiled darkly and shook her head. "I'm not particularly good with court intricacies, so I'm just going to say this to you straight. I have no interest in you or your offer, and I suggest you leave us alone."

He stepped closer.

"Is that a threat?" he hissed, slightly amused.

"It's a promise." Her gaze was cold as ice.

Laila sensed Frej's warm presence appear behind her as he placed a hand on her waist protectively. Out of the corner of her eye, she saw that Mavrik was with him.

"Good evening, Lord Viktor," he said. Despite Laila's confidence that she could handle any unsavory advances made on Lord Viktor's part, it still comforted her to feel Frej's presence behind her. Not because she needed his support and protection—she'd proved very clearly the other night that she could take on a Dragon, or a few—but because Frej's presence made it less likely that Lord Viktor would attempt to harass her in any way. It was the unfortunate struggle of all women, no matter their race or social status. The hard truth was that creeps like him existed in all realms.

Lord Viktor shot Frej a disapproving look. He bit back a comment, noticing that Ragna was watching him like a hawk. Muttering something about a drink, the lord excused himself.

Laila released a breath she had not realized she had been holding. Frej's grip relaxed as well.

"I see my warning came too late," Ragna pointed out.

Laila sighed. "Can we at least try to enjoy ourselves?"

Ragna quickly excused herself, hurrying off to speak with some lord or lady. Laila had the feeling that Lord Viktor would be the topic of that conversation. She accepted a glass from Frej and returned her attention to the dais.

She did not like to be the center of attention. Sure, she need-ed to command respect with her career, but beyond that she was content to observe the drama from the sidelines. That was one of the things she enjoyed when she was out with Ali. Ali had a ten-dency to attract attention. But unlike Laila, Ali always seemed comfortable and in control of the situation. She also seemed to know exactly what to say and could form a snarky reply at the drop of a hat.

Sighing, Laila wished Ali were there. She would know exact-ly how to deal with Lord Viktor, although her methods might be frowned upon by polite society at such a formal event.

A hushed silence fell over the crowd. The king and queen had stepped forward. The king approached the edge of the dais and addressed the crowd.

"I wanted to thank you all for coming. I know that many of you have traveled far to come here, and for that I am grateful.

"When I assumed the throne forty years ago, I was not com-pletely prepared for the position. This is a role I hadn't expected to take on for many more years, and many of you in this room have stood by me as your king through the struggles our country has faced, but none more so than my incredible wife."

He glanced over at her with a warmth that was heart-melt-ing. That look of love and admiration was so pure, so honest, so true that Laila could feel the magic in the air resonate with it. They were truly soulmates.

The king continued.

"A short while ago, we discovered that the Gods had cho-sen to share with us another blessing. It is with great pride and honor that I announce the anticipated arrival of our first child and heir."

The surprised crowd paused a moment before applauding. Laila joined in, but stopped abruptly.

Something was very wrong. It was as if the magic in the air was screaming at her to *do* something. She had never experi-enced anything like it before, and the strangest part was that no one else seemed to be affected.

She scanned the audience, searching for the source of the disturbance. Her breath caught as she sharply inhaled. It was an assassin.

CHAPTER 34

He was disguised cleverly as a lord, and for all Laila knew, perhaps the man was in fact nobility. But the magic crackled around him like static electricity as he wove a deadly spell.

Laila glanced around, willing the guards to do something, but everyone was totally oblivious. In fact, they were all but frozen, moving slowly as though the air around them was solid.

The dagger she had strapped to her thigh early that evening hummed, as if it was urging her to act. Laila realized that she was the only one who would be able to stop the attack in time. By the time the guards took notice, someone would be dead.

Laila reached for the dagger, realizing too late that it was beneath the fabric of her dress. But to Laila's surprise, she felt the hilt of the dagger and wrapped her hand around it.

The assassin had already released the spell, and she could see it slowly flying towards the king.

She was too late.

She raised the dagger and released it at the assassin. Speeding through the air with a blinding flash of blue light, it struck the assassin directly in the shoulder. The blue light coursed through him before shooting out to consume the spell he had cast.

Time returned to its normal speed with a jarring lurch, and Laila stumbled, catching herself on Frej's arm as the exhaustion hit her.

People around her were screaming as guards rushed to apprehend the assassin and to protect the king and queen.

"Someone stop her!" yelled a familiar voice. "She was the one with the knife!"

Guards roughly grabbed her arms. She spun her head to find Lord Viktor smirking at her a short distance away.

"Stop!" Frej roared as the guards dragged her away. But the guards forced him back.

It felt surreal, more like a dream than reality, as she was pulled roughly through the panicking crowd. She could see the king and queen as they slipped out through a side door, and watched the other guards tackle the wounded assassin to the floor. The last thing she saw before she was led out of sight was Lord Mavrik attempting to calm Frej's outrage.

Frej was not entirely sure what had happened. The king was giving his speech when suddenly there was an assassin casting a spell targeting the monarch. An instant later there was a blinding flash of blue light, the assassin was down, and the spell was gone.

Laila had done something to stop him. Frej had never seen such magic before, and as Laila swooned he saw the same flash of blue in her eyes. They had been glowing.

He may not know exactly how she had done it, but it was clear that she was the one who saved the king. So, when the guards took her away as if she were the assassin's co-conspirator, Frej could barely keep himself from shifting and ripping their throats out.

"Calm down!" said Mavrik, who was grabbing Frej by his coat. "We'll figure this out."

Frej wanted to destroy them all. He was an Air Dragon, he was thunder, he could tear those guards apart limb from limb, regardless of whether or not they were his own kind.

But he knew the rage would not help Laila.

He took a deep breath, pushing his primal reptilian urges back into the locked chest in the furthest corner of his mind. He needed to think clearly.

He left the ballroom with Mavrik closely behind, but instead of turning down the stairs towards the dungeons, he took the hallway to the king's private chambers.

A small army of guards waited in the hallway, blocking his path. He approached the nearest.

"I am Sir Frej Ilmarinen, Knight of the Queen's Inner Circle, and I demand entry!" he thundered.

Laila sat on the cold, stone floor of a cell. She was in the subterranean dungeon below the castle. The air was cold, and stank of mold, unwashed bodies, and waste. There were manacles around her wrists, and the room was warded against the use of magic.

If there had been enough light to see by, Laila might have noticed that her beautiful gown was now torn and stained. The guards had not been particularly gentle with her, but frankly, she did not blame them. They were just doing their job and trying to protect their king.

Flashbacks played through her mind, of another time she had been imprisoned, locked away in another small cell...

Her pulse raced. She reminded herself that this situation was completely different. This was all a big misunderstanding. Someone would be down momentarily to free her. Or would they?

She had brought a knife to the ball. Laila didn't know a whole lot about Dragon customs, but surely that was not grounds for such punishment.

Shivering against the chill of the rough stone, Laila thought back to the moment when the assassin attacked. It was as if the magic had spoken to her, which was crazy because magic is not any more sentient than gravity.

The flash of blue light had reminded her of the moment when she had killed Demons with the very same dagger. In both situations, she had reacted without truly choosing to. Was she going insane?

Perhaps it was the dagger, she thought. It seemed to have an unusual effect on her. No one knew where it had come from—it had just sort of appeared at the Demons' complex.

The Demons' complex.

The cries of the audience cheering echoed through the hall of her cell…

Laila pushed back the memories. That was another time. It was in the past.

… A searing pain arced through her body as the cuffs around her wrists electrocuted her…

No. The manacles on her wrists were completely ordinary. They could not shock her.

… A Greater Demon leering at her through the bars of her cell. Marius. The one that escaped…

The walls were pressing in on her. She couldn't breathe.

Trapped.

Trapped.

Trapped.

Her breath came in short gasps. She willed her body to calm down, but she was no longer in control.

Trapped!

Trapped!

Trapped!

It was like a broken recording repeating in her mind, a perpetual loop that could not be stopped. She was gripped by a feeling of dread worse than she had ever experienced. It was far worse than the nightmares, for those she could wake from. With this, she could not tell where she was. Was she here or there? She was lost, stuck, trapped!

… Demons grinning down at her…
Trapped!

Frej glowered across the room. He had finally managed to talk his way into the king's private study. Unfortunately, half a dozen lords were also allowed entry, including Lord Viktor.

He tore his eyes from Viktor and returned his attention to one of the other lords, a rather fat and elderly man. Frej recognized him from other meetings. The man was an expert on all things in his own mind, and at the moment he was explaining why Laila should not be released.

"We don't know the extent of the threat that this Elf poses. Until we investigate further, there is no reason we should risk ourselves by releasing another potential assassin."

Frej caught the man's subtle glance in the direction of Viktor. Frej would not be surprised if Viktor had bought off the man, just to create conflict.

It was over an hour after the attack, and they were no closer to reaching a decision. Frej could tell that the others were growing weary. If a decision was not reached soon, they would all be sent away until the morning, and Frej was not going to leave Laila stuck in a dungeon overnight.

Lord Mavrik cleared his throat. "Has anyone paused to consider the ramifications of imprisoning this particular Elf without cause? Her mother is the Elven emissary. How will that look when word reaches the Elves that we've imprisoned the ambassador's daughter without just cause? What happens to our relationship with the American government?"

"We don't know—" began the elderly lord.

"She saved our king!" Frej roared. "In what way is that incriminating!?!"

The room fell silent.

Frej couldn't care less about offending any of these stuck-up lords. It was not their asses rotting in a cell. This was just another drama to be played out for them, and at this point Frej was done playing their games. They would not offend him like this. He would not allow them to treat Laila like a criminal.

The queen watched him, her grim expression unreadable. If only he had reached her before the rest of these clowns had, perhaps this conversation would be over. He did not know what Lord Viktor was even doing here. He was not a trusted advisor of the king or queen. Yet there he was, and Frej was certain he had something to do with all of this.

Laila was drowning in the torrent of horrors and memories that flooded her mind. Retreating to the farthest recesses of her consciousness, she knew she needed to calm down. The fears were strong, though. Every time she began to surface, they pulled her back down.

Throughout this ordeal, she vaguely recognized voices floating down the hall to her cell. Most of them belonged to unknown persons, either prisoners or guards.

There was a familiar voice, her mother arguing with the guards. Ragna's demanding tone was harsh. With the echo of the tunnel, the words were distorted by the time they reached Laila's ears. It pulled her from her poisonous thoughts for a passing moment, before she was once again overcome by that single, overpowering thought: *trapped.*

As her internal battle raged, Laila was oblivious to the sound of footsteps approaching or the click of a key in the door's lock. Even when the door opened, it barely registered in her mind.

"Laila?"

Frej paused in the doorway of the cell. At first he thought that they had reached the wrong cell, for the woman inside did not react. It took him a moment to realize that the small, trembling figure was in fact Laila.

"By the Gods!" he gasped, rushing to her side. "Laila!"

He reached out to her, but hesitated. She looked so fragile that he was afraid to touch her.

"Gods!" The queen approached behind him. "You didn't tell me about this."

The last part was sharp, accusatory, and stung him like a whip.

"I didn't know. I knew about the nightmares, and she told me she'd been held captive by the Demons, but I didn't realize—"

"She was a prisoner of the Demons?" asked the queen shocked, but after a moment she shook her head. "It doesn't matter now. She's hyperventilating. She needs to slow her breathing now!"

Frej pushed away his feelings of guilt and summoned his magic. Carefully, he reached out and created a barrier in front of Laila's mouth, allowing only a small amount of air through with each breath. Slowly Laila's breathing calmed, but she appeared unaware of his presence. Her body went limp as she slipped out of consciousness.

"She needs a healer," explained the queen. "I'll summon one to a guest suite."

"No, I need to get her out of here." Frej gently scooped up the unconscious Elf.

The queen didn't protest, but followed him up the staircase and to a small courtyard behind the castle where a carriage waited. She waved them through the gate.

The sun was already rising as Frej carried Laila through the door of his house. He was halfway up the stairs by the time Hanna caught up with him.

"Oh my!" she exclaimed. "I'll get the water running!"

Hanna disappeared into the bathroom of Laila's quarters while Frej eased the Elf onto the bed. Hanna quickly returned, instructing him to bring Laila to the large bathtub.

The two of them managed to remove Laila's tattered gown and lower her into the water. Hanna then shooed him out of the room, complaining that he was hovering.

Frej reluctantly retreated as Hanna started to work her magic. As she spun her spell, she hummed a low tune. It was an old song about a girl in the countryside.

Hanna found it was easier to work the magic with a song. She continued to work until Laila's breathing came easier and her body relaxed.

CHAPTER 35

Laila awoke with a peculiar feeling of lightness. It took her a moment to realize that she was actually sitting in a large bathtub.

Opening her eyes, she discovered that she was back in her bathroom in Frej's home. That was odd, she thought, the last thing she remembered was…

Fear gripped her. Water sloshed out of the tub as she clutched the sides. She had been trapped in the dungeon.

"Hey, now!" chided Hanna as she used a spell to return the water to the tub. "Don't go getting yourself all worked up again. There is nothing to worry about right now. You're safe."

Laila took a deep, calming breath before stepping out of the tub. Hanna held out a towel for her.

"Hanna, what was I doing in the bathtub?" Laila asked, drying herself with the towel.

"I can do a bit of healing. It's not quite like what Elves can do. I find that my healing is best done directly in the presence of water. It also has a nice, soothing effect on the soul."

Laila pulled on the thin nightgown and a robe before following Hanna into the bedroom. The curtains were drawn, so it was impossible to tell what time it was.

Hanna lifted the lid of a small pot sitting on the hearth, and Laila's mouth watered at the scent. She joined Hanna by the fire, and the housekeeper passed her a bowl of thick vegetable soup.

They sat in silence while Laila ate. She was not feeling particularly talkative at the moment, and she felt drained. After eating something she felt a bit better, but a part of her was glad that Frej was not there. Laila felt ridiculous about the way she had panicked in the dungeon. She was not sure how much Frej had seen. She only vaguely remembered his voice, but she was certain that she had been a hysterical mess.

"You're thinking too much," said Hanna. "I can see it in your eyes."

"I feel so embarrassed."

"Don't be ridiculous! It's not as if you are the first warrior to be haunted by their past. It's quite common, you know. My brother struggles with it. Even Frej's father struggled with it."

Laila understood, but she did not feel any better. She decided that some sleep would help, though, and fell asleep the moment her head touched the pillow.

A while later, Laila awoke and dressed. She was feeling much better and well-rested. She wandered down the stairs and found Frej writing a letter in his office. He glanced up as she approached.

"How are you?" he asked, rising.

"Fine." She took a seat on one of the leather sofas. "I don't remember much of what happened after they took me to the dungeon. I'm assuming they decided I wasn't a threat?"

"Correct." Frej joined her, taking her hands in his. "Lord Viktor fought to keep you imprisoned as long as he possibly could, probably to spite us."

Laila snorted. "I've been here all of three days and I've already got enemies."

"I have the feeling that he had something to do with that assassin," Frej added grimly.

That would be a pretty bold move on the lord's part. Laila recalled that he had not seemed as panicked as she would have expected when the assassin attacked.

"How did you convince them I was innocent?" asked Laila.

"The queen knew from the beginning that you were innocent. But Lord Viktor had convinced enough of the lords you were a threat, that she and the king had to hear them out before you could be freed."

"I didn't realize how traumatic it would be for you to be locked up. If I had known, I—"

"I don't imagine there was anything more you could have done that you weren't already doing." She rested a hand on his arm. "It's not your fault."

Frej sighed, then turned and looked away towards the window.

"Does my mother know I'm free?" Laila asked.

"Yes, I sent word early this morning. She stopped by a couple of hours ago, but Alfred told her that you were resting, and that she would see you tonight."

"Is that a good idea?" Laila frowned. "To go to the party tonight?"

Frej turned back towards her. "I don't think you are in any danger, and the king wants to officially apologize for having you thrown in the dungeon after saving his life."

"Well, I guess I'll have to get ready, then," muttered Laila. While it would be nice to receive an official apology, Laila was not looking forward to getting all dressed up like a peacock again.

She started to stand when Frej pulled her back down.

"There's no rush," he said, brushing the hair from her face.

Laila could feel heat blossoming in her stomach. She bit her lip and glanced through the doorway to the entrance hall.

"Shouldn't we…?" She motioned at the door.

Frej waved his hand and a light gust of wind nudged the door shut. Laila laughed as he pulled her close.

❖

Once again Laila found herself the object of more attention than she preferred. However, the looks she attracted this evening were more suspicious. They were not exactly hostile, but they were definitely on edge. After all, the last time they had seen Laila, she was being hauled down to the dungeons.

She shook off their looks, reminding herself that she was the one who had saved their king. Whatever gossip had spread, presumably by Lord Viktor, would be of little consequence when she returned to Los Angeles the following day.

Standing by Frej, she silently watched the crowd. She noticed that Lord Mavrik was chatting with a group of young women, who seemed quite flattered. Their escorts appeared less than pleased, but Lord Mavrik didn't seem to notice.

Her mother had arrived as well, but was caught deep in conversation with an older nobleman. It bought her some time, but Laila knew she would have to face her mother's lecture eventually.

Laila shifted her weight, causing the midnight-blue satin to ripple. The gown was simple with a high collar and no sleeves. There was a bit of black lace embroidery around the waist and collar, and around the open back. Laila had felt a little uncomfortable showing the scars on her back, but Frej insisted that the scars reminded others that she, like their queen, was first and foremost a warrior.

Finally, the king and queen made their entrance. As they ascended the dais, Laila noticed that both of them seemed more on edge than usual, and she sensed there was tension between the two monarchs.

The king addressed the crowd, thanking all of those who had made the journey to celebrate with them. Once that was finished, the queen stepped forward.

"As many of you witnessed, last night, there was an attempt

on our king's life. I would like to take this time to dispel any rumor that you might have heard regarding the situation. The assassin has been captured, and rest assured, we will learn the name of any conspirator who hired him."

A heavy silence settled over the crowd as she watched them, her gaze cold as steel. It was a warning to anyone present that the queen would not rest until those responsible were found.

"I am sure you are all as relieved as I am, that His Majesty the King is unharmed after this distressing event. I've already heard a number of rumors circulating through the halls of the palace, and there is one matter I feel is imperative that I address. At this time, I would ask Miss Laila Eyvindr to approach the dais."

Hushed whispers filled the hall. Laila straightened her shoulders, refusing to allow her uncertainty to show. She approached the dais, standing at the bottom of the steps, and bowed deeply as a soldier.

Laila caught a glimmer of approval in the queen's eyes.

"Ladies and gentlemen, this is the woman who saved our king, and my husband's life. She was under no obligation to act, she owes no loyalty to this kingdom, but her quick thinking thwarted the assassin and enabled his capture. For this reason, the king and I wish to apologize publicly for the unjust way that Miss Eyvindr was treated after the incident. We owe her our deepest gratitude, not our suspicion."

To Laila's astonishment, the queen and king gave her slight bows before the queen continued.

"While she is not of our kingdom, we have thought deeply on the matter of how to express our thanks. There is one honor that has not been bestowed in many generations that we find to be fitting." To Laila she said, "Please ascend the dais."

Laila climbed the steps and stood facing Queen Regina. A beautiful sword was brought forth. Its blade and hilt were polished to a high shine, and it was encrusted with rubies. The queen accepted it from the servant.

"Please kneel."

Laila knelt and bowed her head.

"Laila Eyvindr, for your act of bravery I bestow upon you the title of Honorary Knight of the Dragons, an honor reserved for those of our allies who have proved their worth by providing their service to the crown in times of need."

The queen touched the tip of the sword to each of Laila's shoulders.

"Arise, Sir Eyvindr, Honorary Knight of the Dragons."

Laila stood, feeling rather awestruck. The crowd below applauded. She bowed to both the queen and king.

"Sir Eyvindr," said the king, "we offer you our deepest gratitude. Should the need arise, you have an ally in the Dragon Kingdom."

Laila bowed again before returning to the crowd. Whatever parting words the king said to the gathering were lost to Laila's ears. She could not believe that she had just been knighted, let alone in a country that was not her own. Was that even possible? She supposed it must be, but she had never heard of such a thing among Elves.

She returned to her place by Frej as he congratulated her with a look that made her wish she was not currently surrounded by a crowd.

Lord Mavrik joined them, beaming. "You've been here all of three days, and look at you! You're a hero, and a knight!"

"An honorary knight," Laila pointed out.

"Who cares about technicalities?" he said flippantly. "Lord Viktor left the moment you were knighted. He looked none too pleased. I don't think he'll be bothering you tonight."

Lord Mavrik could barely contain his excitement. Laila glanced around, but to her relief found that Lord Viktor was not present. That was one less thing to worry about.

Her mother approached, the very picture of grace and elegance in another one of her many Elven gowns.

"My daughter!" Her smile was radiant. "I am so proud of

you! I cannot wait to give this news to your father. He will be so disappointed he wasn't here to see it."

Ragna did not hug her, but she reached up to cup her daughter's cheek. It was a warm gesture by Elven standards, and just as heartfelt.

"I tried to have you released, but the guards wouldn't hear a word I said." She turned to Frej. "Thank you, Sir Ilmarinen."

Frej bowed then turned to Laila. "I feel it necessary to warn you, this honor is not without a catch." He glanced at Ragna, who nodded slowly.

"You see," her mother explained, "while the crown is at your service, you are likewise expected to be at theirs. Technically they could require you to serve them if you are available in times of need."

Frej nodded darkly.

Laila was beginning to wonder what kind of trouble she had gotten herself into.

"I wouldn't worry about it too much, though," added Frej. "I don't believe that Queen Regina would abuse this power. I believe that the intent behind this was to solidify your alliance with the Dragon Kingdom in the face of a possible Demon invasion. While they haven't pledged their aid to the Elves or the human governments, they will aid *you* however possible."

Laila shook her head. "This is a lot to take in at once."

"Then don't overthink it," said Lord Mavrik cheerfully. "Now is not the time to dwell on the future, but to celebrate the present."

CHAPTER 36

Laila awoke to a warm breeze floating through the open window and the hum of people in a nearby marketplace. Laila realized that she and Frej must have left the window open before they fell asleep.

She started to rise, thinking to shut the window, but a strong arm was wrapped around her waist. Frej mumbled some groggy protest. Laila smiled and allowed herself to be drawn back into his embrace.

The mattress of Frej's bed was luxuriously soft, and Laila would have been content to lie there resting her head on his chest all morning, but one question kept nagging at her.

"Frej?"

"Mmhm?"

"What are we doing? What happens when we go back to Los Angeles?"

"You're overthinking this," he chuckled, nuzzling her ear. "I don't imagine your friends will mind. Ali is Fae, and culturally Erin is too. They are much more open to these matters of the heart than your kind. They're not going to judge you."

Laila knew that Ali seemed rather supportive, but still she was uncertain.

"I think," he said, kissing her gently, "we should see where this path takes us."

She supposed he was right. Surely there was no harm in seeing where this led. She paused and looked into the Dragon's azure eyes.

"You know," she added seriously, "I still haven't seen your Dragon form."

Frej laughed and winked. "All in good time."

There was a gentle knock on the door.

"Come in!" Frej called.

Laila shot him a glare as she pulled more of his blankets around her. She still felt awkward having Hanna enter while they were in bed together.

"Good morning!" she called cheerfully. "A letter just arrived from the queen."

"Thank you, Hanna," said Frej. "I'll read it over breakfast."

"Actually, it's addressed to Laila."

"Oh," Laila accepted the letter. She opened it and skimmed it quickly. "The queen has asked me to accompany her on a tour of the palace gardens at noon." She glanced at Frej. "I should probably get moving. I don't want to keep her waiting."

"Perhaps you want a quick bath?" Hanna handed her a plate of fresh pastries. "The water will be waiting for you as soon as you are finished eating."

After a quick breakfast, and a quick bath, she dressed in her jeans and a nicer shirt before pulling on her knee-high boots and a leather jacket. Jeans were probably not entirely appropriate when meeting royalty, but at the moment her options were limited. She applied a bit of makeup and double-checked her appearance before going out.

The carriage ride passed quicker than she expected, and she soon found herself before the palace. She was alone since Frej had his own business to take care of.

A guard approached and escorted her to the castle and gardens. He asked her to wait by the entrance and informed her that the queen would be joining her momentarily.

While she waited, Laila admired a statue. It was of a little girl and a Dragon who looked down on her protectively. It was made of a polished blue stone that gleamed in the mid-day sun.

"That is one of my favorites," said a voice behind her.

Laila turned to find a woman dressed in pants and a practical tunic. Her hair was slightly disheveled, and perspiration dampened her clothing. There was a hand-and-a-half sword buckled to her waist. It took Laila a moment to realize she was facing Queen Regina.

Laila hastily bowed as the queen approached.

"I'm sorry to keep you waiting. I lost track of time sparring with one of my weapons masters. I intended to wash up before I met you, but…"

Laila schooled her stunned expression to neutral. She hadn't expected the encounter with the monarch to be so casual and laid back. "That is nothing to worry about."

At least she didn't feel so underdressed now.

"Let's walk," the queen suggested cheerfully. "It's such a lovely day, and I expect I'll be stuck indoors with meetings for the rest of the afternoon."

Laila nodded and followed the queen down the garden path.

"I want to apologize again for the distress that we caused you the other night."

"Your men were just doing their job," insisted Laila.

"Even so." She was quiet a moment before continuing. "I wondered if I might ask a personal question."

Laila nodded, unsure what the queen could be so curious about. Perhaps it was her involvement with Frej. The queen held him in high regard, after all.

"Do you have someone you can speak with about what happened to you? That is, whatever you endured at the hands of the Demons."

"Oh," Laila said, somewhat taken aback. "No. I mean, I don't like to talk about it."

The queen nodded silently. The way she held herself as she walked betrayed her military background.

"Sir Eyvindr," she began, "I would like you to find someone to speak to about this. Perhaps a friend, or a healer, or someone who went through a similar situation. I've seen too many good soldiers hide their trauma only to have it build and overwhelm them."

Laila hesitated, "I will consider it."

"No," the queen insisted. "That is an order."

"Yes, Your Majesty." Laila bowed, a little surprised. She supposed she would have to follow through with it now.

"Good." The queen's features softened. "I'm sorry, but I cannot allow you to harm yourself."

Laila was surprised that the queen was so concerned. It was touching, if unexpected.

As they walked through the garden, the queen asked her questions about her decision to move to Midgard, and what life was like there. Laila answered as many questions as she was able to.

The queen was pleasant company. She was down-to-earth and level-headed. At the same time, she was not too serious. She was quick to laugh and had a good-natured sense of humor.

Too soon they reached the end of the path and found themselves at another entrance to the palace.

"I don't suppose you would consider staying here?" asked the queen. "I could use someone like you. I could give you a position with the Royal Guard. You'd be paid very well."

She couldn't believe it. This was everything that Laila had wished for in her own kingdom. She had spent years of training for a position on the Elven Royal Guard but had been rejected. They told her she was too young. It was the reason she had left to join IRSA. Yet, now a position was being offered to her by the Queen of the Dragons.

Laila shook her head. "I'm sorry, Your Majesty. It is a very gracious offer, but right now I belong in Los Angeles."

"Very well," said Queen Regina, a curious expression on her face, "perhaps you will reconsider someday. Before you go, I have a couple of gifts for you."

She beckoned a servant forward with a couple of packages and handed Laila the smaller box. It contained a medal with the royal Dragon insignia.

"This is a medal identifying you as an Honorary Knight of the Dragons. In the event you need to meet with me or the king, this would grant you expedited passage throughout the palace and the kingdom."

"Thank you." Laila bowed her head, but the queen was already opening the second box. From it she produced a leather breastplate. Its appearance was simple, with only a thin, decorative trim in the shape of vines. The surface was matte black leather, and any metal parts had a matte black finish as well.

"Here," she said, handing it to Laila. "Let's see how it fits."

Laila put it on as she was bid. The queen examined it, making small adjustments here and there. The armor fit her nicely. It was lightweight and surprisingly flexible. It was thin enough that she could even wear it under her shirt.

The queen nodded in approval. "This armor was given to me by a sword master I trained with in my youth. It was made by one of the best Dragon smiths to have ever lived. The core is made from Dwarven steel, forged in the fire of an ancient Dragon elder. It is stronger than any metal in existence. The leather is made from the hide of a Pegasus, so it's resistant to magical attacks. It won't stop magic entirely, but it will lessen the impact."

Laila stared in awe at the armor she wore. It was an incredibly valuable gift.

"I can't take this, it's too much."

"Don't be ridiculous," the queen laughed. "My days of adventuring are over. With a child on the way and more to come, I don't think I'll fit into it much longer. Besides, I have access to the best armories in the kingdom." She winked.

"Thank you," said Laila. She knew she would be glad to have it in the years to come.

"Here is your dagger as well. It's a beautiful weapon. I don't suppose you know the maker?"

"Unfortunately, I don't." It would answer a lot of questions if she did, but the dagger's origins remained a mystery.

"Oh, well. In any case, may it serve you well." The queen gave her a pitying look. "I have the feeling that fate has much in store for you."

Laila and Frej planned to make their journey back to Los Angeles the same way they had come, through Ingegard. Since Laila's mother was headed back to the capital, she planned to make the first portal jump with them.

Upon their arrival in Ingegard, an entourage of guards greeted them. Amongst them, one face in particular stood out. He was tall and lean like the others, but slightly older than the rest. He wore the standard uniform of the royal guard. He took a step forward.

"Father!" Laila breathed. She strode over to him, and he rested his hands on her shoulders.

"My daughter!" he cried, checking her over. "I am glad to see that you are all right. Word of your eventful visit to Schonengard has reached me. I needed to see you for myself."

"You don't need to worry, Father, I'm perfectly fine." Physically at least, she thought, but she didn't want him to worry.

He pulled her into his warm embrace. The other guards, she noticed, averted their gaze. They were unaccustomed to such displays, but Laila didn't mind.

"I'm so proud of you," he beamed. "An honorary knighthood is no small feat. You must have made quite the impression on the king."

"On the queen, actually," inserted Frej. "She knows a worthy soldier when she sees one."

"Ah, yes," her father said, releasing her from his embrace. "You are one of her knights, if my memory serves me right."

"Sir Ilmarinen." Frej, offering his hand. Her father accepted it.

"Guardsman Eyvindr. I'm pleased to make your acquaintance, but I understand that there is business that Laila must attend to in Los Angeles."

Laila nodded her head. As happy as she was to see her father, she needed to get back to the city.

Her father led the way, filling Laila in on the latest news from Ingegard, her mother inserting a comment every now and then. It was harder than she expected to say goodbye to her parents. Her mother insisted she come to visit soon, but Laila made no promises. It had been difficult enough to take the time away from work to attend the ball. She was not sure Colin would approve of her taking another trip too soon.

Laila couldn't help it as her eyes clouded with tears. She embraced her father one more time. Then she stepped away and kept her head high as she walked through the portal with Frej. He reached for her hand and gave it a squeeze as they and crossed the expanse to Earth.

As soon as they set foot in LAX, she pulled out her phone and switched it on. It immediately was flooded with messages from Colin, Darien, and Ali, each of them asking her to call as soon as she arrived.

"Crap." She punched the call button on Ali's contact entry. Frej gave her a quizzical glance as they hurried through the airport.

"Laila!" came Ali's voice on the other line. "We need you in the office ASAP. Shit's hit the fan, and we're really shorthanded. How soon can you be here?"

"I'm at the airport. I could probably make it in fifteen, maybe twenty minutes, but I've got Frej with me." She glanced over at Frej as she picked up her pace through the airport.

"Just bring him. Darien's on his way to pick you up. We'll call him a taxi or something from the office. Just get here as soon as you can. There's a Giant on the loose."

❖ 225 ❖

CHAPTER 37

Laila groaned. Why did it have to be Giants? Of all the creatures that inhabited the worlds, Giants loathed Elves the most. There was a long and dark history between the two races. A single Giant could wreak chaos in a city like this, tearing down buildings and crushing civilians. They didn't even have a protocol for dealing with Giants, since they'd never shown interest in, or had the ability to travel to Earth.

"There's a Giant on the loose," she explained to Frej as she hurried towards the door. He swore. Dragons didn't have a particularly good history with Giants either, especially the Ice Giants whose territory bordered theirs to the north.

"I've fought them before," he explained as they reached the exit and stepped into the night. "They're hard to kill and nearly impossible to capture."

"Great," Laila muttered as Darien pulled up.

"He'll have to find another way home." Darien indicated Frej. "The situation is escalating. The Giant is approaching the city."

"I'm coming with you," Frej said, sliding into to the back

seat.

Darien shot Laila a look.

"He's dealt with Giants before," she explained, buckling herself in. "And if this situation is as bad as you say, we'll need all the help we can get."

Darien shook his head but pulled away from the curb, siren blaring.

Laila dug through her duffel bag and found the armor from Queen Regina. She peeled off her leather jacket and buckled on the armor while Darien filled her in.

"A lot has happened since you've left—we've discovered three bodies, including that of Aaron Lawrence, the missing boy from Culver City. The two others were found shortly after in the Old City. One of Ali's contacts found them. Whoever stashed them there probably thought they wouldn't be reported if they were ever found.

"We aren't entirely sure what happened. We wanted an Elf's opinion, but there are no Elves on staff in the morgue. We were about to visit the scenes where the bodies were dumped to search for possible ritual sites when we got the call about the Giant. He's up in Malibu, but he's making his way down to Santa Monica."

Laila shook her head as she pulled on the harness with her gun, magical Taser, and badge that Darien had brought with him.

Darien turned around a corner as fast as he dared while the nearby cars pulled over to let them by. "I also looked into that Di Inferi gang. I've dug up some more information on them including a location that is a likely front for drug deals," he added. "I've got a raid with LAPD's Gangs and Narcotics Division planned for tomorrow. I've kept Colin out of it like you asked."

"I was only gone a couple of days!" she said, exasperated.

Darien shrugged. "That's Los Angeles for you."

After a moment's consideration, Laila buckled the sheath with her dagger to her thigh. It was probably of little use against the Giant, but she felt better with it.

They encountered heavy traffic as they pulled onto Lincoln Boulevard. Darien got on the car's loudspeaker.

"Pull over."

Not that they had time to ticket the humans, but it helped to get them moving.

"Ali and Colin should be there by now, along with Torsten and Donald," the Vampire explained. "Just after you called, LAPD informed us of the Giant's approach into human-populated land."

"How on Earth did he get here?" Laila asked. "I didn't think there were any portals large enough to transport a Giant to earth."

"We're not sure. We thought you might have some idea."

She exchanged glances with Frej, but neither of them had any clue.

As they approached the northern end of Santa Monica, they saw fewer people, and those they saw were in a rush to get out of the area. LAPD was helping to evacuate the city.

Darien pulled up to a curb next to another black SUV. Ali and Colin stood by with Torsten and Donald unloading equipment.

"Thank goodness the cavalry's arrived!" Ali walking over in full tactical gear, including her helmet. She passed another helmet to Laila as she stepped out of the SUV.

"Agent Eyvindr!" shouted Colin. "What the hell are you thinking bringing a civilian out here!?!"

Her supervisor gestured to Frej's tall form that was at least six inches taller than the Werewolf.

"I beg your pardon, sir," said Frej with a bow. "I am a Knight from the Dragon Kingdom, and I have orders directly from my queen to assist your team in any way that I can."

Colin eyed him skeptically.

"He's fought Giants before," Laila added.

The scowl remained etched on Colin's face, but he gave a short nod before stalking back to his SUV.

"What do we have to work with?" asked Laila, wandering over to Torsten's pile of equipment.

"Well, the goal is to apprehend the Giant, but to be honest, I don't have the faintest idea of how to do that." Torsten scratched his head. "I've brought some flash-bang grenades that might have some effect if we can get them close enough, and I've got some heavy-duty artillery if need be."

"Any blades?" asked Frej. "Preferably a long sword?"

"Donald?" he barked. "Anything?"

The Tech Wiz, who had been watching Ali as she checked her weapons, shook himself and searched through the SUV. Torsten rolled his eyes at Laila.

"Um," said Donald, "we've got magical stun batons, a couple of knives… oh! A katana!" He pulled out a round sheath. When Frej stared at him blankly, the Tech Wiz added, "It's a Japanese sword."

Frej shrugged and belted it to his waist.

"Helicopter says it's coming this way!" yelled Colin from the front of the SUV.

"We could set a trap," suggested Laila, examining the buildings on either side. "If we have steel cable, we could anchor it to the buildings up ahead and try to trip the Giant."

"I'll do it," volunteered Darien. "There's a construction site nearby. They should have something we can use."

Colin nodded, and Darien took off in a flash of unnatural speed. "Ali, you and Torsten climb that building across the street with any artillery that could be effective. I'll take the knight and position us on this side of the street."

"What should I do?" Laila asked.

"Stay with Donald."

"What?" she asked, glancing at the awkward Tech Wiz as he nearly dropped a shotgun.

"You heard me."

Colin passed equipment to Frej and motioned for him to follow.

Laila shook her head as the others got into position. Colin was insane if he thought she was just going to wait by the car. Up ahead, she could see Darien lugging around cables, creating a net between the buildings. They were only two stories tall, but it should be enough to impede the Giant. She hoped no one would fall from a rooftop in the gloom.

In the distance, she could hear the Giant's approach, its lumbering steps thundering through the night.

She glanced at the Tech Wiz, whose eyes were wide with terror. "If you have any special skills that could take down a Giant, now would be a good time to use them."

In the light from the SUV, Laila could faintly see the color drain from his face as his mouth opened and closed.

"Um, I'm more of an inventor, I leave that sort of thing to you guys." The case he held rattled as he trembled.

Laila was beginning to wonder why Colin had brought the poor man along. "Okay, well, what else do we have in there?"

He scrambled to look through compartments. "We've got a crossbow. It also has grappling hook attachments. Maybe that could help? We've also got tear gas."

Laila slung the crossbow over her back and clipped the rest of the equipment to her belt.

"Donald," she said seriously as the footsteps grew louder. "I don't think you should be here. Why don't you take the other SUV and wait this out a few blocks away?"

The Tech Wiz looked relieved. He quickly clambered into the SUV and drove off. Colin would probably have something to say about that later, but Laila was not about to watch the Tech Wiz be flattened like a pancake. While Torsten might be able to keep a level head out here, it was clear that his assistant's place was back in the workshop.

Laila stepped out into the street to face the Giant. With any luck, the others could slow him down enough for her to get close.

While a Troll might be two or three times the size of a human, a Giant was five times the size of a fully-grown man or larger. Giants' skin was thick and greyish-blue, with little hair. They were notoriously territorial, particularly the males, and extremely unreasonable.

Laila shook her head. That there was a large male Giant heading directly towards her made Laila suddenly question her life choices.

CHAPTER 38

Laila waited and watched as the Giant approached. She readied herself for a spell, feeling out the magic and elements around her. Reaching out further, she could sense that the others were in position and hoped that Donald had found someplace safe and out of the way to hide.

The Giant reached the buildings where Darien had set his trap. As Laila had hoped, he was oblivious to the cables in the gloom. His feet caught and tangled. As he fell, there was a loud groan and snap as the cables broke free of their anchors. Laila could see a blur of movement as Darien tied more cable around the Giant's feet, trying to further deter him.

The Giant roared in frustration and tried to sit up, but halted suddenly, sniffing the air.

"I smell Elf," he growled in the common tongue. He swiveled his head, which was the size of a small car, in Laila's direction.

"Now!" yelled Colin. He and the others threw flash-bang grenades at the Giant's head. Laila threw up a shield.

The Giant grumbled, rolled over in the street and sat up,

facing away from her. The explosions appeared to have little effect on him, and he swatted at the rooftop where Ali and Torsten were stationed. A corner of the building crumbled away, but her friends made it out of the Giant's reach.

"What's that for?" moaned the Giant.

Laila grabbed the crossbow from over her shoulder and readied a grappling hook with a long line of cable. Aiming it over the Giant's shoulder, she fired. It caught in his thick, canvas-like shirt.

Cautiously she approached the Giant and scaled his back as fast as she could. Partway up, he took notice and tried to shake her off. He twisted, slamming her into the side of a building. Somehow Laila managed to hang on and continue her ascent.

Laila cringed as someone fired on the other side.

"Ow!" the sound rumbled from the Giant. "Awful little creatures!"

As Laila pulled herself onto the Giant's shoulder, it occurred to her that they were possibly making incorrect assumptions about him. He sounded more confused and hurt than aggressive.

"That's my foot!" he cried as Darien attempted to zap the Giant's foot with one of Torsten's magical stun batons.

"Hold!" Laila shouted at the others, waving her arms. That caught the Giant's attention. He swatted at her, and she had to drop to her stomach to avoid his hand.

"Pesky Elves!" he muttered. "They're always causing trouble!"

"Hold on!" she shouted at his ear in the common tongue. "I just want to talk."

He seemed skeptical. Colin fired again, which did not help the situation.

"Please!" she said cringing.

The Giant reached for her again, this time grabbing hold of Laila. She tried to wriggle her way out of his grip, but he was stronger. Her helmet fell from her head and landed far below in his lap.

Dangling her in front of his nose, he examined Laila. She swallowed hard seeing the ground two stories below her and did her best to give him a pleasant smile.

"I just want to talk," she repeated. "That's all."

"And why would I want to talk to you? You haven't been very nice to me, throwing loud things at me, and tying my feet up."

"I'm very sorry about that," she shouted back. "This is all a very big misunderstanding!"

"I'd say so!" he huffed and muttered something about rude little Elves.

"Please? I just want to help," Laila insisted. The Giant gave her a skeptical look, but he carefully opened his hand, allowing Laila to sit somewhat precariously on his palm.

"Thank you!" She gave him a slight bow.

"What the hell are you doing?" shouted Colin from his vantage point.

Laila ignored him and kept her focus on the Giant. "Can you tell me how you came to be in Los Angeles?"

"You mean I'm in Midgard?" he said incredulously. "No wonder I feel so disoriented."

"You have five seconds to get out of there," shouted Colin.

"Colin, *stop!*" she shouted in his direction.

Vaguely she could hear someone else speaking to him—she thought it might be Frej—but Colin didn't appear interested in talking.

"What's going on?" asked the Giant, concerned. "Is that little man trying to hurt you?"

Frej looked from Colin to Laila, unsure if he should disarm the supervisor. Laila shook her head.

"They're confused," explained Laila hastily, "That man doesn't speak the common tongue and he thinks you'll hurt me."

At that moment Ali appeared on the roof of Colin's building. Laila watched as the Fae argued with their supervisor, waving in Laila's direction. Ali and Frej seemed to have things under control though.

"I'm sorry about all this," said Laila again as she returned her attention to the Giant. "Do you remember how you got here? Did you use a portal?"

"I don't think so." The Giant scratched his head. "One moment I'm watering my garden, and the next thing I know, it's like the ground's being pulled out from under me, and I'm surrounded by a bunch of little folk."

"Do you remember anything about those 'little folk?'"

He thought for a moment. "One of them was dead. He was all covered in blood and didn't move. I think he was a Troll or something because I recognized the smell. The others were either human, or from other worlds, except for one. There was something off about him. He just felt wrong. He smelled like a reptile too, kind of like that one over there."

He pointed at Frej.

"Did they say anything to you?"

"Just that there was a city nearby. I don't know what they expected me to do, but I followed the path, and stopped to ask some of the little humans for help, but they just ignored me and ran. Very rude in my opinion."

"I'm sorry about that," said Laila, patting his thumb.

"Thank you, miss."

"Where did you appear surrounded by those men? Was it close by?"

"Over there." He pointed at the mountain range to the north. "Not very far for me, but maybe for you."

"Do you think you could lead us there?"

"Oh, sure, but I don't think I could find the exact place in the dark. There are a lot of little hills out there."

"Do you know why those men would choose to bring you here?" Laila asked.

The Giant shrugged. "I live a simple life in the countryside. I tend to my garden and to my animals. You don't think they brought me here to hurt the little folk, do you!?!" he gasped. "I wouldn't hurt a fly. I swear."

"Don't worry, I believe you." Laila was certain that the Giant had been brought there for that very reason. Luckily, those responsible had clearly picked the wrong Giant.

"I'm sorry to impose," the Giant said sheepishly. "I was wondering if I could go home now. You see, I've got to feed the animals."

Laila racked her brain for a solution. "Um, I don't think that is possible right now. The only portals here are too small for you to access, and I'm afraid we can't send you back the way you came."

"Oh," he said, crestfallen.

"Don't worry, we'll think of something in the meantime."

"Perhaps I could help clean up?" suggested the Giant. "I feel horrible about these buildings, but your little dwellings are so delicate."

Laila nodded. Perhaps that could make up for some of the damage he had caused. "Do you think you could put me down now?"

"Oh, right!" He carefully lowered his hand to the ground.

Darien helped her to dismount the Giant's hand.

"Are you all right?" he asked. Darien didn't speak the common tongue.

Laila nodded. "I'll translate later, but for now we need to find a place for this guy to stay."

Darien whistled. "I'll make some phone calls."

At that moment Colin stormed over. "What do you think you're doing!?!" he fumed.

"Defusing the situation," explained Laila simply. "I realized that the Giant wasn't posing a threat, so I decided to find out what he was doing here."

"That is not your call to make," he growled. Frej bristled behind him.

"I'm sorry that you clearly don't trust my judgement," Laila replied wryly. "However, the situation remains that we've got a

Giant sitting in the middle of the Pacific Coast Highway, and no way to send him home."

"I think I've found a place," mentioned Darien, returning. "I just got off the phone with an acquaintance who has a ware-house in Santa Monica. It's big enough for him to crawl through the doors, and plenty of space for him to sleep inside, so long as he's careful."

The Giant leaned down next to them. "Excuse me, Miss…?"

"Laila," she offered. "You can call me Laila."

"Miss Laila," he said. "I don't suppose there is somewhere that I could eat something."

"Of course." She turned to the others to translate. "We should also find him something to eat."

"I'm not sitting around to babysit a Giant!" Colin snapped. "I can't believe I missed a date for this! I'm going to go investi-gate the crime scenes in Old City with Ali and salvage the rest of my night."

He poked a finger at Laila. "Since *you* are the one who's been on vacation, you and Darien can sort this crap out!"

He stormed off to the remaining SUV, Ali racing after him. The rest of them watched as Colin sped off into the night.

"Good riddance," muttered Darien.

Torsten called Donald on his cell and asked him to bring the other SUV back around while Laila, Frej, and Darien untangled the Giant's feet. He appeared otherwise unscathed.

With Darien driving the SUV as an escort, they made their way to the warehouse. On the way, Laila placed an order at a pizza place, and by the time they had settled the Giant in his temporary accommodations, a very surprised pizza delivery boy arrived with a tall stack of pizza boxes.

"Thank you, Miss Laila," said the Giant, eating an entire pizza in one bite. "This is very kind of you. I always thought Elves were vicious little creatures, but you are very kind."

"Well, I find that people are always surprising me." She smiled and patted his knee. "I never did get your name."

"Oh! How rude of me! My name is Benning."

"Well then, Benning, I'll be back tomorrow, hopefully with news for you."

"Thank you very much, Miss Laila." He gave her an awkward, seated bow.

CHAPTER 39

Back at headquarters, Laila took the elevator with Darien down to the morgue. They had dropped Frej off at the house after dealing with the Giant. Laila wished she could have stayed with him, but there were three bodies waiting for her in the morgue.

The night was warm and generally silent. It was nearly three in the morning and most people would be asleep. An unusual peace hung over the city.

"So, Colin seems pretty serious about this woman," said Laila, breaking the silence.

Colin had a rough past. His wife had been one of the early victims of The Event. He had confided in Laila, before she had been captured by the Demons, that he still grieved. It was the reason he had taken that missing persons case so personally and why Laila had agreed to help him with it.

When he confided in Laila, he had asked her not to speak of it with anyone. Their team was small, though, and the others had spent more time with Colin. Laila had the feeling that the others knew, or suspected something similar.

Darien nodded. "I saw her around here a few times after you left."

Laila had actually been encouraging him to meet people after she escaped from the Demons, hoping it would keep him from dwelling on work-related issues.

"I feel like we should support him," Darien began slowly.

"Yet you sound hesitant," she pointed out.

The Vampire paused and looked at Laila. His expression was troubled.

"Perhaps he's discovered that it is time for him to move on. He could've met some great woman who truly makes him happy."

"But…?" asked Laila when he didn't continue.

"They've been dating for a few weeks…"

Laila realized where he was going with this.

"You think this has something to do with his recent behavior?" she asked, swiveling her head to look at the Vampire.

"The timeline fits," he explained grimly. "I don't know a whole lot about Werewolf biology, but perhaps his shift in attitude has to do with this female presence in his life. Or maybe there's something else we don't know."

Laila could see what he meant. Perhaps he was subconsciously trying to assert his dominance or having some sort of hormone shift. She had heard some SNPs were more susceptible to this sort of thing than others.

"I don't know." Darien shrugged. "Maybe it's just a coincidence. I tried to speak to him a couple of times while you were in Alfheim, but he kept brushing me off. I know something's going on, I just wish I knew what. But what else is there to do?"

Laila shook her head feeling equally conflicted. Whatever the reason, Laila hoped things changed soon. They had enough to worry about at the moment, and they didn't need office drama to distract them from the situation at hand.

They reached the basement level where the morgue was located. There was an office by the entrance where a medical examiner sat at a computer. He glanced up, hearing their approach, and hurried out to meet them.

Jim Cleary, the medical examiner, was human, middle-aged, and short. His hair was slightly disheveled and thinning. Laila noticed that, unlike most humans, the medical examiner did not flinch at Darien's handshake. Working with the dead was bound to desensitize you to some of the eccentricities of the undead.

"Agent Pavoni," said Jim Cleary. "I'm surprised to see you again so soon."

"Agent Eyvindr arrived back in Los Angeles tonight. I want her to take a look at the bodies. Maybe she'll sense something we didn't."

The medical examiner nodded. "Right over here..."

He showed them to three tables. A corpse rested on each, draped in a sheet. He pulled back the first, revealing the body of a woman. The cause of death appeared to be the laceration across her throat, but there were also several shallower cuts across her abdomen that formed strange markings, the largest of which was a pentangle.

"Those lacerations were made before she died, just like the young man you brought in last week," mentioned the medical examiner. "She's a—"

"Hawk Shifter," Laila finished for him. She turned to Darien, shocked. "I've met her."

"That's what we thought," added Darien, "and it gives us reason to believe that whoever's behind this is targeting at least some of the victims."

He nodded for the medical examiner to continue.

"She's the most recent of the murders. It would have happened two days ago. The little boy was from a week ago he's actually part Werebat, presumably on his father's side since the mother knew nothing about it."

"It gets better," continued Darien, "his father was a member of the Di Inferi gang before he died during The Event."

"So it's possible they knew he was a Were," mused Laila.

Darien nodded.

Jim Cleary motioned to the third body. "The man over there was killed about two weeks ago. That makes him the first of our victims."

"SNP?" asked Laila, looking down at the man.

"Human," said the medical examiner.

"The Hawk Shifter and the older male were disposed of in alleys in the Old City," added Darien. "We have yet to find the actual sites of the murders."

"Was there anything else unusual that you found?" Laila asked.

The medical examiner logged onto a computer and pulled up a file.

"That's right, we found traces of calcium powder on each of the victims. I thought that was odd."

"It could have been from the chalk at the crime scenes." Darien lounged against a counter. "There were chalk drawings on the floor of the other ritual scenes we saw."

"What about the young man we found at the ritual scene last week? Anything new on him?" she asked.

The medical examiner opened a file on his computer.

"Just that he was a Shifter as well. Crocodile."

Laila held her hands out above the woman's body. She reached out with her magic searching for any residue. She felt something. It was not elemental magic, but something else.

"More Demonic Energy," muttered Laila. There was a dusting of Demonic energy lingering over the body. It was just on the surface, like a layer of soot.

She repeated the process on the other two bodies, but only the faintest traces of Demonic energy were found, less than on the woman.

"That seems strange," the Vampire deliberated. "What could have caused the residue to appear thicker on one, but not the others?"

Laila shook her head. "It could have settled there in a number of ways. Demonic energy clings to anything in its vicinity. It penetrates anyone or anything that exists in Muspelheim for any period of time. Physical contact with a Greater Demon is sure to transfer it. That's how it accumulates on Lesser Demons, through constant direct or indirect contact."

Laila even found it clinging to her after she had been abducted. It took a week of scrubbing with enchanted soap to finally remove it.

She glanced at the little boy's small form lying beneath a sheet.

"Have the families been notified?" she asked the others.

"Yes," said Darien. "They were notified yesterday, shortly after the bodies were brought in. We haven't told them our suspicions of Demon involvement."

"Nor do I think we should." Laila glanced from Darien to the medical examiner. "I think we need to keep that to ourselves for now."

Darien nodded grimly. "If word of this leaked to the media, there would be mass hysteria. Who knows how the city would respond?"

The medical examiner looked deeply troubled, but he agreed. They thanked him for his time and headed back to their offices.

"How have you been holding up?" asked Darien as they waited for the elevator. "Especially now that we know that there are Demons in the city, and possibly even Marius. I meant to ask you earlier, but…"

"Well, we've known that Demons were likely here for a while now." She watched the display by the door as the elevator slowly approached their floor.

"True, but now we have more evidence of their recent activities."

Laila ran her fingers through her hair in frustration. "I just wish I knew what this was all about. What's the purpose of these rituals?"

The doors of the elevator slid open and they stepped in.

"Perhaps we should contact that Witch you know? Maybe she's seen this sort of thing before," suggested Darien selecting the button for the garage.

"I already have, but we could ask Donald," Laila pointed out. "He's a Witch, after all."

Darien laughed. "We already tried that. He claims that he doesn't specialize in rituals though. Whatever that means. He nearly fainted when I showed him photos of the victims."

She shrugged. "We should go help Ali and Colin with the search for the ritual scenes. We still have a few hours before sunrise."

Laila's cellphone buzzed. Checking the screen, she saw Ali's name on the caller I.D.

"Hey," Laila answered as they stepped into the garage. "You're on speakerphone. Darien's with me."

"Bad news," said Ali.

There was a commotion in the background, but the speaker didn't quite pick up the sound.

"There's a fire in the Old City. The fire department is still trying to contain it, but it's destroyed all three sites where the bodies were found. I'm not sure there'll be any evidence left at this point."

Laila and Darien exchanged glances.

"It looks like they're on to us," Darien warned. "We're going to have to be careful."

Ali continued.

"The fire's spreading fast, I don't know how many people are trapped, but the situation's looking pretty bad here. The firefighters have arrived, but they're barely making a dent."

"They need magical backup," said Laila as she started towards the SUV.

"Exactly…" Ali sounded a little distracted. "Um, sorry to ask, but could someone come pick me up? Our asshole of a supervisor just left."

"What!?!" chorused Laila and Darien in unison, stopping in their tracks.

"What do you mean, he left?" asked Darien stiffly.

"Well," began Ali, fuming. "Colin sort of had another meltdown about missing his date. He stormed off to the SUV. I assumed he was going to cool down, but I just saw him drive off!"

"Son of a bitch!" swore Darien.

Laila shook her head, forcing her anger down. She was done with Colin's shit.

"Send us your location," she said as calmly as she could. "We're on our way."

CHAPTER 40

"I can't believe this," hissed Darien, his red eyes glowed like smoldering coals. "I can't believe that bastard left her in the Old City!"

They sped through the empty city streets. It was late, and Laila was exhausted. It was all too tempting to return home, knowing that Frej would be waiting for her. But as much as she wanted to go home to her nice big bed, she was not about to leave Ali stranded. Plus, she had her job to do.

Perhaps it was all the better that Colin had left. That would be one less problem to deal with.

The ongoing fire would quickly destroy any magical residue left at the crime scenes, not to mention a large section of the Old City. Laila wasn't sure what she could do to help, but if there was a magical cause, perhaps she could counteract it. Meanwhile, every second that passed was precious time lost.

"His attitude was one thing, but this is the second time he's ditched Ali in the Old City this week!" Darien's grip on the steering wheel was so tight, Laila worried he would break it.

"What?"

"Yeah, at least the investigative team was there last time. This time he just took off." Darien took a sharp turn towards the Old City.

"I'm just as frustrated as you are," said Laila as calmly as she could muster. "But you've got to rein it in. There is nothing we can do about Colin right now. Let's focus on getting to Ali safely, and dealing with this fire."

The Vampire didn't say anything, but he took a deep breath.

In the distance, they could see a glow and a large plume of smoke rising into the night. The sheer size of the fire was horrifying. Luckily, that part of the city was largely unpopulated, but there were sure to be casualties nonetheless.

They pulled up to Ali's location. She was standing with a fire captain who was calling out orders, trying to prevent the fire from spreading any further than it already had. But the flames were moving quickly, leaving the entire block charred in its wake.

Laila choked as she opened her door. The smoke burned her lungs and stung her eyes. She held a handkerchief over her nose and mouth.

Ali waved them over. "The captain says we should be safe here. The firefighters have this section contained, but it's still spreading south towards more densely populated areas."

The radio that the fire captain held crackled to life. The voice coming from it was so distorted that the captain had to lean closer to hear.

"Shoot," he said. "There's a building a couple blocks down with residents still trapped inside. The crew can't get in to save them." He sighed and wiped his face with his hand. "This is why this area shouldn't be populated. Nothing's up to code. No sprinklers, nothing!"

Ali's expression was pained as she looked at the others.

"Tell your firefighters I'm on my way." Laila started running down the block.

"I'm coming too," said Darien behind her, but Ali stopped him.

"Are you insane!?! You're a freaking Vampire!" Ali snapped at him. "You're not going anywhere near that fire."

Darien scowled. He was not used to sitting on the sidelines, but Ali was right. If the flames so much as touched him, he could be consumed in seconds.

Ali gave Laila a concerned nod as Laila sprinted down the street in the direction the captain pointed. She still held the handkerchief over her mouth, but it did little to combat the smoke.

The other fire truck came into sight along with a group of firefighters, spraying water on a building in front of them. She could hear screams coming from inside the building.

She stopped in front of the woman who appeared to be in charge. She showed the woman her badge.

"I can help," she explained through a coughing fit. "I can get in there. I'll find the people who are trapped and bring them out to safety."

The woman nodded slowly, her eyes lingering on Laila's pointed ears. "Are you sure?"

Laila nodded.

"You're taking two of my men with you," the firefighter declared. "I can't let you go in there alone."

"Please," she begged the firefighter, "I can protect myself. I don't want your firefighters to risk this."

The other woman ignored her and waved over two men. "The Elf says she can get you in to rescue those inside."

"No, I—"

She indicated for Laila to take her gear. Laila accepted a mask but refused the rest.

"There's no time," she insisted. "I'll be fine."

Laila approached the door of the building with the firefighters. She cast a shield around them as they entered through the door.

"I hope you know what you're doing," said one of the men gazing into the inferno skeptically.

Secretly, Laila hoped she did as well.

She continued onward with the firefighters. They found the staircase more or less intact, and quickly ascended towards the voices on the second floor. Her shield protected them from the reach of the flames and falling debris, but the heat was unbearable.

The hallway of the second floor was completely engulfed in flames. Laila paused, evaluating the situation as the structure groaned and creaked around her. She needed to act fast—the building was about to collapse, and from the look on her companions' faces, they felt the same.

She reached out, feeling the strands of magic attached to the flames that were consuming the hall in front of her. They raged with the power of the fire. Commanding the energy, she ordered it to calm. Massive fires like this were hard to control, though. The fire's energy ignored her, content to destroy everything in its path. She needed to find a way to soothe it, a way to enhance her abilities.

There was a loud crash somewhere in the building.

"We need to move!" The firefighter grabbed her shoulder. "We're going to be buried!"

An idea occurred to her, something Hanna had done. She ripped off her mask, closed her eyes, and sang. The song was in Elvish and spoke of taming an angered spirit. The melody was very old and haunting.

Slowly she walked forward down the hall. As she sang, she wove the magic, forcing the flames to her will and pushing the deadly smoke away from her. This time the flames listened, and she swore they flickered in time with the song.

The firefighters followed her, checking the apartments as they went, but found no one.

Only one apartment remained. A firefighter checked the door, but the handle was glowing red. He looked hesitant to enter, but Laila sang louder, her voice carrying through into the room beyond. It would be enough to prevent the fire from flaring outward as they entered. She motioned for him to break down the door.

As she waited, she continued her song, fearful that she would lose control of the fire if she stopped. It seemed to appease the fire, which felt odd to Laila. Fires of this realm were not typically sentient, yet this one acted almost as if it were.

The door splintered, and Laila followed the firefighters into the room. A quick glance revealed no one, but there were doors leading to other rooms. The firefighters went to investigate.

Something felt very wrong to Laila. They could still hear the screaming, but where were the people?

A blue light caught her attention by the window, and she carefully picked her way through the room, avoiding burning furniture to investigate.

On the windowsill sat a black box. It was a recording device, and the source of the screams. It was surrounded by an enchantment protecting it from the heat of the inferno.

"It's a trap!" she screamed, but the second she broke off her song, there was an explosion as the fire roared back to its full force.

CHAPTER 41

Laila coughed and sputtered as she struggled to her feet. Luckily her shield had protected her from the brunt of the explosion, but the firefighters had stepped out of its protection, into the other rooms.

Snatching the recording device from the windowsill, she rushed as fast as she could into the first room. The firefighter in this room seemed relatively unscathed thanks to his equipment, but his coworker in the other room was in worse shape.

They found him sagging against the far wall. Not only was he unconscious, his mask had been ripped away. Worse still was the wall of flame separating him from Laila and the other firefighter.

"What do we do?" yelled the man next to her over the roar.

"I'm thinking!" she shouted back.

The firefighter proceeded to bellow a string of profanity at her. Laila ignored him, trying to focus on controlling the fire, but the magic slipped from her grasp.

That was when she noticed it, a vaguely humanoid figure standing in the thick of the flames.

It watched her laughing as flames lashed out, trying to scorch her. No wonder she'd had so much difficulty controlling the fire. It was literally alive.

"Foolish Elf!" it cackled, its voice like the sound of snapping wood. It was a Fire Elemental, and a powerful one at that.

She shuddered, despite the heat. They were legendary beings residing in Vanaheim, the realm of the ancient Gods. These ancient Elementals were said to be the origin of younger races with the ability to use elemental magic, such as Elves. However, these Elementals would abide by no mortal rules. They were completely untamable, and extremely dangerous. Most of the time they kept to themselves in remote corners of Vanaheim, slumbering, but somehow one of them had emerged into Los Angeles.

Laila knew they were as good as dead if they lingered any longer, but she was not willing to leave the unconscious firefighter behind.

She cast a blast of icy magic at the Fire Elemental, but it burned up before it reached halfway across the room. The Fire Elemental laughed louder as the flames engulfed the doorway behind them.

Laila's shield that protected her and the firefighter standing beside her was failing, as its energy was slowly eaten away by the fire. She couldn't sustain it much longer.

She turned to the man next to her. "I'm sorry!" she cried, as the flames breached her failing shield.

Flames surged, wrapping themselves around her arms like the tentacles of a great sea monster. They squeezed her, burning through her shirt and scorching her arms.

She screamed as the blinding pain hit her. It hurt more than anything she had ever experienced in her life. The firefighter next to her cried in agony before slumping on the ground, lifeless. The Fire Elemental roared triumphantly, feeding off her pain. In the flames, she could see its intentions. It would kill her slowly and painfully, while feeding off her energy. It would then go on to ravage the entire city, leaving nothing but dust and ashes behind.

Not if Laila could help it.

There was a shift, something awakening from within. She felt a sudden surge of energy and released a wave of blue flames that ate through the Fire Elemental's grip.

"Not you!" the Elemental hissed, backing up.

She took a step towards it, blue fire flaring around her hands. The blue flames did not scorch her. She was its master. Instead its touch was like a gentle, loving caress. But even as Laila moved she had the strangest sensation that she was no longer in control of her body, simply an observer within.

"Your kind does not belong here!" boomed Laila. Her voice echoed through the room with power. "You will pay."

"Please!" hissed the Fire Elemental. "Mercy!"

But Laila knew there would be no mercy for him.

She clapped her hands together, and from them reverberated a shock wave of blue fire. It tore through the room, eating up the fire in its path. When it washed over the Fire Elemental, it screamed and writhed in agony, until its own flame was extinguished. The blue fire then surged out through the building and into the city.

Gods, what just happened? She wondered. Laila had no idea she was capable of a spell that powerful.

Laila glanced around the room. It was no longer burning. There were nasty burns on her arms where the Elemental had seared through her flesh. She should be screaming in pain, but something held it at bay. There was still a job to do.

The man who had been standing next to her was nothing but a charred corpse. She turned her attention to the man lying on the floor and knelt by him. There were burns on his skin, and he had inhaled too much smoke, but he was, by some miracle, alive.

She reached out to touch him, but gasped. The flesh on her arms was nearly charred to the bone.

In the corner of her eye, she caught a glimpse of a familiar glowing figure. She had seen this figure before, the unnamed Goddess. Laila bowed deeply. In that moment, the force that had guided her actions left her body. The pain in her arms hit her suddenly, and she fell to her knees.

She screamed.

"Breathe easy, little Elf," said the Goddess, approaching Laila as she writhed in pain. "You have done well."

The Goddess knelt beside her, her hands hovering by Laila's arms. The air around them shimmered, and when the light faded, smooth skin had replaced the charred flesh. The pain had vanished, and all that remained were shimmering blue scars that wrapped around her upper arms like the blue flames. They were the same color as the scars on her back.

Laila looked up to thank the Goddess, but she was gone.

The firefighter coughed, and Laila rushed to his side. She used her magic to help pull the worst of the smoke from his lungs. He coughed up the rest.

"What happened?" he wheezed.

"There was a Fire Elemental, but it's gone."

She was not entirely sure how she knew that the Elemental was gone. She didn't even know it was possible to destroy one, but somehow, she had done just that. Or was it the Goddess working through her? She recalled the feeling of not being in control at the time.

She cautiously helped the man up and through the charred remains of the building. They made it out the door and across the street to where the rest of the firefighters, including the captain with the other truck, and her teammates were waiting.

"I don't know what you did," said the captain, approaching. "But the entire fire was put out in that flash of blue."

Laila shook her head. "I'm so sorry, I couldn't save him, I couldn't save the other one."

The color drained from the captain's face.

"Where is he?"

"The second floor."

The captain rushed with two of the others back into the wreckage while the paramedics loaded the survivor into an ambulance.

"Gods!" exclaimed Ali, dragging her aside. "What in the worlds happened?"

Laila glanced down at her clothes. They were singed, and the sleeves of her shirt had been burned away. Curiously enough, the Dragon armor she wore was untouched. Perhaps Pegasus leather was impervious to fire. Her boots were also destroyed, and she cringed as she felt the singed ends of her hair. So much for growing it out.

"Let's go," Laila said, as she was hit by a wave of fatigue. "We won't find anything else here tonight, and I could really use something to eat. I'll explain what I can over dinner."

CHAPTER 42

The three agents slid into the booth of a twenty-four-hour diner. A grumpy-looking waitress slapped some menus down on the table before stalking back to her post behind the counter. They were the only customers in the place.

Laila picked up the menu, which was unpleasantly greasy, and looked over her options. The menu contained a variety of fried food.

After waving the waitress back over, Laila ordered a veggie burger with a large side of fries. Ali ordered an enchilada plate, but there was nothing on the menu for Darien.

"So, what happened?" asked Darien quietly, so the waitress wouldn't overhear.

Laila took the small electronic recording device out of her pocket and placed it on the table in front of them.

"It was a trap," she explained grimly. "Whoever set the fire wanted to lure people into the burning building where a Fire Elemental was waiting. They made sure the fire wouldn't destroy this recording, too, because it was warded. Probably the work of a Witch."

Darien whistled low. "Seems like there is a lot of suspicious Witch activity going on these days. You don't think that friend of yours could be involved?"

Laila shook her head. "Lyn's too clever to get involved with something like this without warning us."

At least Laila hoped so. She didn't know Lyn too well, but Laila was certain the Witch wouldn't be involved in anything as destructive as this.

"I think I should pay her a visit tomorrow," Laila continued. "She might know something about these incidents."

Ali sighed. "I can't shake the feeling that this is all connected. It seems too coincidental. I mean, three bodies are discovered dumped in the Old City. Then before we can even go back to investigate, a Giant mysteriously appears, diverting our attention. When we finally make it out to investigate the crime scenes from the murders, a fire has started thanks to a Fire Elemental, destroying the evidence and everything around it."

Darien and Laila nodded. Laila had been thinking along the same lines. It seemed that someone, most likely a Demon, was sending them on a wild goose chase.

"By the way," said Ali, "what happened to the Fire Elemental? How did you escape it?"

Laila hesitated as the waitress delivered a couple of waters. She waited until the waitress was back out of earshot.

"I think I destroyed it."

Ali choked on her water.

"What!?!" the Fae spluttered, staring at Laila as if she had grown a second head. "How is that possible!?!"

Darien glanced back and forth between Ali and Laila. "Okay, I'm missing something here. What's a Fire Elemental?"

"It's an ancient type of SNP that's immortal, and crazy powerful. It's basically fire incarnate, and can incinerate an entire city within a matter of hours."

Darien cocked his head at Laila. "So, you destroyed an immortal?"

"I guess," said Laila, trying to process it herself, "but I think I had help. That Goddess I met when I was imprisoned up north intervened. She helped me to stop the Elemental and the fire. That's where the blue flame came from. She also healed my burns." She indicated the blue markings on her arms.

"Unfortunately," she continued, "she didn't extend the same courtesy to the firefighters."

Laila felt horrible. She'd done what she could, but if it weren't for the Goddess's intervention, she would be dead as well.

"You tried to talk them out of it," Darien reminded her. "You didn't force the firefighters to go with you."

They sat in pensive silence as the waitress brought their food. After they ate, Ali finally broke the silence.

"I don't know what's more terrifying, that random SNPs are showing up unannounced to destroy the city, or that you've captured the attention of a God." She shuddered.

"I know," sighed Laila. "But if the Gods are willing to help us, shouldn't we be relieved? The Demons or whoever is behind this have been one step ahead of us the entire time."

She pushed the remaining fries around her plate, stabbing them with a fork.

"You're right," mused Darien suspiciously, "it's almost like they know what is going on in the office."

The color drained from Ali's face. "You don't think…"

Darien and Laila waited as she trailed off.

"What?" asked Laila, encouraging her to continue.

"That there's a mole in the office?" Ali finished.

Laila and Darien exchanged glances.

"I know it sounds paranoid," continued Darien, "but we've been trying to track down Demons in the city for several weeks now, and every lead we find gets us nowhere. What if that's because someone's feeding them information?"

"Well, shit." Ali rested her head in her hands. "If you're right, then we're in trouble. Who knows what information they have?"

"We have no evidence, though," Laila pointed out.

"I know," Darien said. "It just occurred to me, though. That would explain our recent streak of bad luck. We should err on the side of caution, though. In case there is a leak, we need to be careful about what we say, and who we say it to. We should keep any further information we discover between the three of us."

Laila frowned. "What about Colin?"

"I hate to say it, but given his recent behavior, I'm not convinced we can trust him. Especially after tonight."

Ali nodded slowly in agreement.

"Wait, you don't actually think *he's* the leak, do you?" Laila couldn't believe what she was hearing. Sure, Colin's behavior had been obnoxious and irresponsible. Even if he was becoming a liability, treason was something else entirely.

Ali sighed. "I have to agree with Darien. Even if Colin isn't the leak, he's still a liability. I mean, he ditched me in the Old City, for goodness' sake! Who does that!?!"

Ali had a point. Colin had been more of a hindrance and a distraction than anything. But to even suspect that Colin had sold them out seemed outrageous. Colin had established their office and created this team. Why would he sell them out and throw everything he worked for away?

"I don't know!" groaned Laila. "It's been a rough night."

Darien glanced out the window. "It'll be dawn soon."

"It's settled then." Ali pulled out her wallet. "We are officially done for the night."

They paid the waitress and hit the road. Already people were on their way to early morning shifts.

"So," began Ali from the back seat. "What's the plan for tomorrow?"

Laila shifted in her seat to face Ali. "I was planning to speak to Lyn. Maybe you should come with me just in case. We should also see if Benning, the Giant, can take us to the location where he appeared."

"Sounds good," said Ali. "We should be able to get that taken care of by dusk at the latest."

"Don't forget, we're investigating the Di Inferi tomorrow night," added Darien. "I'll do some more research during the day and make some phone calls. Hopefully we'll have more information by this time tomorrow."

"What about Colin?" asked Ali. "Does he know about that?"

Darien shook his head. "I've kept it between me and the LAPD, and now you two."

"Okay," Ali yawned. "I'll convince him to come with me to interview witnesses and check out the aftermath of the fire. I doubt we'll find anything useful, and it will buy you two time to deal with the Di Inferi and any new leads they give you."

Laila nodded and stifled her own yawn. There was so much to do, but she was bone-weary. Whatever else came their way would have to wait until later.

Darien dropped them off at the house. They entered the kitchen quietly and found Frej sleeping on the sofa. There was a cold cup of tea next to him and a book open on his lap. He must have been waiting up for them. Laila felt a twinge of guilt.

Quietly the two women crept past him. They had just reached the stairs when he mumbled, "You two smell like you got into a fight with a Fire Dragon."

"Close enough," muttered Ali as she continued up the stairs.

Laila paused to explain but realized that he had already drifted back to sleep. She let him be and retreated to her room. There would be plenty of time for explanations in the morning, and currently she was too exhausted.

Cringing as she caught a glance of her singed hair in the mirror, Laila stripped off the remnants of her outfit. Examining her boots, she sighed. There would be no saving those. It would give her an excuse to go shopping with Ali, but who knew when they would have time for that?

Once again, she marveled at the condition of the armor from the Dragon Queen. It was completely unaffected. She examined it thoroughly but could not find a single burn mark.

She turned on the shower and stepped into the steaming hot

water. It felt good to scrub away the layer of ash that turned the water black.

Laila paused and examined the markings on her upper arms. They had faded now and only held a slight hint of shimmery blue. She wasn't a fan of tattoos and body art, but then again, she supposed that it was a small price to pay considering how badly burnt her flesh had been. By all rights, she should be lying in a hospital bed right now.

Why did the Goddess save her? Not that she was complaining, but the Gods only intervened when they deemed it necessary. Most people, even long-lived Elves, would never interact with a God, unless they befriended one the way that Ali had the Goddess of the Black Forest. But that was a rare exception.

She was certain the Goddess had a reason for keeping her alive, since she had been saved on two occasions now. But she worried about the motive behind the Goddess's actions. Mortals who caught the attention of the Gods tended to find a series of misfortunes befalling them. They could be taken back to Asgard, never to see their loved ones again, or become cursed. The Gods, she knew, did not intend to be cruel in most instances, but they simply had a different understanding of time, just as Elves had a different perspective on time than humans.

Reluctantly, Laila turned off the water and stepped out of the shower. She just hoped that whatever plans the Goddess had could wait. Or perhaps the Goddess would forget about her. After all, Laila had enough on her plate at the moment.

CHAPTER 43

It was nine o'clock in the morning when Laila's alarm startled her awake. She had only gotten a few hours of sleep, but it would have to do.

She applied a bit of makeup and pulled on a fresh pair of dark wash jeans and black, knee-high leather boots. Looking at the black leather breastplate, she decided that a little extra protection wouldn't hurt, so she pulled on a grey blouse before sliding into the thin armor.

Her hair was a mess. It was uneven, and the ends were visibly burnt, but she did not have time to stop at a salon to have it fixed either. She quickly gave up and just let it be.

Down in the great room, Laila discovered Frej was still sleeping on the sofa. She made coffee as silently as she could and searched the cupboards for bread to toast. Apparently she was not quiet enough, though, because Frej shifted to a sitting position on the sofa.

"Good morning," he mumbled, rubbing his face. "I had the strangest dream that you fought a Fire Dragon."

"No Dragons, just a Fire Elemental." Laila stuck the bread in the toaster and depressed the knob.

"Wait," said Frej, his expression serious as he walked over to the counter. "You're joking, right? It's hard to tell sometimes...."

"Um, yeah." She pulled a clean mug from the dishwasher. "After the Giant, we sort of had an incident with a Fire Elemental."

"And by 'incident,'" called Ali from the stairs, "she actually means that she charged into a Gods-damned burning building and took down a Fire Elemental with only two humans for back-up."

Frej cast her a disapproving look.

Laila threw her hand in the air. "I didn't *know* there was a Fire Elemental in there. It tricked us into thinking there was a group of humans trapped inside." She shook her head. Only an insane person would knowingly enter a burning building to fight an Elemental.

Frej shook his head. "Trouble really does follow you. First the assassin, and now this."

"Assassin?" Ali cocked her head. "What assassin?"

"Laila didn't tell you?" Frej asked. Laila caught the amusement in his eyes. "She thwarted an assassination attempt on the Dragon King and was given an honorary knighthood."

"What!?!" Ali's mouth dropped open.

"Yes, she is now Sir Laila Eyvindr, Honorary Knight of the Dragons."

"Yeah, I only received the honor after I was thrown in a dungeon all night," Laila reminded the Dragon. He simply shrugged.

Ali laughed. "Only *you* could go on vacation and insist that you are still on duty. Lucky for that king though."

Laila rolled her eyes, grabbed the remote control, and switched on the television in hopes of a distraction as she returned to her breakfast.

Ali searched through the refrigerator and pulled out a box of leftovers. She stuck it in the microwave and punched the "minute plus" button a few times.

"What?" Ali asked, noticing the others watching.

"Nothing," said Frej. "I just didn't realize Pad Thai was considered to be a breakfast food."

A door opened down the hall, and out came Erin dressed in a pair of sweats, grumbling.

"Since when are you morning people? What the…?" Erin trailed off, looking at the television. "Whoa, is that L.A.?"

All three adults turned simultaneously to look at the television. A newscaster spoke as the camera panned down the street showing the extent of the damage to the Old City.

"Unfortunately, yes," muttered Laila. "Which is why Ali and I need to get moving."

She set her plate in the sink.

"Give me just a couple of minutes." Ali indicated the microwave.

"I'll go get my things." Laila headed to the stairs.

She ascended to her room and searched for her weapons. She strapped on a belt with her badge and holsters and strapped her dagger and sheath onto her thigh. She glanced around to make sure she had not missed anything and realized that Frej had followed her.

"Perhaps I should go with you." He frowned, leaning against the doorframe. "I don't know what's going on, but that fire looked pretty bad. I'm sure you could use the help."

"Don't worry," she said lightly. "We'll be fine. Besides, I'm sure you and Erin have a lot to work on."

"That can wait." Frej, stepped closer. "I don't want you walking into a dangerous situation without backup."

Laila bit her lip nervously.

"Frej," she began gently, "I don't want your feelings to interfere with your responsibilities. Erin *needs* your guidance right now. She's finally starting to make progress."

The Dragon stood there shocked for a moment. She saw a flicker of emotion cross his eyes.

"Of course," he nodded, taking a step back.

"It's not that I don't welcome your affections," explained

Laila hastily. "I definitely do. I just… It's not fair to her."

Frej took a tentative step forward. "Laila, I promise that I will not shirk my duty to Erin, but that doesn't mean that I can't help you."

He gently caressed her cheek. She leaned into his hand and did not protest when he pulled her in for a kiss. It was intense, and Laila could feel his mixture of desire and fear. She pulled back before his emotion overwhelmed her and rested her forehead against his.

"It's my duty," she whispered.

"I know," he said gently.

She knew he understood. After all, he walked a similar path to her own. He knew that risk was unavoidable.

"Then I'll see you tonight." Laila stepped out of his embrace and returned to the kitchen, knowing that the longer she lingered, the less she'd want to leave.

"There you are!" Ali smirked. "I was wondering if I'd have to send a search party."

"We'd better go." Laila grabbed her keys.

"Have a good lesson," called Ali over her shoulder to Erin and Frej as she followed Laila to the garage.

They took off in Laila's car towards the beach.

"Well, it looks like you had an eventful trip. A title, new fancy armor, a boy toy…" Ali gave her a sly grin.

Laila blushed. "I'm not sure why you are so keen on pairing Frej and me up, but I'll admit, it seems to be working."

"Eeee!" squealed Ali. "I knew it would happen!"

"And this is so exciting because…?"

"Because you could use the distraction. You need a way to blow off steam, and you are a little more reserved about your sexual relations than I am, so—"

"Okay!" Laila cut her off quickly. "I get the idea. But you know I can always spar with Darien."

"That's definitely not the same." Ali reclined in her seat.

"Did Erin find anything useful in the books Lyn sent over?"

"Not really, but she's just started the last one. Maybe there's something in there that would help us understand the purpose of these rituals. I told her she should focus on reading it today."

A few minutes later, Laila pulled into a parking space a block from Lyn's shop. As they walked to the storefront, Laila hoped Lyn would be there. She hadn't called ahead of time, but since the Witch lived above her shop, Laila was fairly certain she would be close by. They tried the door, and the bell jingled as the door swung open.

Lyn poked her head through the beaded curtain at the back of the shop, her arms full of bottled potions.

"Oh, hey!" She frowned. "You look pretty official today. Is everything all right?"

"Not really," Laila said, stepping into the shop. "We need your help with that case involving rituals."

"The one you asked me about last time?" she asked as she restocked one of the shelves.

Laila nodded. "A couple of bodies turned up with strange markings, and we think they are victims of ritual sacrifice. I hoped you would be able to identify the markings now that I have photographs."

Ali passed Lyn her phone, showing her a picture of the female victim. Lyn's frown deepened. She also showed her the pictures from the one ritual location they'd managed to photograph.

"Give me just a minute." The Witch returned to the back of her shop. She emerged with a dark leather tome. It was dustier than most of the books Lyn had lying around. She opened it and flipped through the pages. "How many victims are we talking about?"

"Four so far," said Ali, "but there are possibly more in the Old City that we haven't found."

Laila nodded, she feared that there were far more victims.

"Damn," Lyn swore. "This is bad. I mean I thought it was bad from your description before, but this is *really* bad."

"What does it mean?" asked Laila as she and Ali stepped

closer to examine the book.

The color drained from Lyn's face as she found the passage she was looking for. She flipped back and forth through a segment. She shook her head, mumbling something that Laila couldn't quite hear. Finally, she glanced up at the agents.

"I can't be certain, but if this is what I think it is, then we're screwed." Lyn took a deep breath to steady herself. "Was there anything unusual about the location they were found in? Maybe more symbols?"

Ali grimaced. "Unfortunately, most of the sites have yet to be discovered."

"This is the only one we've been able to document." Laila flipped back to the photos from the hotel lobby and showed them to Lyn.

Lyn's frown deepened. She ran her fingers through her curly hair as she turned back to the book, lost in thought.

"Was this the work of a Witch?" asked Ali.

"Definitely, but I have no idea who it would be." Lyn flipped frantically through the dusty tome on the counter as she searched for a page, sending a cloud of dust into the air. "I could try to set up a séance with one of the victims, but that would take time, and there is no guarantee that the information we get would be accurate."

It was the first time Laila had seen Lyn so visibly shaken. After all, aside from selling the usual magical trinkets and potions, Lyn dealt with Ghosts and other minor Supernatural disturbances for a living.

Laila could feel the tension rising in her body as she watched the Witch pace back and forth. She was practically trembling.

"Are you certain there aren't any witnesses?" asked Lyn.

Laila started to shake her head, but stopped

"Wait," Laila turned to Ali. "What about the Giant?"

"Giant? You mean the Giant on the news?" asked Lyn as she stopped in her tracks.

"Yeah, he said he saw a body at the spot where he appeared."

"You mean they summoned *him?*" asked Lyn incredulous.

Ali shook her head. "What do you mean, 'summoned'?"

Lyn stalked over to the book and pointed to a drawing. "If I'm right, it means that someone is summoning Supernaturals with black magic. See the symbols? They are a type of rune used exclusively by black magic practitioners. Before black magic was outlawed, one thing those practitioners were known for was summoning Supernatural creatures."

Ali and Laila stepped closer to examine the page. On it was a sketch of a corpse with similar markings at the foot of some terrifying beast. The creature was standing in a circle surrounded by more of the same runes and candles.

"Essentially," explained Lyn, "they open a small portal that pulls a specific being through. Witch communities have banned black magic spells for centuries because they use blood sacrifices and it occasionally pushes the boundaries of Necromancy, but there have always been Witches that walk darker paths."

Laila glanced at the contorted figures on the page in front of them.

"Well," said Laila as she glanced at Ali, "it looks like we've discovered another way the Demons have been getting to Earth."

CHAPTER 44

Lyn shook her head. "I should have thought of this sooner. I'm so sorry. There aren't many practitioners of black magic these days, especially after The Event. All that research, and the answer was literally right under my nose." She scowled at the black, leather-bound book in front of her.

Ali pulled out her phone. "At least we have some idea of what the Demons are doing now. I'm going to call Darien—he'll want to hear this."

She stepped over to the other side of the shop to make the call. Laila turned her attention back to Lyn.

"Would you mind coming with us now? We are on our way to speak to the Giant. If he was summoned by the Demons, he should be able to lead us to the location of the ritual."

"Of course." Lyn carefully shut the book on black magic. "I'll need a minute to gather my things, but I want to see this location for myself. Maybe then I can help identify the Witch."

Lyn rushed upstairs while mumbling something about spells and irresponsible Witches.

Laila massaged her temples. How many of these rituals had

the Demons performed? For all they knew, they could be summoning a whole Demon army. This case had suddenly gone from bad to worse.

❖

At the warehouse, the three women were greeted by a group of disgruntled security guards who waved them through a gate.

"Oh, good!" one of them exclaimed, striding over to where Laila parked her car. "I'm assuming you've come for him."

The man jerked his thumb towards the building.

"We're here to see him." Laila, locked the car.

"Oh," he replied, crestfallen. "I'd thought…"

Ali gave the man a dazzling smile as she walked around the car. "Don't worry, we're working on finding more comfortable accommodations for our friend, but we really appreciate your help in the meantime."

The man blushed and stuttered, "Oh, uh, thank you! It's nothing!" before retreating to his post.

"Damn!" said Lyn appreciatively. "I wish I could do that."

Ali winked.

Laila led them through a door and into the warehouse. It took a moment for their eyes to adjust, but when they did, the massive form of a sleeping Giant was sprawled out before them. It appeared that he had had a restless night's sleep, because there were several nearby shelves that had been knocked over or pushed aside.

The Giant mumbled in his sleep as they approached, but didn't wake.

"He's friendly, right?" asked Lyn quietly. "He's not going to try to grind my bones into dust or anything?"

Ali shrugged. "He seemed nice last night."

"He only speaks in the common tongue though," added Laila.

"No worries, I've got a charm for that." Lyn produced what

appeared to be a small adhesive patch. "It's a temporary English spell."

"That sounds handy," said Ali as Lyn stuck the patch to the Giant's skin.

Laila walked over to his ear.

"Good morning!" she called.

The Giant woke with a start, looking around for the source of the noise.

"Um, down here!"

"Oh! Miss Laila!" He grinned. "Good morning to you too."

"I'm sorry to disturb you, but my colleagues and I are pressed for time, and we were hoping you could take us to the place where you arrived. You met Ali last night, and this is Lyn."

"It's a pleasure to make your acquaintance, Miss Lyn." He looked as though he wanted to shake hands, then thought better of it. "Of course I can take you there. We'll just have to mind all of the other little folk."

"Don't worry, we've got that under control," said Ali. "We'll give you an escort, but you'll have to tell us how to get there."

The Giant started to stand, careful not to bump his head on the rafters or work lights. "Well, if Miss Laila rides on my shoulder, she could tell you where to go with one of those special talking boxes."

He pointed to the phone in Ali's hand.

"Right," said Laila. "Our cell phones."

Benning led the way out of the warehouse and into the parking lot, stretching in the open space. Laila handed Ali her car keys and looked up as the Giant carefully scooped her up.

Laila's stomach twisted in knots as she saw the earth fall away below her. Reaching his shoulder, she cautiously clambered into a sitting position. Searching for a viable handhold, she apologized as she grabbed a fistful of his hair.

She then pulled out her phone and called Ali.

"Are you ready up there?" Ali asked.

"Um, not really." Laila cringed as she looked down at the

car. "Let's just get this over with."

Ali took the lead. There were no emergency lights installed in Laila's car though, so Laila improvised with a spell that created blue and red lights in the grille of the car.

Pedestrians pulled over as they passed. They stared at the Giant and pulled out their phones to record the strange phenomenon. Laila wished she had brought a hat or hood to hide her face. She didn't need videos of her riding around on the Giant's shoulder circulating on social media. Hopefully, the bystanders would be more interested in the Giant.

Ali led them north via smaller, less crowded streets for as long as possible before cutting over to the coast and the Pacific Coast Highway. From there, they relied on Benning's memory.

They continued along the coast until Benning stopped and pointed into the hills.

"That's it up there." The Giant pointed off the main road.

Laila relayed the information to the others, who pulled off the highway and onto a side road. A minute later they had reached a clearing, and the Giant carefully set her down.

There was white powder covering the earth. The wind had blown it across the clearing but there was still enough left to be able to identify the black magic runes. Laila crouched down and cautiously examined the circle. But this time, there was no body in the center.

"The markings are the same as the other sites." She looked up at Ali and Lyn.

Ali pulled out her phone to request an investigative team.

The Witch produced her book on black magic from the backpack she wore. "Chalk or chalk powder is standard for this sort of spell. Salt is pretty common too. It traps the entity inside a circle so they can return it to its home-realm. In this case they must have omitted the salt from the circle, and freed Benning into this realm. Was there anything unusual found at the other sites?"

"A Lindworm," replied Laila, taking photos.

"I see," said Lyn. "They must be struggling to get the spell right. I bet the Witch who's helping them has no idea what they're doing. A halfway decent Witch would know better than to mess around with stuff like this."

Lyn opened her book and began comparing the faded symbols drawn in chalk dust.

In the meantime, Laila and Ali continued to take photos of the scene. Laila reached a spot where the ground was a darker shade of brown. The scent of blood caught in her nostrils.

"Hey, Benning," she called. "You said there was a body here, right?"

"Yes, Miss Laila. It was lying right where you are." The Giant gave her a solemn look. "But it didn't seem right to leave him lying here in the open like that. I moved him under those leaves over there." He pointed north towards a cluster of trees.

Laila shook her head. At this point there was no use in lecturing the Giant about crime scene preservation. She set off in the direction he pointed. As she drew closer, the reek of death filled her nostrils. The body of a Troll was partially covered in a layer of leaves and detritus just under the trees that bordered the clearing. It had been picked over by scavengers, leaving little behind. She photographed that as well. She doubted there would be any evidence left on the body to help them at this point.

"Found it," she called to Ali, "but I'm not sure how they're going to transport a Troll."

"The investigative team is on its way."

Ali's phone buzzed, and she answered it.

"Whoa, slow down." Ali waved Lyn and Laila over. "I'm going to put you on speakerphone so the others can hear, okay?"

Ali held her phone out so that Laila and Lyn could listen.

"Okay, Erin, can you repeat that?"

"Yeah," said Erin on the phone, "so I'm reading the last book that Laila gave me. It's in Latin and talks about really old spells. There's a story here that mentions someone who used animal sacrifices to conjure Supernatural creatures."

"Go on," encouraged Lyn. "What else does it say?"

"Well, it looks like the bigger the sacrifice, the greater the being that can be summoned. An insect summoned a Pixie, a dog summoned a Hellhound, that sort of thing."

"What kind of Supernaturals were killed at the other sites?" Lyn asked Laila.

"The other one I saw was a Crocodile Shifter, where we found the Lindworm."

Ali flipped through the autopsy reports on her phone.

"Here are the others: Werebat, Hawk Shifter, and a human," Ali listed them off from her phone screen.

"Sounds like someone was trying to summon a Dragon," replied Erin, who was still on speakerphone.

"Why summon a Dragon, though?" asked Lyn. "Unless they are trying to summon a Dragon from Hell."

"This book mentions that a Dragon-like creature can be used to summon something else, but the translation gets funny here..." Erin trailed off.

"Erin? You there?" called Ali.

"Um, yeah, sorry. There've been some guys that have been hanging out across the street all day. They look kind of sketchy. Anyway, the Dragon-thing is supposed to summon a 'Fake God' or 'Demon God.' Whatever that means."

Laila gave Lyn a questioning look, but by her confused expression, the Witch didn't seem to have any idea what that creature was supposed to be.

"Thank you, Erin," said Laila before Ali hung up.

Lyn shook her head. "This is really bad. I don't know what this 'Demon God' is, but it can't be good. I might have a way to track this Witch, but I'll need a map."

"The investigative team should be here any minute," added Ali. "Once they arrive, we can head back to headquarters. We've got plenty of maps there."

While they waited impatiently, Laila returned to the blood-stained patch in the clearing. Reaching out, she examined the magic in the area. She could feel that a distinct disruption had occurred. The invisible strands were tangled and moved in an unusual manner. Many of them felt off to her as well, almost sickly, just like at the previous site she'd examined. She voiced her concern to Lyn.

"Yep, that's black magic." Lyn wrinkled her nose. "It pollutes the natural magic and takes a long time to dissipate. I can't sense magic in the way you do, but I can still feel the black magic here like a disturbance in the air."

Laila noticed something else as well—the faint remnants of Demonic energy as there had been on the bodies in the morgue.

The crew arrived, and Laila informed them that the Giant had discovered the Troll's body in the area yesterday, leaving out many of the details of the situation, just in case someone in the crew was feeding information to the Demons. She had called them primarily to handle securing the crime scene, to ensure it would be cleaned up, and to see that the body was transported. How they would manage to transport the body, she didn't know.

Lyn gave her a quizzical glance but didn't say a word about Laila's short report.

Just as she finished, her phone rang. This time it was Darien.

"Hey, I'm out at the crime scene still," she said.

"You and Ali need to get back to the city immediately. There's been another incident."

CHAPTER 45

Siren blaring, Laila sped back into the city with Ali. Benning was left with the investigative team back at the crime scene, but Lyn had talked them into bringing her along.

From what Darien had said, there was an unidentified SNP raging through a shopping mall, destroying displays and antagonizing humans. They had about an hour of sunlight still, so Darien was stuck in the office while they handled the situation.

They pulled up in front of the mall, parking along the curb by the mall's entrance. People were rushing out of the building, running for their cars in the early evening heat. Screams could be heard from within.

"Okay, Lyn," Laila began, climbing out of the car. "You need to stay back. We don't know what we are dealing with."

"Don't worry about me," Lyn winked. "I came prepared." She patted her backpack.

Laila and Ali cautiously entered the building, Lyn taking up the rear. The occasional fleeing human passed them, but there was no sign of the SNP. They reached the end of the corridor that opened up into the cavernous mall.

Here benches had been knocked over, shopping bags abandoned, and merchandise scattered about. They passed a lingerie shop whose window had been shattered. The mannequins were trampled, and several racks upturned.

Ali sighed. "Why did it have to be the mall? Why not a fitness studio?"

Lyn raised her eyebrow.

"What?" Ali shrugged. "I like this mall."

"Shh!" Laila hissed and pointed at a store up ahead. There was a crash from within.

They crept closer, using a large, raised planter for cover. From within the store they could see what appeared to be a mass of clothing lumbering through the shop, knocking over shelves and clothing racks. A terrified clerk was cowering behind the counter.

"What in the worlds?" whispered Ali.

"It has large horns and walks on two legs, but that's all I can make out." Laila peered around a plant. "It has little to no magic ability either."

"Then we should just confront it," determined Ali, standing. "There are three of us and one of it, after all."

Laila and Lyn stayed in place and readied themselves for trouble while Ali slowly approached the store.

"Stay where you are and put your hands where I can see them!" barked the Fae.

The creature didn't react.

Ali tried in a few different languages. The SNP didn't respond, but its head turned towards her. It advanced in her direction, picking up speed as it moved.

Ripping a dress from its face, the creature revealed the head of a bull with the body of a man. Its horns descended as it charged Ali.

"Shit!" yelled Ali, running for the cover of the planter. "So not good!"

Laila pulled her behind the planter as the bull sped past.

Ali scrambled upright as the bull turned. "What the hell *is* that!?!"

"A Minotaur—I think," said Lyn, bewildered. "I didn't think they actually existed."

"Well, this one looks pretty real to me!" Laila scrambled on top of the planter as the bull-like creature tossed its head and prepared to charge again. She shot a magical ball of fire at the Minotaur, trying to discourage its attack, but it dodged the flames and charged again.

"How did it get here?" asked Ali.

"Probably one of those summoning spells," guessed Lyn. "Who knows how many creatures they summoned?"

Laila helped the others scramble over the planter just before the Minotaur crashed into it with a boom that shook the ground.

"Here." Lyn passed Ali a couple of glass vials.

"Do I drink it?" asked Ali skeptically.

"No! Throw them at it! It should stun the Minotaur. Just don't hit us with it." The Witch went back to rummaging through her bag.

The head of the Minotaur loomed over them as it stood on the planter.

"Run!" Laila pushed Lyn in front of her.

Ali followed quickly behind. There was the sound of breaking glass, and Laila glanced over her shoulder. Ali tossed another vial, but it missed.

Laila reached out, turning the floor in front of the Minotaur to ice. The creature slipped and landed with a thud.

"Do it now!" she yelled.

Ali tossed the two remaining vials, which shattered on the floor in front of the Minotaur. Blue smoke curled upwards, engulfing him. When it cleared, the Minotaur sat frozen, turned to stone like a statue.

"How long does this stuff last?" Laila asked the Witch.

"No idea, but that's why I've got this." She pulled out a

coiled rope. "It's been soaked in a binding enchantment."

"That might not be necessary." Ali produced a pair of handcuffs. "But maybe we should double up. He looks pretty beefy."

Laila allowed her ice spell to dissipate so they could approach the Minotaur. Luckily his hands were close together so they could be cuffed. Lyn tied the rope over the cuffs and passed the end to Ali.

Laila pulled out her phone and dialed Darien's number.

"Hey, Darien," she said as he answered. "We've apprehended the Minotaur, but we are going to need a larger transport vehicle for him."

"Those things actually exist?" asked the Vampire in shock.

"It's sitting here in cuffs as we speak." She eyed the creature.

"Well, I'll be damned! I'll get a truck there right away."

True to his word, a truck arrived less than ten minutes later. Lyn's spell still held, so the Minotaur had to be wheeled up a ramp with a dolly. Ali accompanied the driver back to headquarters in order to help.

The mall was a mess, but the damage was repairable. The vendors were cautiously emerging from the back rooms where they had been hiding, looking shaken. Some of the humans were injured, so Laila called an ambulance.

Laila and Lyn were preparing to leave when Laila realized how hungry she was. She made a quick decision and ordered several boxes of Chinese food to go.

"So how do we locate these Demons?" Laila wondered out loud as they climbed back into her car. Much to her horror, the sun was close to setting. The day was almost gone, and she needed to get back to the office to prepare for the Di Inferi raid with Darien. She was pretty sure that the Minotaur was just another distraction the Demons were using to buy time.

"I have a spell," Lyn suggested. "I can enchant a map but I'm going to need some time."

"Time's something we're short on. Do you need anything from your shop?"

"Nope." She patted her backpack. "I've got everything I need."

"Okay, I'm going to get you set up in one of the rooms at headquarters. I'll have to leave you for a few hours."

"That's fine," she said, sorting through her bag. "It'll take a few hours for me to get the spell working. There's no way in hell I'm letting Demons walk around the city using black magic."

As they were pulling up to the IRSA building, she spotted Colin in the courtyard between headquarters and the hospital entrance. There was a woman with him in a grey pencil skirt and a pink silk blouse. Her hair was pulled back in a French twist, and she wore a pair of designer stilettos.

"Who's that?" asked Lyn as they approached.

"Colin, my supervisor," she explained.

"So, I take it the sexy librarian's his girlfriend?"

Laila watched, feeling somewhat embarrassed as Colin wrapped his hands around the woman's waist and pulled her in for a long kiss.

"Yeah," Laila stepped on the gas and headed towards the garage. "He hasn't introduced her to us yet."

"Well, they seem, um, passionate," snorted Lyn, but her expression darkened as something caught her eye.

"What?" asked Laila, glancing over at the Witch.

"Nothing," she shook her head. "I'm pretty sure I've seen that necklace she's wearing before, but I can't remember where. It's got some sort of a winged woman on it, I've got the strangest feeling about it, like I've seen it before."

Laila glanced in the rearview mirror and caught a glimpse of silver around the woman's neck. "Maybe it's religiously significant? Like an Angel or something?"

"Maybe…" Lyn trailed off lost in thought.

Laila parked the car and unloaded the takeout she had purchased.

"Speaking of Colin," she added, "don't say anything about the new developments we've made in the case. He's been a little… unreliable lately."

She didn't clarify further. Not that she found Lyn untrustworthy, but the office drama was something that was best kept to the team.

The Witch shrugged and followed her upstairs.

CHAPTER 46

"Ready to go?" asked Laila when she found Darien waiting in the hall. He leaned against the doorway in a leather jacket and dark wash jeans. "I'm going to get Lyn set up in the conference room before we go. She's working on a spell for us, but Colin will be up shortly."

"I don't know about that. He looked pretty busy to me," added Lyn with a smirk. Laila rolled her eyes.

"Great," muttered Darien. He pushed off the doorframe and returned to his desk.

Laila showed Lyn to the conference room.

"You can use whatever maps you need." She indicated the maps plastering one of the walls. "I've got to go, but call Ali or ask the others in the office if you need anything."

"Just some time and a bit of luck." The Witch started unpacking jars and magical objects from her bag.

Laila sighed. Both time and luck seemed to be in short supply around the office. She just hoped Lyn could help them find a lead before more people were murdered and more destructive SNPs were unleashed upon the city.

Back in the hall she found Darien and Ali waiting.

"Here you go." She passed a bag of takeout to Ali. "I know you haven't eaten since breakfast."

"Ah yes! You're a Goddess!" Ali found a pair of chopsticks and dug into the first box she found, not bothering to check what was in it.

"We've got to go," Laila said, grabbing a black leather jacket from her office. "Can you take care of the Minotaur and Colin?"

"I've got it." Ali passed a takeout box to Laila with a pair of chopsticks. "You guys get out of here."

Laila took the box of food and headed down to the garage. Once they were in the car, Laila dug into the food as Darien drove.

"Do you think it's safe to send them out to that interview? Especially with Colin in his current state?"

"They won't find much." The Vampire sped down the street. "The guy they're looking for probably didn't even witness anything, but he was in the area at the time of the fire, and it'll buy us some time."

Laila explained what they'd discovered about the summoning rituals and the black magic as they drove, the lines on Darien's forehead deepening all the while.

"Well," he said when Laila had finished, "hopefully we can get the information about the next summoning ritual out of these guys."

Darien called their contact with the Gangs and Narcotics Division. They were already in place near the third location, an antique shop on the edge of the Old City.

They drove along abandoned streets with crumbling asphalt. Thanks to Darien's superior low-light vision, they traversed the road much faster than Laila would have dared. It was only fifteen minutes later when they pulled into an alley a couple of blocks away from the antique shop. A pair of LAPD officers waited for them in the gloom.

The elder of them stepped forward as they approached.

"You must be Captain Anderson." Laila offered her hand.

He nodded solemnly. Laila suspected he was in his late forties. The skin that was visible beneath his shirt and bulletproof vest was leathery and marred with a handful of visible scars. While many of the humans who survived The Event were hardened and grim, Laila could tell this man had been a survivor long before that.

He warily eyed Darien, who was standing next to her, and crossed his arms.

"I'd heard of your team before. There were rumors that the group of you weren't exactly human."

"Lucky for you we aren't." Darien examining a scratch on the bumper of their SUV with a bored expression.

"Have your officers been able to determine how many people are in the building?" asked Laila.

"Maybe six. Two in the front of the shop, and more in the back. It's hard to say for sure, though." He scratched the back of his head.

"I'm not sure how much Darien told you," she said, zipping up her jacket to cover her armor, "but in addition to a possible connection with Demons, we believe these guys are connected to a string of ritualized murders. There could be another one happening somewhere in the city as we speak, so getting the information out of these Di Inferi members is of the utmost importance."

The captain nodded.

They each hid a wire in their clothing to record and send the conversation to the captain. Laila also had an earpiece, in case the captain needed to speak to them. She unhooked the hair from behind her ear to cover the earpiece.

They locked their government-issued pistols in a safe inside the SUV before heading out. The captain stared in shock, but Laila shrugged.

"We don't need them. They'll only make the humans in there suspicious. We need to get them to talk, and to make sure that we've got the right people."

The captain nodded slowly.

"Besides," added Darien, "it's not like we need guns to take them down." He smiled, showing off his fangs.

The captain frowned at the Vampire as the two SNPs headed towards the shop on foot.

The street on which the antique shop was located appeared deserted at first, but small signs of life and activity revealed that a handful of the buildings were still in use. Light from the shop in front of them filtered through grimy, barred windows.

A bell jingled as they opened the door. As the Captain had told them, two men stood behind glass display cases. They watched Laila and Darien suspiciously before approaching.

"Can we help you two?" asked one of the men, a hairy human with an unkempt beard.

"My girlfriend has peculiar tastes." Darien indicated Laila as he spoke. "She's fond of old human artifacts that are pre-Event."

The man glanced at her skeptically. Laila shrugged.

"We don't have video games where I come from." She noticed a variety of old gaming consoles behind the glass.

"What exactly are you looking for?" asked the other man. He was more muscular than the first.

Before Laila could speak, Darien rattled off a list of devices. She'd never heard of them, but the muscular human clearly had. His eyes lit up, and he carefully selected a variety of items to show them.

Laila nodded as he explained to her the condition of the various electronic devices. When he offered one to her, Laila glimpsed a tattoo of a three-faced skull on his arm.

"These seem great." Laila subtly indicated the tattoo to her partner. "I wonder, though. Surely you don't keep your best items out front here..."

The two humans exchanged glances.

"Everything for sale is on display," said the hairy man firmly.

"But the arcade game—" started the other.

"A vintage arcade game! Does it actually work?" Laila asked enthusiastically. "You have to show me!"

She waited impatiently while the two humans debated whether or not to allow them in the back. Darien gave her a slight nod of approval.

"Never mind, my dear, I've heard that a shop in Santa Monica sells them in pristine condition." Darien wrapped an arm around her waist and guided her towards the door.

"Wait!" The muscular human stopped them. "We'll show you! Please! I can guarantee that I'll give you a better price."

Laila and Darien looked at each other as the man gestured for them to follow.

A small hallway led to a storage room that was converted into a living space of sorts. Seated around a table were a handful of men counting money. They scowled as Laila and Darien entered the room, and she saw one of them pocket something, presumably drugs. Laila immediately recognized one of them. There was a picture of him pinned to the bulletin board in her office. It was one of the men from the traffic camera photo.

They followed the human behind a pile of junk. Laila could immediately see that the large video game machine was in really bad shape.

"Oh, ugh, that's not exactly what I had in mind." She wrinkled her nose at the smell of rat droppings. They were probably nesting inside the device.

She turned around to find him pointing a gun at her.

"What kind of Elf gives a damn about video games?" he spat at them. "Why are you really here?"

"Hey, man," said Darien, "we don't want any trouble, I—"

The man pulled the trigger, and Laila threw up a shield just in time.

"We need backup!" shouted Laila, hoping the microphone would pick it up.

"On it!" replied the captain in her earpiece.

Darien disarmed their attacker and handcuffed him while

Laila turned to face the others. The men at the table scrambled to grab the cash and shove it in their pockets before rushing out the door. Laila followed after them, avoiding the trash can one of them shoved in her path. They pulled out more weapons preparing to attack.

"I wouldn't do that." Laila stepped forward, conjuring glowing orbs of light that illuminated the back alleyway. "Drop your weapons."

Officers advanced from down the alley blocking their escape, but the gang members weren't going down without a fight, and they fought viciously.

Laila used her magic to superheat the guns of the two armed gang members. They howled and dropped the burning hot metal. She then froze the men in place.

Another grabbed her from behind. She rammed her head back and heard the crunch of his breaking nose. Then she grabbed him by the arm and threw him over her shoulder, where he landed with a thud. Rolling him over, she cuffed him while two officers cuffed the men she had frozen.

CHAPTER 47

Watching through a one-way mirror in the police department's interrogation room, Laila tapped her coffee cup impatiently as a detective questioned one of the human gang members, just as he had the previous three.

They needed the gang members to talk. Captain Anderson who was standing beside her was not optimistic though. The gang members were remaining tight-lipped, and not a single one seemed ready to cooperate. They had also been unwilling to admit their involvement in vandalizing the bar, even after they were confronted with evidence left at the scene. The gang members were completely content to keep their mouths shut and take the fall.

Laila was growing irritated with their lack of progress. They didn't have time for this. They were murdering people and unleashing creatures into the city, and Laila was no closer to figuring out the locations of the Demons, or the rest of the gang.

That was until they brought in this current man to interrogate. He also had a Di Inferi tattoo on his wrist, just like the man who had attacked Orin's bartender. He was also the man in the photograph from a traffic cam pinned to her bulletin board back at headquarters.

She had allowed the police to do the work up until this point, but they needed to speed things up.

She hit the button on the microphone in front of her.

"Detective, a word, please?"

The detective glanced at the mirror before excusing himself from the room.

"What's this about?" he asked, entering the room. If he intended to hide his annoyance, he did a poor job of it.

"My partner and I wish to speak with him." She inclined her head towards the interrogation room.

The detective hesitated.

Darien stepped forward. "This man's connected to an ongoing IRSA investigation that is extremely time-sensitive."

The detective looked at the captain, waiting for his support. Captain Anderson nodded.

"Do it. Maybe they'll get him to talk."

The detective grudgingly nodded and held the door open for the two IRSA agents.

They entered the interrogation room. Darien chose to stand in the corner, so Laila took the chair across the table from the human. She placed a couple of folders on the table between them.

She took her time looking the man over, and remembered him from the fight. He was the man who had grabbed her from behind. As expected, his nose was broken. Someone had set it for him, but it was swollen and bruised under the bandage. He glared at her but didn't seem interested in speaking.

"I'm Special Agent Laila Eyvindr, and this is my colleague, Special Agent Darien Pavoni. We work for the Inter-Realm Security Agency."

The man didn't react so Laila continued.

"I'm going to get straight to the point here. You're already looking at charges for possession of illegal drugs. You also fit the description of a perpetrator who severely beat a man an outside the Club La Fae last week prior to breaking into the club, vandalizing it, and leaving a message threatening Supernaturals."

"Drug possession, battery with great bodily injury, vandalism, criminal threats, don't forget about assaulting a federal officer," listed off Darien from the dimly-lit corner, "and we're just getting started. I'm sure we'd find more if we keep digging."

"I don't know what you're talkin' about," said the man as he stared blankly at Laila, but she could see the uncertainty creeping into his eyes.

Laila ignored the response. "Lucky for you, we're more interested in the people you work for." Laila folded her hands on the table in front of her. "If you're willing to cooperate, we might be able to work out a deal."

"I can't tell you what I don't know." He shifted in his seat.

"Why did you vandalize the Club La Fae?" asked Darien.

"I don't know, man," he snapped. "I don't actually know these things. We do what we're told, take our cuts, and mind our own business. There's a lot of us, I don't keep tabs on them."

"So you admit to your involvement with vandalizing the club," said Darien with the ghost of a predatory smile. "Good to know."

The gang member opened his mouth to protest, then shut it again. He glowered at the Vampire.

"Why are Demons involved with Di Inferi?" she asked after a moment.

He returned his attention to Laila. "I don't know nothing about no Demons. I try to keep my head down, and I don't ask too many questions. Those who do, don't stick around too long."

"Who should we ask, then?"

"No one. Not unless you want them to come after you."

"We need names," Darien hissed.

"Like hell I'm tellin' you shit." He glared at Darien. "I tell you that, and I'm a dead man."

After a minute, Laila opened the first folder she'd brought and pulled out a copy of the photograph. She slid it across the table, so he could look at it more closely.

"Who was the man in the car with you?"

"I don't know," he insisted evenly.

"I find it unlikely that you pick up strangers off the street and drive them around the city."

"I don't remember."

Darien chuckled from his corner. It was a slow, intimidating sound.

"What's so funny?" The gang member turned to look at the Vampire. Darien was definitely having an effect on him.

"Oh, nothing, but your pulse jumped when you looked at the photo. It jumped again both times you answered."

"So?" he asked uneasily.

"So, you're lying. I can smell it." He gave the human a dark smile, baring his fangs. The human swallowed hard.

"Look," Laila said, "this would be a whole lot easier if you would just tell us how the Demons are involved in your gang. We see no reason why Di Inferi should get involved with Supernatural affairs, yet here we are."

The human just stared at her. She could tell he knew something, but he didn't appear ready to speak. She decided to switch up her tactics.

"That looks painful." She indicated his broken nose. "I could fix it for you."

She held up a hand, conjuring a warm, healing light to surround it. The human's eyes grew large as he watched her, and he appeared to consider the offer.

"Fine. Fix my nose, then we'll talk."

Laila waved her hand in front of his face, easing the pain momentarily as the she healed the nose partway. It was just enough to show him that she could fix it, but she cut off the spell abruptly. The pain returned instantly and the man groaned as he clenched his teeth.

"You tell us what you know first, or no healing." She leaned back in her chair.

He grunted.

"Fine," he began. "I don't actually know much. We get calls from one of the lieutenants. He's way higher up than I am, and I've never seen him in person. I don't even know his name. He told me to pick that guy up." He nodded towards the picture.

"Who is he?" asked Laila again.

"I dunno!"

"What *do* you know?" hissed Darien in his ear, causing the man to flinch.

"Look man, I got a call, picked this guy up, and that's it."

"Where did you pick him up?" asked Laila leaning closer.

"The airport."

"And where did you take him?"

"A house in the Old City."

"The address." Laila passed him a notepad and pen.

The huffed in exasperation, as he debated whether or not he should comply. He shook his head finally and wrote down the address.

"Tell us about him," said Laila taking the pen and paper from him.

"I don't know, he didn't say much, just read through this old book with weird symbols."

Laila flipped through a second folder and removed a picture from one of the ritual sites.

"Did they look like these?" she pointed at the runes around the circle in the picture.

"Yeah."

Laila glanced at Darien, wondering if the other man was the Witch performing the summoning rituals. She opened a second file and pulled out the pictures of the ritual victims from the morgue and slapped them down on the table in front of the gang member.

"Recognize them?" she asked.

He blinked at the photos.

"You recognize them, don't you," growled Darien in his ear.

"No." He flinched. "I mean, yes, just one of them."

"Who?"

The man was silent.

"How many crime scenes will we find your fingerprints at when we run them through the system?" purred Darien.

The man inched away from him.

"Look," said Laila, "right now we know you know a hell of a lot more than you're saying. We know you're involved, but if you cooperate, maybe we can cut you a deal and help you lighten your prison sentence. We might even get you transferred to another state. But we need names and locations. Now."

"I don't know!" he blurted out. "That guy was Di Inferi, that's all I know!"

Laila looked at the picture he pointed to. It was the young, male Crocodile Shifter.

"He was in the gang?" she asked, surprised.

The Di Inferi member nodded.

"Why would other gang members kill him?"

"Because he wanted them to. He said it was for a greater cause."

"Who?" asked Darien. "The boy?"

"No, the snake-man." The guy shuddered.

"Who is that?" Laila leaned in closer.

"This creepy dude that turns into a snake. I've only actually seen him once or twice, but he appeared like six months ago and started takin' charge."

Laila unlocked her phone and pulled up a picture. It was from a low-quality security camera, and the image was a bit grainy, but one could still make out the suspect pretty well. He was bald and had on an expensive suit. The picture had been taken the night she was abducted.

She showed it to him.

"Is this the guy?"

The man nodded.

Laila turned to Darien. "It's the Lesser Demon. The Snake

Shifter from the fight-ring kidnappings."

"How do you—" started the gang member.

"Because she's the one who took them down," said Darien, "so I'd spill everything you know, now."

"I—"

"What are the rituals for?" Laila demanded.

"I already told you, they don't tell me stuff like that."

"When's the next ritual?"

"I don't know, probably tonight."

"Where?"

"I don't know!" he cried.

Laila frowned at the man with disdain.

"We're done here." She opened the door.

"You guys are gonna help me, right?" he asked frantically. "If they know I told you anything, they'll kill me! What about my nose!?!"

Laila reached out to the magic and the cartilage mended itself as she left, Darien exiting behind her. The door shut with a click.

Captain Andersen joined them in the hall, "Now what?"

"We need to find out more about this gang," explained Laila. "They're involved with the Demons, and that makes them dangerous. If they're planning another ritual tonight, then we need to move fast, starting with that building where he dropped off the passenger in the photo. I have a feeling he's our Witch."

"I can have one of my officers lookup the building," suggested the captain. "If there's no registered owner, then you won't have to bother with a search warrant."

One of the laws that was put into effect after The Event granted law enforcement officers access to abandoned buildings, so long as no one had stepped forward to legally claim them as their own. Registering as the building's owner wasn't terribly difficult or expensive these days, so long as they were able to properly maintain the building and keep it up to code. But those who chose to occupy a building without registering forfeited their privacy. The law was intended to discourage people from occupying potentially unsafe buildings or conducting illegal operations in them. Still, there were so many abandoned buildings in the Old City that it was a waste of time to search them without intel of criminal activity.

"Sounds good," said Laila as she gathered her things from a chair. "See what else you can get out of him and the others. If anything new comes up, please let us know."

"I've got a feeling that Di Inferi's got their fingers in a lot of pies." The captain massaged the bridge of his nose.

Laila and Darien exchanged glances.

"Thank you for your help." Laila shrugged into her jacket.

"Sure thing," he said, distracted as he looked at the door to the interrogation room.

An officer looked up the address they had been given. Sure enough, there was no registered owner. He showed them out of the building.

CHAPTER 48

Darien punched in the address the Di Inferi member gave them into the GPS while Laila reviewed some notes she'd taken after the interrogation.

"Should we call for backup?" asked Laila as Darien pulled out of the parking lot.

"Who would we call?" he asked. "Ali's with Colin in the Old City, the investigative team has their hands full with the crime scene you found today and the arson investigation."

Darien was right, they should be able to handle the search themselves. They'd just have to make sure there wasn't a group of gang members or Demons lying in wait.

"Well, now we have our confirmation, Di Inferi is definitely working with the Demons." Laila tucked her phone into her pocket.

"Yeah, and two of the victims were connected to the gang." Darien drove under the 405 freeway and into the Old City.

"Hopefully this Witch is the link we need to connect the two, and to lead us to the Demons. With any luck we'll have them in custody soon."

Laila leaned her head back against the headrest as she tried to think through the information they had.

"We know they're trying to summon a creature with the rituals, possibly a Dragon or something from Muspelheim."

"And that the Witch is probably from out of town," added Darien.

He turned onto a street and slowed the car to a stop.

"That's it." He nodded to a small apartment building across the street.

"Looks deserted." Laila frowned.

There were no lights on in the building, and many of the windows were broken. Laila reached out to feel the magic inside. Something felt off in one of the second-floor apartments. Someone had been using a lot of magic there, including black magic.

"I think this is it." She stepped out of the SUV and walked around to Darien's side. "I don't sense anyone in there, but we should be careful. There could still be lookouts or other inhabitants inside."

They left the SUV and crossed the street. The hair on Laila's neck stood, and she hoped it was just a reaction to the black magic, and not something else. She prepared a shield spell just in case. Darien drew his gun as they approached the building.

He tried the door, but it was locked.

"This is the Inter-Realm Security Agency," barked Darien, "open up!"

They listened, but there was nothing but silence within the building. Darien tried again, but still nothing. It seemed that no one was home.

Laila stepped forward and unlock the door with a spell. There was a click as she shifted the pins and tumblers within the lock. This time when Darien tried the door, it opened easily.

Laila conjured a light as they stepped into the hall. Systematically, they searched each of the apartments on the first floor, Darien taking the left while Laila checked the ones on the right. The doors were unlocked but the apartments appeared maintained, although the contents of each apartment were coated in a fine layer of dust. The furnishings were basic and mismatched. She suspected they'd been salvaged from different residences.

"All clear," announced Laila as she joined Darien down the hall.

"Same here," said Darien as they started climbing the stairs to the second level. "Is it just me, or does it feel like these are ready to rent out?"

"That's exactly what I was thinking." Laila cautiously peered around the corner of the second-floor hall, but it was deserted as well. "Maybe the Demons were using this for anyone passing though the city?"

They quickly searched that floor as well, but one of the doors on the right was locked.

"Someone's been using black-magic in there." Laila pressed her hand against the door.

She tried to use magic on the lock, but it was enchanted against spell work.

"Looks like we're doing this the old fashioned way." Darien shoved his body weight against the door. On the third try, the doorjamb gave out with a large crack as the bolt broke through the wood. He brushed splinters off his leather jack as he stepped into the apartment.

Like the other apartments, it was relatively small with a random assortment of furniture. The kitchen was small, grimy, and covered with bits of herbs and food on the counters. There was a sofa with an open suitcase sitting on top of it. A large table sat in one corner of the room, cluttered with old books, scraps of paper, magical tools, and a laptop.

"You think he was smart enough to have a password?" Darien asked, pulling on a pair of nitrile gloves.

He flipped the screen up, and sure enough the computer had only been in sleep mode.

"Jackpot!" he said grinning at Laila.

She shook her head and examined the objects on the table. Some of them she recognized from Lyn's apartment, such as carving tools and magnifying glasses. One of the books was lying open, but rather than neat print, there was messy handwriting scrawled across the pages.

"I think these are notes." Laila picked up the book with gloved hands.

Darien looked over her shoulder. "That's probably his grimoire, his personal book of spells. A lot of the Witches I've met keep them."

He went back to searching through the computer while Laila flipped through the grimoire. The first part of the book didn't contain much of interest, just general spells for protection charms and wards. The further into the book she went, the more disturbing the spells became, involving blood-letting and animal sacrifice. Finally, she found what she was looking for, a summoning ritual spell. On the page was a sketch of a circle and runes matching the ones from the crime scenes. There were more notes on these pages, many of which had been crossed out and revised.

"Well, this is definitely the Witch we're looking for, these descriptions are an exact match," said Laila as she glanced at Darien.

"Yeah, his emails are pretty interesting too. There's a conversation back and forth here between the Witch and someone called C. Ubel. Sound familiar?" he asked.

Laila shook her head. Then again, they didn't have many names of the people involved.

"Me either. In their brief correspondences, C. Ubel tells the Witch when he'll be picked up, but not much else." His expression darkened as he scrolled. "Shit, I'd say there's been at least twenty homicides from these emails, nothing about locations though."

Laila didn't know what to say. Demons were cruel and despicable. There was a reason why they had been damned in the first place. After her own experiences as their prisoner though, the number didn't surprise her.

"Is there anything else?" asked Laila as she placed the grimoire in a plastic evidence bag.

"They talk about Izel in here," he added, scanning the earlier emails.

As far as they could tell, Izel was a powerful Greater Demon who was above Marius. They'd found a letter written by her back in Marius's office that seemed to indicate that she was still trapped in Hell.

Darien continued, "The Witch asked what Izel is, but the other seems reluctant to say. He tells the Witch that he will provide the sacrifices, but check out the most recent email the Witch sent."

He took a step to the side so Laila could read:

This isn't working, reptilian and flying creatures just won't cut it. You need an actual Dragon if you want to summon Izel. Nothing else is working. If you want more Trolls and other creatures, I can do that for you, but forget about summoning Izel without a Dragon.

"They're not trying to summon a Dragon," breathed Laila, "they need a Dragon to summon Izel."

Darien nodded.

"Erin found a passage in an old Latin text," explained Laila as she started to pace, "it spoke about a summoning where a Dragon-like creature could be used to call a Demon-God. What if Izel is the Demon-God?"

"I—" began Darien, but a noise below silenced him.

"Someone's here," shouted a voice from downstairs, "search the place."

Multiple pairs of feet could be heard shuffling through the building.

"There's too many," whispered Darien grabbing the computer, "quick, the window."

Unlike the door, the windows were left unwarded. Clearly the Witch hadn't expected someone to climb through a second story window. Laila pushed it open with a spell. Darien stuck his head through before jumping out the window. Laila followed with the grimoire, as footfalls in the hallway drew closer.

She landed in a crouch with a small thud, and sprinted to the SUV while Darien covered her, watching for anyone coming from the apartment building. Laila got in and slammed the door as Darien took off. Gunshots and swearing were heard behind them, but Darien was already turning the corner.

"That was close." Laila buckled herself in.

"We won't be going back there tonight," said Darien. "We'll have to come back for the rest of the evidence later."

Laila glanced at the clock, it was almost three in the morning.

"Lyn should be done with the tracking spell she's preparing, we should head back and see what she's found."

Back at the office there was no sign of Colin and Ali. They were probably still out in the Old City.

Laila knocked quietly on the door to the conference room before entering. She found Lyn painting runes on the map while chanting softly under her breath. She didn't acknowledge Laila's presence.

The Witch finished her incantation and picked up the book on black magic. She lifted the book, holding it in front of the map, then blew on it as if to clear away dust—only instead of dust, a little cloud of black magic wafted towards the map, vanishing into its surface. Lyn took a step back and put the book down.

"It's done," she declared, stifling a yawn. "I've imbued the map with an enchantment to track any significant appearances of dark magic in the city."

"Let me get Darien. He'll want to see this."

She returned seconds later with the Vampire. Lyn beckoned Laila closer and pointed to a spot on the map north of the city.

"Here's where we were today. There are still trace amounts of black magic in the area."

Sure enough, Laila saw a grey haze covering that location on the map. There were some other areas of light grey in various locations on the map.

"But those are all remnants of old spells." Lyn waved at the map. "An ongoing or very recent spell would be much darker."

"Like this one?" Laila pointed to a new dark cloud forming over an area south of the airport.

"Shit! We need to get over there." Darien rushed out of the room. Laila was about to follow him when her phone rang. It was Frej. She felt bad since he had tried calling her multiple times and she had not been able to call back. She hit answer.

"I'm sorry, Frej, but I'm kind of in the middle of something—"

"This is an emergency! Erin's been kidnapped!"

CHAPTER 49

"What!?! Are you sure?" Laila didn't know what to think. Erin was fairly independent. Perhaps she was just out for a walk.

"Yes, they took her," gasped Frej, out of breath.

"Who?"

"Those guys who were watching the house grabbed her."

"Oh, Gods." Laila's gut twisted. Erin had mentioned the men earlier, but no one had thought much of it.

"Darien!" she yelled. The Vampire was there in a flash. "Ali's sister has been kidnapped."

The horror in his reaction reflected her own. The Demons had found their Dragon. Her hands trembled as she switched the phone to speaker and set it on the table. Even Lyn stopped what she was doing.

"Frej, you're on speakerphone. Ali is out interviewing a witness. I need you to tell us everything that happened."

"We noticed the group of men loitering down the street. Erin hadn't seen them before, and it made her anxious. I convinced her to focus on her lesson, and thought they would leave, but they were still outside when we took a break.

"There was a commotion on the street. It sounded like an accident, and a woman came to the door asking for a phone to call for help. Erin opened the door to help, and the men from down the street came barging in and attacked. I tried to fight them off, but two of them grabbed Erin and ran. They got into a white van and drove off, but I followed them."

"How?" asked Laila. He didn't know how to drive a car, and all they needed was for Frej to cause an accident while trying to save Erin.

"I flew. Don't worry, I was cautious, I don't think they saw me. They took her to a tall building south of the airport."

Lyn gasped. She got up so fast she knocked over her chair. "Did you see any street signs?"

"Yeah, I saw one that said Mariposa."

"That's where the black magic is spiking." Lyn pointed to a black splotch on the map.

"Frej," said Laila, grabbing her things. "I need you to keep an eye on that building, but don't go in. Those were Demons that kidnapped Erin. We're leaving now. See if you can tell how many people are in there, where they are, and if there are any lookouts guarding the place. We'll be there soon."

She hung up, and the three of them rushed down the hall. Darien was already on the phone, calling the investigative team for backup.

"You should stay here," Laila called over her shoulder to Lyn.

"No, if there is a Witch involved, you might need my help."

It was hard for Laila to argue with that logic, but she didn't want Lyn to get hurt like the firefighters had. Reluctantly she nodded.

"Okay, well, we found the Witch's grimoire, maybe you can figure out how to stop this ritual." She passed the book in its plastic bag to Lyn.

"On it," said Lyn.

They climbed into Darien's SUV and sped out of the garage, lights on and siren screeching, but he switched them off as they passed the airport. This section of the city was uninhabited. The roads would be all but empty, and they didn't want to alert the captors. Darien's night vision would be enough to guide them.

Laila attempted to call Ali, but there was no answer. Laila left a voice message explaining what had happened and that she, Darien, and Lyn were on their way. Meanwhile, Lyn flipped through the grimoire looking for anything that could help.

"This guy's seriously screwed up," muttered Lyn. She shook her head at one of the pages before moving on.

They pulled down a side street about a block away and parked. She sent their location to Frej and suited up while they waited.

Darien opened the trunk and unlocked the miniature armory chest he kept in the car. He removed the case that held his sniper rifle. Laila selected one of Torsten's magical stun batons. She hesitated a moment, then selected a small shield. The extra protection wouldn't hurt. They also set up their radio coms.

Frej appeared around a corner. He was battered and bruised, and his clothing was torn in places, but he seemed relatively uninjured. Darien passed him the katana the Dragon had used the previous night.

"Thanks," whispered the Dragon. He seemed calm and cool, but Laila could tell he was in battle mode and ready to fight.

Laila checked her phone, but Ali hadn't returned her call.

Frej led them quietly down the dark, empty streets. Old hotels loomed around them in early stages of decay. They were dark except for one where flickering light came from the top floor of the building through filthy windows.

"That's it." Frej, followed her gaze. "I don't think they expected anyone to follow them. There's no guard on the bottom floor of the building, and only two cars parked in front. It looked like there were several of them up there though."

They stopped, surveying the building in front of them.

"I'm going to set up on this roof of this hotel." Darien nodded to the building next to them. "I'll get eyes on the situation and see how many I can take out if need be. Frej's with me, since he can fly. I want to be able to get over there and he can make it happen, but I don't want to leave you alone, Laila."

"I'll go with her," insisted Lyn. "I need to be close enough to counter any spells their Witch has already cast."

"We should also wait for backup," said Darien.

Laila shook her head. "We can't waste any time. I am NOT letting Erin become some ritual sacrifice! We need to move now."

"But last time—"

She waved him off. The last time she had gone into a situation like this without backup, she had ended up as a gladiator. But her instincts screamed at her to get in there now.

Darien nodded and then climbed through the broken window next to him, with Frej following. They vanished into the gloom as Laila waited. She needed to give Darien enough time to get into place.

Frej struggled to keep up with the Vampire. The stairwell was dark, and the Vampire was naturally faster than him. He clung to the handrail to keep from stumbling.

At this point he was functioning on adrenaline alone, and he was determined to save Erin. He hadn't been there for her father when he had been attacked, and that guilt had lingered with him for ages. There was nothing he could have done—at least that's what Queen Regina had told him.

This time he would be there. He would save Erin.

They reached a steel door labeled ROOF. It was locked, but Darien kicked it in with one powerful blow. Frej crept to the edge of the roof as Darien opened the case he carried.

"If anything happens," said the Vampire, preparing a sniper rifle, "get Laila out of there. We can't afford to lose her."

"Do you know that my queen has offered her a place in my kingdom?"

Darien glanced up. "What?"

"She saved the king from a would-be assassin. Rarely have I seen the queen so impressed. Laila would've been welcomed by my people, but she declined."

"Why'd she decline? Wouldn't that be better than this?" Darien gestured to the decaying city around them.

"Possibly, but she insisted that this is her duty." Frej saw the Vampire smile in the gloom.

"Yeah, she may be a little stoic at times, but she's a good partner and dedicated to the team. I always know she's got my back."

"I see them up here," said Darien through her earpiece. "Erin's tied to a chair in the middle of the room. She's in the center of the chalk circle. The Shifter's there and the Witch, plus half a dozen other men armed with guns."

"Are they human?" Laila asked as she and Lyn crept through the shadows and towards the hotel.

"I can't tell for sure. They *look* human."

"Let's be cautious, then." Laila glanced through the entrance to the building. "We're heading in."

Laila didn't see movement in the darkness. She reached out with her magic, feeling for any spells, but did not sense anything. Cautiously she crept into the building. Lyn followed, holding a staff engraved with runes in one hand and a glass vial of something in the other.

After a quick check of the first floor, they found nothing, so they proceeded to the stairwell.

She eased the door open, and they slipped into the darkness. The stairwell was black as pitch, and the only light came from the doorway several stories above them. Laila conjured a dim blue light, just bright enough to see by, and ascended the stairs, Lyn trailing behind.

Snippets of conversation drifted down towards them, but they were faint and distorted. The women had to climb slowly to keep quiet, and the ascent seemed to take hours.

They finally reached the second to last floor. They hadn't encountered a single guard, which led Laila to believe that Frej was right, and that the kidnappers really weren't expecting them.

Laila motioned for Lyn to stop, as she extinguished her light. She closed her eyes and concentrated on the floor above them as she reached out of her body and felt the magic.

She hissed, recoiling. The fresh black magic burned like acid. She cautiously reached through its coils to feel the other energy in the room. Erin's was red-hot, burning with anger and fear. Most of the others were human, or magic-less Supernaturals, but tainted, and not just by the black magic.

Opening her eyes, Laila signaled for Lyn to wait as she ascended the last few steps.

CHAPTER 50

Erin pulled at the ropes that bound her wrists. They were raw, and the friction burned, but she clenched down on the gag in her mouth and kept pulling. She even tried conjuring a small flame to burn through the rope, but to no avail.

She knew there had been something suspicious about the men hanging out down the street, and she was right. Now she was bound to a chair, while some human chanted in shitty Latin about opening gateways and conjuring spirits, as he drew on the ground with chalk. She had seen enough horror films to know that she was in trouble. If she couldn't find a way out of there, she would probably end up possessed by something, or worse.

The boss man, as she thought of him, noticed her squirming. He grabbed her jaw and leaned in close. His eyes shifted, his pupils becoming long slits like a cat's. His teeth grew long and thin like a snake's.

She tried to scream, but the gag muffled it.

"Stop squirming, little girl, or I'll inflict more pain on you than you can possibly imagine," hissed the man.

There was noise by the door, and he swiveled his head away.

Erin lashed out, kicking him in the balls. The man-snake thingy howled in pain as Erin grinned. After all, it was his mistake for not tying her feet.

Laila covered her mouth and held still. She had not intended to gasp, but when she saw the Shifter in person…

The last time she had seen him, he was in a dingy law office behind a bar when he had drugged her and sent her to the fight ring. How many others had he sent to be tortured and killed?

Laila holstered her stun baton and removed her gun from its holster instead.

There was a dull thump, and a man's cry of pain. She took the opportunity to step into the doorway, taking cover behind the shield on her arm.

"ON THE GROUND! HANDS WHERE I CAN SEE THEM!!!" Laila aimed her gun at the Shifter.

There was a moment of confusion in which the henchmen glanced at each other uncertainly.

"NOW!" Laila fired into the floor by the Shifter's feet. The others flinched, but not the Shifter.

"I know you." His nostrils flared as he breathed in her scent. "You're the Elf I sent to Marius."

"Release the girl *now*!" Laila snarled.

"Or what?" he hissed. "You'll bring in that human hiding downstairs—"

Bang.

The Shifter howled, grabbing his thigh where Laila had shot him. The blood oozed between his fingers and dripped to the floor.

"This is your last chance." She aimed at his chest.

Two of the henchmen charged her, blocking the shot. She sent a burst of flame at them, which deterred their approach.

"Back to work," spat the Shifter to the Witch, who quickly

began drawing on the floor while muttering to himself.

"Darien," she said through the coms, "don't kill the Shifter."

Laila didn't wait for a response. She holstered the gun, replacing it with the stun baton before diving into the fight.

Erin watched as Laila walked head-on into the advancing group of human cronies. Laila ducked as the first one grabbed for her, easily slipping out of his reach, and bashed his knee with her baton. The man shuddered and collapsed like he'd been shocked, but Laila was already moving onto the second one, ramming him in the face with her shield, while smashing the baton into the head of a third.

The men were gaining the advantage, though, and Laila was outnumbered. Meanwhile, the scrawny man in front of her seemed to be finishing his incantation.

The glass shattered behind him, but the male Witch barely reacted. Erin's eyes grew wide as he reached into a bag and pulled out a dagger. She tried to scream, but with the gag in her mouth it was useless.

Glancing over at Laila, she saw the Elf had lost her shield, and switched to her dagger. She was slowly fighting her way through the men.

There was no way Laila would be able to save her in time.

As the man approached, Erin shut her eyes, relaxed, and imagined reaching out into the space around her. She could see the warm, glowing strands of magic, the fire. Erin didn't know what to do. She had never cast anything larger than a small ball of flame. Hoping something would happen, she grabbed as many strands as she could and pulled, willing them to obey her.

Her eyes shot open, and she could see the man standing over her with the dagger...

Laila ducked, punched, whirled, and stabbed her way through the men. Glass shattered, and one of them dropped. Darien must have taken him out.

She plunged her dagger into a set of ribs on her right, and blasted another man with lethal ice shards. Darien's sniper fire took out another.

Laila was down to two when she felt the energy in the room shift. She was barely able to throw up a shield as a blast of fire tore through the room. Looking up, she saw Erin fall backwards in her chair from the force of the magic.

"Yeah!" Laila shouted, but her triumph was short-lived.

The air in the middle of the circle, over the now-dead body of the Witch, swirled in a dark vortex. Erin, who was still tied to the chair, shuffled out of the way as quickly as she could.

"LYN! You better get in here!" Laila shoved her way through the fallen men to reach Erin's side. She cut the ropes that bound Erin, and the Dragon hastily removed her gag.

"Snake!" Erin screamed, pointing over Laila's shoulder. Laila spun and faced the SNP.

In her peripheral vision, Laila saw Lyn rush into the room and toward the spinning vortex of black magic. She hoped Lyn could stop the spell before whatever was trying to come through the portal succeeded.

Laila locked eyes with the serpentine Lesser Demon. She wanted to make him pay for all the suffering he had caused those he had sent to the arena, but she needed him alive. He was the direct connection to the other Demons, including Marius and Izel. She needed him alive.

He shifted partially, allowing his fangs to lower, like a Vampire. They glistened as they dripped venom. He reached out to strike, but Laila was prepared. She stepped out of his path and shoved him, forcing his weight onto his injured leg.

He hissed, collapsing to his knees. Without missing a beat, he struck again. But Laila had anticipated this as well, dodging again and slicing across his cheek with her dagger.

The Lesser Demon swept her feet out from under her, and she landed hard on her back. He was on top of her immediately, wrapping his hands around her throat. Laila clawed at his eyes as she tried to hold him off, but the Shifter was incredibly strong.

There was a blur of movement above them and a loud crash before the Lesser Demon went limp. Laila cautiously rolled him off her to find Erin standing above them with a broken chair.

"We need to get out, now!" shouted Lyn over the noise of the vortex. The whirl of air had mixed with the sound of deep, thunderous laughter, and it was growing louder by the second. "I'm counteracting the spell, but when I break this vial, all this energy is going to erupt into a magical explosion. You need to get your friend out now!"

The Witch held up a glass bottle as the vortex spun faster.

Laila pulled Erin to the window and looked out into the night. She turned to Erin and grabbed her by the shoulders.

"Do you trust me?" she shouted.

"Yeah, why?"

"Then jump!"

"What!?!"

"NOW!" Laila grabbed the girl and flung herself out of the broken window.

For a beat of her heart, the air rushed past them as they fell. Then they landed with a thud, and Laila scrambled to hold herself and Erin onto the scaly back of the fully-grown Dragon.

Frej beat his large wings carrying them higher into the night sky. He landed on the building across the way where Darien waited. The Vampire caught Erin as Laila released her.

"We have to get Lyn," Laila said, seating herself more comfortably on Frej's back. He huffed in acknowledgement before taking off again.

He beat his wings, gaining altitude before swooping towards the broken window where Lyn was standing. Once the Witch spotted Laila, she smashed the glass bottle and leapt from the window. Laila caught the Witch, but Frej dipped dangerously low. He recovered with another beat of his wings, pulling them up and away from the building.

An explosion boomed behind them, shaking the earth. Laila glanced back and briefly glimpsed a humanoid figure before it was sucked back through the portal, which dissipated. Whatever or whoever the Demon had summoned was gone.

Frej landed back on the other building and crouched so the women could dismount.

"We can't let the Shifter escape!" cried Laila. But Darien just shook his head.

"He's gone, Laila. He shifted when you jumped, and I lost track of him."

Laila felt as though she had been punched in the stomach.

"I'm so sorry, Laila," continued Darien, resting a hand on her shoulder. "We'll find him. Don't worry."

Laila nodded and straightened herself.

"Laila!" Erin plowed into her, wrapping the Elf in a big hug.

"Are you okay?" Laila asked, checking her for any sign of injury. She saw the friction burns on the girl's wrists and healed them with a quick spell.

"I'm fine," she insisted, stepping back and looking rather sheepish. "How did you know Frej would catch us?"

She turned, facing Frej who was still in his true Dragon form. He was huge. Not including his tail, he was the length of two SUV's, with azure blue scales that matched his eyes. He was magnificent, if a bit frightening. The Dragon shuddered and shifted back into his human form.

"Because she knew I would never let you fall," he said, stepping forward.

The sound of sirens in the distance caught their attention.

"We better get down there." Darien snapped his gun case shut before leading the way down the stairs.

Another SUV pulled up in front of the building as they emerged, and Ali jumped out of the passenger's seat.

"Erin!" she screamed as she saw her little sister. Ali ran to embrace her, sobbing. "I'm so sorry! I should have listened. I—"

A strangled cry caught the words in her throat as she held her sister in her arms.

"See, Ali?" Colin gave her an exasperated look as he stepped out of the SUV. "I told you everything was under control. We could have stayed and interviewed that witness."

Ali's head whipped around to face Colin. Laila could practically feel the seething anger rolling off her. In a flash Darien was at her side, resting his hand on her shoulder to keep her from attacking Colin. Laila was ready to strangle him as well, but she forced her ire down.

"Laila?" he called tightly over his shoulder. "Why don't you see to the others? You should probably be checked out by a medic as well. Colin and I will wrap things up here."

Laila gently motioned for the others, including Ali, to follow her to the ambulance that was just pulling up. She watched from a distance as the investigative team arrived to secure the scene, feeling lucky that she was off the hook.

She also noticed that Ali was glaring in Colin's direction. Laila had a feeling that she and Darien would not be able to keep her in check much longer. While Laila was not entirely convinced that Colin didn't deserve a punch in the face, she knew they were going to have to find a solution sooner rather than later. Preferably one that wouldn't result in battery charges being pressed against them.

But that would be a battle for another night. She'd just taken down a group of Lesser Demons, and Laila was finished fighting for tonight.

CHAPTER 51

Laila borrowed Darien's SUV and headed home with the others, dropping Lyn off at her shop along the way. The Witch was bone-weary and muttered something about taking the rest of the week off.

Once home, the rest of them silently made their way into the house. Laila collapsed onto a bar stool, resting her head on the counter. Erin searched through the refrigerator, pulling out some bread and jam while Ali fussed over her.

"If you want to help, find some peanut butter," huffed Erin. "I'm hungry enough to eat a cow."

"Well, you are a Dragon," Laila pointed out from her resting place on the counter.

"One thing's for certain, we need a security system." Ali stalked over to a cupboard and retrieved a jar of peanut butter. "Preferably top of the line."

"I'll look into it for you," said Frej, who started slathering slices of bread with jam. "It's the least I can do."

A silence fell over the room like a dark veil. The guilt was tangible, and as Laila lifted her head she could see that Ali was struggling as tears flooded her eyes.

Reaching across the counter, Laila grabbed Ali's hand and squeezed it as the tears rushed unbidden down her friend's face.

"This is not your fault," Laila insisted. "No one here is to blame for what happened, only the Demons. They are the only ones responsible. Even if we had come home earlier, before all this happened, nothing would have changed."

"But why Erin?" asked Ali pounding her fist against the counter, "Why not one of us?"

Laila knew she meant one of the IRSA team members.

"They needed a Dragon to summon Izel," explained Laila. "Darien and I discovered that just before we got the call from Frej."

"Was that thing coming through the portal Izel?" asked Erin as she cut a sandwich in half.

Laila shook her head. "No, from what Darien and I could tell, only a Dragon's blood would summon her. Who knows what that creature was."

"I thought I was going to lose you!" Ali choked on a sob as Erin hugged her.

"Why don't we take these to go?" Erin took two of the plates, and the sisters climbed the stairs to Ali's room.

Laila watched them until they disappeared around the corner.

Frej pushed a sandwich across the table, but Laila just stared at it.

"You need to eat too," insisted Frej. "You know you'll feel better once you do."

She sighed and took a bite. He was right, but she had no appetite. While they had caught the Demons in the act of opening a portal, it was far from a victory. They had almost lost someone they cared about dearly. It had been way too close for comfort. The Demons had just made this personal, and Laila would stop at nothing to send them back to Hell.

"Are you all right?" Frej watched her closely.

"Yeah, sorry. This has been a really long week." She massaged her temples. "Do you mind cleaning up? I think I should go lie down."

"Of course," he said gently.

Laila trudged up the stairs and to her room, where she flung herself on the bed. Her headache was growing, and all she wanted to do was sleep for a week. Or maybe take a vacation to some secluded beach where no one talked about Demons. Or both.

A knock on the door startled her. She rolled over with a groan and sat up.

"Come in."

The door eased open slowly, revealing Frej standing in the hall with a steaming mug.

"This should help your head. It's one of Hanna's remedies."

Laila nodded, too tired to argue. He passed her the mug and sat on the bed beside her.

Laila sniffed the steam. It had a tangy, herbal scent to it. She sipped it, and immediately it relieved the tension in her shoulders. Whatever Hanna put in this blend was certainly effective.

"Thank you. Laila glanced at him.

"I know this is a lot for you to deal with. I just want you to know that I'm here."

Laila nodded silently as Frej continued to watch her closely.

"I also know you're hesitant about our growing relationship, and that you worry that it will affect Erin and her studies. If there is one thing that I've taken away from the horrifying events of this evening, though, it's that Erin is incredibly strong. You all are, and your friendship and love make you all the stronger."

He reached over and tucked a stray hair behind Laila's ear, his fingers lingered as they brushed against her skin. "If this makes you happy, then please let yourself be happy."

"There are literally Demons attacking the house!" said Laila, exasperated. How could she justify the time and energy that a relationship would take? There was so much she needed to do.

"That is all the more reason to find happiness where you

can." Frej gazed into her eyes. "This threat isn't going away. We *will* deal with it. I swear to you that I will do everything I can to help. But in the meantime, life continues, and you can embrace every moment of it or you waste it waiting."

He had a point. As much as she wished that the issue with the Demons could be quickly resolved, she knew that it would take time.

"If we continue with this," began Laila slowly, "you have to swear that you will back off if this effects Erin negatively in any way."

"Of course," he said, hope bringing a light into his eyes.

"Then I suppose there is no harm in this." She leaned over and kissed him lightly, teasing him. He wrapped an arm around her waist and pressed her to him, hungry for more.

Quickly, she set the mug onto her nightstand before Frej pulled her back into his embrace. Laila felt the tension in her body ease as she allowed herself to be caught up in her desire. As she ran her fingers through his hair and he lowered her down onto the bed, she realized she truly wanted this. She wanted him

"You failed," snapped a voice as cold as ice. Its owner's face was obscured by the darkness of the abandoned building.

"Please," begged the Shifter, "I didn't know we had been followed, just give me another chance…"

"Another chance to do what? Your job was simple, use the Witch to open a portal and bring Izel through. Thanks to your sloppy abduction, not only did you fail at bringing Izel through, but you let our Witch die in the process."

The man stepped forward, and a beam of moonlight that filtered through the window and fell on his fine Fae features and platinum blond hair.

"Not to mention," continued the Fae, "your traps to kill the Elf have all failed miserably."

"S-she's cunning. Please, Marius! I—"

Marius picked up his knife and was about to draw it across the Shifter's neck when a voice behind him intervened.

"Wait!" called a woman's musical voice. "Do not kill him yet, we still have need of him."

Marius turned to face the scrying glass where the woman watched.

"There are too few of us," continued the woman. "I have heard his influence has a wide reach, something we will need in the months to come."

"Very well, Your Greatness," said Marius with a bow. "Then maiming should be sufficient."

"No, please!" the man screamed, and backed away.

Marius motioned for two men to approach from the shadows. The first pinned the Shifter to the table while his companion held the Shifter's arm in place. Marius picked up a saw from the table and slowly, calmly began the task of sawing the Shifter's hand off.

The Shifter screamed, but there was no one to hear him. His blood splattered the Fae as he severed an artery. By the time he had finished, the Shifter was curled into a ball cradling the bleeding stump that was once a hand.

Marius turned and faced the scrying glass.

"That will do, Marius." The woman examined her nails with disinterest. "I've got an appointment to keep, but I expect to hear from you soon."

"Of course, I will inform you as soon as I have news, Izel."

EPILOGUE

Laila paused in the doorway of the café. She knew she needed to do this, but she was not quite sure if she was ready.

Ali squeezed her hand encouragingly. "Are we going to go in?"

Taking a deep breath, Laila nodded and pushed the door open to find half a dozen men waiting for her. They recognized her immediately and stood to greet her.

After speaking with the Queen of Dragons, Laila had realized that it was time for her to reach out for help in dealing with the demons of her past. She had spoken to Torsten, and between the two of them they had been able to convince half a dozen of the other prisoners from the Demons' arena to join them, including Mato and Henrik, two of the men who had shared their cell block.

Mato embraced her with a hug that lifted her off the ground. Henrik hugged her as well, but both men were tripping over each other to be introduced to Ali. Ali pretended not to notice, but Laila knew she enjoyed the attention.

Laila walked over to the circle of chairs they had set up in the empty café and took a seat. Ali joined her quickly.

"Thank you, everyone, for coming," Laila said, taking time to look at each individual who was present. "I know that this is not an easy thing to do, but it was recently brought to my attention that I was hiding from what happened, pushing it aside like it didn't affect me."

She paused to take a deep breath before continuing.

"The truth is that this *did* happen to us. We endured a horrible fate. I did things that I never would have done if I hadn't been placed in that situation. I hate it. I hate how they controlled me, and I hate how they still control me."

The others nodded, and slowly each of them shared insights about their lives now, and the things that happened back when they were imprisoned. Even Ali shared how her sister's kidnapping had affected her.

It had been nearly two weeks since that horrible night. They hadn't found the Shifter, and the other Demon henchmen who had survived were not talking. It frustrated Laila to no end, but they seemed determined to face life in prison, or worse, life in Muspelheim with sealed lips.

Eventually, the café owner came over and politely told them that she needed to close up for the night. She even gave them a platter of pastries left over from the day.

Laila and Ali said their goodbyes to the others and took the leftover pastries to go.

"So, who do you think will ask me for your number first? Henrik or Mato?" Laila asked as they crossed the street.

"Seriously?" Ali rolled her eyes, shifting the tray.

Laila's phone buzzed as she glanced at the screen. "Oh! It's Henrik!"

They climbed the steps to the main entrance of the building that housed the Inter-Realm Security Agency.

"Just because you are perfectly happy with a handsome Dragon-knight-in-shining-armor does not mean you need to play matchmaker for me."

"It's called payback."

"But," continued Ali, "he was pretty good-looking."

Laila laughed. It felt good to laugh. There were so many questions still left unanswered, and an increasing list of problems. She still had yet to discover why there was a Goddess watching over her. Laila knew she should speak with Arduinna about it and ask for her advice, but there were so many other things to think about.

They stopped short as they saw Colin embracing his girlfriend just in front of the door, blocking their path.

Ali coughed as they approached, catching the attention of the pair.

"Oh, excuse us," sniffed the woman as she cast her appraising gaze over Ali and Laila. "You must be the women that work for Colin."

"Oh, right," said Colin, hastily, "Lorel, this is Ali and Laila. Ladies, this is my girlfriend, Lorel."

"Yes, we're his coworkers." Ali forced a smile.

"It's nice to meet you." Laila extended her hand.

"Yes," said Lorel ignoring the hand. She smiled, but it didn't reach her eyes.

Laila noticed she was wearing a silver necklace. As Lyn had pointed out, there was a winged woman carved into it.

"We should go," muttered Ali stiffly. Laila followed her through the door with a final nod to the couple.

"What was that about?" asked Laila as Ali pushed the button for the elevator.

"Something about her seems off." Ali shook her head. "I don't know what it is."

The doors of the elevator opened.

"Lyn mentioned something about her," said Laila, frowning as she selected the button for their floor, "It was about her necklace. She said it looked familiar."

"Interesting."

They stepped out of the elevator and into the hall and nearly ran into Darien.

"Really?" he exclaimed as he stared longingly at the pastries. "More food I can't eat? Are you trying to torture me?"

Ali tried to swat him but stopped short so she would not upset her stack of sweets.

Laila shook her head. "As if we don't know that you keep a stash of blood in your office." She led them into the conference room where they prepared for their meeting.

"But it's not desserts!" whined Darien. "This is the worst part about being a Vampire."

"Hey, everyone!" said Colin cheerfully as he entered the conference room. "I've got some great news. I know we've been feeling a little overworked as of late, so I got in touch with D.C. I know that the Witch, Lyn, was a huge help with the last big case, so I've brought on an agent in training to help us in the field."

Movement by the door caught Laila's attention, and in walked a figure that was unmistakably familiar. His skin had a cool silvery glow which complemented his long hair that was black as onyx.

"Hey, princess," the words rolled off his tongue like honey as he sauntered into the room.

Her jaw dropped and time blurred. All she was aware of was the man standing before her.

"Jerrik," she breathed.

❖ 325 ❖

❖ 326 ❖

ACKNOWLEDGMENTS

Each book I write is a journey. As much as I love to travel the world, I find it is not about the destination, or even about the journey, but those you meet along the way. I want to take this moment to thank the people around me who have supported me throughout the adventure of writing this book, and the Laila of Midgard series in general.

To Rene, Eric, Lizz, and Sophie who are the best friends anyone could ask for. From giving me feedback to listening to my crazy ideas, I always know I can count on you guys.

To my family who has been there for me all along. My family members are truly amazing for supporting this dream of mine, particularly my parents who are truly my biggest supporters. Also to Cindy, whose feedback is much appreciated.

To Jenna E. Johnson who keeps me sane. You

rock!

To my editors Mindy and Natalie with The Crimson Quill who are more than just editors. You go above and beyond. You two remind me why I'm telling these stories.

And finally, to my readers. Your support means more to me than you can possibly know.

CHARACTERS

Laila Eyvindr – An Elf hired by the Interrealm Security Agency (IRSA). She is young for an Elf and appears to be in her mid-twenties by human standards but she is really 83 years old. She is a trained warrior and has a good amount of magical training. Laila is determined, hardworking, caring, and passionate.

Colin Grayson – A Werewolf in his mid 30's with brown hair, short beard and grey eyes. He is a descendent of Shifters who have lived amongst humans in hiding for generations. He is the supervisor of the IRSA team, and has been a part of the organization since it's foundation.

Alastrina Fiachra (Ali) – A Fae woman with long curly golden hair and purple eyes. Like Laila, she is an IRSA agent, but she has been around for much longer and has adjusted to life in Midgard. Ali's parents died a few years ago, so she cares for her adopted little sister, Erin. She knows how to have a good time and loves the Los Angeles nightlife.

Darien Pavoni – A male Vampire with black spiky hair, pale skin, and red eyes. Another member of Laila's IRSA team, he is arrogant, and may not always make the most professional decisions, but he genuinely cares about the work he does. In 1724 he died in a duel and was turned into a Vampire.

Erin Fiachra – A young Dragon who is trapped in her human form. She is Ali's adopted sister, and appears to be about thirteen, but she is actually around sixty years old. She's had difficulty contacting other Dragons to discover why she's stopped aging.

Arduinna – The Celtic Goddess of the Black Forest in Germany. She is down to earth and wise, and is a friend of Ali and Laila's.

Sir Frej Ilmarinen – An Air Dragon and a Knight from the Dragon Kingdom. He has chosen to stay in Los Angeles to train Erin.

Orin – The Fae man who owns the Club La Fae. He's cheeky, but a reliable informant.

Lyn – A human witch who lives in Los Angeles. She owns a shop in Venice Beach called Lyn's Charms and Remedies, and helps Laila with the occasional case.

Jerrik Torhild – Svartálfr (plural: Svartalfar) or Dark Elf who was imprisoned in the same cellblock as Laila. He and Laila had a short-lived romance until he left without a word

Torsten – A fatherly Dwarf that was also imprisoned in the same cellblock as Laila. He now works for IRSA developing weapons and tools to make the agents' jobs safer.

Donald – A male Witch, or Tech Wiz, as he prefers. A local witch hired to assist Torsten in enchanting equipment for the IRSA team.

Unknown Goddess – Appears to be watching Laila.

Snake Shifter (Name: Unknown) – A Snake Shifter and a Lesser Demon, who was capturing and sending Supernaturals to the Demon-run fight ring.

Marius – A.K.A. the Master of the Games. He's Fae and was the Greater Demon in charge of the illegal fight ring. He escaped IRSA's raid, and is still at large.

Izel – Unknown. Connected to Marius and the Demons.

Alfred – An Earth Dragon and Frej's butler.

Hanna – A Water Dragon and Frej's motherly housekeeper.

King Ingmar Hildegard – An Earth Dragon and King of the Dragons.

Queen Regina Halvard-Hilgard – A Fire Dragon and Queen of the Dragons.

Lord Issac Mavrik – An Earth Dragon and a close friend of Frej's.

Lord Viktor – A Fire Dragon, and a lord who seems to be involved in shady activities.

Ragna Eyvindr – An Elf and Laila's mother who works in the court of the Elves.

Andor Eyvindr – An Elf and Laila's father and a member of the Royal Guard of the Elven Kingdom

J.D. – A Human and one of Ali's informants in the Old City. He's a burn victim, and never speaks.

Benning – A Giant who was sent, by the Demons, to terrorize Los Angeles. In reality, he wouldn't hurt a fly.

Captain Anderson – A Human and captain of the LAPD's Gangs and Narcotics division.

Lorel – A Human and Colin's girlfriend.

Carlos – A Human who was one of Ali's informants in the Old City until he was assassinated while meeting with Ali and Darien.

Mato – A Bear Shifter who was imprisoned by the Demons

in the same cellblock as Laila.

Henrik – A Mörkö (ice creature) who was imprisoned in the same cellblock as Laila.

WORLDS

Asgard – World of the Gods.

Vanaheim – World of the Ancient Gods.

Alfheim (pronounced "ALF-hame;") – World of the Elves, Fae, Dragons and nature related beings. Large cites of note include:
> Ingegard – Elven City
> Tír na nÓg – City of the Fae
> Schonengard – City of the Dragons

Earth (or Midgard) – The world of the humans. For Millennia it was off limits to the other worlds as humans and other creatures of this world were not gifted in magic or strength. Over time, the humans have become a force to reckon with as they created amazing technologies that rival the magic that others possess. The people of Alfheim were the ones who proposed the truce that would keep the human world safe from the other worlds. There are creatures like human Vampires, human Shifters, and a hand full of other creatures who have managed to stay under the radar during the era before The Event.

Svartalfheim (pronounced "SVART-alf-hame;") – The world of Dark Elves or Svartalfar, Dwarves, and creatures of the earth. They are known for their mines and craftsmanship.

Jotunheim – The world of brutish creatures like Trolls and Giants. They are constantly at war with the races of Alfheim or other worlds.

Muspelheim – The world of the Dammed. The inter-realm prison where the worst criminals are banished. There is a political organization that has risen to power within this world known as the Demons. They have begun to gain connections in the other worlds, particularly Earth, and have begun to plot their escape and rise to power.

❖ 339 ❖

CAN'T WAIT FOR MORE?

Want monthly access to advance announcements, exclusive content and more? Check out Kathryn Blanche's Patreon page for more information!

patreon.com/kathrynblanche

ABOUT THE AUTHOR

Kathryn Blanche writes novels in her favorite local cafes when not indulging her love for travel. Aside from exploring the world, this California native may be found designing for the theatre, reading, fencing, or teaching. *Summoned by Demons* is the second novel in her Laila of Midgard series.

Website: www.kathrynblanche.com
Email: contact@kathrynblanche.com
Facebook: @LailaofMidgardSeries
Instagram: @kathryn_blanche
Twitter: @_kathrynblanche

DID YOU KNOW...

Did you know that leaving a review is one of the most helpful things a reader can do for any author? If you have a moment, please leave a review online.

THE ADVENTURE CONTINUES IN...

INFILTRATED
BY
DEMONS

LAILA OF MIDGARD
BOOK 3

BY

KATHRYN BLANCHE